I0628763

An Alien Exchange

Book 1 of An Alien Exchange

Keri Kruspe

StarChance Productions

Copyright © 2018 by Keri Kruspe

eBook ISBN: 978-1-7326584-0-0

Paperback ISBN: 979-8-9873726-0-9

All rights reserved.

This book is a work of fiction. Any names, characters, companies, organizations, places, events, locales, and incidents are either used in a fictitious manner or are fictional. Any resemblance to actual persons, living or dead, actual companies or organizations, or actual events is purely coincidental.

No portion of this book may be reproduced in any form without written permission from the publisher or author, except as permitted by U.S. copyright law.

I dedicate this book to those who are alone in a crowd. To those who are desperately trying to right a wrong they've done in the past. Sometimes taking a chance may seem crazy, but you'll never know until you try.

CONTENTS

Also By Keri

CHAPTER ONE

Aimee

A imee knew she'd made a mistake the minute she sat down. The music in the crowded sports bar was too loud, the lighting was too dim, and the air was thick with a mixture of greasy food, sweaty bodies, and desperation. She glanced at her fellow managers from the credit union. These were the people she now called "friends," not that any of them knew it.

Seated at the round table was "on-the-prowl" Melissa, who sat next to the group's smart phone addict, just-out-of-college Emily. Good-looking, middle-aged "manwhore" William, was making some moves to grab Emily's attention for the umpteenth time. He had his sights on the younger Emily while he ignored Melissa's not so subtle attempts to get his attention. Then there was Mary, who started at the credit union when women had to wear pearls and nylons. Mary was in an ongoing, low argument with Mr. Reed, their "still in the closet" suave CEO.

Watching her coworker's made Aimee's chest squeeze. She had no business pretending she wanted to be there, surrounded by people but all alone. Why had she come in the first place? Oh yeah, she was trying to make it back to the human race after the violent deaths of her parents in a mass shooting last year. She ached that she'd never see them again. Coupled with the breakup of her five-year marriage, it was hard for Aimee to reconnect with others. Life-long friends from college had either married or moved away until one day Aimee realized they were all gone. As a manager, she couldn't make friends with her staff, so her only choice was her peers sitting at this table.

She took a sip of the wine spritzer and grimaced when the water-downed drink left a bitter taste in her mouth. She tilted her head and watched the others. The clueless trio was still...ah...clueless. Mr. Reed waved a forefinger at Mary, who sat back with her lips pursed and her arms crossed.

It was hard to breathe. Aimee had to get out of this darkened den with these people she barely knew, except on a professional level. Then it dawned on her, she really didn't want to get to know them.

"Um, sorry guys," Aimee stood. "But I gotta go."

Mr. Reed frowned. "But we haven't ordered dinner yet."

"Yes," the mulish expression on Mary's face deepened the lines around her mouth. "It's tradition. Which should be sacred around here." That statement came with a glare that she stabbed in Mr. Reed's direction.

Mr. Reed opened his mouth but Aimee interrupted.

"I'm really sorry, but..." The waiter approached with pad in hand. Time to escape. "I'll talk to you tomorrow." Aimee directed that to no one in particular. The walls were closing in. The atmosphere stale and moist, her lungs seized. With hand to her throat, she gave a quick nod and sprinted out to the parking lot. She put her hands on her thighs and gulped in breaths of fresh air.

Straightening, Aimee glanced around the crisp, late spring air and noticed for the first time a twinge of ozone. The tension in her shoulders loosened as she observed a full parking lot of empty cars. She headed to her ten-year-old hybrid car sitting in the weak light of a lone lamp. Nothing sounded better than going home to a frozen dinner and a book. Maybe she'd step it up, watch a movie, and splurge with a glass of wine. At peace with the decision she'd made in leaving, she swallowed her pity-party, got in the car, and headed home.

After her uneventful, if somewhat tasteless dinner, Aimee turned in for the night. She relaxed and moaned in relief into the soft cocoon of her bed. Within the soothing, dim light from the lamp on her nightstand, she settled in the nest of pillows, her electronic reader ready to go in one hand and a glass of Zin in the other. She had to escape...and what better way than to faraway galaxies? She'd return to the story she started yesterday and forget the night's near disaster. Where was she? Oh yeah, wrapped in a sexual fantasy on a space station...

His tongue stroked in lavish circles around the swollen bundle of nerves as he inserted a thick finger into her trembling passage. Searching, probing, caressing before he found the sensitive nest under her clit. His glorious mouth massaged the stiff, protruding bud displayed proudly between the silken folds. One, two circular rubs were all he gave before he his mouth surrounded, then furiously sucked her clit into his mouth to give her an unexpected violent orgasm. She screamed his name, closing her legs around his ears. She pushed against his head to control her intense pleasure.

He ignored her feeble attempts at interruption by holding her raised hips with steady hands. In control, he continued to drink her nectar before inserting another finger to join the first, spiraling her into blinding ecstasy.

Aimee gave a loud snort. Yeah, like that ever happens in real life.

Good God...maybe she was too tired to read tonight, especially after the emotional upheaval at the sports bar. Drinking the rest of her wine, Aimee put the glass on the nightstand. She switched the power off the tablet and put it next to her empty glass before turning off the lamp. She wiggled farther until her butt found the comfortable dip she'd spent countless nights creating.

She lay there, hands under her head. Instead of thinking about her emotional breakdown earlier, she decided she'd rather think about the story she'd read and her dubious reaction to it. The reason she loved alien romances was they told of a male devoted to just one female. Okay...added truth. She also liked the fantasy of the human woman getting a mind-blowing orgasm quicker than most human men took to unzip their pants. Yeah, she'd jump at the chance to find an alien lover, especially if she could escape the nightmare her life had become on Earth.

Crap! The bright, red light on the alarm clock chastised her. How'd it get so late? She should have gone to sleep at least an hour ago. She groaned. It was her own fault for scheduling a staff meeting so flipping early. Note to self, stop at the store, and get donuts on the way to work. Best give everyone a sugar high before blathering on about compliance regulations.

She burrowed farther into her warm nest and dreamed about a gorgeous, alpha alien male who'd take her to the stars and declare to the galaxy she was his in a true mating bond.

Aimee jolted awake from a sound sleep in a bright room with her heart pounding and her mouth dry with fear. What woke her up? She scrambled around a narrow, hard cot before she stumbled out of it to land flat on her butt. She jumped to her feet with her knees bent and her fist up. The details of the cramped room were an afterthought for her overexcited brain except for white. White bed, white floor, and surrounded by white walls except for the large black partition in front of her. Where was her normal bedroom of a cool, pastel blue?

Her arms pebbled and her body shivered in the flat, crisp air.

Not seeing any door or windows added to her nervousness, and the glaring white theme didn't help much. The black wall unfolded and expanded. She was about to touch it when a loud chime made her jump with a squeak of alarm. It lifted and expanded into a 3-D picture in front of her. The black square blossomed into a colorful geometric pattern, swirling in high definition.

The dizzying pattern made her nauseous.

"Welcome, Aimee Elizabeth Gwiazdowski. Please do not be alarmed. You are in no danger." A low synthesized voice vibrated throughout the small space. As it spoke, the geometric pattern floated and spiked with each word.

Well, shit. The disembodied voice not only knew her name, it even pronounced it right.

Deciding it'd be a little hard for an empty room to attack, she straightened and dropped her hands to her sides. It wasn't as if she had any personal experience in self-defense. She had to look like an idiot, crouched in the oversized T-shirt she'd worn to bed.

The silence unnerved her. Why wasn't the voice saying anything? Maybe it waited for her to answer.

"Okay?"

Great. Intelligent response, Aimee. But come on, no way was she going to let on she was scared out of her mind. Hold on…act as if cooperation was your middle name. She didn't believe for one minute she wasn't in danger. No telling what kind of sick pervert was behind the voice.

She'd watched those scary *Saw* movies.

Crossing her arms under her breasts to stop the nervous sweat, she waited for the response. It didn't take long for the voice to continue.

"Excellent. We have a proposition for you. Are you amiable to discuss your future?"

What was she going to do—say no? Like that was an option when she was stuck in a small room and no obvious way out.

"Yes," she croaked through a dry throat. It was interesting the voice said "we." Maybe there was more than one person involved.

Humph. Reality check. It didn't take a genius to figure out it took more than one person to kidnap her from her bed to bring her to…wherever she was. Not to mention how they did it without waking her up.

"Excellent!" the low metallic voice repeated. "We are pleased you are amiable to open a dialogue." The swirling image expanded, giving her a holographic version of her adult life in various stages. At work, at a coworker's birthday party, and even one of her getting a renewal of her driver's license last month. Stomach acid churned and crawled up her throat at the implications.

My God, who were these people and what did they want with her?

"Are these not correct representations of your day-to-day existence?" If she wasn't mistaken, there was a twinge of smugness in that distorted voice. "I can assure you we have researched your circumstances and believe we have a proposition that will benefit you." The voice paused before it continued as the pictures rolled by. "You live in Grand Rapids, Michigan, are a thirty-six-year old divorcee, no children, and no living relatives since your parents were killed in a tragic mass shooting. You were close to them, weren't you?"

A rhetorical question since the voice didn't wait for an answer.

"You keep yourself busy as a branch manager at a local credit union, the same job you've had for over a decade. You have not dated since the break-up of your marriage. Your strong friendships have declined, resulting in no close relationships."

The voice paused before asking, "Are these statements true and accurate?"

Cold panic immobilized her as she searched for something to say. Yes, everything the annoying voice said was true. Those few short sentences clarified if she disappeared, no one would miss her.

No one.

Her heart thudded as a new trickle of sweat beaded between her breasts. Her dry throat made it hard to swallow as she concentrated on controlling her rising panic. She sure as hell wasn't going to give them any more information if she could help it.

Aloud, she answered, "Yes."

"Excellent. So would it be safe to say you might be open to changing your circumstances?"

Okay, now that just pissed her off. She clenched her fists under her elbows and shuddered. She had to grind her back molars to keep her temper under control before she gave another short retort.

"Maybe." *Ha!*

"Excellent."

Stupid voice didn't seem to know any other word.

"Are you familiar with these literary works?" The narrative continued as various covers from the erotic sci-fi romances downloaded on her electronic reader floated in front of her. "Do you not have these in your possession and read them?"

What the hell? Her face flushed as she realized someone hacked into her reader. Now she experienced violation on a whole other level.

"Yes," she whispered in a strangled tone.

"Excellent." If nothing else, their hearing was good. "Tell me, how would you feel if you found yourself in a position to have one of these alien males choose you? Would that interest you?"

Wait—what? Okay, now she was confused. "Um, I don't know?" Were they giving her some kind of choice of...alien men?

"Excellent."

Cue in the eye roll. How was "I don't know," excellent?

"So are you willing to explore the possibility?"

How laughable was it she continued this asinine conversation with a faceless coward hiding behind a computer? She needed to step it up. "Please explain."

"Think of it, your dreams coming true when an alien male claims you, giving you the chance to leave the pain of Earth behind." The random pictures changed. Now the scene showed buff bodies from the covers of the books she'd read, seductively flaunted in various stages of undress.

Eerie how many of her favorite pictures lingered.

Don't say it...don't say it... "What do you have in mind?" Okay, she'd said it. It didn't matter, she'd show them. She put her hands on her hips and a stern demand in her tone. They didn't need to know she was *freaking the hell out right now!*

"Excellent!" The belligerence went up a notch. Aimee growled under her breath in reaction. "We propose to you a reality you assumed was a fantasy." The video changed. This time the 3-D images had the various alien males in their "natural habitats." She had no trouble recognizing the different species and planets (or dimensions) being shown to her.

"The various cultures and their circumstances described in every story you've read on your electronic reading device are based on reality. There are thousands of cultures looking for their respective mates and it has been discovered the females of Earth are more than compatible with the majority of these species."

The pictures continued, but now the males were walking around her as if in the same room. Large, primal, sexy bodies her fingers itched to touch.

"As a result, the Exchange was created by the Federation Consortium to aid these worlds who desperately need females. We give human females the option to leave Earth and take part in this Exchange. There you will meet all the males you've read about." A meaningful break in the speech. "We assure you, this is done without the inconvenience of being forcibly kidnapped." The irony wasn't lost on her. Most of her favorite stories were of aliens kidnapping human women.

A metallic sigh sounded sincere. "Please understand human women are unique since your DNA adapts to a good portion of the humanoid males in the galaxy. The human genome disappears so the non-human species survives." An adoring sigh came next. "That is why human females are revered and adored throughout the Milky Way."

The pictures of the males disappeared and the geometrical pattern resumed, gathering itself to swirl in front of her.

"I can assure you, we are from a civilized galaxy and human females cannot attend unless they agree to be a part of this Exchange. The choice has to be yours."

Wow, that was some speech. What kind of idiot did these people think she was to fall for this load of crap? Even if she, for one second, believed this bullshit—each story she'd read about the coupling of alien men with human women were as different as, well, as men and women.

"Let me get this straight," she said, ticking a finger off with each statement. "Are you asking me if I want to leave Earth, go to this Exchange, find an alien man, and then mate with him and have his child?" Her heart thundered as she wished, even for a second, what they said was possible.

"Affirmative," the faceless voice replied. "Why not take a chance to change your life for the better? You'll gain the family you're yearning for and have a devoted mate as well. We are giving you the opportunity to find him among the deserving males of the known galaxy."

"Imagine it. One male just for you. One who will cherish you as the valuable female you are and one who would never forsake you for another. Say 'yes' right now and you'll never have to worry about being alone again. All your dreams will come true."

Okay, that's it! No doubt about it, someone was jerking her around. She'd rather be tortured with hot pokers than stand here and listen to this. Her arms dropped to her sides as she gripped her fingers, knuckles cracking. She had no idea why someone was trying to make her believe what she'd read in those books was based on reality. At this point, she didn't care. She wasn't a brainless idiot and didn't appreciate someone treating her like one. This whole thing was ludicrous. She didn't care where they came from, no male wanted a lifelong commitment with the tantalizing promise of making miracle babies and him being grateful for the privilege.

Time to jump off this merry-go-round.

So, without thinking, she crossed her arms and blurted, "You know what I think? I think you're trying to take advantage of me for some sick, twisted reason. While I'm sure there are aliens in the universe, I doubt you're one. You might've had me believing in some of your bull, but then you spouted off nonsense about how males in the galaxy are desperate for females and are willing to do anything to get them. To top it off, you want me to make a life decision right now?"

With fists still clenched, she exhaled nosily through pursed lips. Yeah, so what if that grunt coming out of her mouth wasn't lady-like. *Jerks.* "I tell you what. Let's try something simple first, hum, Mr.

Wizard? There's only one way I'll believe your stupid story. You say you're an alien?"

She took in a deep breath and plunged ahead.

"Prove it."

Qay

"Qay, get your butt down here." The rude request sounded in Qay's inner ear when he subconsciously opened the communicator in response to a soft ping.

Sitting on his work lounger in his official room off the bridge of the merchant ship the *StarChance*, Commander Qayyum A'agnan E'etu was engrossed in an important systems program through his ocular implant. His private chamber may have been small, but it had more than enough room to fit his comfortable work lounger, desk, and various bookshelves. He'd commissioned the paneling and walls to display rare natural woods and in the background, a soothing sound of white noise meant to stimulate the intellectual centers of the brain helped to keep him focused.

Qay's favorite hot beverage sat in a steaming cup on the desk attachment. The nutty aroma and flavor helped to keep him alert while it satisfied his waking hunger. He'd eat once they left Earth's orbit and were on their way back to the Zerin homeworld.

Right now he was engrossed in analyzing the experimental reactionless engine that created a propellantless drive. So far, it generated unlimited power with a minimal amount of stress to the integrity of the ship. The engines were performing better than he'd hoped, but with a few tweaks here and there, they'd be able to...

What was that annoying racket? Oh right, his cousin D'zia was trying to get his attention. At first, Qay did not intend to stop his dissection of the fascinating report, but he had to admit it was unusual for D'zia to contact him at this late stage. Not only was D'zia his second-in-command but he also had the added responsibility of being in charge of the human women brought aboard the

StarChance. The Exchange deadline was tight and losing a single female at this late stage would put them behind.

"What is it now, D'zia?" Qay responded, keeping the impatience out of his voice. He blinked in the ocular implant to halt the program.

"Well, you insisted on knowing if there were any problems with the remaining females. You've got to see the new one who insists we 'prove it' before she decides." Amusement laced his cousin's tone.

"Prove what?" Qay's patience thinned. The demand for the human females to attend the Exchange had doubled this time around. They had a hundred humans on board, the largest group ever attempted. The crew had thirty days to train and acclimate them to the Federation Consortium laws and regulations before they reached the Exchange on the Zerin moon of Urim. He wasn't in the mood for cryptic scenarios.

Qay rubbed the throbbing pulse in the middle of his forehead. On top of organizing the Exchange, the Imperial Forces of Zerin gave him a directive to uncover the illegal human trafficking rumored to be involved with the Exchange. His reputation, not to mention his home planet, was at stake. It was imperative he find out who was behind the disgusting practice.

The voice droning in his ear reminded him his cousin was talking about...something.

"Well, when she was told the standard line about males wanting human females, you should have heard her! Anyway, that's not important. What is important is she ordered I prove aliens were real," D'zia chuckled. "No one has demanded that from us before they'd agreed to go to the Exchange first. What do you want me to do?"

Qay stifled the urge to roll his eyes in exasperation like a human. By the Sacred Goddess, now he was picking up humanistic behaviors from his cousin. It was okay for D'zia to act like that—he had to work with the humans.

Qay didn't.

"I don't understand the problem," Qay activated the previous program to continue his evaluation. "Why are you bothering me with this? Why aren't you consulting the liaisons? Or do I have to call in Ki?"

"Oh, come on! There's no reason to get mean and threaten me with his holiness," D'zia whined. "I just thought you'd like to look at this one yourself."

Qay paused his reading. "Why would you think that? I've never seen an Earth female in person before, nor do I want to." The information in front of him claimed his attention once again. "Just handle it and let me know when we're ready to go."

"Qay, you've got to see this one in action. I bet you'd find her amusing." D'zia's tone was teasing. "You've been over-extending yourself and a little diversion might be good for you." That last statement came out flat.

Qay snorted at the absurd statement. Since when did it matter if he over-extended himself?

"Come on. It won't hurt for you to get away from your hibernation for a few clicks. I wasn't going to say anything, but the crew needs a break from your, ah, grumpiness. Besides, I need someone else's opinion about this woman." A short grunt came next. "I don't want the liaisons to look at her—they'll pronounce her "unfit" and then we'd have to take the time to look for another one." Now came the drawn-out, dramatic groan. "If we do that we won't make our quota in time...."

D'zia had his full attention. One annoying female stood in the way of them making their quota? More than likely his cousin was manipulating him, but there was always the chance he wasn't. Damn everything to the depths of a black hole and back.

"All right, you win. As usual." Resigned, he blinked off the input and let out a loud breath. "I'll be there in a few clicks." He tapped the communication off in his ear and left his workroom to enter the bridge.

"Lieutenant, you have the authorization." He strode to the transportation tube to take him to his cousin's communication center on a lower deck.

"Yes, sir." The female officer stood and saluted with her right arm crossing over her chest, acknowledging the transfer of command. She left her assigned work lounger to sit in the commander's and took control of the bridge.

Qay inspected the heart of the *StarChance* and smiled in satisfaction. The ten crewmembers were at their various workstations—each in their loungers sitting side-by-side in a U formation. Together they created a relaxed and professional atmosphere. Qay glanced at the vid in front of the loungers to admire the 3-D display of their orbit around the green and blue planet covered in white clouds. The sight would have been riveting except for the space debris covering a large part of the view.

Leaving the bridge, Qay considered what his cousin said about him being "grumpy," whatever that meant. His cousin's proclivity for spouting off Earth slang confused him.

In spite of D'zia's assumption of his mood, Qay enjoyed every phase of this assignment. He relished the trial of running experimental engines, along with the strategic challenge of closing in on an illegal slave ring. Best of all, he enjoyed a sense of self-satisfaction to know he provided fellow citizens a means to save their species. Qay grinned. If he was successful, it would also pave the way to rescind his exile status.

Speaking of plans, when this was over, he'd search for his True-Bond in the Southern Providence this time. If he got her pregnant right away with his heir, he'd have a better chance at reclaiming his birthright. Definitely something he'd have to consider later.

His mind wandered back to his cousin. Qay thanked the Sacred Goddess D'zia elected to join him in his exile. He shuddered to think how lonely and empty his life would have been if he'd been alone while outcast from home. He appreciated having D'zia around, even when the stubborn *eztli* bragged the only reason he stayed with Qay was to keep him out of trouble.

Of course, D'zia shadowing him for the last fifty years wasn't only for Qay's benefit. The credits D'zia made over the years were incentive enough. Sacred Goddess willing, both of them would return to their families as successful males.

Lost in his musings, Qay was surprised to find he was already at D'zia's office. The doors opened and he entered into the communication area where D'zia "welcomed" the human females. Not that those humans had any idea they were on an alien ship. The goal was to keep them calm and isolated to minimize any danger to them or his crew. If the females didn't say "yes" to their proposal, they woke up the next morning in their own beds. Thanks to a small memory inhibitor given to them, they would wake, thinking everything had been a remote dream.

"Okay, I'm here."

Trust D'zia to be sitting back on his lounger with his feet draped over the arm to rest on top of a separate console. D'zia waved to open a vid program to formulate in the middle of the designated area on the floor. The chamber D'zia used for this phase of the operation was larger than Qay's workroom on the bridge. It held D'zia's lounger, a long rectangular table, and several comfortable chairs for group meetings.

"Show tape 148-Z from the beginning." D'zia rubbed the end of his warrior braid as his intense stare stayed on Qay.

Qay didn't trust the unusual expression D'zia had. He wasn't sure what his cousin was up to, but since he was here he might as well see what was so important. He pulled up a chair and leaned back with one ankle crossed over his thigh to watch the 3-D display.

At first, it was hard to follow the conversation since the exotic beauty of the human caught his attention. Holy Goddess, she was a captivating little creature. Her firm calves tapered into round thighs, with enough softness to tempt a male to sample the delights they promised. She had a narrow waist that flowed into round, shapely hips. Her skimpy covering reached the top of her thighs and didn't do much to conceal her magnificent, large breasts. She stood with her legs apart to brace her body with her arms crossed. A hint of dark nipples poked through the light cloth.

His throat dried at the sight of those luscious beauties.

Her soft tresses were wavy and brushed the top of her shoulders. The multifaceted color was a combination of rich brown with a dazzling mixture of gold and umber. Her hair boasted a two-inch-wide white streak on the right which brought out the pale cream of her face. He wondered if it was natural or a possible birthmark.

Qay took in the rest of her mesmerizing face. Her eyes were wide, the irises a strange mixture of gold, brown, and green—and sharply focused on what was happening around her. Dark mink eyebrows arched over those expressive eyes framed by thick lashes. Her pert nose topped a full, lush mouth.

A mouth stiffened in a tight frown that matched the deep furrows across her forehead.

Her terse answers struck him as somewhat strange. Normally the human's shrieked for help or babbled their life's story. She appeared to be nervous, but kept her cool. He didn't get the impression she was scared.

He would love to play *cabaza* with her alone. Forget credits, they'd use articles of clothing for their wagers.

The vid caught up to real time when she demanded they "prove it." He activated his audio to give him access to talk to her. Good thing she had the nano translator in place so he didn't have to worry about any miscommunication between them.

"What is it you want to be proven?" She was like a small *Grapple* pup snarling fearlessly at a larger predator. The feisty little human would get a minimal amount of questions answered until she agreed to participate in the Exchange.

Maintaining protocol was necessary.

No matter how adorable she was.

Aimee

"What is it you want proven?" The synthesized voice was different enough to make Aimee believe another person was speaking. The inflection was deeper with a hint of an accent. Her spine shivered in an unexpected reaction. At the same time, Aimee got the distinct impression she was the butt of some kind of joke.

"I beg your pardon?" Her face heated as she growled. "I want you to prove aliens exist. That should be easy enough. True?"

A pause before the metallic voice answered. "What happens if we prove aliens exist? What then?"

Aimee tightened her arms across her chest and rubbed them. The room was a little too cool to be comfortable. "Well, then maybe I'd be open to discussing things further."

Not.

Great, now she was channeling her inner '80's girl.

"I'm afraid we'd need something more than that, Ms. Gwiazdowski. You have to agree to go with us first before this discussion can go any further. Once we reveal ourselves to you, you cannot go back to Earth." She was sure the brief dramatic silence was for effect. "Ever. This is it, I'm afraid. As you humans like to say, it's now or never." This time a small chuckle lightened the drama. "Really, you strike me as the type of person who isn't afraid of taking chances. Think about it, if what we say is true, you'll have your own devoted mate. One who will love and adore you your whole life.

"Or you can go home. You'll think this has been a dream and you'll resume your life as if nothing has happened. You will wake up in your bed none the wiser."

A sense of dread flooded her. With those few words, a vision of a long, lonely life stretched out before her. Every day...the same thing over and over, with little to no chance for anything to change.

"Don't you have a staff meeting to look forward to in the morning?"

Baffled, she didn't know what to do. She dropped her hands to her sides and hugged her waist. She had a hard time trying to come to terms with their proposal.

Wait, what was she thinking? How was this a problem? It wasn't as though there was an alien offering her chance to live with the man of her dreams. Since there were probably, maybe—um, conceivably no such things as aliens, what would happen if she agreed?

All right, all right, quit waffling. Besides, she didn't want to stay in this stupid room for the rest of her life. It was time to put on her big girl panties and finish riding this train all the way to Crazyville.

Decision made. "All right, I'm in. Bring in an alien for me to meet."

"I assure you, you've made the right decision, Ms. Gwiazdowski. I will be down in a few clicks. Please do not be alarmed when I arrive."

Damn, she wasn't sure what a "click" was, but she suspected she didn't have much time to get her head out of her ass for her first encounter with an actual, live alien. Her stomach tightened in anticipation. As usual, her big mouth got her into trouble. Prove there were aliens? She must be out of her ever-loving mind.

Everything would change when the "person" behind the distorted voice came into the room. Didn't matter if he was an alien or not.

If he weren't an alien, he was probably a perverted sociopath who wanted to cut her up and wear her eyeballs as trophies.

If he were an alien, she at least had a fifty-fifty chance he wasn't hostile and wouldn't kill her. Maybe—just maybe he was gorgeous and wanted to "mate" with her.

Yeah, that'd be good.

If he were hostile, who wasn't to say he didn't want to cut her up and wear her eyeballs as trophies?

The idea of getting a weapon popped into her head. She whipped her head back and forth, trying to find something to use. No such luck. The bed was a solid cube fused to the floor and offered a flat pillow with an attached thin blanket as its sorry companion.

Yep, all she had to do was take the sad pillow and whap him on his head. Oooh, better yet, she'd twist it and flick him with the sharp corner. Hah, if she were lucky she might give him a small welt. Yeah, that'd sure show 'em.

A little devil on her shoulder whispered in her ear. Wouldn't it be great if she met one of the aliens she'd read about? What species could he be from? She gripped her trembling hands as her mind raced, thinking about some of the very delectable alpha men of her fantasies.

Okay, okay, knock it off, time to get serious and stop this back-and-forth crap. She didn't start this but damn it, she sure as hell was going to finish it. Now was her chance to get out of this godforsaken room. There wasn't any other way out as far as she could see.

She jerked in surprise as the entire wall in front of her vanished. There, down the dim hallway, a tall figure walked toward her.

Qay

Qay chuckled. He shouldn't let the little human goad him into doing something reckless, but after talking to her, he had to meet her in person. Maybe one look at him would jolt the feisty little attitude right out of her. He admitted it might be fun to see her reaction, even without D'zia's goading.

"I assure you, you've made the right decision, Ms. Gwiazdowski. I will be down to meet you in a few clicks. Do not be alarmed when I arrive." Qay waved off the communication and turned to D'zia, who sat there with his mouth open and his eyes widened in a look of horror. His feet plonked off the console hard enough to make him lose his balance and jerk in the chair. Qay struggled not to laugh.

"You're going to see her yourself?" D'zia squeaked. The continued shock on D'zia's face was well worth leaving his office. It had been a long time since he'd been able to catch his cousin by surprise. Qay had forgotten how good it felt.

As if to make sure no one else was around, D'zia leaned in, "Do you think that's a good idea?"

Qay savored the lightness in his chest of doing something unexpected for a change. He probably had a stupid smile on his face too.

"Why not? She's agreed to take part in the Exchange and will have to meet one of us anyway. I want to be the one to see the look on her face when she realizes the truth. And, to be honest, I can't wait to make her travel down a wall."

The tortured expression on D'zia's face was priceless until his expression lightened. "Ah, you mean up a wall. You can't wait to drive her up a wall."

Qay waved his hand dismissively. "Neither expression makes sense, so it doesn't matter. I want to see her face when she takes a good look at me. Besides, what could it hurt?"

CHAPTER TWO

Aimee

Aimee smoothed her damp palms down the top of her naked thigh and sucked in a breath when he came closer. *Damn.* She wished she had something to cover herself. The cot didn't have any removable blanket or sheet to use. Oh well, the T-shirt she'd worn covered the important parts. She crossed her arms over her chest as she watched the figure come closer.

Walking through the shadows, he was at least humanoid in appearance; two arms, two legs, a torso with a head between broad, muscular shoulders. Holy moly, he was tall. He had to be at least a foot taller than her average five-foot-five frame. As he got closer, she decided he didn't walk but glided in a controlled, fluid manner like someone comfortable in his own skin. Sucked into his laser-like gaze, he reminded her of a predatory animal with prey in sight. He stopped several feet away inside the well-lit room. No longer thinking of making a run for it, she drank in his unusual features.

She stared at his booted feet and the thick black material that protected his calves and ended under his knees. His thighs...thick and firm were covered in a formfitting dark blue cloth that hugged his powerful frame.

Without pause, her eyes roamed upward. Yep...there a massive bulge sat at the apex of his thighs. If he was that big at rest, what....*no, don't go there, Aimee.* She swallowed in a dry throat as her gaze skipped to a waist defined by a large black belt made of the same material as his boots. A lighter formfitting blue shirt covered his expansive chest framed by a black vest matching the boots and belt. His powerful arms crossed a thickset, muscled torso.

Star struck, she gawked at him with her mouth open. Any preconceived notion she had about masculine beauty changed. His overt, exceptional maleness matched the images she's conjured while reading her sci-fi romances.

His skin was a light russet brown nestled by a pearlescent sheen. Hair black as midnight layered with strands of cobalt blue reflected when he moved. A subtle widow's peak crowned a smooth, wide forehead. A tiny intricate braid at his right temple ended in a long curl at the front of his crotch, framing his manhood. Pulled hair bared ears larger than a human's, the tips ending in a slight point. A small gold hoop pierced the left tip, twinkling as it danced and teased in the light. Aimee's lips moistened as she envisioned savoring the combination of warm flesh and cool steel.

She took in his matching black eyebrows. They rose up and down like an upside down V over his almond-shaped eyes framed by a set of thick lashes. Instead of black, his pupils were a dark iridescent green, oval-shaped and surrounded by a ring of dual color. The first ring was a dark emerald with the outer ring a contrasting shade of lighter green. His full lips parted in a patronizing smile and displayed small fangs where human eyeteeth were.

He pulled his arms away from his chest and she noticed he had three fingers on each hand instead of four. Those fingers were long and thick, one digit not any shorter or smaller than another— his thumbs no different than a human.

She sighed, trying to picture how many toes he had.

"Satisfied?" His amused accented tone left no doubt he was making fun of her. "Believe in aliens now?" He leaned against the wall as he crossed his ankles. His dual-emerald eyes caressed and devoured her in a lazy roll.

His casual attitude bugged her. On one hand, she was glad he was an alien and not some sociopath wanting her eyeballs as trophies. He straightened and ambled toward her with a small grin on his full lips. On the other hand, his amusement at her expense was irritating.

A few feet away he stopped. A gape of shock replaced the grinning smirk.

He took in a deep breath and stepped closer. He raised a hand toward her as if he weren't aware of his actions. Those bright emerald orbs bore into hers with widened pupils before he pulled his hand back and shuddered. Clutching his fingers into a fist, he straightened his back, turned around and left without saying a word.

Whoa, what in the world just happened?

"Wait!" Panicked, she ran after him to grab him by the upper bicep. For some strange reason, she choked with dread at him leaving. "Where are you going?" She moved back a step. Her touch stopped him as he swiveled his head toward her. Staring, she got lost in the desire behind his expansive pupils. Her right hand caressed its way down his arm until she grasped the exposed skin on his wrist. He was warm and his pulse pounded, picking up speed.

"What will happen to me now?" she asked in a low tone. She couldn't believe her intense reaction toward him. And what in the world was that wonderful smell? A warm spicy scent...mellow sandalwood interlaid with a hint of tangy citrus. His musky aroma surrounded her and settled deep inside. She responded to his nearness physically as well as emotionally. Her nipples tighten as her womb clenched in anticipated pleasure.

He stepped closer as his nostrils flared and his eyes blazed emerald fire. "What do you want to happen?" His words were low, a secret whisper as his body heat caressed her. "I believe you came here to find yourself a mate." He moved closer. "Did you not?"

With each syllable, her over-stimulated body shivered. Everything faded into the background as she focused on him...her mate, standing right in front of her. "Yes—a mate." It was hard to talk and breathe at the same time. Her voice came out hoarse—she couldn't take her eyes off him. Instinctively she stepped farther into his personal space. Chill bumps coated her arms and the hair on the back of her neck stood at attention. Now Aimee believed the whole "finding your mate with one look thing." A mate, yes, he was her mate...any doubt she might have had about going with the aliens dissipated like a warm fog in the late morning.

With a light touch, his fingers, long, broad at the base, slender at the tips covered her hand. She pressed her body against his to strengthen their connection. When those fingers tightened and removed her from his arm, her stomach dropped as bittersweet confusion followed. He stepped back, her smile faded.

"Then we must indoctrinate you into the Exchange program right away." He motioned to a female crewmember Aimee hadn't noticed waiting in the background. His body twisted as he moved to leave again.

"But..." How could he walk away after something so powerful had begun between them? She wanted—no needed—to get to know him, *damn it!* He had to be as aware of their mutual attraction as she was. It was there in the way his body swayed toward her. It was there in the burning desire in his mesmerizing eyes. And it was there in the darkening of his skin as he licked his full bottom lip before he backed away.

He took the warmth away with him. The cool air between them brought a pungent scent of pain. It fanned—sharp and bitter around them like a splash of ozone before a major storm.

Aimee blinked. How in the world would she know what pain smelled like?

"Please take her to your tutorial section," he told the alien female who stood next to Aimee. The glittering gem of his exotic, dual-emerald eyes rested on her again. "May the Goddess bless and reward you with many offspring for you and your destined mate." He gave a slight formal bow before going through the wall opening.

Aimee stopped at the threshold to watch him walk down the hallway. The pain of his sudden departure made her clutch her stomach to control the heavy fluttering. While she wasn't sure why he'd left abruptly, she noticed how his thick hair pulled at the nape of his neck tapered into a long braid against his spine. The heavy mane rested above his tailbone and swayed across a taut backside. On silent feet, he disappeared into another wall opening a few feet away.

Qay

When Qay first entered the holding room, what caught his attention was her flabbergasted expression. He had to admit he enjoyed her open mouth, widen eyes, and struggled not to chuckle aloud. For the first time in a long time, Qay's lips curled into a playful smile that he directed in the female's direction.

When she'd checked him over, he had to return the favor. Since his duties didn't call for him to personally interact with humans, he'd never been this close to one before. He was going to take the opportunity to look at one up close.

What surprised him was how attractive he found her. She was shorter than a normal Zerin female, but her figure was in perfect proportion to her size. She was a luscious little package for an alien. An expected flush rushed through his body. He gave an impatient grunt and dismissed his brief internal dialogue. It was time to focus what was important, not how he felt towards the pretty human. With her on board, the quota was finished. Now they could leave orbit and head home to get the Exchange running on time.

And not too soon. Thank the Goddess everything was on target and under control.

At least that's what he thought until he'd stepped into the room and took in a deep breath. The female's enthralling scent of creamy vanilla musk snared him. Shocked stupid, he faltered in his tracks. His olfactory senses overloaded and he was flooded with an over-whelming instinct to possess and claim her.

He'd never experienced such a strong reaction before. He swallowed another deep breath as his senses came alive. He had to stifle the urge to get closer because all he wanted to do was wallow in her feminine allure and start the TrueBond process.

He didn't care that the female in front of him was human, and he didn't care she was off limits. Now his goal in life changed, the only thing he wanted to do was claim his TrueBond.

Right here, right now.

Common sense reared its ugly head as a painful, pounding erection became impossible to hide in his formfitting uniform. He cursed the known Gods and Goddesses and threw in a couple of obscene words for good measure. He closed his eyes and clenched his fists to get a grip on his out-of-control emotions. Her intoxicating spice became stronger the closer he got.

He popped his eyes open and unclenched his fists to take a tentative step back to eliminate her feminine pull. He had to get out of here. What started as a joke between him and his cousin was turning into something else.

Now the joke was on him.

Before he'd left, the human female ran up and grabbed his fore-arm. Her boldness stunned him.

"Wait!" she cried. Her soft breasts smashed against his arm when he stopped. Her innocent touch sent shivers up his arm as he glanced at her in alarm. Didn't she know she shouldn't touch him? Didn't she have any sense of self-preservation? She needed to be careful when approaching unknown males!

Conflicting emotions bubbled and swirled. He would like nothing better than to grab her and run, but the urge to run away *from* her was just as strong.

"Where are you going?" She moved in closer, her fingers holding on to the bare skin of his wrist. His heart thudded hard in reaction.

"What will happen to me now?" The huskiness in her voice lured him toward her.

Before he knew it, he stepped closer. Her light feminine scent continued to beckon.

"What do you want to happen?" Was that his voice coming out in a low, silky hum? What in the nine systems was wrong with him? He should be getting away from her, not trying to get closer.

Out of desperation, he stated, "I believe you came here to find yourself a mate." His feet moved toward her, the small space between them shrinking. "Did you not?" Yes, she had to attend the Exchange. The longer he was next to her, the more he wanted to stay.

Her visible shiver struck a satisfied male cord within him. Her voice quivered when she faced him straight on. "Yes, a mate."

It took every ounce of strength he had to remove her hand from his arm and take a needed step back. "Then we must indoctrinate you into the Exchange program right away." Grabbing at anything to help him escape, he spied the liaison, Aja, hovering behind Aimee and motioned to her. "Please take her to your tutorial section." Just one more glimpse. "May the Sacred Goddess bless and reward you many offspring for you and your destined mate." He stiffly gave a courteous bow and left, no matter how painful it was.

Alone in the transportation tube, he bowed his head in silent despair.

Aimee

"But, but..." Confused, Aimee faced the alien female standing behind her. "What in the world just happened? Why did he have to leave?"

The woman shrugged her shoulders in a stilted human gesture. "I have no idea. It's unusual for Commander Qay to even talk to you." Her skin tone was a much lighter reddish-brown than his, the translucent overtones shimmered in the ship's muted glowing light.

She was tall for a woman, over six feet, with long, dark wine-red hair bound in several braided dreadlocks reaching the backs of her thighs. It must have taken forever to put it in such precision since her hair was so long. The thick strands flowed in a symmetrical swish with a life of their own.

With her hair in a tight weave, it prominently displayed her pointed ears. Multi-colored crystallized earrings dangled in a single rope that started at the tips and ended an inch from each lobe. Her eyes were almond-shaped, the irises a darker shade of yellowish green followed by a light shade of khaki. Her long, thick lashes matched her rich eyebrows, the same deep burgundy of her lustrous hair.

The alien's outfit was the same style as the man who'd left, but hers was a cream color. She had a figure Aimee would kill to have. She had small, high breasts, a tiny waist, and legs that went from here to eternity.

She was a striking individual, like an exotic butterfly with tiny fangs.

Something the other woman said caught her attention. "He's a Commander? Are we on a ship?"

In response, the attractive alien ignored her question and extended her hand in a stiff greeting. "Yes, we are on a space going vessel named the *StarChance.* My name is Aja and we are from the planetary system of Zerin. During our trip, I will be your liaison. I wish to welcome you aboard and am looking forward to working with you."

If Aimee wasn't mistaken, the woman had a little snap in her greeting as if she were offended. Aimee hesitated before she returned the handshake. The three fingers gripping her hand weren't awkward and her skin was warm. Aimee let go and took a step back.

"I'm surprised you shook my hand. I'd have thought that was a human gesture." Aimee rubbed her arms. The room had gotten cooler since Qay left and she was breaking out in chill bumps.

"It is, but I've been trained in several of your Earth societies to make your transition as comfortable as possible. My specialty is in your American culture." The plastic smile dropped as she gestured to a small pile of clothes she had in her other hand. "Please change into these clothes." A forced smile that didn't quite reach her eyes made Aimee uneasy. *Okay, okay, stop with the judgments.* After all, this whole thing was a little stressful and maybe she should give the alien the benefit of the doubt.

Aimee took the offered clothing with a tentative smile. There was a long tunic with matching loose pants made of soft, iridescent grey material. Kind of like the sheen on the Zerin's skin that reflected several shades when catching the light. Though grey could be a depressing color, not so with these clothes. The refraction of light displayed a colorful array, from white to deep black.

Aimee loved it.

Included in the pile were a pair of panties and a small circle strip of cloth. Puzzled, she held the flimsy band out and showed it to Aja. "What in the world is this?"

"I believe you humans prefer to wear something else over your mammary glands under your tunic." Aja gave a small grimace of distaste. "Why you prefer this I do not understand."

Huh? Mammary glands? Oh... "You mean my breasts?"

Aja's stoic face became eerie in its stillness. "Isn't that what I said? I know your nano translators were installed correctly." She gestured to the thin strip. "I believe you call it a bra."

"You're kidding, right?" Aimee decided not to go into the whole nano translator-thingy—she'd circle back to that some other time. Right now, she was more concerned about the itty-bitty bit of grey cloth. She held it against her very healthy, full breasts over her T-shirt. The one-inch cloth wouldn't cover her nipples much less hold anything up.

Aja's eyebrows lifted in classic condescension. "I do not kid," was the terse reply. "You put it on like you would any other such garment and the fabric will do the rest."

Well, alrighty then. *Note to self—the alien woman doesn't have a sense of humor.*

"Um, ok. Where do I change? Here?" Not going to happen. No way was she going to strip in front of someone she didn't know. Well, at least not until they bought dinner first.

"Yes, you are to change here."

Was this alien talking to her as if she were a small child? Yes, yes, she was. "Well, I'd prefer to do it in private, if you don't mind." So what if she wasn't in any position to make demands? She kept her face blank waiting for Aja's reply.

The phrase "stink eye" came to mind before Aja responded. "If you insist. I will step out for a moment and be right back."

Without another word, Aja left. As soon as she passed through the doorway, the wall came back in place, leaving her trapped in the bright room. Aimee whipped off the T-shirt and boy panties to put on the alien clothes. No telling how long she'd be alone. The new panties were easy enough. Now for the small piece of fabric that was supposedly a bra. She examined the circle of fabric one more time before she pulled it over her head and draped it over her breasts. Maybe there was a way to adjust it to her boobs. As soon as the material touched her nipples it expanded and matched the exact shape and size of her breasts, and at the same time it gave them the nice lift she'd always needed in a bra. It was comfortable and supportive...hard to tell she wore anything. As an added bonus, it didn't need shoulder straps to hold her up. Carrying around the weight of her boobs had been giving her a backache for years. The tunic and pants went on next.

Yeah—this alone was worth leaving Earth.

Next came the ballerina slippers (which confused her at first, scrunched as they were into a small, tight ball the size of a marble). Once she put them on her toes and heel the fabric enveloped her foot with surprising ease. They were warm with a supporting sole to cushion her steps.

Annnnd....everything was right and just in the universe. What woman (or man) wouldn't give anything to have comfortable, non-pinching clothes and shoes to help get them through their day?

So what if you had to leave your home planet and marry an alien? Ha...easy choice.

Aimee straightened when the wall disappeared and Aja stepped through. "Are you ready now?" Impatient much?

Aimee wasn't going to let Aja ruin her good mood. The only downside so far was the Commander's subtle rejection. No matter, she *was* going to see him again. Anyone who could make her tingle and shiver just by being near her deserved a second look.

Aja motioned Aimee down the same corridor Qay used. "Please follow me so we can meet the rest of your group for orientation." She turned her back on Aimee and strode down the hallway. Her wine-colored braid swayed across her back with the motion of her hips.

Aja's actions were confusing. She said the right things, but her tone and body language contradicted her statements and made Aimee uneasy.

Aja's actions toward her aside, Aimee was enjoying looking around her. No doubt about it, she was acting like a complete dork as she followed Aja around down a spacious corridor, staring at everything in wide-eyed interest. The golden floor shimmered in a spongy material that blended with the recessed lighting and glowed in an easy amber color. It was weird how soothing and warming it was. The walls glistened of the same golden material, muffling the sounds the two made as they walked at a brisk pace.

Damn...how cool was it she was on an honest-to-god spaceship?

There was something missing... "Where is everyone?" The corridor was large enough for four people to walk side by side, but it was just her and Aja. "I thought there'd be more people on a spaceship."

Aja gave her an unsmiling look over her right shoulder as she answered. "This deck is for human females. Since you are the last one of your group to come on board, everyone else is already at orientation."

"Orientation?" What, she was starting a new job? "You said that before. What does it mean?"

Aja slowed to match her stride with Aimee. "There are over one hundred human females on this thirty-day trip to the Exchange. We'll use this time to acclimate you to the various alien cultures you may encounter. At the same time, we'll indoctrinate you to some preliminary laws of the Federation Consortium."

Before Aimee opened her mouth to ask another question, Aja halted and stood beside a blank wall. She furrowed her brow and gave Aimee a stern frown. "Know this, *human*. This is it for you. As you humans like to say, *there's no going back now*." Without another word, she placed her palm on a small indentation in the wall. It disappeared to create a doorway for Aja to walk through.

Maybe staying at home would have been better than putting up with this crap. Aimee sighed and closed her eyes to rein in her temper. No matter, she would make the best of the decision she'd made. She threw her shoulders back and followed Aja to the other side.

Qay

Disheartened, depressed, and disgusted, Qay made it to his workroom with no one stopping him. Good, he didn't want to talk to anyone right now. All he wanted to do was figure out what just happened.

Keeping the lights off, Qay headed for the bathing chamber to wash off any trace of the human. He had to get rid of any possible evidence of a beginning bonding scent. He jerked the formsuit apart, tearing the fabric away from his body. As he pulled it off, a faint suggestion of her feminine bouquet reached him. He brought the blue suit to his nose and inhaled. Subtle notes of vanilla musk combined with an alluring unknown sweetness had him spellbound. He stood there with the clothes clutched in his fists and his eyes closed as he savored the waning fragrance.

He shook out of his reverie to sit on the commode to take off his boots before he put the whole mess into a recycling receptacle. He grabbed a cleansing cloth to wipe his arms and chest before tossing that into the same repository. Naked, he went to his wardrobe in the outer room and pulled out another formsuit, once again dressing for the day. He pulled on a different pair of boots and collapsed on his lounger in another part of the other room to figure out what to do.

Glad he'd kept the room dark, he rubbed his eyes before pinching the bridge of his nose as he sat in the simulated safety of his private room.

Damn everything to the nearest black hole and back.

At least the uncomfortable erection he'd been sporting had gone down when he'd washed off her scent. Gone too was the urge to stroke the ridged flesh to relieve the pressure.

Thank the Goddess for small favors.

Now back to the problem at hand. He would not go against what he held dear as a Zerin to claim her as his instincts screamed for him to do. He refused to contemplate the uproar he'd cause if he took her out of the Exchange.

More important, taking her as a TrueBond would undo the hard work he'd done over the last fifty years. Everything he'd accomplished since leaving Zerin would be for nothing.

Maybe he didn't have to worry. The chances of their brief encounter solidifying the TrueBond were slim, so all he had to do was stay away from her. Which shouldn't be too hard, since he didn't normally mix with humans. So far, there wasn't any reason for him to start. As long as the TrueBond MalDerVon tattoo didn't make an appearance, he had nothing to worry about.

If it did—well, then he'd deal with it then.

The one good thing about all of this was he didn't have to take time off to take that trip to the Southern Providence to look for his TrueBond.

Damn everything to the depths of the nearest black hole and back again.

Aimee

Boy, what a letdown. Where was the weird alien technology to overwhelm her? All Aimee saw was a handful of human women sitting in a U formation in a circular room made of the same golden material as the corridor. The women stopped talking and stared at her when she came in.

Good thing that wasn't awkward. Yep, nothing, like walking into a room full of strangers and having each one of them give you their undivided attention. They were lounging nonchalantly in a variety of neon-colored chairs. Every one of them wore the same grey tunic set she did. The chairs that they sat on were something between a recliner and an old-fashioned school desk, complete with a small tabletop.

Great, there wasn't anywhere for her to sit. She sure hoped no one thought she was going to park her padded butt on that bright green blob lying flat on the floor with its mountain range of small lumps. It was like an old-fashioned beanbag chair her parents had once, except with only one or two beans inside.

Before she asked Aja where she was supposed to sit, one woman piped up, "Just sit in it, girl! You're gonna love it."

Several fingers pointed to the green blob. Oh sure, like she was going to fall straight on her ass for everyone's amusement. Before she opened her mouth, several of the women laughed and encouraged her further.

"Man, it's the best damn chair I've ever sat on!"

"Go ahead, it won't bite!"

"YOLO, baby!"

Okay, the last one was just weird. Resigned, she gave into the peer pressure, walked over to the mess on the floor and gave it a closer look. Maybe if she nudged it with her toe—wait, was it moving? Undulating?

The loud girly squawk coming out of her mouth wasn't about to win her any dignity awards. She backed away, which made the other women laugh like cackling hens.

"Don't mind them, honey." The pretty, thirty-something blonde-haired woman next to her reassured her with a smile. "We had the same reaction when we first got here." Nice to know she wasn't the only one who reacted like a schizoid. The woman waved her hand toward the goopy, bright green mess. "Turn around and sit down like normal. You'll be surprised how comfortable it is. Trust me."

Looked like it was her day to take giant leaps of faith and trust what others told her. Aimee sucked in a deep breath for courage, closed her eyes, and braced for the painful impact of falling straight on her butt.

Instead of the expected sharp pain in her tailbone, the green glob rose up to meet her tush and enveloped her in a snug, yet supportive, manner. It formed to her specific dimensions, from the backrest to the actual seat. It had to be by far one of the most comfortable chairs she'd ever sat on. A small, desk-like protrusion popped out, perfect in length, width, and height for her right arm.

Best of all, the chair was warm and pulsated against her lower back and got rid of a nasty kink that had bothered her for quite some time.

Woo-hoo, she'd died and gone to sitting heaven. First the bra, the shoes, and now this insane chair. All she had to do was to figure out how to take everything with her to—wherever she ended up.

An unbidden vision perked up. She and a naked Commander could make the best of the perfect height the chair had for him to kneel between her thighs...

"Now that we're all here we should get started," Aja said from the center of the room, jolting Aimee from her daydreams and bringing her back to reality.

Damn! It didn't take much for her to zone out on this cuddly green work of genius.

"Tutoring will be done every day in this room and these are your colleagues for our trip." Aja's no-nonsense tone continued as Aimee's mind checked out.

Peeking around the room, Aimee was happy to note they were an eclectic bunch. A mixture of light, dark, and various skin tones in between. Some were around her age, some in their early-to-late twenties and one who appeared to be in her forties.

Aja continued as the corners of her full lips pulled into a semblance of a smile. "I can't tell you how exciting it is to meet you all and help you find your destined male. To do this, we have set up what we call an Exchange program where the males in our galaxy in need of mates can claim Earth females. This will take place on the Zerin moon of Urim. There, all of you Earth women will be put into one big room and the males will come in and meet you."

They spent the next few hours in introductions and strict rules of "what was allowed aboard the ship and what wasn't." Mornings were in the instruction chamber studying various alien cultures with a huge emphasis on taboos they might encounter. Break for a small lunch and afternoons were devoted to physical activities, everything from various alien dance lessons to physical defense.

Dinner would be a group affair, with the Earth women on board going to a single location to enjoy a meal and socialize. All one hundred women representing various Earth countries would be there.

Before Aimee knew it, it was time for lunch. The wall across the room disappeared and a young Zerin woman stepped through, followed by a hovering tray. The silver tray was flat, and the woman controlled it by a series of small, colorful lights flashing on the side.

"This is Taliyah and she will serve your lunch." Aja introduced the younger woman to the group. "This is her first tour of duty aboard our ship and she has been assigned to work with me as another one of your liaisons." Aja nodded her head toward Taliyah to indicate she wanted the food to be distributed.

Taliyah's youthful appearance was in stark contrast to the efficient manner she adjusted the tray. She was tall, with hunter green eyes around the iridescent pupil and a lighter shade on the outside ring.

Her light walnut brown hair gathered in an intricate French braid tapered to rest above her tailbone. Her formfitting suit was identical in color to Aja's but Aimee decided it complimented her darker iridescent skin tone much better than the older Zerin.

"Today we will be serving Earth food, specifically your American salads and sandwiches. We'll introduce you to 'alien' cuisine as we progress on our journey. Tell Taliyah what you would like and she'll program it for you." Aja instructed before she sat in her own bright sunflower colored chair. There she ignored the group as she blinked and the irises of her right eye changed into veins of silver. Her eyes would dart back and forth and her lips moved with silent words. Maybe the alien was plugged into some computer implant she accessed by her eyes. Aja remained engrossed with whatever she was working on until Taliyah finished serving the food and informed her she was finished.

Getting up from her seated position, Aja told the group she and Taliyah would return within an Earth hour to resume their orientation. After that announcement, both alien females left, closing the open wall behind them. With the Zerins gone, the atmosphere in the room lightened and everybody took the opportunity to get to know one another better.

Aimee inhaled the mouthwatering scents of the various foods ordered. Pizza mingled with vegetable soup, chicken, and various hot and cold sandwiches. It was like sitting down at a familiar diner. It gave her a sense of home and comfort.

"I'm still in shock." This confession came from Lora, a thirty-something, dark blonde-haired woman from Sioux Falls. "One minute I'm falling asleep in my own bed." She paused as if to weigh what she would say next, a tense frown pulled the corners of her mouth and caused her deep dimples to disappear. "And the next thing I know I'm here going on an exciting adventure with all of you!" Her light grey eyes lit up with the last word as she focused back at the group.

Aimee tilted her head and studied the rotund woman with a nagging suspicion she'd seen her before. There must be more to the story than what Lora shared.

"You know it, sister," African-American Chloe from Chicago agreed with a smack of her palm on the desktop. Her tuna salad sandwich jumped off the plate before landing back with a small splat. Her hair was in a short bob, enhancing her pronounced cheekbones and round, expressive dark eyes.

Her eyes flashed in annoyance as she talked about former boyfriends. "I'm thirty-two and I've sworn off looking for Mr. Mc-Dreamy!" She snorted in disgust. "I can't believe the crop of mamma's boys out there. They are always whining about every damn thing from having to do their own laundry to help keep the apartment clean." A satisfied smile crossed her lips. "Give me one of those big, beefy alien men any old day of the week." She leaned in as if to share a secret, her ample breasts pushed to the limit of her shirt when she propped them on the desk edge. "I'm hoping for one of those big purple ones—you know the ones with the big...." Her fingers closed in a wide circle as if holding a large penis and pumping it up and down.

There was a round of shared laughter at Chloe's insinuation.

A redhead, Shannon from Bangor, nodded in agreement before adding, "I know what you mean." She gave a small, shy smile. "I've never been with a man but I'm looking forward to being with someone who only wants me."

"Jeez girl, how old are you?" An auburn-haired woman, a thirty-something from Phoenix named Sherrilyn, asked in disbelief. "How can you be a virgin in this day and age?"

"I'm twenty-one. And I'll have you know I am waiting for the right man." Shannon sniffed in a defensive tone as she sat straighter in her chair.

"There's nothing wrong with waiting for the right man, or um, alien," Lora reassured with a wide smile.

"Yes, but I want to join one of those clans, you know, the ones that have three men for every woman?" Shannon agreed with an exclamation.

Shrieks of laughter filled the small chamber.

"That's right! You get 'em, girl!" Chloe roared with glee. "The virgin and the clan!"

Far from being embarrassed, Shannon beamed.

The talk was light and focused on the various aliens they'd read about who fueled their fantasies.

Aimee rested her cheek on her palm. The lunch hour was not long enough.

Taliyah and Aja returned, and lunch break was over. They brought with them a pair of virtual goggles for each woman that had their personal information inserted to disperse their assets. They were to leave everything behind since they couldn't take anything from Earth. The Zerin's would then erase each woman from their prospective government databases and make them disappear.

Aimee picked up the glasses and inspected them before she placed them over her eyes. The control was easy enough—a couple of blinks here and her prior life vanished. Job, home, and all her possessions. Nothing was sacred, everything gone as if she'd never existed.

Her throat clogged and she had to fight back tears. Even though Aimee was glad to be on this trip, it was hard to see her entire existence on Earth disappear...just...like...that.

After returning the glasses (or as Aja called them, "VDU's—video display units"), there was a small, sobering lull in the conversation. Taking advantage of the silence, Aimee confronted Aja about some of the things that bothered her. She cleared her throat to get attention before she spoke up.

"What happens to us if we don't find a male?" Several heads bobbed in agreement.

Aja gave her an absentminded smile as if the question was ridiculous. "My dear, the Zerin people have run this Exchange over twenty times and not once have any of our selected females been left behind." The human shrug she gave was creepy as hell. It came out stilted and awkward. "Do not worry. Human females are in high demand. It isn't possible for any of you to be left behind." With a wave of her hand, she called up the holographic image of the first alien race they were to review.

Aimee doubted anything was that simple.

"Um, excuse me Aja," she insisted, interrupting Aja's droning voice.

Aja waved a finger to pause the 3-D image of a green-scaled male who defined blonde and beautiful, in a hunky, drool-worthy way. "Yes, Aimee?" There it was again, the unmistakable sharp tone.

She didn't care if she irritated Aja. There were important things she had to know.

"Okay, what about your people, the Zerins? Are you part of the Exchange? Will we be able to visit your planet or mingle with the crew?" Maybe Aja wouldn't put two-and-two together to know what, or who, Aimee was asking about.

Not a muscle moved on Aja's face. "I'm afraid not. Law forbids any interaction between Zerin males and the human women. Humans are here for those races in desperate need of repopulation, and I can assure you my people are not one of those. Therefore, there is no reason for us to ever, ah, mingle as it were." She gave a small, stiff smile before she continued. "Of course, I'm not talking about the female liaisons assigned to this deck."

Wow, xenophobe much? "But shouldn't we know a bit about your culture as well? After all, we will be living together for the next thirty days."

The rigid smile on Aja's face stayed firmly in place. "I can appreciate any interest you may have in our culture, but I'm afraid that's not possible." She narrowed her eyes as if to emphasize her next point.

"Nor is it needed." With a finger wave, the new image of a barbarian male from a different dimension holding a pulsating, crystal bridal necklace came into view.

Aimee folded her arms across her chest and slumped in her chair as she lost interest in the drone of the computerized voice interacting with Aja. If she were being honest, she'd already chosen her "alien mate" and didn't want to go to the Exchange. She wanted Qay.

Well, now what?

There had to be some way she could at least see him again. No way had she imagined the powerful attraction between them.

Okay, decision made. Aimee took in a deep breath and glanced around the room. She half expected someone to comment on how she wasn't taking part, but no one paid any attention to her. Everyone was engrossed in the bounty of masculinity in the middle of the room.

The first day of Aimee's new life wound down and it was time for Aja to take them to their assigned living quarters. Which was conveniently close to the training chamber. Aimee smirked. The Zerins weren't taking any chances of someone getting lost, or doing any unscheduled exploring.

One by one, Aja led the human women to their own small accommodations. Besides the normal bedroom suite, each was equipped with a replicator that could make anything from light snacks to replacements of clothing they wore. The replicator doubled as a waste receptacle, complete with recycling those discarded foodstuffs and clothing material. It was a handy thing to have on a space-going vessel.

Aimee loved the light scent of her room and the slight breeze that kept the air circulated. She adored the color scheme. The walls and floor were in a soft silver with recessed lighting. The queen-sized bed was dark blue with purple inlay designs that matched the indigo throw rugs. The walls were devoid of artwork—except for the far-thest wall that had a mosaic of living outdoor scenes. Some were of Earth, some of exotic, alien landscapes.

Before dismissing the women, Aja met them in the hallway for last-minute instructions. "You will each have one hour to get your-self settled in before Taliyah takes you to the dining hall. There you will join all the human women on board for the evening meal. We will see you then." She tilted in a small bow of dismissal.

Aimee started to leave, but Aja blocked her in front of the door to her quarters. "Enjoy your new living quarters, *human*." She sneered the word "human" like a curse in a low voice. "For now."

Aja whacked her hand on the indentation to open Aimee's quarters, inches away from her head. Aimee jumped in surprise at the loud smacking sound as the door opened and Aja stomped away. Aimee's cheeks heated at the violent display, shocked at the level of the alien's frustration. Well, shit—good thing the Zerin slapped the stupid door instead of her.

By the time Taliyah gathered the group to walk to the dining hall, Aimee was a seething jumble of nerves. Between Aja's unexplained animosity, an uncontrollable urge to find Qay, and last, but not least, the stress of losing her prior life took its toll on her fluctuating emotions. Excitement and worry had her jumbled in knots and she was afraid she'd snap.

Her fellow humans didn't appear to be having any problems. The other women laughed and teased each other as if they'd been best friends their whole lives. Aimee couldn't ruin the group's fun by expressing her sense of dread. What good would it do besides make her feel better and upset the others?

Aimee stopped with the others in front of a large archway into an enormous chamber. Peeking over the shoulders in front of her, Aimee's eyes bugged out in astonishment before she joined them in a burst of laughter. It was wonderful how the pinching tension at the back of her neck went away with each chuckle.

The freakin' dining hall was done up like a high school gym, complete with rolled back bleachers, basketball hoops and flags dripping "Go Team" in several color combinations: bright blue and gold, red and black and the ever-popular green and white. What was more surprising was the banners were in different Earth languages.

It was bizarre on so many levels.

Her laughter turned to awe as Aimee stared up at the high, invisible ceiling. Racing stripes of blazing stars streaked by as pinpoints of lights moved overhead. It was like flying through space unimpeded. She'd never seen anything so captivating in her whole life.

Loud female voices echoed in the large chamber and brought her attention back to where she was. A hundred women sat at long tables and ate, various Zerin women with their blank trays placed food they programmed in the middle of the table.

Aimee didn't think the Zerins had to serve the food. Maybe they did it to make the humans feel comfortable, which would be weird. Looking around the gym it was more than obvious the Zerins didn't understand that most of these women hadn't been in high school for decades. If she were to guess, most of the people here would rather forget those years.

Good to know the aliens weren't perfect.

Following behind Taliyah, her group ended up at an empty table in the back. And look, oh joy—there was Aja waiting for them.

Ignoring Aja and concentrating on the mix of the various foods the Zerins were putting down had her nose twitching in appreciation. When she walked past the tables, she tried to see what was on them. Humph, Earth dishes. No matter, she was hungry and there was nothing better than comfort food.

Settling on the hard, backless bench, she sat between Lora and Sherri, with Chloe and Shannon in front. The whole group smiled at each other as several Zerin women placed plates and utensils to use. It was home-style service at its best.

Glasses were in front of each place setting, filled with a clear liquid. Aimee took a sip and frowned at the cool water.

"Hey, where's the cocktails?" Sherri smirked as one of the females placed a tumbler in the middle of the table.

"No alcohol, miss," the polite reply came from the young alien. "Only nutritious food and drink are allowed on board."

Sherri gave a loud snort echoed by Chloe. "You've got to be kidding me!" Sherri pleaded to Chloe for support.

Chloe winked at Sherri. "What kind of nutritious food?"

Aja walked up and stood behind Aimee, close enough for her to feel the alien's body heat. "Is there a problem?"

The hair on the back of Aimee's neck stood in unexpected suspense. After the way that woman acted before dinner, she couldn't help but be skittish around her. Wait, did Aja touch her behind her neck? Aimee twisted around and grabbed the back of her neck to see if anything were there.

There wasn't.

Okay, she must have imagined it. Besides, why would Aja touch her? Aimee moved her head back and forth to see if something were there. Nope, nothing moved. She pressed her fingers against the back of her neck. The thought of the female alien touching her creeped her out. To be safe, she scooted her butt over to the left a couple of inches to turn and keep Aja in her sights.

Ignoring Aimee, Aja clasped her hands in front of her as she interacted amicably with the group. When Aja was speaking to the other women, she was nice and warm.

What had she done to make Aja dislike her so much? Didn't matter, she was going to trust her instincts and keep a close eye on her.

And never be alone with the alien.

CHAPTER **THREE**

Qay

Yes, "justifiable homicide" sounded nice. And if Qay couldn't get away with murder, torture was always a viable option. There were varied and delicious ways to administer pain to someone who made you miserable. A skill he'd learned in his previous life and not something he could use now. Qay gnashed his teeth. The only option he had in this situation was to glare at his tyrant of a cousin. Too bad all the glaring in the world wasn't going to shut D'zia up.

"Will you go away?" Qay growled at the younger male who stood over him. This was the umpteenth time in the last fifteen clicks he had to demand that question. Not his fault his tone came out with more heat than he intended. "I'm sure you have other things to do besides harass me, don't you?" D'zia's grin had better disappear before he wiped it off for him.

"But cuz, nothing is more important to me than your welfare." D'zia's light and dark aqua eyes twinkled in amusement.

It was scary how his cousin wasn't bright enough to realize he was close to losing his temper. Qay rubbed the bridge of his nose. His workroom should be a place of blessed privacy for him. The old-fashioned natural wood tones of the walls and floor were a soothing balm for his busy soul. He kept a bookcase of rare bound books on one wall. A prized collection from around the civilized galaxy he indulged in at every opportunity.

But now an unwelcome irritant invaded his sanctuary. Qay answered his cousin with a snort of disbelief. "No, you just want to harass me." He grumbled and rested against his work lounger. He pushed his braid over his shoulder. "I am fine. Nothing, I repeat, nothing happened between me and the human." He glanced at his cousin with a frown. "What makes you think otherwise?"

D'zia shrugged in that human habit again. "Qay, you seem to forget I was watching you on the monitor and saw the look on your face when you stood next to her." He grabbed a spare chair next to the lounger and set it in front of Qay. He mounted the chair with the backrest in front to lean on. "I have never seen you react like that to a female before." He rested his folded arms on the backrest. "Is she your TrueBond?" He said it in a low whisper as if afraid to voice the forbidden question aloud.

Qay growled and jumped out of his lounger, which caused it to fly across the room and hit the wall with a loud bang as it bounced off the impenetrable surface. Qay surprised himself by that automatic, vicious reaction. D'zia's eyes and mouth opened wide.

"Don't say something like that!" Taking deep breaths, Qay glowered at his cousin. His heart raced as the tension in his hands made his fingers clench into a tight fist. By the nine systems, why was he losing control like this? He cleared his throat and straightened his shoulders. He had to calm down or D'zia would use it as a reason to keep pushing. This ridiculous topic had to end now.

D'zia straightened, his lips set in a firm line and his eyes narrowed. He opened his mouth to say something when the wall disappeared and another figure strode through with heavy, authoritative steps.

The only other person with unfettered access to Qay's working room was his Chief of Security, M'alalu Ki E'eur. He and D'zia called him Ki—the rest of the crew addressed him as "Chief."

When Ki entered the room, the pinch between Qay's shoulders loosened. The bigger man had always had a calming effect on him. Which was a Goddess-given talent whenever Qay needed it. Like now.

Ki was large for a Zerin. He was a little over seven feet tall—three hundred pounds of adversary or a loyal ally. His unusual eyes were navy blue around the luminescent pupil with the outside ring a dark hunter green. Rumor had it he had alien DNA in his family, but no one had enough courage to ask him about it.

Ki kept his unbound dark mahogany hair a shocking shoulder length, considered unacceptable in their culture. Zerin males did not cut their hair or keep it short unless they were disgraced or suffered an unbearable loss. Either way, it never mattered to Qay. He respected the male too much to ask about it. If Ki wanted him to know, he'd tell him.

The most impressive feature on the big man was the ragged scar that bisected his face from the top left of his forehead, diagonal over his eye, down his nose and ended on the bottom right of his prominent cleft chin. His strong jaw sported a full mustache and close, dark beard. The facial hair covered some of the puckered skin, but the scar remained prominent and noticeable.

In Qay's previous, less respectable life, he'd come upon Ki in a brutal fight with a group of greedy Friebbigh. When he saw a fellow Zerin outnumbered by the tiny horde of the repulsive things, he had no choice but to jump in and help. With relish, he and his new friend rid the galaxy of some of the disgusting lawbreakers.

Instead of parting ways, Ki made a surprising move by pledging his undying loyalty to Qay. He'd been astonished Ki was willing to leave a lucrative bounty hunter enterprise to stay by his side. Ki's continued sense of duty and honor humbled Qay more than once over the last solar years.

When Ki agreed to join him on the *StarChance* and become the Chief of Security, Qay thanked the Goddess Ki hadn't left. It was comforting to know he had another person he could count on.

Now if only Ki would quit letting D'zia provoke him....

Stopping after he entered the room, his Chief of Security crossed his massive arms and focused a laser-like glower at D'zia. "What have you done now?" His deep voice boomed with each syllable.

"You are so adorable when you stomp in all protector-like." D'zia gave him a kissy face. "So big and strong." He batted his eyes at Ki.

Ki frowned at him in confusion. "Have you been hanging around the humans again?" He unfolded his arms, placed his knuckles on narrow hips, and scowled at Qay. "I can't understand half of what he says anymore."

Qay gave a yelp of laughter. Trust the two of them to put things in perspective. Their friendly back and forth banter was a great stress reliever. "I know, I know." He grabbed the hapless lounger and brought it back before he sat down. "He's just leaving."

D'zia slumped in his chair and crossed his arms with a narrow stare. Qay wasn't the only stubborn E'etu family member. "No, I'm not. We will discuss this whether or not you want to." D'zia glanced up at Ki. "Now that his holiness is here, we can have a real conversation." He gestured at another chair against the wall and invited Ki to sit.

"Stop calling me that," Ki gave his usual absent minded retort to D'zia. He brought the chair over and sat, spreading his large legs and resting his forearms on his thighs. "Now, what's going on?"

"Nothing." Qay tried his best not to be irritated all over again. He just wanted to forget the encounter with the luscious, mouth-watering—female—*shit*! He had to stop thinking about "The Human" as he called her in his mind. He'd hoped by not using her name, he might keep their brief encounter impersonal.

He'd use any tactic to stop the TrueBond.

A cheerful thought occurred to him. Qay never considered if a Zerin could form a TrueBond with a human, maybe it wasn't possible. Bah! What did it matter—any discussion about "The Human" wasn't open for debate with anyone. Not even himself.

"You're impossible." D'zia dismissed Qay with a disgusted snort. He accessed the ocular VDU and shared the 3-D display on their personal units before Qay could stop him.

Ki watched and listened without a comment. When the short encounter was over, he blinked to cancel the vid and glanced over at Qay with a stoic expression.

The silence stretched for several clicks.

Qay gave an unwavering stare back.

"Goddess above have mercy and save me from these two," D'zia implored looking up at the ceiling. "So...Ki...what do you think?"

"It doesn't matter how I view it," came the gruff reply. "It depends on what Qay thinks."

Both men gave Qay identical expressions of patience with arms crossed over their chests.

Qay mirrored their body language as he considered the two males in front of him. This line of thought was starting to get out of control. The idea of him having a human TrueBond came with too many possible consequences to contemplate.

"Nothing happened. It was fun to tease the human." He accessed the program and blinked to archive the damning vid. "End of story." He went into full commander mode as he dismissed the topic by straightening his back. He blinked to retrieve the engine-reporting program in his OVDU. "I'm convinced the both of you have more important matters to attend to. I suggest you go over the contingencies we've discussed to make sure nothing has been left out." He glared at them before stating, "You're dismissed."

Ki and D'zia glanced at each other in rare accord.

"Yes, sir!" D'zia's lips thinned in displeasure. He stood and gave a crisp salute with his right hand over his heart before he bowed and left without saying another word.

Qay refused to feel guilty at the hurt look on his cousin's face. Even if he wanted to confide his suspicions to D'zia, he wouldn't.

He refused to put D'zia in a precarious position just so he could feel better.

Ki stood and paused behind Qay, placing a reassuring hand on the younger man's shoulder. "If you need anything, you know where I am," he said in a low tone before he left.

The silence was a heavy weight in the small chamber. Qay picked up a stylus from his desk and twirled it around his fingers as he reclined in his lounger. Indecision was a rare thing for him but he had to admit he didn't know what to do if all of his efforts to remain unbound didn't work.

Aimee

The training session the next day gave Aimee a searing headache. When it was time for dinner, she was more than ready for a change of pace.

That night as they entered the crazy gymnasium, it cheered Aimee up. The place was so unreasonable it lifted her spirits with its glorious, star-filled ceiling and tacky décor.

She settled in her usual place between Sherri and Lora, with Shannon and Chloe across from them. The warm aroma of Earth and alien food made her stomach rumble and her mouth water as she licked her lips in anticipation. Shannon was eating turkey with all of the fixings next to Sherri happily munching on a colorful Mediterranean salad. Chloe gave an excited yelp and grabbed a bowl of some unknown gray gelatinous stuff that wiggled like Jell-O with bits of orange globs mixed in. She piled several mounds of the jiggling food on her plate before she plopped a spoonful in her mouth.

"This is great!" she exclaimed with a rapturous grin. "It's better than I thought it'd be." She downed a couple more bites with her eyes closed in bliss before she opened them again. "What? You gonna try some or not?" She huffed at their dismissal as she continued to enjoy the bounty in front of her.

The noise in the hall increased as a hundred women's voices competed with each other. Between laughter and the clinking of dishes and utensils, it was hard to hear the conversation between them.

"Anyway," Lora raised her voice after everyone had started to eat. "Aimee, were you having problems in your cabin today?"

Surprised by the random question, Aimee paused with a forkful of spicy shrimp burrito as she scrunched her nose in confusion. "No, why do you ask?"

Lora shrugged her shoulders. "Well, I think I saw a Zerin man walk out after we all went to our physical classes this afternoon." Aimee's heart pounded. Qay? Was Qay looking for her? She put a hand over her rumbling stomach.

"A Zerin man?" Chloe squeaked in excitement. Her loud tone caused heads to turn in their direction from a couple of tables over. "You saw a live Zerin man?" She paused and shoved her plate aside to lean in with folded hands on the table. "What'd he look like? Was he gorgeous or just a plain ole stick man?"

The group stopped talking to hear Lora's answer, their intent palatable. Aimee glanced around and was surprised to see those nearest to them had stopped talking to listen in.

Aimee pictured Qay in her mind and refused to feel guilty she hadn't shared their meeting and her strong reaction to him. Then she'd have to tell them how he rejected her. It was embarrassing enough that Aja had been there when the whole thing happened—she didn't need her new friends to know.

"He was no stick man, believe you me." Lora's face flushed. "He was absolutely gorgeous, tall—around six-two, maybe six-three—with lean muscles bulging in a dark blue formsuit. He had light brown braided hair topped in a man bun." She gave a dramatic sigh worthy of any swooning maiden as she rested her chin on her open palm. "He had the most beautiful dual-colored turquoise eyes I've ever seen and the deepest, most gorgeous dimples ever." Lora's eyes glazed over as her own dimples peeked out.

Aimee frowned as her mind raced. Turquoise eyes? Light brown hair? It didn't sound anything like her commander with his pitch-black hair and stunning emerald eyes. He had to be taller than six-two—at least six-five or more.

"Did he see you?" Aimee asked. "Say anything to you?" Why would some Zerin man be in her quarters? She took a bite of her burrito, oozing with spicy red sauce and cheese.

Lora jerked and gave a quick nod. "Hum? Yeah. As I was coming out of my cabin we came out at the same time." The small smile was back as her eyes unfocused again.

Lora remained silent, oblivious to everyone around her.

"Well?" Sherri slapped a palm on the tabletop to get Lora's attention. "What did he say?" There were murmurs of consent from several voices.

"Huh?" Lora shook out of her reverie. "Oh, well, nothing really. He wished me a good afternoon and walked away." She gave soulful moan. "He had the most adorable lips you'd ever seen with the richest accent you've ever heard." She glanced at her companions with wide-eyed innocence. "And the most delectable, mouth-watering, firm ass in existence."

There were snorts and chuckles of laughter.

Ha! Bet Qay's ass was better. Aimee's eyes unfocused as she relived the image of him walking away from her as the muscles in his ass cheeks flexed deliciously. Boy, she loved those aliens wearing tight suits. It gave a girl some great eye candy to look at.

Back to the conversation, Aimee asked, "Did he say why he was in my cabin?" Something wasn't right about the whole thing.

Lora shook her head. "No." She gave a sheepish grin. "I'm afraid I was too busy drooling over him to fire up any brain cells to ask."

"Maybe he was maintenance and had to fix something," Sherri gave a reasonable suggestion.

Lora shook her head again. "No way was that hunkalicious working maintenance." She paused. "He didn't have any tools on him either."

"Well." Chloe sat back and stabbed a piece of light-colored meat with her fork. "When you get back to your cabin, Aimee, be sure to look around and see if anything looks weird or not." She popped the chunk into her mouth and chewed before swallowing. "There isn't any reason for a Zerin to hurt you so I don't think he was there to do something bad."

Sherri pursed her lips as she narrowed her brown eyes. "I think we should go in the cabin with her just in case to help her check it out. What do you think, Aimee?"

Aimee's shoulders relaxed at Sherri's suggestion. It was nice to know the others cared about her, but she didn't think it would be necessary. "No, I'm good. But thanks anyway, guys."

"No worries, it's all good," Chloe agreed before she gave Lora a piercing glare as she pointed an empty fork at her. "Now missy, let's hear every excruciating detail about this hunkalicious of yours."

After saying said goodnight to her friends, Aimee entered her room with more caution than usual. She stepped over a small pile of discarded dirty clothes and sat on her unmade bed. Another reason she didn't want her friends to come: she was a bit of a slob and hadn't cleaned up before she'd left this morning. Great, nothing like letting a mysterious Zerin man know how messy she was. Oh well, nothing she could do about it now.

Out of the corner of her eye, she noticed something black peeking out from under her ink colored blue pillow. She threw the pillow off a pair of VDU wraparound glasses. Was this why the guy had been in her room? To give her these? Squirming to sit at the head of the bed, she leaned against the cushiony wall and put them on. They operated on the same principles as the glasses she wore in the training class. Good thing it didn't take a genius to navigate through the displayed files.

One file stated "Monitors" and another said "History." Compelled, Aimee navigated to the one saying "Monitors." There another list popped up: "Dining Hall, Medical, Bridge, Training, and Commander's Workroom." She touched "Bridge" and stood on an obvious ship's bridge. The layout was different from what she'd seen in the movies; this one reminded her of a small theater. There were ten lounge seats shaped in a U pattern with a large, similar chair behind them. The front wall showed the passing galaxy, a 3-D display like the ceiling of the crazy dining gym.

She glanced around—afraid someone would notice her and call an alarm. When no one shouted that a crazy human invaded the bridge, she relaxed and remembered she was in a virtual world and not standing in the actual room.

She ignored everything around because there...there was the object of her continued fixation—Commander Qay. Her heart pounded as she checked out his bent form over a console attached to the back wall. His long, thick braid fell over his right shoulder and draped to sway enticingly around his crotch. His formfitting admiral blue suit caressed his body and showed off his maleness.

Unexpected tears welled as a great weight lifted from her shoulders. She went over to stand next to him and sighed with relief. She'd begun to believe she'd dreamed him up. But really, no way was her imagination good enough to come up someone like him. Added to her relief that she wasn't going crazy was how she wanted, no—how the intense *need* to see him overwhelmed her. The urge to be with him went against everything she'd ever believed of herself as a sane, rational person.

Unconsciously she reached out to touch him as she whispered, "Qay." Her finger passed through the scruff of his lower jaw.

Oh yeah, she had it bad.

The burden of the last twenty-four hours came crashing down. She was so tired it was hard to sit up. She took off the glasses and put them on a small table near the bed. She got up to take off her clothes and added them to the pile on the floor. Maybe she'd get to them in the morning. Aimee grabbed a one-piece sleep tunic from the receptacle unit to wear. Exhausted, she crawled between the covers and laid her head on the soft pillow. The fresh linen smell lulled and relaxed until she fell asleep with Qay on her mind.

The next day was the same as the day before. Meet everyone at the training chamber for breakfast and morning lessons. Lunch served, another hour of information dump before heading out to various physical classes. Dance, defense, an alien version of yoga or plain old calisthenics were offered before having dinner in the gym.

Aimee tried to hide her impatience. All she wanted to do was go back to her room and the VDU glasses. She wasn't sure if others noticed her impatience, but she didn't care. She ignored her conscience anytime the word "stalker" popped into her head. She wasn't hurting anyone, she told herself, so her conscience should just buzz off.

After an eternity, she was finally back to her cabin. She changed into nightclothes and ignored the small pile of the discarded wear from the morning that took up space at the foot of the bed. She got in bed and kicked the clothes off. She settled in and put the glasses on to search. She began at the bridge, before moving on to his private workroom. No luck. It wasn't until she touched the training link that she found him in a dojo.

He was practicing a mixture of martial arts with a huge male Zerin at least half a foot taller and fifty pounds heavier. The man's mahogany, shoulder-length hair matched his close-cropped circular beard and mustache. He sported a wicked-looking scar bisecting the left side of his face and ending on his right chin. The scar might be intimidating, but he wasn't. He was attractive in a badass, biker way. It wouldn't be hard to imagine him astride an oversized Harley, riding down a dark road with his massive arms draped over ape handlebars.

Her unsubstantial form stood close to the circling pair, able to observe them in momentous detail. They wore minuscule loincloths to cover the interesting bits—their feet, thighs, and massive bare chests glistening in the soft light. She laughed at her whimsy of what Qay's toes looked like. His feet were beautiful in symmetry, with one big toe and three smaller ones. Both males balanced and spun on their toes when they revolved around each other in their dance for dominance.

It was fascinating to watch as they gauged each other's strengths and weaknesses in graceful movements. They circled in a slow, predatory manner, unable to take their eyes off one another. Their moves were a mixture of martial arts, sword fighting, and dancing as they swung a three-part wooden staff connected by metal rings. The staffs became an extension of their arms to strike, flail, and block, with different sections of it acting simultaneously. Inserted at the end of each staff was a sharp blade or a ball the size of their fists embedded with sharp spikes.

As they continued to circle, each had a determined look of concentration with several cuts and body blows bruising. Their iridescent, bronzed torsos gleamed as their large chests heaved with exertion. Muscles flexed and moved in a steady, synchronized rhythm as their firm, hardworking muscles simultaneously caressed and contorted with each movement.

Her mouth and eyes became dry as sandpaper. No wonder, since all of her body fluids headed south to pool between her legs. Sweaty palms twitched as she rubbed them up and down her bare thighs in agitation. What she wouldn't give to be there in person and inhale in all that musky testosterone goodness.

A nasty blow struck Qay's right shoulder. Her heart pounded and she screamed, her muscles readied to protect...to protect him. *No!* She touched him. Crap! She was a virtual ghost, as her hand went through him.

As if they heard her, they stopped in complete synchronization and stepped back to stare at each other. They gave each other with an incredulous stare before they broke out into shared laughter and grasped each other's forearms.

Oh, for the love of God. She took a step back and crossed her arms. Stupid idiots loved to beat the shit out of each other and call it good when someone got hurt. The spiked ball had punched Qay's shoulder and several perforated holes bled small tracks down his muscled arm.

Well, if nothing else, Zerins bled red like a human. She cursed the soundless image since it didn't come with audio. She'd give anything to know what they were saying.

All too soon the little things she hadn't noticed before distracted her. Like how Qay's nose was long and regal but had a small bump in the middle as if it hadn't healed properly. She liked the tiny gold hoop earring piercing the tip of his left pointed ear, with small intricate etchings around the jewelry. She took in the stubble on the lower part of his face and decided she liked him a little scruffy.

He was an animated talker, using his hands as if to punctuate a particular point he was trying to make with his companion. The three-finger thing at first startled her, but being around the female Zerins for the last couple of days she didn't notice it as much.

She gave an involuntary moan as Qay and his companion walked out of visual range. She watched their naked, muscled backsides writhe and bunch with each step. With firm strides, they crossed the room and left.

Best. Eye. Candy. Ever. Giggling at the absurd notion, she chastised herself for giggling. What was she...twelve?

Show over, she blinked to disconnect and took off the glasses to set them on her lap. One thing was for sure, observing her alien interacting with his friend made her grateful for taking a chance to come on this trip. Watching Qay and his friend renewed her desire to connect with others, especially him. She was positive he was the one for her. Thank god that strange Zerin left the glasses in her room. Why he did was a mystery, but who was she to question good fortune? At least it gave her a way to get to know Qay, even if it was in secret. Now all she had to do was ignore the creepy stalking factor of her plan and focus on the optimistic turn of events.

Yep, with someone helping her, things were looking up and going her way.

As one day blurred into the next, Aimee found she was impatient for each one to end so she could go back to her cabin and spend the evening watching Qay. It was hard for her to pay attention to the daily activities; she'd rather daydream on how Qay moved when he sparred, how warm he appeared when he interacted with his friends, and the mouthwatering way he fought practically naked. *Damn*, worse than some starry-eyed preteen with her first crush.

As usual, she ignored the changing landscape on one of the walls and her growing pile of discarded clothes to change into a night tunic. She jumped in bed and put on the glasses. Settling with her back cushioned by a collection of pillows and the soft wall, she swiped through the file menus.

This particular evening, instead of checking out Qay's day, her eyes latched on a file titled, "Commander Qayyum A'agnan E'etu" and another one that said "Exchange Information." Eagerly she opened the first one to learn more info on him. She scrolled through it. The accompanying list was long, but one titled "Deliverance of Gloth U48R" with a jumbled line of numbers caught her curiosity. Hooking up the file, she dove in—

—and found she was smack dab in chaos. Thick smoke she couldn't smell engulfed and swirled around her. She wasn't on the *StarChance* but a virtual perspective of an underground cave lit with primitive torches along craggy walls. A myriad of alien species rushed around— and through—her holographic image. She was smack dab in the middle of a panic rush...terror surrounded her.

Mouths were open and moving, probably shouting and screaming to one another.

Straight ahead, Qay rushed in her direction as rivets of red ran down his blackened face. His dirty clothes were in tatters, a loose shirt hung in ribbons from his shoulders. His dark pants had holes in the knees and various areas around his thighs. He carried a long shovel in one hand and some type of gun in the other.

The fierce determination on his handsome face alarmed her. His eyebrows were slanted in a stern line, his teeth pulled back to expose his sharp fangs. He raced through her, giving her no choice but to follow.

His long, black braid flew behind him as she pushed her virtual legs to keep up. He stopped, dropped the gun and started swinging with the heavy-looking shovel. He wasn't digging dirt—he was using the shovel as some sort of weapon on the small, slimy bodies trying to block him.

Aimee held her breath as she took a good look at the little creatures trying to fight Qay off with their long, spindly arms and hands. She'd swear those little aliens looked like one of the "Greys" she'd read about in UFO abduction stories. They had large, bulbous heads, huge black almond-shaped eyes, little skinny arms, legs, and torsos. Thin, nondescript lips set in a horizontal line opened as forked tongues snaked out when he'd hit them over the head.

Repulsed, Aimee shrunk back when a small group of Zerins ran through her and followed Qay. As the group passed, her heart dropped when she noticed small children, a couple of older females, and one older male who took up the rear. He picked up the weapon Qay had dropped.

With growing concern and admiration, Aimee watched Qay protect and save the small group of hapless Zerins. After he dispatched the grey aliens, he herded the other Zerins through the dark tunnels, the small children given the responsibility of holding tubes to light the way. The little ones were crying but kept moving as the women encouraged them.

The small troupe ended up at a jagged cave opening. Aimee's heart dropped when a throng of those grey aliens blocked them. They raised their weapons at Qay and those behind him.

Aimee squealed as she watched in horror when Qay stood in front of the shivering Zerins with his arms raised at his side as if that would protect them.

"NO!" she screamed, rushing toward him. What good she could do, she'd never know because the grey aliens disappeared in a puff of smoke.

Shocked, Aimee blinked at the new scene. Through the haze and ash, tall humanoid beings in metallic colored battle-suits and triangular helmets stopped in front of Qay.

He lowered his arms and brought them over his chest. He spoke, but Aimee couldn't hear what he said. It became apparent the new troops were the good guys when they lowered their weapons. Qay had saved his ragged little band.

The window closed and she was back at the menu she'd been in before, sitting on her bed in the comfort of her cabin.

Heart racing, she closed her eyes to get her bearings. Qay's determination to save the helpless group made Aimee's admiration grow. Okay, her admiration didn't just grow—she practically swooned at his heroism. He'd been alone, against horrible odds but didn't shy away from protecting those in his care. She wished she could hear what they were saying because she would love to know the whole story.

She blinked her eyes to the right to back out of Qay's menu. Next, she went to the file of "Exchange." Maybe there she'd find something to help her learn how to "mate" with her Zerin—no matter what Aja said.

"Now that's odd," Aimee mumbled as she found another link hidden on the page. She kept seeing the name "Friebbigh" regarding one species taking part in the Exchange but no reference to human women mating with them. Thinking back, she was sure she never noticed that name in the information given to her by Aja or on any other link she'd read.

After trolling through a couple more links, she found a written description that matched the grey aliens from Qay's heroic adventure:

"Description: The Friebbigh are male/female hybrids originally from the planet Fibona in the North Western section of the galaxy. They are grey in skin color with a large bulbous head, big almond eyes, and a black pupil. Two vertical slits for a nose and one small horizontal slit for a mouth. It is small in stature, around four feet, five inches tall with thin, stick-like arms and legs. They wear a skintight suit the same color as their waxy grey skin, giving them an unclothed appearance.

They communicate telepathically with each other but do not do so with other species, which they deem inferior. To converse with other races, they have a "voice box" attached to their suits that transmit their thoughts into speech.

Their reproductive process is unknown.

Warning: They are criminals within the Federation Consortium, wanted for arms dealing, kidnapping, slavery, and war crimes. This species is suspect in several outstanding assassin warrants with each of the known civilized members. It is against Consortium law to interact with this species in any manner other than to kill or arrest. Interactions with this species are a treasonable offense and will be prosecuted to the fullest extent of the law."

Well, isn't that weird. Aimee took off the glasses and settled in for the night. How could they be a part of the Exchange when they were criminals and "Their reproductive process is unknown"? It wasn't as if she could go up to a Zerin and ask them. How could she explain how she'd gotten the information in the first place? She doubted Aja would let her keep her VDU glasses if she told her about them.

The Exchange was coming up in less than two weeks and she was trying to figure out how to talk to Qay and avoid Aja before then.

Aimee frowned as she contemplated Aja's hostility toward her. Every day was worse than the day before, but she decided it didn't matter. It wasn't as if the alien woman was a threat to her or anything.

Aja

Deep in the bowels of the *StarChance*, Aja moved unsanctioned computer files away from prying eyes, growing increasingly annoyed. She hated it when she had to take extra steps for protection she hadn't counted on.

Idiot human! Aja uncovered Aimee's efforts to gain information about the Zerins and the Exchange in a classified database. She didn't have time for the human's stupid little attempts to find out how screwed she was. Who gave her the ability to access the mainframe, anyway? Aja's ocular implant had a hard time keeping up with her furious pace as she deleted files and put false ones into place. That would take care of the annoying little *jazbitz*.

She wrote a program to frame Aimee for the human trafficking that Aja was going to commit on board the *StarChance*. To complete the conspiracy, she created a vid showing Aimee in collusion with the Friebbigh to sell out her fellow humans.

Satisfied, Aja smiled at her plan to implicate the annoying human. She pulled up her final list of human women from the StarChance slated for the slave market on FiPan. Thank the Goddess this was the last bunch she had to hand off to the Friebbigh for quite a while. Once she settled her numerous debts, she'd have enough credits to satisfy Chancellor U'unk. Then she'd be able to leave the fake life behind and begin her promised job in working for the Chancellor. Within a short period of time, she'd end up as one of the most powerful Zerins in the galaxy, second only to the Chancellor, who was the current elected official running the Consortium.

She shook back to the present. Her plans were foolproof and everything would work as scheduled. She double-checked the safeguards and was confident it would be impossible for anyone to find out what was going on underneath their noses. Much less connect it with her.

If by some miracle they did, she'd be long gone and Aimee would be responsible.

Qay

Qay lay in his comfortable bed with his mind racing—too many images fought for attention as he tried to fall asleep.

Uncertainties about "The Human" aside, he had bigger worries than whether or not he illegally bonded with an alien. The directive from the Imperial Forces to find the criminal slave ring operating with the Exchange was taking up more time than he'd expected. So far, they weren't able to find any shred of evidence the slavers were using the *StarChance*, much less finding out they weren't.

Good thing the experimental engines worked with flawless precision—one less concern.

The slavery problem heated up with the latest rumor of human slaves up for auction in the outer rim territories. The timing coincided with the *StarChance's* arrival on Urim for the Exchange.

Qay growled in frustration. He intertwined his fingers beneath his head as he continued his internal dialogue and stared at the blank ceiling. It infuriated him how someone was profiting on the sale of sentient beings illegally, and used the Zerin people to do it.

Rubbing his tired eyes, Qay thought about her, "The Human," the beautiful Aimee. If he had any sense of self-preservation, he wouldn't give her another thought. Too bad, he wasn't that smart. Like tonight, in the quiet dark of his personal quarters, he activated his personal OVDU and followed her around, watching her in her routine. When she attended class, when she was in the training center, and when she was in that Goddess-awful dining hall with the other human females, their voices raised in laughter and excited talk.

Good thing there wasn't a vid system in her quarters because he was pathetic enough to view it if it'd been available.

Before falling asleep, he enjoyed his nightly ritual of when they met. He'd lay there for hours, envisioning being with her when he should have been sleeping. He remembered the way she moved, the soft glow of her pale skin, and the way his body responded when exposed to her unique scent. Watching her exotic eyes dilate as they caressed his face was nothing short of mesmerizing. And the softness of her body when she'd unconsciously moved closer as they brushed together...

Did she experience the same pull of the TrueBond as he did? Were her nerves strung so tight she had to do something—anything to bind them in a tight, unbreakable embrace? Holy Goddess, he had to stop from going down this morbid pit that would take him to his eternal damnation.

He grimaced in exasperation as he gave a grunt of impatience. *Fruk*, he was as miserable and maudlin as an old one. Since when was he so disgustingly poetic as to bemoan his eternal damnation? His morose thinking got him up from his cozy bed to go to the lounger in the other room. Time to focus on something other than "The Human."

His personal quarters were a direct contrast to his old-fashioned workroom. Here he preferred straight lines and blunt edges. The floor, walls, and ceiling were in a matte silver while the fabric covering his sleeping pad was a deep black. His lounger matched the bed, an onyx so deep it was hard to distinguish the stitching on the faux animal hide. The chair was strong, durable, and withstood his absentminded treatment.

Flopping in the personalized lounger, he powered his ocular VDU and called up the reports from earlier. Something he'd read bothered him. The engines continued to work with precision accuracy, but a nagging at the back of his mind had him wondering what he was missing.

After a few frustrating attempts, he didn't find anything out of the ordinary. He was about to give up when he had a better idea. Why should he be the only one up late at night? Guess it was time to share his late-night insomnia with someone who deserved it.

"D'zia," his voice snapped into the internal communication. "I need you to run another analysis on the T-192 report and compare it to the first one we did before we started this voyage. It has to be done immediately."

There was dead air. Qay waited for his cousin to answer and got a response faster than he expected.

"What is *wrong* with you?" D'zia grumbled. "Go to sleep and leave me alone." There was a rustling noise in the background and a purring female voice demanded D'zia come back to bed. D'zia answered his companion in a low growl that he'd be right back. "I don't report for duty for another three hours. So, as humans liked to say, *fuck off*." The communication ended.

Qay didn't know if he was offended or amused at his cousin's answer. He tried to decide when his communication beeped with an incoming call. It was Ki.

"Yes, Ki? Everything okay?"

Ki's grunt told Qay of his impatience. "Hard to say. I've been trying to run a comparison analysis on the T-192 report, but it's off and I have no idea why." Qay imagined Ki sitting with his visual display unit in his security office. He doubted the male ever slept.

"You know, funny you should mention that report. I just called D'zia to run a diagnostic on it."

Ki's bark of laughter was infectious and made Qay smile. "I'm sure that went over well."

Qay gave a chuckle of his own. "Hardly. He was busy with some female and he told me to *fuck off*. Whatever that means."

"Sounds like the human slang he keeps using." Ki paused. "I don't like how we can't discern when the Friebbigh might come in contact with the *StarChance*. It shouldn't be hard to figure out, but something is eluding us or someone is sabotaging our records. I need your permission to run a full spec analysis on the key system so I can look deeper."

Qay gave Ki's question serious consideration. "How long would it take to do a complete analysis?"

"Well..." Ki's hesitated. "We have less than two weeks before we begin our descent home. My guess is they'd have to make their move between now and then. I think its best we don't inform the crew and keep this between us for now. So I'll need your cousin to help. That is if he can fit me into his busy schedule." His dry tone was unmistakable.

"I assure you, he's all yours. I'll reassign his other duties so he can be at your complete disposal. Day or night."

Ki's low, evil laugh was a hefty promise to take advantage of Qay's offer before he signed off. Qay smiled in satisfaction before he popped his jaw with a loud yawn. Damn, he was tired enough to sleep now. Knowing D'zia was at Ki's tender mercies for the next couple of days was better than a sedative any night of the week.

If nothing else, it was better than—what did D'zia say?

Ah, yes—to *fuck off.*

Chapter **FOUR**

Aimee

Three days before the Exchange, Aimee woke up with her stomach fluttering in excitement. This was the day Aja had taunted Aimee and her friends about a "day off." The liaison repeated more than once that they'd love what the Zerin's had planned for them. Aimee and the others were to meet her and Taliyah at the entrance of the dining hall first thing that morning.

Aimee could only hope they'd gotten rid of the stupid high school gym. That would make it a good "day off."

She rushed to meet everyone as fast as she could, but she was still the last to arrive. Good thing no one commented on her tardiness—they all were too busy commenting on what the day off meant. Aimee glanced around the room and noticed the vacant feel with the deflated chairs dotting the floor. Like colorful neon polka dots in a perfect U shape.

"Aja here?" was Aimee's first question. She was in such a good mood when she woke up she cleaned her quarters and replicated a new tunic and leggings set. This one was in a cheery goldenrod blonde, with amber piping around the three-quarter sleeves, tunic hem, and the flared material at her ankles. She had matching slippers in the same color and trim.

"Nope," Chloe stated. The multi-colored beads in her short hair tinkled as she shook her head. "The day is lookin' up, my friends!" Chloe's tunic and pant set was a bright teal with lime green trim. The colorful outfit set off her umber brown skin to perfection.

The others laughed and agreed except for Shannon, who stayed back from the group and was quiet and withdrawn. Aimee frowned as she made a mental note to talk to her the first chance she got. Being the youngest couldn't be easy, but that didn't explain why she wasn't acting like the bubbly, confident woman she'd been when they'd first met.

No doubt it was Aja's fault.

"Shall we depart, gentle ladies?" Lora quipped. She made an old-fashioned bow with a swirl of her hand and her right foot at a smart angle in front of her. Her tunic was lavender with silver trim, setting off her shining grey eyes and thick blonde hair. Laughing, the group left for their promised adventure.

The trip to the dining hall was full of teasing laughter. It was great to cut loose and relax for once. In no time Aimee and her friends reached the dining entrance, crowded with other human women. The shut door caused them to mill around in the crowded hallway.

"I wonder what the holdup is," Sherri said. She placed a hand on Lora's arm as she stood on her toes, trying to see over the heads of the women in front. Her tunic set was a double length top—the first layer in a red-orange, the lower layer in a burnt orange and the pants in the matching color to the top tunic. The edgy bob and wispy bangs of her auburn hair swayed when she moved her head back and forth.

"Do you see anything?" Lora held the other woman's elbow. Sherri shook her head and dropped back to the soles of her feet.

The sudden deafening silence gave Aimee pause.

The bottleneck broke as women pushed each other into the open room. Unable to get free, Aimee stumbled until the surge stopped.

At first, she wanted to laugh at the identical looks of horror on the faces around her.

That is until she saw what everyone else did. And wished she hadn't.

The enormous room was a visual hodge-podge in Picasso-like proportions. It was as if Las Vegas threw up on a '50s sock hop and mixed up with some kind of disco roller rink trying to cozy next to a Cinderella ball dreamed up by Rob Zombie. Individual pieces sort of made sense, but the whole thing was an attack on all five senses.

The mishmash of scenery overwhelmed Aimee as it came at her from too many directions. A mix of offensive smells burned her nose—spoiled food combined with the gritty corn of old socks. An ear-splitting blast vibrated through the soles of her feet and shot out the top of her head. The humidity clung to her skin and made her flesh crawl as her clothes stuck to her skin. To top it off, the air had a rancid taste of thick goop, slithering down her throat before it settled in her stomach like a heavy knot. Which, of course, wanted to come back up in dry heaves.

No one said a word. Not that she could tell if they did between the thumping, twangy alarms going off. She was nauseous, dizzy, and faint simultaneously.

She couldn't breathe.

A painful squeeze on her arm made her turn to the person next to her. Shannon grabbed onto her with a death grip, shaking in wide-eyed terror. Aimee gave her a reassuring clutch as she hoofed her feet backward, taking the other woman with her.

Shannon joined her step-by-step without uttering a single word.

Like a hive mind, all of the women backed up in unison to make a beeline for the doors and freedom.

Before Aimee took another step, the large walls closed behind them. The screeching noise cut off as the room plunged into inky blackness. The ringing silence became an assault all on its own. Between one breath and the next, a welcoming breeze blew through and replaced the stench with a cleansing scent of lemons and fresh air. Like a rising sunrise, a warm glow replaced the garish flashing lights. The room transformed into a park-like scene, complete with a warm yellow sun and fluffy clouds dotting the blue sky above. Fresh green grass cushioned her feet and a soft jazz song whispered around large oak trees. A multitude of beautiful, bright blossoms dotted throughout and bought her a sense of comforting peace.

From the corner of her eye, an older Zerin female Aimee had never seen before hurried to one of the small hilltops in front of the crowd. She wore the normal tan formsuit covered in a long brown vest with dual panels in the front and a solid one draped over her back. Her coffee dark hair had a splattering of light yellow at her temples and hairline, giving testament to her advanced age. Her face remained unlined and carried an air of maturity and serenity. She stood faced toward the crowd.

"Oh my Goddess, we are so sorry!" Face flushed, she fluttered her hands to her breasts in a human gesture of dismay. "We do not understand what happened! That program was for a different delegate we transported several years ago before we made trips to Earth." She waved toward the other Zerin women in the back of the room, gesturing as if to make them move. "We wanted to give you a nice picnic day so you could relax." Her voice wobbled.

Aimee expected the distraught woman to burst into tears.

Overall, she found the Zerins attitude a welcome change from the cold-hearted personality Aimee endured from Aja. She couldn't help but feel sorry for the woman.

"Please forgive us," the poor thing continued as she wrung her hands. "We have wonderful food prepared over in that corner." She pointed to the back right. "And plenty of fresh juice and cool water for you to drink throughout the facility."

She folded her hands in front of her. "There are comfortable chairs for you to relax in to use the VDU devices filled with Earth books and videos." She waved over to her left. "Outdoor games, and a slow-running swimming chute to enjoy a tranquil ride down a small creek. There is also a nature trail you can hike if you desire." She clasped her right arm over her chest with her fist covering her heart.

"Avail yourselves of today's repast and we pray you forgive the scare we have unwittingly given you."

The Zerin female left the hill to join her shipmates. From where Aimee stood, the stern glare she gave the others was unmistakable. She was glad she wasn't going to be on the receiving end of that tongue-lashing.

Aimee grinned as she faced the others. "Well, that was fun. Whaddya say we not do that again."

She snickered when Chloe rolled her expressive eyes.

"Ahmen to dat sistah," Chloe said with an exaggerated urban drawl. "Let's go see about havin' us some fun!"

Aimee joined the fray, laughing and trying to decide what to do first. It turned out to be one of the best days she'd had in a long time. In fact, it was hard to remember the last time she'd enjoyed a day off with friends so much. Laughing, joking, and being as carefree as a child.

When the day came to a satisfying close, Aimee was positive one of the large inner tubes floating on the lazy river had a permanent imprint of her butt. She'd played a variety of outdoor games—ones she hadn't enjoyed since she was a child: ping-pong, volleyball, horseshoes, and shuffleboard.

When it was time to leave, Aimee joined her friends to walk back to their quarters. She laughed as everyone bragged about the adventures of the day.

At first, Aimee didn't notice anything wrong. But something kept nagging at her subconscious before she paid attention. She searched the group talking and laughing before it dawned on her what was bothering her.

Someone was missing.

"Hey, where's Shannon?" She stopped in the middle of the hallway. "Has anyone seen her?" She glanced around as if the redhead dragged behind them.

"Oh, jeez—she's probably still there." Asian-American Christine planted her slender fists on her slim hips. "Oh man, I don't wanna go back and get her, I'm beat. I'm dying to crawl into my wonderful bed and sleep for a week."

"Whine much?" Lora smacked the small woman playfully on her shoulder. "Big baby. Come on, Aimee. You and I can go and get her. The rest of you head back and we'll meet up with you in the morning."

Grateful mummers voiced as the rest of the group walked off down the dimming hallway. Nighttime was coming to the *StarChance* and the lighting on the ship reflected the change in cycles to help ward off space sickness.

The dim light added to her urgency. "Come on, hurry up." Aimee started back the way they'd come. Worried sick about Shannon, she jogged back to the large hall.

"Crap, Aimee, what's the hurry?" Lora groused as she struggled behind her. "You afraid she won't be there or something?"

"I don't know!" Aimee hated to say it, but her nerves were screaming at her to *hurry, hurry*. "I've got this terrible feeling..."

The closed wall loomed ahead. Lora put her hand on the wall to pant a couple of times before she put her hand on the indent to open them.

Nothing happened.

"What the hell?" Subtlety wasn't a factor here. Aimee bumped her shoulder on Lora's and gave a quick shove to push her aside.

Same result.

"Hey, assholes, open up!" Panic choked as she pounded on the metal door with the flat of her palm. The chance of the doors having flimsy construction wasn't high, so it would be hard for someone on the other side to hear her futile attempts at getting their attention. Aimee pounded on the door a couple of times. All she got for her troubles was a sore palm and a hoarse voice.

"Damn it!" Aimee wanted to kick the steadfast door in frustration. She was upset, not stupid. Crunched toes were not on her to-do list today.

"Do you think she already went back to her cabin before us?" Lora asked a reasonable question in a reasonable tone.

Something was wrong, but in all fairness, Aimee had to admit her blonde-haired friend was probably right. She had to be overreacting. It was late and Shannon was more than likely asleep in her bed where she should be.

Aimee agreed with Lora and they headed down the dusky corridor to go back to their quarters. Maybe Shannon was okay and she was just imagining things. Why was she overdramatizing the whole thing anyway? She'd never been so emotional before she came on this trip.

Great—now she'd lost her mind and no way to find it.

Aja

Aja's pace quickened as she approached an unused portion of a small, cargo bay to meet with her Friebbigh contact—the criminal alien holding the human women she'd sent to it. She was grinning like an idiot because the stressful part of her plan was over and all she had to worry about was the hefty credits coming her way.

Best of all, it was only a matter of time before that *puntneji* Aimee was discovered as an accomplice in working with the Friebbigh in kidnapping her fellow humans. Yes, the last of her plans were falling into place nicely. A piece of cake as the humans liked to say. What a stupid saying. What did cake have to do with anything?

Just the memory of that human trying to TrueBond with Commander Qay had Aja believing in the human superstition of luck. If she hadn't seen it with her own eyes, she wouldn't have believed it was possible. At first, she'd been disgusted the Commander was weak enough to bond with an inferior alien, but after giving it serious consideration, it opened an excellent opportunity for her.

She'd give them enough time to continue the TrueBond process, which would destroy any chance he'd have in reinstatement on Zerin. Once accomplished, such a TrueBond would put an end to the damnable E'etu family and advance the Chancellor's agenda by several decades.

Then the Chancellor would have no choice but to recognize how she'd single-handedly brought this glorious victory to him sooner than he'd planned. Basking in his respect and admiration would be worth the pain and sacrifice she'd endured throughout her life.

"Aja-ne L'len R'oxk, Equerry to the Chancellor" had a nice ring to it. Too bad it wasn't her real name. Not that the name itself mattered, she'd be happy to use whatever name she came up with to run the empire.

Musings aside, she focused on putting this part of the plan in motion. When she got to the supposed unused hangar, she put in her programmed code to open the door.

Stale air and dark shadows littered around the bay and the small egg-shaped ship. The ship was no bigger than an escape pod and it took up half the area. The dampening fields she'd erected around the room held steady and the computer program she'd bypassed was working with perfect precision. No one on the *StarChance* would know she harbored an illegal vessel inside.

A small figure separated itself from the dark outline of the ship and slithered toward her.

Aja straightened her posture. The greater goal was worth the repugnance of dealing with the Friebbigh.

"Any problems?" she asked the small grey being. She crossed her arms in a human-like gesture of defiance.

The short creature stared at her with a steady, unblinking glare in its wide black almond-shaped eyes. "They arrive. I put in cage," its tinny voice replied. It stood in front of her with a stillness unnatural for a living organism. The Friebbigh were an intelligent, sentient race, but they spoke to other species with as few words as possible. As if each syllable wasted on another race was a crime against their nature.

Who cared? As long as it did its job, she couldn't care less how it talked to her. "Take me to them now. I want to make sure all ten showed up."

"Yes."

The Friebbigh led the way. Aja kept a discreet distance behind it, keeping a concealed weapon in the folds of her long black tunic, her finger on the trigger. First rule: Never trust the filthy little things. Aja made sure she had her blaster whenever she was around one. Though she'd dealt with this creature more than once, she wasn't taking any chances.

A small doorway opened in the indistinguishable hull of the ship and she had to bend at the waist to enter. The interior air was sour and gritty to her sensitive nose. With small, deliberate steps, Aja moved toward the rear of the single-room ship. There along the back wall were the women she'd targeted to sell at the slave auction.

All of the humans were catatonic from the drug she'd placed on the backs of their necks earlier. Aja grinned at how easy it'd been to get these stupid cattle into this pen to sell. She'd swapped the "Earth picnic" program for one they'd used for the aHxxjt delegation from five solar years earlier. That holoprogram provided a perfect distraction for Aja to place a tiny nanobot on the back of each woman's neck. The nano-program made the recipient leave the festivities within an Earth hour and head to this hangar. It also took away their free will and placed them in a trancelike state for the duration of their trip before dissolving harmlessly into their bloodstream. The bondage collars the Friebbigh put on each one would keep them tethered together until they reach FiPan.

It was a long two-month journey for these females, and Aja was satisfied to see all ten accounted for. Including the annoying redhead that had been part of the group assigned to her. What was her name again? Shirley, Sabrina, Sally? It had to be some stupid, forgettable Earth name.

"Good." Aja gave final instructions. "I will monitor your progress until you reach the waystation on FiPan. There you will meet with the Dread Pirate Maynwaring's contact and he will pay you for your services."

The grey alien stood unmoving as she continued. It never blinked.

"However, I have a new opportunity for you." She stared into its bottomless black eyes to command its attention. "One that will double your credits."

The Friebbigh remained motionless. "How?" It answered her through its voice box at the center of its flat chest.

"There is one more Earth female to be picked up on the night of the Exchange." When it gave her a sideways blink, she knew she had its attention. Aja continued. "It will be dangerous to come at the same time as the other males, but this female will bring triple credits if she can be successfully taken that night. Would any of your people be interested in taking the risk for such a high reward?"

Its black eyes remained unblinking and Aja assumed it communicated with its people. Within a short span of time, its side eyelids blinked open and shut from right to left.

"Akoobjie."

Yes! The Goddess blessed her with a streak of good fortune when it told her the name of the Friebbigh who would take the job. As the undisputed leader of that criminal race, Akoobjie was one of the best slavers in the galaxy. With it taking the job, the sale of the exiled prince's TrueBond would generate a hefty price.

"That is acceptable." She kept her voice passionless. "The agreement will be sent to the usual place once you leave this ship. I will expect a communication from Akoobjie within twenty-four solar hours before the Exchange for instructions."

With a parting glance at the comatose humans, her shoulders released her tense muscles as her chest became light. Now all she had to do was mix up the Earth groups and their liaisons so no one would notice the missing women.

She glared at the Friebbigh and gave it one last bit of instructions. "These humans are to be delivered in good health with as little damage as possible. We won't get a high price at the slave auction with damaged goods." She took the blaster out of the folds of her tunic, placed it across her chest and pointed the barrel upward. "Do I make myself clear? Half of the last shipment ended up malnourished and suffered from multiple breaks and contusions. That cannot happen again or you forfeit your share of any profits." She leaned toward the smaller alien. "Understand?"

She'd swear the vile creature smirked at her through its nonexistent lips. Aja straightened and thumbed the blaster barrel again. The Friebbigh's base emotions were greed and self-preservation, so she was pretty sure it would agree.

It gave a clipped answer. "Understood."

It raised its many-jointed index finger and pointed to the hangar door. "Leave. I go."

Aja gave a warning scowl before she left the stuffy atmosphere of the alien vessel. She reached the door and heard an insistent, weak female voice stutter. "My clan will come for me."

Aja sighed. Curiosity was a weakness of hers. She should keep going and ignore the repulsive human, but she couldn't resist making sure they knew who took their miserable lives away. Empowered, she strolled to the invisible barrier and raised a sardonic eyebrow at the redheaded female.

"Is that so?" Aja put a bite in her tone. She faced her blaster down with one hand and placed her other hand on her hip. "I can assure you, you disgusting *puntneji,* no one is coming for you." How could this stupid alien be awake? She should be unconscious with the nanobot Aja put on the back of her neck.

It amused Aja to see the human's face twisted in hatred. "Doesn't matter what you think." The female's voice cracked. She crawled closer to the forcefield. "They will come for me. My clan will find me and *kill* you."

Aja's laughter echoed around the small chamber. "You've got to be kidding me!" She waved her free hand to include all of the females. "There is no way for any 'clan' to find you, you stupid idiot. But do I have a treat for you! When Akoobjie brings Aimee to FiPan after the Exchange, you and your little friend will be pleasure slaves together. Won't that be fun?"

"My clan will find me."

Now, see? This is what she got for talking to an annoying human. When would she ever learn? Bored with the conversation, Aja left and motioned to the Friebbigh to shock the human to shut her stupid ass up. Hopefully the pain would stop the annoying alien from talking. She was such a persistent little *norakthed* insect.

"My clan will find me!" the human shouted as the Friebbigh activated a shock wave that affected everyone in the cage.

Delusional and stupid. No one would find the captives unless Aja or the Friebbigh let them.

With a light step, Aja walked away from the pain-filled screams echoing behind her. Once she cleared the hangar, she put her blaster away in a holster strapped to her back. She punched in the codes to allow the Friebbigh's ship to drift out the hangar doors to open space. The cloaked ship would follow the *StarChance's* wake for a few parsecs before drifting away to the outer rim.

Finally—finally those who had it all would end with nothing.

Those who had nothing would have everything.

Aimee

Chaos.

Confusion.

Mayhem.

The next morning, those words rattled in her brain while under her breath she muttered "Son of bitch" and the ever popular, "Are you fucking kidding me?"

One minute she was sound asleep in her comfy bed and the next a loud voice in her ear startled her awake. Before she could squeak in alarm, a female Zerin she'd never met before stood over her and exclaimed, "Wake up! It's moving day! Isn't it great?" She clapped her hands and jumped up and down in little steps like a child.

Where was a gun when you needed one? The cheerful disposition of the crazy alien made Aimee want to shoot her—right between the eyes. No one should have to put up with this kind of abuse first thing in the morning. She hadn't even had a cup of coffee yet. No coffee...no talkie.

Aimee groaned and threw an arm across her eyes to blot out the bright light the idiot alien turned on. "Who are you...why are you in my cabin...and how soon are you leaving?"

"Gosh, don't you know?" The tall female pulled off Aimee's ink blue bed cover and then had the audacity to pull Aimee's arm off her face. "It's moving day. I'm sure your previous liaison told you all about it."

Aimee lifted one eye half-mast to peer at the lunatic in front of her. "No, I'm afraid it must have slipped her mind. And why in the hell are you here so damned early?" she groaned and took her time to sit up. If she'd gotten three hours of sleep last night she'd be surprised. She had other things to do besides sleep. She'd rather watch her favorite commander going about his daily routine rather than sleep.

"You know, moving day! All you Earth people just love moving day!" The unknown Zerin yapped on and on in her cheerful...high...squeaky voice. "You get to mix with the other humans, and at the same time learn about your possible mates on a whole other level!" Enthusiasm gushed with each word.

Ugh. Anything was better than this torture. Aimee swung her legs for her feet to touch the floor. The female handed her a blue tunic set, complete with fresh bra, panties, and matching slippers.

Aimee glared and once more contemplated murder. How well could the replicator handle an annoying Zerin's body? "Again I ask what moving day is and what's so damn exciting about it?" She grabbed the clothes out of the woman's hand and got off the bed. She jerked her sleep tunic over her head and put the clothes on. So what if she dressed in front of a perfect stranger? No shower, no coffee, meant no manners. She put the matching slippers over her feet last.

"Oh, you're just teasing me." The poor delusional idiot was oblivious she was *this close* to getting her annoying smile bitch-slapped into another dimension.

Since violence wasn't the answer, Aimee settled for an eye roll and the truth. "No, I'm not."

"I don't understand. You mean you don't know what moving day is?" The female frowned. Which disappeared as her bright, sunny smile took its place again. Her light and dark spruce green eyes twinkled.

"Oh, I know! Maybe I'm not saying something right. Moving day is the next step in acclimating yourself to different cultures and environments. It'll help you with the final transition to becoming a Consortium citizen." She shook a finger at Aimee. The woman could work in a preschool with those skills.

"Becoming a citizen of the Federation Consortium is one of the highest honors any sentient being in the galaxy can accomplish. Who wouldn't be excited about that?" The unknown Zerin patted Aimee on the back before she opened the door.

She gave Aimee a gentle push to join the throng of human women strolling down the hallway at a fast pace with excited voices raised. "Now go out there and enjoy your new place. Bye!"

After that cryptic shot, a helpless Aimee stumbled into a stream of chattering, laughing human women. Her previous cabin disappeared and she was soon lost.

Strangers in the crowded corridor jostled Aimee. She suffered a painful jab to her upper arm, shoved back and forth and squished between bodies. The air was thick with pressed bodies and various levels of perfume.

She couldn't see any of her friends in the noisy throng.

Confused about what was happening, Aimee mumbled curses at Aja. The mean bitch should have told her and the others about the next step in the Zerin training program. Why keep it a secret?

Someone yanked her arm and dragged her into a new room with nine other humans she'd never met before. Good, maybe she'd find some answers here. It turned out moving day was what it sounded like—the humans switched from their previous cabins and tutoring chambers to new ones. This included getting a new liaison. Keziah was older and a lot nicer to her than Aja ever had been.

With a sinking feeling, Aimee realized she'd left her VDU glasses behind. When she'd asked Keziah if she could go back to her old quarters to get something, the elderly Zerin assured her anything left behind was long gone.

Damn it! Aimee's eyes filled. How could she go through her day knowing she wasn't going to see Qay again? It was silly, wasn't it? It wasn't as if she had any claim on him. He was as elusive as any fantasy.

Alone that night in her new cabin, Aimee stood in the center of the room in dismay. On the surface, it appeared to be the same, but it wasn't. Instead of the ink-blue coverlet on her bed, this one was a sunny yellow. Her friends weren't next door or across the way. She couldn't pop over and meet with them to laugh at the day's antics or complain about Aja.

Oh my God! She'd forgotten all about Shannon! Did she make it to her cabin last night? On the way back to their cabins the night before, she and Lora met a female Zerin guard in the hallway. With a gentle admonishment, the guard had told them to stay put for the night. Aimee figured she was overreacting about Shannon and agreed with Lora that they'd check on the younger woman in the morning. With a frustrated grunt, Aimee made a mental promise to find Shannon tomorrow, no matter what.

The next morning, the first thing Aimee did was ask her new liaison how she could contact her other friends.

"I'm sorry, my dear." Keziah's tone was gentle but firm. "There isn't any time for such nonsense. We must focus on the rest of your training. Everything is behind because of moving day."

As if she needed another reason to hate moving day.

Keziah explained instructions had to double in the short time left to get ready for the Exchange. Which, she stressed, was coming up in two days.

"Besides," she admonished. "It's not as if you could take your friends with you when you leave, now could you?"

That advice sounded reasonable, but Aimee wasn't going to drop the whole thing, and she had no idea why. How could she forget about Shannon? Aimee was positive something bad had happened to the younger woman. There had to be someone who could help her.

Alone in her cabin that night, an outrageous idea popped into Aimee's head. Who do you go to if you want answers? Why, to the top, of course! She'd tried her liaison, so...now was the time to go up the chain of command. Maybe going to Qay wasn't the brightest thing to do, but how could she live with herself if she didn't at least try? Hadn't she watched him every night for the last few weeks? Everything he did showed her he was a fair and respected commander.

Her dying to see him had nothing to do with it.

Heart thumping, she stepped out of her cabin and glanced around to make sure no one was in the corridor. All of her spying for the last several weeks paid off since she had a good idea where Qay might be if he stuck to his normal routine. She'd go to the maintenance tube at the end of the hallway, as that would bypass all of the security protocols. The maintenance tubes had directional labels and all she had to do was follow the markings.

With nerves stretched tight, she entered the service corridor and began to climb up a steep rung of steps. She'd find Qay and he'd help her. Besides, who better to ask where someone was on the ship other than the commander?

No one...that's who.

Qay

WHACK!

I will not let her distract me.

WHACK, WHACK!

I am better than this. I will not lose my focus.

WHOMP, WHACK—THUMP!

Which was what happened when he let his inner dialogue run amok: lose focus when sparing with the master of the three-section weapon and end up with a well-deserved thump on his left temple when the said master wields the weapon. Because the master was also Qay's *gnotdile*-bastard of a cousin, he wasn't going to get any leniency as the session continued.

The hollow sound of the WHACK, WHACK echoed throughout the dojo as Qay and D'zia battled for supremacy. A throbbing headache aside, Qay was determined to teach his younger cousin a lesson in respect. Whirling his sanjiegun in opposite propelling motions, he circled around the other male, seeking for an opening in his defenses.

Unfortunately, there weren't any.

Well, he'd make one. Feigning right he shifted to the left and dove for D'zia's battle hand. At the same time, he rotated the wooden staff and plowed it into the meaty flesh of his cousin's palm. It should have been an admirable move, but D'zia struck back at Qay in a lightning attempt meant to immobilize his opponent. He'd seen D'zia use that move before and Qay was ready for it. Frustrated growls filled the air.

Evenly matched, they simultaneously threw their sanjiegun's aside and came at each other in an undignified wrestlers' grapple. With sheer masculine joy, they stripped away any pretense of civility as they morphed into sheer testosterone mayhem. Rolling on the floor like young ones, they brawled. Fists flying and elbows punching, they were having the time of their lives working out the frustrations of the last couple of weeks.

When D'zia landed a lucky elbow to Qay's nose and it gushed a red, bloody mess, they stared at each other in shock. A piercing scream added to the surprise as a savage yell echoed throughout the empty chamber. A blur of color launched itself on an astounded D'zia and clung to his back. Sharp blows landed with smacking thuds to his neck and shoulders.

"You son of a bitch!" a feminine scream immobilized the stunned males. Strong legs wrapped around D'zia's waist, fists rained around his head. "You hurt him! I'll mess you up!" Rows of scratches bloomed on the back of his neck as D'zia made a frantic attempt to twist back and forth, trying to grab the offender who eluded his grip.

D'zia's bellows of pain blended with the higher pitch of the females screams. The sound in the room escalated as the noise competed with each other.

Qay stared dumbfounded at the bizarre scene in front of him. He sat on his butt and pinched his bloody nose, trying to decide what in the nine systems was going on. If he didn't know any better, he'd swear a savage *danka* beast was doing its best to dismember his poor cousin. D'zia wasn't getting much traction in fending off the squirming monster on his back.

At a full run, Ki came into the room and grabbed the screaming mess off D'zia—who plopped on his ass. His cousin moaned and clutched the top of his bleeding left ear. As far as Qay could tell, a small chunk of the sensitive organ was missing below the tip.

The writhing, screaming dervish in Ki's arms wasn't the least impressed by the mammoth Zerin. Qay's eyes widened when he recognized it was "The Human" screeching.

"Let go! He's hurt! I've gotta help him!" Qay wasn't about to let the situation turn violent. He raced over before Ki had to take an aggressive measure to get her to calm down.

He grabbed her from Ki's massive arms. Not easy since she squirmed and kicked to get loose. Once Ki realized Qay was trying to take her, he let go. The momentum of switching arms startled her enough to become motionless. They locked gazes.

Qay couldn't help but stare at her exotic appearance as the surrounding background faded. He tightened his hold on her as she wrapped her arms around his neck and her legs around his waist.

She shouldn't be in this section of the ship, and she definitely shouldn't be anywhere near him. He was already infatuated with her and being this close heightened his need.

He drowned in the unusual hazel color of her single irises, now absorbed by the widened pupils. Her skin was warm and soft, her scent tantalizing and intoxicating. Not to mention her supple breasts melded seamlessly into his hardened chest. The heat generated from her core on his lower stomach caused his dick to stir in avid interest.

He had to put a stop to this insane chain of events right now.

He hugged her close before he pushed her off. Her eyes and mouth opened wide as he set her down. For good measure, he took two steps back. When she made a move toward him, he put up his palm in a universal gesture of "stop." She did, but not before her expression dulled.

"I'm so sorry. I know I shouldn't have done that," she whispered. Her gazed stayed on her feet as she kept her hands clasped behind her back. "I thought that guy was trying to hurt you. Are you okay?" She tilted her head as her gaze raked over his face.

"I'm fine." He lowered his hand and brought his fingers to his tender nose again. Thank the Goddess the bleeding had stopped, but his face, chest, and hands were sticky with blood. Ki handed him an absorbing cleansing cloth before he had to ask.

Qay didn't dare glance at his head of security or the expression on his friend's face. He didn't have to look at D'zia to know what he was thinking.

"Holy son of an ass wipe, female!" his cousin complained. He got up off the floor with his fingers pinching the tip of his offended ear. "Did you have to take out a chunk of my ear?"

"Oh my gosh, I am really, really sorry!" Her voice came out in a pleading, mortified rush. She went up to him and laid her fingers on his forearm. "I have never, in my whole life, ever been so out of control." Tears filled as her eyes darted over D'zia. "I don't know what came over me." She made her appeal to all three of them. "I lost control when I saw Qay bleeding." She gave D'zia's arm a squeeze.

Out of the corner of his eye, he watched Ki give her a thoughtful frown. With hands on his hips, his focus turned to Qay.

Qay ignored him. Hearing the beautiful human say his name for the first time filled him with pride. The pride turned into resentment at the sight of her hand on his cousin. She'd better let go of his cousin *right now*—or he would not be responsible for his actions. For the first time he understood the human term "seeing red."

Good thing Ki read the emotions in the room and interceded between Aimee and D'zia. With a gentle hand, he pulled her away from the grimacing D'zia before doing the same to the younger male.

"Qay, I'll take D'zia to the medical unit." Ki tapped D'zia between the shoulders to walk in front of him. "While I'm gone, ask her why she's here and how she accessed the restricted area. I'll bring an escort with me to take her back to her assigned quarters." Before he left, Ki gave Qay a pointed look of warning between him and the female.

He might have expected the caution from Ki, but D'zia leaving without a word wasn't. He tilted his head back and gave a loud sigh before he crossed his arms to face "The Human."

"What are you doing here?" The words came out sharper than he intended, but he had every reason to be irritated. She wasn't supposed to be in here and she'd damn well better have a good explanation.

She appeared nervous, biting her bottom lip and wringing her hands. She cleared her throat. "I have to talk to you about Shannon."

Qay stopped trying to wipe the drying blood off with the used cloth to stare at her. "What or who is a Shannon?" With luck, his spilled blood would mask any lingering scent of her off his skin.

"Okay, look, Shannon was in our group and the last time I saw her was at the picnic and then she didn't leave with us but because the whole moving day happened I didn't see her that morning and when I asked Keziah about it she blew me off and I couldn't ask anyone else since I can't find them and now I'm with a bunch of people I don't know so I can't very well ask them now can I?"

She took in a breath, and before Qay could speak, she was off again. "What's with this stupid moving day, anyway? Did you have something to do with that? Of course, you probably did but how am I supposed to know if Shannon is okay or not? I just know something bad has happened but no one will take me seriously and let me know she's all right but then I thought you're the commander of this ship and you should know where everyone is and all you have to do is look her up and tell me she's okay because I've got a really bad feeling something bad has happened to Shannon!" She ended the rambling sentence with a high-pitched wail and a stomp of a foot.

Qay blinked in confusion with his mouth open. "I'm afraid I have no idea what you just said. Is your nano translator working properly?"

She took in a deep breath, which moved her amazing breasts and caught his undivided attention. He zoned out for a few clicks before he noticed she was talking in a calm, rational manner.

"....and because of moving day I have no way to find her to make sure she's okay." Her feminine shoulders slumped and her eyes stayed on his. She wrung her hands.

"You should talk to your liaison about what is upsetting you—not me," he said. He dismissed her concerns with a wave of his hand. Small changes started to stir in his body and he had to get away from her before he became overwhelmed. "I'm sure you are aware human women may not mingle outside of their designated living quarters." He backed away, trying to put as much distance between them as possible.

Her expressive eyes narrowed as she glared at him. Placing her hands on her rounded hips, she stepped toward him and pointed an index finger at his chest. She poked him for emphasis.

"Look, buster, I've about had it with you and your attitude." Her voice was firm and tight. She stalked, forcing him back. "I came here for your help and you're damn well going to give it to me." She stopped her advance and stomped her foot in agitation, her fists clenched. "Will you stay in one place so I can talk to you?" She crossed her arms over her glorious breasts to glare at him.

Qay stopped and stared at her in shock. No one talked to him like that. His face and neck heated in agitation. "I'm afraid you're confused." He stalked and forced *her* to back up. "Let me tell you how things run on this ship." He crowded her as she hit a wall. Standing with a few inches between them, Qay let his temper out. "One, you have a liaison to go to for your little problems. Two, you are to stay in your designated area, to never—ever—leave it. And more important, you must *stay away from me*." As he spoke those angry words, it never occurred to him how close they were. Her sweet scent flooded his senses and caused his heart to race. He stopped inches away as her lips parted with a surprised squeak.

At the sound, his eyes focused on her lips. Tempting and plump, a taste—he had to have a taste—just one. Mesmerized, he leaned in and surrounded her with his palms flat against the wall, inches from her head. He placed his lips on hers. At first, she remained passive, pressed against him and the wall. Then she parted her lips in invitation. Her palms laid flat against his naked chest. Her soft tongue licked his, bringing with her a burst of unexpected, sensual flavor.

When they touched skin-to-skin, lust, bright and sharp, sizzled and caught him by surprise. Her alluring sweet scent of vanilla musk invaded his senses. Qay was no stranger to the art of lovemaking, but he'd never experienced the connection he had with Aimee. He prided himself on being a male who seldom lost control, but with her, his mind blanked with the urge to deepen the kiss. Pulling courage from deep within, he pushed away.

"Get away from me." The words came out in a guttural tone, but he knew she understood him as her eyes widened. She stared back, her hands suspended in front of her as if she were touching him.

"What?" she asked. Her brows knitted as she lowered her arms.

He cleared his clogged throat. "I said..." He kept his voice steady so there would be no misunderstanding between them. "Please, go away. I can't have you near me." He stepped back before he straightened his shoulders. Any hint of a tender lover had to disappear.

As he spoke the last word, Ki walked into the room with two Zerin security guards and went to the human female. She glanced away when Ki stood in front of her.

Ki gave her a slight bow of respect. "These men will show you the way back to your quarters, *Rouva*." Granting her a female title of respect, he held out his elbow for her to take and escorted her to the men waiting at the door. With a decisive nod to the guards, he positioned her between them.

"Please follow us." The younger guard gave an invitational wave down the corridor to guide her out of the room.

"But, but what about..." Her last beseeching look at Qay pierced through his resolve to remain aloof. He stepped toward her as she disappeared through the door with her escorts, her voice trailing.

Qay's heart gave a painful squeeze as he recalled his harsh words to Aimee. He hated the look of pain that crossed her face. But he had to be strong. Neither one of them could afford the consequences of having a TrueBond between them.

Time to focus his anger on something else. He strode over to his security chief and barked, "Will you please tell me how in the nine systems she got in here?"

Ki's anger was as palatable as his own. "Believe it or not, she came through one of the service corridors, tripping an alarm. I apologize I couldn't get here fast enough to stop her."

Qay fisted his hands on his hips and glared at his longtime friend. "And how did she know what a service corridor was?"

The large male raised a sardonic eyebrow. "I think the better question is how she knew where to go once she was there. If I didn't know any better, I'd swear she could read Zerin." Ki muttered the next words as if he didn't want Qay to hear.

Qay pinched the bridge of his tender nose to ease the pulsating pain. He wished he could do the same to the pounding headache between his eyebrows. "Fine, change of subject." He didn't like where this conversation was going. He'd rather avoid any talk about him and "The Human." "How is D'zia?"

"D'zia is just fine," D'zia stated as he entered the room. The other man's face flushed as he touched the regrowth on his bitten ear. "Freaking *danka* beast. Someone should snip her fangs." He gave Qay an angry glare as if he blamed Qay.

"How is this my fault?" Qay grumbled at the other man. "Aren't you the one in charge of the human women?"

D'zia's lazy smile raised the hackles on the back of Qay's neck. "Obviously not all of them."

"What's that supposed to mean?" Qay took a step toward him, his face hot with irritation.

Arms crossed, Ki stepped between the two. "Enough."

D'zia waved Ki aside. "Thanks for your protection, big guy. But we've got more important things to worry about right now."

Qay forced the tension off his body so he could concentrate on what D'zia hinted at. His volatile emotions were out of character and he had to get under control. Clenching his fists, he faced the other male. "Tell me."

A deep crease formed between D'zia's eyebrows. "We've run a personnel test on the humans and have come up with at least ten missing." Ki growled as D'zia continued. "With the unexpected confusion of moving day, we're behind in generating a personnel report on them. I found the discrepancy after I compared their current living quarters to the list of when we first left Earth."

Qay frowned in confusion. "I'm not sure I follow you. Are you telling me there are human women missing?" Didn't "The Human" say something about a missing friend?

"I'm afraid so," the younger male admitted. "It's as if they disappeared the night before this moving day so no one would notice they were gone." He shook his head. "It's the damnedest thing I've ever seen. One day they were here and the next it's as if they'd never been in our database. My only conclusion is the Friebbigh ship was here the whole time and as soon as it got its cargo it left within the last twelve cycle period."

Fisting his nails to cut into his palms, Qay held on to his patience. "I want to know how this happened and I want to know it now. Run a complete analysis on every crew member for the last twenty-four cycle blocks." He stopped to consider what to say next.

"And I want a complete report on every human female that boarded this ship when we left Earth and compare it to who is left. Above all, I want a thorough analysis on who has had access to our security mainframe besides the three of us." He widened his stance as if facing an unforeseen opponent. "I want this traitor found so we can request help from the Imperial Forces in finding those women before they reach the outer rim territories." His nostrils pinched as he imaged what the human women under his protection now had to endure.

Things were getting worse and worse.

D'zia waved an impatient hand between the three of them. "Change of subject. What did the female say to you?" he asked.

Qay swallowed his annoyance at the change in conversation. "I honestly don't know. She was talking so fast I had a hard time understanding a word she said."

D'zia cocked his head. "Are you sure that's the only reason you didn't understand her?" A faint smile crossed his lips. For the first time, it wasn't about teasing as much as it was relaying a sense of affection.

Qay grunted. "I don't see what that has to do with the problems we're having right now."

D'zia gave a human-like shrug. "Maybe it doesn't, but now we'll never know because you couldn't be bothered to ask her. You know, it's strange she felt it was important enough for her go out of her way to find you. Why didn't she just go to her liaison?"

Ki grunted in agreement. "Do you remember anything she said? It might be important."

Qay paced before be answered. "She was upset somebody named Shirley or Susan or something was missing and she needed help to find her. She was also distraught about moving day..." Now that he thought about it..."You know this moving day was a great way to create confusion. It mixed up the humans and made it easier to hide those who ended up missing. She hinted I might have had something to do with her friend's disappearance." He grimaced.

He stopped walking and focused on D'zia. "Get in touch with her liaison and see why she hasn't taken care of this situation." He stared hard at his cousin with his arms folded. "And, make sure the liaison knows humans are not allowed around the restricted areas of the ship. I want her held accountable for this breach. At the same time, check on the female and make sure she's getting whatever she needs. Are we clear?"

D'zia gave a sloppy salute. "On it!" He left.

Qay eyed his security chief. "I want you to look into who orchestrated this so-called moving day and the reason behind it. Sort this out and find out where that damned ship was hiding. Do you need extra personnel to help you?"

Ki's brow furrowed as he rubbed his bearded jaw. He shook his head. "I don't want to involve anyone else since it's hard to know who to trust. D'zia and I have enough to go on to get you the answers you need."

Qay gave him a curt nod. "All right, but if you change your mind, advise me as soon as possible. I know I don't have to stress how important this is, not only for the reputation of the *StarChance* but also for the Zerin people. Our number one priority is to find these women. If rumor gets out we are involved in selling human women as slaves, the ramifications could be catastrophic for the stability of the Federation Consortium." Qay closed his eyes and tapped a thigh with nervous fingers. "I can't afford to be distracted right now. Too many lives are at stake, mine included." He opened his eyes and stared at the dried blood on his hands and watched brown flakes crack and fall around him. "I'll be in my quarters getting cleaned up if you need me."

Ki grunted in acknowledgment. He gave Qay a comforting pat on his shoulder before they left the dojo. They parted and Qay headed to his quarters.

It was the sleep cycle for most of the ship and the corridor was deserted. Qay rubbed his chest with the now ineffective cloth, glad there weren't any prying eyes around.

He contemplated having a relationship with "The Human" but it would be impossible. If he pursued her, the best he could hope for was continued exile—at worst, both of them executed.

Too many lives were at stake, and he had no choice but to keep her away from him.

No matter how much he wished it was different.

Aimee

Walking between the behemoth Zerin guards, Aimee tried to match the military precision of the long steps beside her. She ignored the stares of the smattering of other human women eyeing her in the corridor and at the rare sight of the male Zerins beside her. She kept her eyes straight ahead and pretended she wasn't dying of embarrassment. It was mortifying to be treated like a naughty child sent to her room.

Besides, she had better things to think about other than who was looking at her. For God's sake, why in the world did she attack the younger guy? Humiliation, hard and heavy, settled at the bottom of her stomach. And...ew. She bit off a piece of his ear. Seeing Qay hurt flipped some kind of trigger in her head and she went ballistic. When blood gushed out of Qay's nose...BAM! Higher cognitive thinking ceased and a primitive banshee took over. Her focus had been to protect Qay.

Crap. All she did was make herself look like an escapee from a funny farm. What she wouldn't give to crawl into the nearest hole and hide for a decade or so.

Well, there was a bright spot in this debacle. Since he'd wasted no time in telling her to stay away from him, she didn't have to worry about being embarrassed the next time she saw him.

But, for one brief, shining moment there was a hint of longing in his eyes before his lips met hers. She didn't doubt he'd wanted her. Warmth soothed the cold tension in her body as she relived how everything clicked into place between them. They were made for each other, as cliché as that sounded. She mourned the loss.

Emotions crashed, eyes became hot. There was no way she wanted to join the other women in the Exchange. She'd found her alien mate and didn't want another. It didn't matter he rejected her. Her heart wasn't in it.

Maybe there was a way she could get out of going to the Exchange.

Okay, maybe that wasn't a good thing to think about that right now. She had to focus all of her efforts on finding out what happened to Shannon.

The guards stopped and stood in front of the door to her quarters. The door disappeared when one of the Zerin's placed a large palm on the indent.

"We wish you a good evening, female," the young guard stated. Aimee gave a double take at the gleam of appreciation in his dual pear-green eyes. Before she could react, both of them gave her a slight bow and left the way they'd come.

Aimee blinked. Maybe she hadn't seen what she thought she did.

Baffled, Aimee entered her sunny yellow room. Ugh, the color got on her nerves. Discouraged with the way the evening progressed, Aimee pinned her arms against her stomach. Guilt pulled as the door closed behind her. What did she accomplish tonight? Nothing—that's what. Well, except pissing Qay off. She was an expert in getting him to reject her every time she saw him.

Aimee sighed and pinched the bridge of her nose. She not only didn't get any information about Shannon, she couldn't find anyone to help her either. She glanced around the sterile room and its lack of welcome. Disheartened, she got ready for bed.

Rumors were flying the next morning about missing women. Aimee overheard two of her classmates talking about a mutual friend they'd had and couldn't find. So far, no one had any idea how many were missing or how they might have gotten off the ship.

After listening to the others banter worse-case scenarios around, Aimee decided it was time to ask Keziah how she could get out of the Exchange.

After Aimee posed her question, surprise widened Keziah's light and dark hunter green eyes. She gave a slight shake of her head, her brown braid falling behind her back. "Why would you want to do that? The whole reason you are here is to find yourself a mate. Wasn't that your dream?"

"Yeah, well, sometimes things don't work out the way you think they should." She stuck her nose in the air and crossed her arms. She should be ashamed of her infatuation with Qay. After all, he didn't have any trouble making sure she knew he wanted to forget her. But, she was big enough to admit she didn't want anyone one else. She'd rather go back to Earth and forget the whole thing.

Keziah pursed her lips as if she didn't believe Aimee. "Now that's an odd thing for you to say. Even if you meant it, you don't have a choice. You have to go through with the Exchange."

"Why? Aren't you going back to get more women?" Aimee winced at the whiny, desperate tone in her voice.

Keziah shook her head. "Actually, we're not. We aren't going back to Earth for quite some time since the ship has to undergo detailed maintenance. There would be no place for you in the meantime."

"But what about all of these women who've disappeared? I don't want anything to do with this anymore. I want this whole freaking nightmare over."

Keziah frowned. "Do not pay any attention to that ridiculous rumor. How could anyone disappear from this ship while traveling in space?" She waved her hand. "The Exchange is tomorrow and everyone is scheduled to attend." She put a reassuring hand on Aimee's shoulder. "Things will work out fine, you'll see." She gave her a pat and walked away.

For some reason, Aimee doubted anything would be fine again.

CHAPTER FIVE

Ki and D'zia

In the evening before the Exchange, D'zia was busy with several arrangements that had come up while in in his communications room. A strange file popped up that caught his attention in his OVDU. He opened it to read the contents in growing horror. *Danka shit!* This report was going to push his cousin over the edge. He activated a private audio to Ki. If anyone could stop the disaster about to happen, it would be the security officer.

"Ki, open the new file we've just gotten. We have to get to Qay before he sees this. I'll be right there." D'zia bolted out of his office to the nearest transportation tube. By the time he'd gotten to Ki's lounger on the bridge, the big male was already heading for Qay's workroom.

When D'zia joined him, Ki growled. "Has Qay seen this yet?"

"Goddess, I hope not," D'zia had a sinking feeling they were too late. "We need to get to him before he does. There's no telling how he'll react if we aren't there to stop whatever stupid thing he'll do."

"Agreed," Ki responded. They stood at the closed door to Qay's private office and glanced at each other with a nod. Ki placed his hand on the opening indentation, not waiting for an invitation. The doors whooshed open to his worst fears. Qay was not in the room, but there was plenty of evidence he'd left in a hurry. At the desktop extension, an overturned cup of Qay's favorite savage tea ran in dark rivulets to drip on the unique wood floor. A bound tome of ancient Zerin history lay upside down on the floor next to the lounger, a strain on its delicate binding. Good thing the tea was dripping on the other side and not near the rare book.

"*Puntneji*!" D'zia cursed. He rushed to the empty lounger as if to stop what had happened before they got there. "He must've taken the emergency exit to avoid people seeing him." He gave the other male an agonized gaze. "Where do you think he went?"

Ki wiped a palm down his close-cropped beard as a thundering growl rumbled out of his throat. "He must be on his way to the human's cabin." Goddess knew how this nightmare would play out. If Qay was in a TrueBond with the human, as Ki suspected he was, they might be facing an enraged, out-of-control male. Qay would be fighting against his natural impulses to protect her, even though he believed she was one of the organizers on Earth setting up the slave trade with the underworld at FiPan. He'd be next to impossible to subdue.

They had to get to Qay before he did something he'd regret.

Ki activated the communication device by touching the back of his right ear. "Commander Qay, please respond."

Silence.

"Commander Qayyum A'agnan E'etu, this is Security Officer M'alalu Ki E'eur. Please respond." The formal announcement of their names should have generated an immediate response.

Silence.

D'zia confronted him when he failed to contact his cousin as well. "We don't have any choice. We've got get to the human's quarters and see if he's there."

"I agree. Let's go through the same emergency exit to keep this as private as possible."

A pinched look crossed D'zia's face. "Do you think the human is his TrueBond?" He lowered his voice as if he were afraid somebody would overhear him.

At first, Ki didn't want to answer. He went to open the emergency exit. "I hate to admit it, but I'm afraid so."

"Well, the humans have a great saying for this type of situation." Following Ki through the emergency exit, D'zia gave a self-depre-cating chuckle. "What a *clusterfuck* this is turning out to be!"

Ki grunted in response. He didn't need that translated and agreed with D'zia and his colorful way of putting things.

Aimee

Aimee indulged in the heated water as it sluiced down her body. While she soaked, she absently mused how the ship used water for bathing. However they did, she was grateful for the comfort. The last day of harsh training combined with the morose disaster with Qay made her muscles tense and compounded her constant headache.

She palmed the tile to turn off the spray from the shower. Grab-bing a water-absorbing towel, she wrapped her hair in a turban before taking another one to wrap around her damp body.

Going into the bedroom, she undid the towel around her head and rubbed the moisture from her hair. Hard to believe the Exchange was tomorrow. Dismay weighed as she admitted there wasn't any way to get out of it. It was hard being around the other excited women when all they talked about was finding true love. She'd lost hers before she ever had it.

She was about to pull the other towel off when the doors to her chamber opened. She jumped and gave a sharp squeal as she gripped the cloth tighter. Her eyes widened in surprise. Standing in the doorway was the last person in the galaxy she thought she'd ever see again.

Inexplicable joy coursed through her. He'd come for her! Ah—no. That was a definite no if the thunderous glower on his face was any indication. "What?" She squeaked as he stomped over to her and grabbed her by the arms to give her a shake. Aimee clutched the front of the towel to keep it from flying off.

"How dare you!" He gritted his teeth as he gave her three firm shakes with each word. "What kind of person are you to sell out your own people? You've condemned all of them to a life of sheer torture at the slave markets! Were the credits worth it?" He'd stop shaking her, but his look of desperate anger terrified her.

"What are you talking about?" She pulled the towel closer and tried to squirm out of his hold. "Let go of me, you moron. You're hurting me!"

His fingers released their hard grip, but he didn't let her go. He pulled her closer to the heat his enraged body gave off. "Are you mentally deficient? Is that it?"

Aimee's body tensed and quivered as her own anger heated up. "If you don't let me go right now, I'll make you." She widened her stance to give her the advantage to dislodge him.

His snort of disbelief was his undoing. Aimee did not hesitate to twist her body to throw his bulk over her shoulder. Oh my God...it worked!

Whoo-hoo...lookie...lookie who's the badass now.

Her twisting movement dislodged her cover, which now draped over his face. The poor towel didn't deserve the excessive force he used when he gripped the damp cloth and flung it across the room. He pushed up, but his eyes landed on Aimee. The arm he had been using for leverage snapped as he flopped back on his ass. His mouth and eyes went wide and had Aimee laughing at his comical expression.

Then it dawned on her what he was looking at.

Oh, shit! She was standing in front of him naked as the day she was born. Aimee's body reacted to the tense expression tightening his face. Her nipples hardened into tight little points as her pussy plumped in anticipation. She tried to cover up by placing one arm across her breasts and one hand over her mound, but it was impossible to hide her abundant feminine curves.

Between one blink and the next, his entire demeanor changed. Gone was the furious male with the cold flinty eyes. Now his beautiful dual-emerald orbs were half-lidded in a gleam of unbridled desire. Hunger dominated his features and presented the classic image of a hunter seeking his prey.

Aimee backed up in an instinctual gesture of self-preservation. She got in a few awkward steps before he pounced. They sailed through the air and landed on her soft bed. He'd taken the brunt of their combined weight by landing on the bottom before he rolled them, giving him the dominant top position.

He shifted his weight so her body accommodated his girth.

"Open for me," his voice whispered. His knees nudged her legs open to allow his pelvis to settle in the cradle between. A groan of satisfaction rumbled as he settled over her bare breasts. The sensitive skin around her nipples puckered tighter to applaud the attention. "Hum—your scent is addictive."

He buried his nose in the crook of her neck and licked the delicate skin beneath her ear. Strong fingers plowed along her hairline with a deep massaging motion, sending shivers down her spine.

His body tensed and a loud snarling noise replaced the sexy growl. He jumped off the bed and crouched in front of her as if to protect her. He'd moved faster than anyone she'd ever seen before. Standing in the open doorway were the two Zerin males Qay'd been with the night they'd kissed.

The bigger one with the beard and facial scar held out his palm in a gesture of submission as he lowered to a bended knee and bowed his head. "My Lord, we mean you no harm." The smaller man next to him mirrored the other male's gestures as he knelt with his palm outward and lowered his head.

Well, at least his ear was whole again.

"Get...out." The guttural order that came out of Qay wasn't civilized.

"My Lord," the large male tried again in a calm, sensible tone. He kept his head down. "The female cannot possibly be to blame. I suspect someone made it look like she was involved. You are operating on sheer emotion—please think this through. Come away with us before you go too far."

"It's already too late," the smaller man mumbled to the floor.

Too late for what?

Aimee twitched when a throaty snarl pulsated out of Qay. He shook his head. "I said...get out." He demanded in a gravelly tone.

When the other man placed a firm palm on his chest, the younger male raised his head and opened his mouth.

"Qay, please..." The smaller man's pleas died when Qay answered in the same thick tone. She understood the Zerin language, but she couldn't get what Qay told them. As if in silent agreement, the kneeling males stood, stepped back and gave slight bows in unison. The door whooshed closed, shutting them out.

Which left Aimee alone with the testosterone-laden, large alien.

She should be afraid, but his dominant display to the other males was a complete turn-on. It was weird how excited she was to be alone with him.

When he faced her, her heart stumbled before it thundered with excitement. He widened his stance as he licked his full lower lip. His intense stare caught her. Reaching down, he pulled his boots off without taking his eyes from hers. The vest was next. In one fell swoop, he opened the seam of his dark blue uniform to peel the fabric away from his chiseled chest. The hills and rolling muscles across his brawny pecs glistened in the soft light. His steady gaze never moved as he unwrapped his lower half. Aimee sucked in her lips in response. *Holy Mother of God*, the man had a body she'd never before seen in person.

"Do you like what you see?" He reached to give his dark erection a firm, rounding stroke, his eyes lidded as he watched her. "You and I will experience extraordinary pleasure together." He came to the bed and towered over her. A purr rumbled past his parted lips with a tilt of his head. "Would you like that, my lovely human?"

Oh. My. God. She couldn't answer. Any cognitive ability she had died as she watched the naked man in front of her. He fulfilled every lustful fantasy she'd ever dreamed of—and more.

A sharp squeeze of pleasure contracted her sex. Her gaze stayed glued to the bounty of male perfection in front of her.

His body was big without the unnecessary bulk, fluid muscles proportioned to his size. As he joined her on the bed, his long braid slipped across his back and lay in a coiled pool next to her. She had always been a sucker for stories about men having long hair and was dying to untie his to run her fingers through the silky strands.

He had a light smattering of dark hair that covered his pecs and trailed to the soft down around his groin. She didn't get more than a quick peek before he placed his body over hers. The impression she got was wide girth complemented by a ridged staff, curling at the end. It would be damn near perfect for finding that little spot inside. Aimee whimpered at the promise of her fireworks shooting off quickly.

He nudged her legs apart to regain his position of cradling his pelvis within hers.

"Yes, that's it." His iridescent pupil was dilated, the dual emerald irises merged. He lined their groins with care. "Ah, perfect. Yes, together we are perfect." His lips burrowed into the sensitive skin between her neck and shoulder.

Soon his body became slick, his skin secreting warm oils on his chest, palms, and groin. With every caress, squeeze, and touch, the added friction heightened her pleasure.

A savory scent of spicy sandalwood between them tickled Aimee's nose and created a flood of renewed desire as her sex tightened in expectation.

She groaned with him as he took his time in licking and sucking her neck, behind her ears and down her throat. "I can't fight it anymore. All I can think of is holding you like this, savoring you, taking you in every way a male takes a female," he murmured into her hair. He grabbed her wet tresses with one hand to move her neck over. "You have no idea how hard it has been for me to stay away from you." A masculine rumble reverberated as his mouth and tongue continued their exploration.

"Oh." Aimee shifted to give him better access. She stroked and petted every inch of his delectable skin she could reach. The ridges and valleys on his back were a playground made in heaven for her fingertips until both hands ended up on his glorious ass. She gave the firm muscles a squeeze as she urged him closer and wrapped her right leg around him—an open invitation for them to join. Her lower body expanded in a riot of sexual anticipation.

A self-satisfied chuckle escaped as he worked his way down to her puckered nipples. "Slow down, *Ahyoka*. I need to taste all of you first." He moved their bodies out of alignment so his mouth had free reign to give full attention to her quivering breasts.

When he'd moved, her hands lost their favorite occupation of caressing and molding his firm ass cheeks. She had an unobstructed view of the top of his head, which included the pointy tips of his ears. She had to touch them. She reached over to caress the firm point between her forefinger and thumb. He bit down in reaction with enough pressure from the tips of his pointy teeth to break her skin and draw a few drops of blood. He groaned and his back bowed, causing his groin to push against her sensitive clit. A flash of pleasure and pain caused her to groan in reaction. She gripped both sides of his head as the sensation washed over her.

"Please," he panted. "*Ahyoka* do not touch me there. I want to relish our time together, not have it over before we begin." He gave a lopsided grin and licked his lips as if to savor her taste. He reached around and enfolded her in his massive arms.

Aimee gave him a tentative smile. "Okay, I'll leave your ears alone, but only if you let me play with them later." Her fingers slid into the silky strands of his now-freed midnight hair. Her eyes widened when the strands roped around her wrists in a firm grip.

"We'll enjoy struggles for dominance later." He warned with narrow eyes as his hair released its hold. Her breasts claimed his attention next. His mouth and tongue worshiped them before he continued his journey down her torso. He sucked on the indentation of her waist and plunged his tongue into her belly button. His slick palms left a trail of sensitized skin behind as traitorous lips stopped above the slit of her mound.

He paused at her sex. On Earth, she'd kept her curls trimmed into a landing strip, but since leaving she hadn't been able to. Her face heated with embarrassment until he stroked the area with a forefinger. "Lovely," he crooned. He made his way to part the folds, exposing the pink skin within. Inhaling, he lowered his head to lap at the distended clit.

Warm, raised bumpy ridges on the surface of his tongue caressed, from tip to middle. Aimee lurched with a yelp.

"Oh my God, do that again!" she pleaded.

He chuckled as he complied, taking his time. His lubricated palms rubbed sensuously on her lower belly before his tongue began its decadent work again. He alternated between drawing, stroking, and rolling the responsive nerves between his teeth, tongue, and lips, making her body spasm in record time. Her lower body tightened as the soles of her feet burned in pleasure.

"No—no—wait!" she wailed. One final nip and her body combusted in white fireworks. Pushed over the edge, she flew through the stars with abandon as her inner explosions released their tension.

Was that ungodly noise coming from her?

Floating in serene bliss, Aimee came back to reality. No doubt about it, an alien male *could* give a human female an orgasm in less time than a human man could unzip his pants.

Lucky her, her lusty alien lover wasn't finished. His talented tongue kept a leisurely pace sampling her outer juices before thrusting inside. Not to be outdone, his fingers on her overly sensitive clit mimicked the plunging move his tongue was making. The warming oils of his fingers created an unexpected depth of sensation and forced her pussy into mini convulsions.

Round two caught her by surprise and she verged on a blackout. Now the noise she made sounded more like a squealing pig than a woman in the throes of orgasmic completion. Taking in deep gulps, her body floated.

"Now, isn't that pretty? Your pussy is nice and wet, quivering for me to fill it. Isn't it?"

He didn't wait for her reply as he moved away from her lower half to stake his masculine claim with another part of his anatomy. He lowered his groin snugly against hers. With her head between his large hands, he tentatively brushed her lips with his. The soft pads of his lips demanded admission, which she happily conceded.

Aimee's musky taste lingered in the warm cavern of his mouth and gave her the unique blend of their combined flavors. She stroked the rigid tongue that had given her so much pleasure. Lifting his pelvis up, he grabbed the head of his cock to penetrate her slick entrance. Because of his size, it was snug at first. Between his natural lubrication and hers, it took two strong, sure thrusts before he filled her.

She moaned in reaction, the sensation of his wide member had her gasping. She wrapped her legs around him as her hands plunged into the onyx strands of his thick, unbound hair. The dark curtain created an atmosphere of privacy where they existed only for each other.

He broke off the kiss, his gaze latching onto hers. His dark moss iridescent pupils were wide as his lips tightened. He pulled out, then in, and lowered his head to watch. He repeated the motion, each surge closer to the perfect rhythm she craved. His arms were under her shoulders as he cupped the back of her head in his large palms.

"That's it, *Ahyoka*, take all of me." She was caught in his dual emerald gaze and demanding speech. Aimee allowed her body to release the tension into each push as he stroked the sensitive walls of her body. Connecting with another person on this intimate level was the most awe-inspiring experience she'd ever had. Tears gathered as she made love with the missing half of her soul.

Qay's heavy-lidded stare never wavered as he pushed deep. "Yes—give yourself to me." His growling demand combined with the angle of his cock caused her body to spiral into another mind-altering orgasm that caught her by surprise. Qay was right there with her, roaring his own completion as his hot seed spurted into her quivering passage.

Quiet moments passed—her body languid and satiated, Aimee reached up to caress his beloved face when he stiffened and yanked his head out of her reach. With a jerk, he pulled out of her which had her gasping in surprise. He scrambled off the bed and tugged on his clothes in rapid succession.

Alarmed, Aimee sat up. She watched him dress as her chest tightened. "What are you doing?"

With his back to her, he closed his formsuit. "I would think it's obvious. I'm leaving."

"Leaving?" She hated the desperate tone of her voice, but his actions started to scare her. She cleared her throat and reached for the blanket to cover her naked body in a defensive move. The rapture faded and something dark took its place.

With his back to her, Qay sat on the bed to put his boots on. He teetered on the edge of the mattress as if he wanted to be as far away from her as possible. "I have got to get out of here." It sounded like he was talking to himself until he spoke again in a louder tone. "I have to take care of things before you attend the Exchange tomorrow." With a jolt, he stood up and whipped his head back and forth as if he were searching for something.

"Oh?" There went her temper. "After what we just did, you want me to attend the Exchange?" Did she somehow misinterpret what happened between them?

He located his vest, which had gotten under the covers. He straightened up and stared at her for the first time. "It's the only way I can think of to protect you from what you've done." He pressed his lips until the plump mounds became bloodless. "I'm sorry I let us get carried away, but I can't have someone like you in my life." His face twisted in a wince before his expression flattened into a stony scowl.

Rage, red and hot, had her clenching her fingers into a tight fist as she got off of the bed. She didn't care that she left the blanket behind as she walked toward him naked, his seed trickling down her inner thighs. "Someone like me? Let me make sure I understand you correctly. You come in here, ready to tear my head off. Then you tell me you can't fight 'it' anymore. You say you've dreamed of holding me and being with me. Then you change your mind again and now you can't have someone *like me* in your life?"

"You don't understand!" He gripped the tops of her arms and gave her a quick shake. "I'm going against everything I hold dear by letting you go to the Exchange when I should turn you over to the Imperial Forces." He stepped back and frowned. "I should hate you for what you've done, but I can't stand the thought of you dying." His face contorted. "Then again, I can't stand being around you either. You represent everything abhorrent to me."

Her stomach dropped at his mean statement as her face flushed in disbelief. "Really? Why you smug son-of-a-bitch! Get out," she whispered. If she raised her voice she'd scream like a shrew. Pain, destructive and sharp, squeezed her chest as her eyes filled with uncontrollable tears and spilled down her cheeks. Mortified, she stifled the urge to retaliate in kind. Instead, she held her head high and pointed to the door with a trembling finger. She repeated, "Get out."

For a brief nanosecond, there was shared pain in his eyes. Aimee refused to give him a chance to say anything. She went to the door and pressed her palm to the indentation for it to open. Let everyone in the corridor see her naked, she just wanted this humiliation to end.

She pointed her finger out the door for him to leave.

And...without another word, he did.

Aimee awoke the next morning resigned to the fact that she had no reason to avoid the Exchange. Any hope of a relationship with Qay was long gone. Why would he say those things to her? Was he repulsed because she was a human?

A sharp pain constricted her chest as she relived the hateful words along with the stony expression on his face. Tears blurred her vision before slipping down her cheeks. Oh God, how can she still want him? She thought she'd shed all of her tears the night before. Throughout the night she'd told herself to stop crying, he wasn't worth it, and she deserved so much better. Not only that, but she was going to find her true love at the Exchange. All she had to do was get up and get going!

Dragging out of bed, Aimee ignored her inner cheerleader. Burying her anguish deep inside, she stood straight and pulled back her shoulders. The only thing to do now was make the best of the situation and put it all behind her.

Aimee chose a tunic set with matching slippers in a dark, flat black color to fit her somber mood. Maybe the stark color would wash out her features so no one would see her in the room with the other excited women.

Glancing around the tiny cabin with its bright yellow bedspread and happy landscape one last time, she took in a deep breath and walked out to the crowded hallway. She joined the others and headed for the transport station that would take them to the Exchange on the Zerin moon of Urim. The trek didn't take long and soon she and the rest of the women ended up in a large circular room on the other side of the ship. Mirrors, which would be their transportation from the ship to the moon, lined the walls.

The mirrors scrambled their molecules from one place to another in less than two heartbeats. She had to admit it was freaky, but since several dozen women had gone ahead of her, it didn't look like she was in any danger.

With stubborn resolve, she ignored her screaming instincts to turn around to find Qay. She watched herself approach an enormous mirror and dispassionately observed her appearance. The dark tunic set washed out her pale skin the way she'd wanted, her hazel eyes dull. She'd left her shoulder length hair loose, the white birthmark framing the right side of her face.

Sliding her eyes away, she went through the mirror with a dozen women, led by a cheerful Zerin liaison. At first, it was like walking into a cool pool of water, but the sensation didn't last long enough to become uncomfortable. Soon she was in another room and the temperature was warmer and the gravitational pull heavier than aboard the *StarChance*.

What a letdown. Underwhelmed best described her new environment. This wasn't any different from the place she'd left. All around her were large mirrors in a circular room. It was as if the group had gone nowhere. She considered trying to find her friends until a loud gong reverberated. Heart thudding, she joined the rest of the women to face in one direction as a lone elderly Zerin female stood in front, her body stiff and formal. She was the one who had apologized to them at the beginning of the disastrous picnic.

"Ladies, may I have your attention please." The room went silent. "The time is finally here! Through these mirrors, your destined mates will join you. As we've discussed before, all you have to do is stand right where you are and they will find you." She gave them a gentle maternal smile with a hand over her heart. "I can't tell you how much the Zerin people appreciate you letting us be a part of your finding true love. May the Goddess bless you with Grace, Contentment, and Glory."

With a sweeping Zerin bow, she left through the mirror behind her.

Aimee jumped as a loud pop reverberated in the room. The wall of mirrors erupted as a hundred various alien males poured inside. All had determination stamped on their expressions. Their heavy footfalls and low growls permeated the atmosphere. At first, the differences between the males entering were hard to distinguish, but soon their diversities became clear as several walked past her.

It was fun to recognize most species passing by from the books she'd read. On her left was a large prince from another dimension with his pulsating bridal collar. On her right was a dragon shifter with his golden panther symbiont at his side. Ahead of her was a dark purple male with shoulder-length gray hair that enhanced his unearthly beauty. Next to him was a magnificent blue barbarian with white-blonde hair, horns like a ram and a tail like a lion. Aimee held a hand to her throat as copper-skinned, three-partnered clansmen walked near in masculine purpose. Their purple cat eyes scanned in unison around the crowd for the fourth member to complete their family group.

Rushing by her was every conceivable color of the rainbow in skin tones. Yellow, different shades of blue, reds, greens, and an unusual pink shifter caught her eye. The most startling ones were a pair of males who walked side by side. One had a wiry build, his skin an unimaginable endless shade of blue-black. The male next to him was a behemoth whose skin color was the palest hue of blinding white.

The din in the room exploded as males and females met in joyful abandon. Squeals of delight, shouts of triumph, and cries of happiness echoed throughout the large chamber.

At the corner of her eye, Aimee saw one of her friends, Native American Karen, staring into the eyes of an approaching male. His neon blue eyes zeroed in on her; their laser-like intensity brightened when their eyes clicked. His onyx skin grew tight across a mountain of muscles as his fingers clutched a thin, round silver band in his right hand. He sauntered toward the immobilized woman and stopped inches from her. He bent and whispered a word Aimee couldn't catch, but Karen did— tears rolled down her face and she nodded yes. His handsome face creased into a wide smile, showing two sets of upper fangs. With a gentle motion, he brought the circular jewelry to the top of her head and placed it on her long, wavy espresso-brown hair. The band glowed to match the hue of his platinum hair, the enveloping radiance covering them both.

A squeal behind her caught Aimee's attention. An auburn-haired pixie of a woman ran through the crowd toward a male little bigger than she was. He had dark hunter green skin, complete with an impressive set of compact muscles. His clothes were a tan leather loincloth, barely covering all of his interesting bits.

When he met up with the woman running to him, he picked her up and kissed her as if his life depended on it. The woman was no dummy since she returned the caress with enthusiasm and wrapped her legs around his waist. Lips locked, he moved them through the transportation mirrors and disappeared.

Again and again, Aimee witnessed the same scenario. Couples (some with more than one male) met, instantly connected, and left together with beaming smiles and groping hugs. Aimee was so busy watching what was going on around her that she didn't have time to worry about someone trying to claim her.

It wasn't until the room emptied that Aimee became uneasy.

Oh my God, this couldn't be happening to her!

She hadn't wanted anyone to choose her, but never in her wildest dreams did she think she wouldn't be. The rejection caused her mouth to twist as her ears flushed. All too soon, Aimee was alone with a corpulent woman she'd never met before in the large, empty chamber. The woman bounced from one foot to the other and wrung her hands as she murmured, "They are coming. I know they are." With a determined glint in her eyes, she stared at the transportation mirrors. "My light and dark twins, they are coming for me."

No sooner had the words left her mouth than a set of identical male twins, one with blonde hair and one a brunette, raced through a mirror making a beeline straight for the waiting woman. Her face lit up as she gave a happy squeal of laughter and raced toward them in the middle of the room. Jumping into their hefty arms, they caught her easily enough between them and held onto her as if daring anyone to take her away.

Together they left out the same mirror they'd come through, leaving Aimee alone in the massive chamber. The resounding silence made her shiver as she glanced at her reflection multiplied in the mirrors around her.

This latest rejection hurt as much as Qay's did. Well, at least now she didn't have to worry about turning anyone down. It was hard enough to have the one your heart cried out for cast you aside, but to have the rest of the galaxy reject you was just too much. Trust her to be the only human unclaimed at the Exchange. It didn't matter she that hadn't wanted anyone to claim her. Her eyes filled. It still hurt.

Now what? She was at a total loss about what to do next. Standing there like an idiot only made her nervous. Movements from the side of the room made her glance in that direction. At first, she wasn't sure what she was seeing, but all too soon it became clear who came toward her.

Aja.

Self-pity morphed into a boiling wave of anger. Lifting her head in defiance, Aimee refused to let the other woman get to her. She stood with her arms crossed and waited for the alien woman to speak.

"Well, well, well, what do we have here?" The self-satisfied sneer on Aja's mouth was enough to make Aimee want to slap it off. "Not able to attract a mate, are we?" Aja had the temerity to walk in a circle around Aimee. With hands clasped behind her back, she sneered as if she examined a bug. Her tunic set was a deep garnet and she kept her wine-colored hair in a loose braid behind her back. Delicate ear ornaments swayed with each step as the red crystals glinted in the bright light.

"What do you want?" Aimee ignored the snarky comments Aja made as she kept an eye on Aja's every move.

"What do I want, what do I want?" Aja crossed her arms and raised her left index finger to tap on her lips as if the question puzzled her. The yellowish green of her inner iris expanded and diminished the outer ring into a light shade of khaki. "Now that is a very interesting question."

Aimee wasn't about to play into this wacko's game. She'd be damned if she would give her the satisfaction of getting any reaction out of her. With thin lips, she glared back.

Aja ignored Aimee's attitude and continued with her one-way conversation. "There is so much that I want." Loud, phony sigh. "But fortunately for me, you are the one person who will help me get it."

Before Aimee knew it, Aja jumped and locked a choker around her neck. It snapped closed with an audible click.

"What the hell?" Aimee clutched at the cold metal as it bit into her flesh. "What are you doing?" The more Aimee tried to rip it off, the more the metal shrank and pinched the fragile skin around her throat. A slight scent of burnt flesh made her sneeze.

"Now, now, no need for that." Aja pulled a small black box out of the folds of her tunic. "With a push of my finger, you will do anything I tell you to." Before Aimee reacted, Aja flicked her raised finger over the box.

Pain, deep and profound, blasted through every particle of Aimee's body and brought her to her knees. The agony held her hostage and caused her to shriek. Never before had she experienced anything like the bubbles of hot lava scratching and clawing under her skin. A vise squeezed her temples as thoughts scattered.

Through the roaring in her ears, Aja's laughter pierced her skull. "Stupid human. You thought you were good enough for our crown prince, didn't you?" After an eternity, Aja waved her finger and gave a maniacal chuckle. Aimee fell to rest on her hands and knees, gasping for breath as the pain ebbed away.

God, the insane laughter that came out of Aja's mouth was as painful as the activated collar. Nausea churned. It would serve the obnoxious bitch right if she threw up all over her.

"The prince would never claim you, even if he wanted to," Aja blabbed as she walked around before she crouched on the floor close to Aimee's head.

Great, no way to miss the ugly words coming out of Aja's mouth, even with Aimee's head bent to the floor.

"It was so easy to manipulate him into thinking you were the one working with the Friebbigh selling humans at FiPan. How he thought someone as stupid as you could pull it off is a mystery to me. But..." Her tongue snapped in a clicking sound and made Aimee look up. "Obviously he did since you're here." She chuckled as she surveyed the empty room. "What does impress me is the other galactic males are smarter than I thought. None of them wanted you either." She clasped Aimee's chin with her fingers. "You know you only have yourself to blame. You should never have gotten involved with him in the first place. Being a royal, he values his privileged life way too much to be with some repulsive human."

"Who in the hell are you talking about?" Aimee jerked her head away and wheezed out of a dry throat. *Idiot!* Everyone knew you never interrupted the villain when she spouted her evil plan. Let the psychopathic, crazy person talk and it might give you a chance to think of a way out of this mess.

Aja snorted and stood. "Not so clever now, are you? I saw the way you two reacted to each other when you first met." She nudged Aimee onto her back with the toe of her boot. "It was absolutely disgusting to see a member of the royal family forming a TrueBond with someone like you."

Aimee lay there and took in a deep breath. Tense muscles relaxed as the pain subsided. A quick internal check told her there weren't any lingering effects. Aja kept her one-sided conversation going, but it was hard to pay attention to her— Aimee was too busy trying to figure out how to get away from the bat-shit crazy alien.

Hopefully, a brilliant idea would pop into her head any second.

Aimee rolled over to sit on her knees and laid her hands on her thighs as she eyed the alien in front of her. "Why are you are obsessed with some stupid prince and what does it have to do with me?"

Aja's face twisted in anger and she gave Aimee a shove with her booted toe to put her on her butt again. "Ignorant piece of trash! As if you didn't know. Remember this—he's like everyone else in the royal family. He's uncaring and unable to do anything for anyone but himself." She leaned in and bared her fangs at Aimee.

Aimee crab walked backwards. "Back off, bitch! And take whatever 'prince' you're talking about and shove it up your ass." Her head pounded, her vision blurred, and she had a hard time comprehending anything coming out of the alien's sneering mouth.

With fingers of steel biting into her upper arm, Aja hauled Aimee to her feet.

"You…" Her dual-khaki eyes widened before she laughed and shoved Aimee away.

"Oh, this is just priceless! He actually bedded you." She narrowed her eyes as if looking into Aimee's soul. "And yet here you are, aren't you? He threw you away like the piece of trash I've been calling you." She glanced around the empty hall. "And now no one else wants you either." With her back to Aimee, Aja headed for the mirror she'd come through. "Bad for you, good for me. Follow along, little slave. It's time to meet your new master. I can't tell you how anxious it is to meet you. As you'll soon learn, the Friebbigh are not known for their patience."

It? Was she was calling someone an "it"? Wait, that name, Friebbigh rang a bell. But with her head splitting, she couldn't remember why. At least Aja had stopped talking about some prince. Maybe the Zerin was having a breakdown—one could only hope.

Aimee didn't want to follow the bully, but her body reacted as if there were invisible tethers between them. Great, the choker was not only a wonderful torture tool but as an added bonus, it acted like an invisible leash.

This time walking through the mirror wasn't as easy as it was before. Going through a doorway with your own frightened, disheveled face looking back at you was bad enough, but now Aimee ended up in a dark, freezing room. At first, it was hard to see anything. It took time for her eyes to adjust to the dusky lighting. She wished she hadn't bothered.

Before a scream of fright jumped out of Aimee's mouth, Aja pressed another button making her mute.

To her utter horror, standing in front of her was the typical large-headed grey alien so prevalent in human lore. Was this the Friebbigh Aja mentioned? The small, bulbous grey alien had large, shark-like black eyes. It wore a skintight seamless covering that heightened its asexual appearance. Completing the spine-chilling image were its long skinny arms and three-digit fingers.

Aimee recalled the file she'd read when she'd first found the VDU glasses in her quarters and shivered. Aja was giving her to an alien gangbanger.

"Ah, Akoobjie. Good, you are right on time." Aja's syrupy tones made Aimee hyperventilate. She swallowed to gain control.

"Prince mate?" A tinny voice came out of a small silver box hanging off the Friebbigh's neck. The metallic translator did the talking but the patronizing intent behind the words was more than clear with its unblinking stare aimed in her direction. "Not much worth. Will charge double."

Aja raised a thin wine-colored eyebrow. "Not going to happen. We will stick to the arranged price." She leaned toward the smaller creature and hissed. "I suggest you rethink your attitude about trying to coerce me into paying you more. Remember, I work for the Chancellor and it would be a shame if he was to learn your full identity." The curl at the corners of her mouth was chilling. "We wouldn't want that to happen, now would we?"

The Friebbigh's unblinking stare didn't waver during Aja's tirade. The tension in the room climbed and Aimee was afraid the two might come to blows. It was fleeting, as the grey alien gave a subtle nod. "Agreed."

"Good, good. I'm glad you see things my way." Aimee imagined Aja patting the smaller creature on its head and treating it as if it were a small child. She didn't know why, but Aimee had a feeling if there was an altercation between the two, Aja wouldn't fare as well as she thought. Nothing was scarier than being around an idiot who didn't know she was in over her head.

But, being under control of the idiot didn't mean she was doing any better.

"She's all yours, Akoobjie. Please make sure she ends up in a most disagreeable place. I would be quite disappointed otherwise." With those parting instructions, Aja handed over the little black box to the small, leathery humanoid. The mute hold on her disappeared.

"Well, as you humans love to say, parting is such sweet sorrow." Aja gave Aimee one last up-and-down look of disgust. "Maybe this will teach you a lesson and not try to rise above your station in life."

"Aja." What did she have to lose? She might as well ask the question bugging her since they'd first met. "Why do you hate me so much? What'd I ever do to you?"

At first, it didn't look like Aja would answer, but with a smug smile, she did. "Nothing."

Pivoting on her heels, Aja left the way she'd come, through the transportation mirror.

Wow, if nothing else, Aimee had to give Aja credit for knowing how to make a great exit.

Left alone with the small being, Aimee peeked around to see if there was any way for her to escape. Too bad she couldn't outrun the choker or black box. She doubted the Friebbigh would go along with her "great escape" plan.

"Enter ship." It gave the command and swept its long fingers over the black remote. Through no control of her own, Aimee found her body moved to its command. The opening was small, and she had to bend into the egg-shaped ship. At least the little maggot gave her enough control to squeeze in.

A flat and coarse atmosphere greeted Aimee. Coupled with the faint light in the interior, it could be enough to send her into a depressed spiral. Nope, she refused to become more of a victim than she already was, so she concentrated on examining for a possible way out. With a little bit of time and a lot of luck, she might get out of this stupid predicament.

There wasn't much to see in the little vessel. The ship was small, with barely enough room for her to stand straight. The gnarly little dweeb behind her prodded her back with a metal pole to herd her in a specific direction. She ended up facing a blank wall, which cut her trip short. She turned to ask it where it wanted her to go when a soft humming noise and a slight wave came between her and her jailer. It reminded her of heat waves coming up off the floor.

"No touch," it gave its short command. It waved its long, skeletal fingers at the air between them. "Will burn. You hurt, I no fix." A final word of warning before it left and closed the wall behind it.

Aimee was discouraged to see nothing in the six-by-six space. There wasn't anything to sit on, no cover to ward off the chill, and worst of all, nothing to use when she had to go to the bathroom.

Backing up to the furthest wall away from the invisible force field, Aimee slid down until her butt hit the floor. She pulled her knees up under her chin to lay her head down. She wasn't going to cry.

She wasn't.

Sniffling, she sat and concentrated on each breath until she fell into a light, troubled sleep.

CHAPTER SIX

Qay

The morning after the Exchange, Qay sat in his personal quarters in the same position he'd started in the night before. He reclined in a deceptively relaxed pose on top of his sleeping pad, his back leaning against the wall. One leg laid flat, the other bent with his right arm on top of his knee. He wallowed in the lack of light, trying to calm his chaotic mind.

When they'd made port around the Zerin moon of Urim for the Exchange, he decided he didn't need to be on the bridge...or anywhere else for that matter. Qay snorted—that's what he had a crew for. What he had to do was figure out what was important.

He contemplated and re-evaluated each move he'd made for the last thirty solar days. There was no doubt in his mind he'd handled his TrueBond in the worst way possible. From the first time he'd met her to the last. Speaking of last, he cringed how he'd misjudged that report. If he'd been in any rational state of mind, the vid evidence of her involvement with the ten women taken off the *StarChance* was pretty slim. For the love of the Goddess, he'd never heard of the Friebbigh working with others outside their species—much less with an Earth woman.

Qay choked as an image of Aimee's alluring features crossed his mind. He'd never seen anything so captivating as the expression on her face when she'd come apart in his arms. Her skin flushed a rosy hue with her eyes shut and her mouth rounded in an erotic moan. Her rapturous image would haunt him for the rest of his life.

He pounded a clenched fist on the soft mattress. He didn't even give her a chance to defend herself. He'd left with unashamed arrogance without asking any questions. Much less stopping to hear what she had to say. What kind of an idiot did that?

Qay grunted. An idiot like him.

When he'd woke up this morning, he had a rude surprise when he saw himself in the reflective vid. His physical appearance changed with the evidence of the natural TrueBond process he shared with Aimee. He sported a wide, white stripe in his hair, mirroring the one Aimee had. It started from the roots on the right to end in his warrior braid. His dual irises now had a swirled combination of gold and brown mixed in with the emerald while the dark sheen of his skin had become lighter.

But it was the appearance of the MalDerVon scroll around his right temple with its prominent E'etu royal crest that left no doubt he had a TrueBond. The elegant lines of the scroll curled from the middle of his forehead down his right temple and rested below his cheek in prominent purple ink.

In the center of the MalDerVon scroll at his temple, a normal Zerin heir crystal would be brilliant and, clear-faceted, reflecting a rainbow of prisms when the light hit it. The one Qay had nestled in his skin was a brilliant shade of viridian green—a proclamation to the galaxy that his son was growing within his mate's womb.

Qay's heart pounded. His child. He'd lost his child—the next heir to the E'etu family line. He tried to tell himself he'd rebuked her to protect her in that fleeting moment when he'd been certain she was the traitor. Regardless, he never would have turned her over to the

Imperial Forces. He couldn't let her suffer incarceration or death. Sending her away was the only thing he could think of. At least, that had been his excuse.

To make matters worse, it was his own fault he'd sent his True-Bond to the Exchange and into the arms of another male. Someone else had the privilege of loving and cherishing his female when he refused to do so.

Scalding anger seized him at the mere thought of another male touching her. His violent reaction surprised him, causing a tremor to run down his spine as a low growl escaped.

Qay pinched the bridge of his nose as he recalled Aimee's crushed expression after he'd treated her in that callous manner. Now everything was circling back to him not talking to her and him reacting without thought. Around and around he struggled with the damning thoughts whirling in his mind. In the low light of his bedroom, he admitted his real problem.

He'd been scared.

He was afraid of having a human as a TrueBond. He was afraid being with her would prevent rescinding his exile. And, most of all, he was afraid of how she made him feel. He'd been out of control with her, a little wild, lost in primitive throes that took his breath away.

The ironic part of all of this was his father would have admonished him to discover the truth first before sending her away. He would expect Qay to figure out how to keep her and regain his birthright simultaneously. Being a part of a TrueBond pair was never a hindrance—the joining was a treasured gift in Zerin society.

That's what intelligent males did...and that's what kings did.

He not only failed Aimee, but also his father, his people, and now his unborn son.

To add to his guilt, precious time had been lost since he hadn't found the traitor on his ship. Not to mention finding a way to retrieve those abducted human women. Goddess, those poor women's fate weighed on his conscience. Never before had he ever experienced such failure as he had during this trip. He should have checked in with his heart instead of his ego. If he'd followed his instincts and claimed Aimee instead of trying to avoid her, everything else would have fallen into place.

He snorted. If he'd concluded this yesterday, he might've been able to find Aimee before she went to the Exchange. He'd have grabbed her and damn the consequences. Initially, she might be mad at him, but he'd take her to a private place and slowly change her mind about him...

At first, Qay ignored the soft chime ringing in his room, telling him someone outside wanted him. He refused to answer as he leaned his head back on the wall and closed his eyes. Whoever it was could go to the depths of the nearest black hole and be done with it.

The chime was insistent, coming in increasingly longer bursts. Well, good. Looked like the annoying person needed a taste of his fists to leave him alone. Qay gave a disgusted grunt as he got up and donned a pair of casual pants strewn on the floor. Burning adrenaline filled his nervous system, giving him the perfect tool to vent his frustrations.

Smacking his palm on the indent to open the door, he was ready to throw the first punch when Ki pushed him aside. He stomped in and barked for the lights to come on. The bright light pierced Qay's eyes as he put up his hands to shield them from the glare. "What do you think you're doing, you maggoty bastard?" He lowered his hands as his vision adjusted to the change.

Ki glanced at the tattoo markings on his commander's face but showed no reaction. "We have a volatile situation that needs your immediate attention. So get off your ass, get dressed, and come with me to your workroom." The bigger man picked out a uniform hanging inside the wall unit and threw it at Qay's head.

"Wait, quit throwing clothes at me," Qay muttered under the clothes before he flicked them off his face. He took off the dirty pants he wore and put on the clean formsuit. "Can't you take care of it?"

Ki's tone was uncharacteristically terse. "While you've been moping around in this room for the last twenty-four solar hours, we've had a lot of shit to deal with. Something has come up that only *you* can take care of. So let's go."

Before Qay had a chance to respond, Ki left without a backward glance. Asshole assumed he'd follow, which of course Qay did. *Smug bastard.* In record time, they reached Qay's workroom on the upper deck. Going through the door, he was shocked to see a large male from a neighboring sector holding what appeared to be a dead Friebbigh in a bruising grip around its neck. Its large bulbous head flopped to one side, its milky eyes white in death. Its pink, forked tongue hung out the small slit of its mouth. As Qay passed him, the male shook the flaccid carcass at him in anger before he flung it at Qay's feet.

What in the nine systems was going on? Qay stared at the corpse splayed in a heap on the wooden floor before he jerked his attention to the imposing alien in front of him. Their species was one of the first to enter the Exchange because, without viable females, their race would become extinct within a generation. They'd faced the possibility for so long, their family clans were comprised of three males to every female. They were a large race, with dark mahogany skin, purple cat-like eyes, and razor-thin fangs used to inject their prey with an intoxicating substance. Despite their frightening appearance, their race was a favorite among the human women who attended the Exchange.

Now this big male, whom Qay suspected as the leader of his clan, was here on the *StarChance* with a dead Friebbigh. "Why'd you bring that here?"

"We highly respect you and your people, Prince E'etu, but we've become aware that some of your people have been trafficking female humans to the outer rim." The male came close to Qay, invading his personal space. He bent to force Qay to look him in the eye. "As you know, without the human women my species will die out. We cannot afford to have any of the humans used for profit. We refuse to ignore the fact that these women are being exploited while your race looks the other way."

Heat infused Qay's neck and face, but before he responded, the furious alien exposed his razor-sharp, needle-thin fangs. "So we took matters into our own hands. We've been following your ship since you left Earth and monitored your movements to catch these..." with a sharp kick to the corpse, he continued, "...disgusting slave traffickers in the act." He stepped away from Qay. "Which, of course, we did." He barked out a guttural command in his own language.

Two other males of his species entered the room, one carrying in his arms a redheaded human woman either asleep or unconscious. The other male, a few inches shorter with a slighter build than his partner, was the lethal one and the protector of his clan. Which left the one holding the human as the caregiver of the group, a no less a formidable opponent.

"Where did you get her?" Qay crossed his arms and assumed an open stance. He ignored a sense of dread as it crept up his spine to threaten his composure. He appreciated the years of training that allowed him to deal with tense situations. He pointed to the corpse in a negligent manner. "And, where did you get that?"

"We took its ship a few parsecs after it left yours. We discovered it not only had our lifebringer, but nine other human women who were shackled together in a small room barely large enough to hold one of them," the leader stated through clenched teeth. A low growl rumbled out of the throat of one of his clanmates behind him. The leader continued and ignored the threatening noise. "We thought it prudent to let you know what we found, to put you on formal notice so you would take steps to put an end to their illegal activities."

The large male mirrored Qay's commanding stance. "Of course, we will keep our female and the others we found since you were careless enough to lose them in the first place. Rest assured, they will live a life of comfort and ease before they are well enough to join one of our clans." A sardonic smile crossed his full lips with his last statement.

The male began to leave when the small, light voice of the female stopped them. "Wait. I have to tell him something." Her imploring tone softened the stony face of the mammoth holding her. At the same time, she gained the full attention of the other two.

With evident care, the leader caressed her bruised cheek. "You don't owe him anything, precious one."

Now that Qay's attention was directed at her, he was appalled to see how abused she was. Mottled yellow and green bruises dotted her face and her lip was split, a coat of dry, crusted blood forming around a scab. He wasn't able to see the rest of her body, but it was clear one of her wrists had been broken—it laid unmoving and bent unnaturally on her lap. The horror he experienced for her overshadowed any hesitation in believing what the clan had told him.

Shaken by her abused appearance, Qay strived to remain un-threatening as he came closer and kept his voice in a low tone. "What do you need to tell me, gentle one?"

The clan protector growled in warning. Qay ignored him but stopped a respectable distance from her. He gave her his full atten-tion to encourage her to continue what she'd been saying.

"Aimee, they have Aimee." She coughed weakly as if speaking wore her out. The clan leader made a move to leave, but with her good hand, she waved him back. "No, no I have to tell him."

Qay couldn't breathe. Horror seized as panic lodged in his throat. "Aimee was claimed at the Exchange, wasn't she?" Crazed, he im-plored Ki for confirmation. Out of the corner of his eyes, he noticed D'zia in the room. The stoic look his friends passed between each other made him speechless. His terror escalated. The human had to be mistaken. Aimee was safe and happy with some other male, going on to a new life without him.

She had to be.

"No, I overheard Aja planned to have another one of those—things." She pointed to the dead grey alien sprawled on the floor. "To come for her the night of Exchange—someone named Akoo...Aka...bee or something. I really couldn't hear what the name was." She groaned and with adoration on her face, she gazed up at the one holding her. "I told Aja you'd find me." She snuggled deeper into his large arms and closed her eyes.

At first, Qay tried to understand what she said, but the horrific realization of the name she was trying to say had him hyperventilating. His TrueBond was in extreme danger.

Akoobjie.

Akoobjie was the undisputed leader of the ruthless Friebbigh race. If it had Aimee, the hopes of her surviving were less than slim. Tamping down his impulsive male instinct to lash out, he concentrated on his next words. "Could the name have been Akoobjie?"

Without opening her eyes, she nodded yes.

"Did you happen to hear where they were taking her?" His voice came out in a whisper as his heart thundered in pain. He gripped his fists and a trickle of sweat rolled over the MalDerVon scroll on his right temple.

The redhead opened her exotic single-colored blue eyes and scrunched her nose. "I'm not sure. I think they said something about a frying pan?" She leaned her head back on the male's broad chest. "I'm sorry, that's all I know." She sniffed. "Can we go now? I'm really tired."

"Absolutely." The two males left with her, leaving only the head of their clan. The leader crossed his arms as he addressed Qay. "I assume this will help you, Zerin. If we can be of some further assistance, please do not hesitate to contact our Consulate." With a slight bow and a stern glare, he left the room.

In the wake of the devastating news about Aimee, Qay found the nearest chair and dropped into it. He rubbed his eyes, trying to understand what to do. It was good news the abducted women were no longer missing. The better news: they had the name of their traitor.

Aja.

Qay took in a deep breath as his spine straightened with purpose. Now he had a focal point to concentrate on. He jumped off the chair and paced, his nerves strung tight.

"D'zia, you find Aja and bring her to me immediately." His cousin gave a nod and rushed out of the room. He stepped over the dead body of the Friebbigh and activated his ocular communication console. Opening a secure channel, he paused the communication to give Ki his own directives. "Ki, get someone in here to get rid of this thing." He pointed to the corpse on the floor. "Then you need to get a ship ready so you and I can go after Akoobjie and my TrueBond."

Qay tuned Ki's voice out as he contacted the guards to come and get the body. No sooner had Ki finished speaking when two guards entered the room. Ki commanded them to put the body into cold storage to help build evidence against the Friebbigh Empire. They both acknowledged his orders before one of them picked up the alien's body and draped it over his shoulder. Without a word, they left.

"Any thought what ship you'd like me to make ready?" Ki stood in front of Qay with a long-suffering expression and crossed arms.

Qay raised an eyebrow at the aggressive stance the other male had. "No, whatever you think is best. But keep in mind speed is of the essence and we have to find her as soon as possible." He had to make sure he was looking at all of the ramifications before he continued. "I'd prefer it if we kept this between you and me." He paused. "And of course, D'zia. I don't have to tell you how precarious this situation can become."

Ki's left eyebrow rose. "Indeed? To which part of this situation are you referring?" He used his thumb and forefinger to stroke the sides of his beard at the jawline.

Qay snorted at the sarcastic statement. He sat in his lounger and leaned back to reply with a sarcastic tone of his own. "Well, I don't know, let's see. Could it be we had a traitor working on board and we didn't know who it was until now? Could it be we had an illegal Friebbigh ship on board the *StarChance*? On the other hand, are you referring to the situation I find myself in personally? About me ignoring your advice that she wasn't the traitor and believing she was, which in turn allowed her to get kidnapped and taken to Goddess knows where to be sold as a pleasure slave on the black market?" He tilted his head to regard his friend and confidant as he finished admitting his failures. "So, what do you think? Do any or all of these count as a situation?" Shame heated Qay's face at the angry tirade he'd spewed at the undeserving male.

Ki gave a mocking grin of his own. "Of course." The simple, answer caught Qay off guard. Ki was the last person to use humor in a tense situation.

"Asswipe." Qay allowed a small smile to show. His strain eased. "But seriously, we have to do damage control quickly. I have no choice but to contact my father for the first time in fifty years and explain everything going on and throw myself on his tender mercies."

Ki stiffened as he regarded Qay. "No matter the outcome, I will stand by you." He put his massive arms behind his back and clasped his hands.

Qay offered a wave of thanks toward his friend. This wasn't the first time he'd been grateful toward Ki and hopefully not the last. "I can't tell you how much I appreciate your support."

D'zia walked in to hear Qay's last comment. "Oh spare me. You two are getting awfully mushy. If I didn't know any better I'd say you guys were a TrueBond pair." He gestured to the scroll on his cousin's temple. "Speaking of which—how does it feel?"

"Are you really interested or are you just trying to stir shit up?" Qay rested back in his chair as he narrowed his eyes at his cousin. Now it looked like D'zia was trying to use humor to lighten the tense situation.

His cousin shrugged with a tilt of his head. "A little of both, I guess. I'm sorry to have to tell you this, but I can't find Aja anywhere. Not only is she not on the ship, but right after the Exchange she completely disappeared from all Zerin records."

"Well, isn't that convenient? Okay, I want to know everything about her from birth to now. Any known associates, friends, family—anything to help us find out where she could've gone."

"Already done. She may have been good at erasing her records, but I'm better." D'zia sat on a chair facing Qay as he curled a lip at a standing Ki. "Sit down, big guy, this is a story you'll want to hear," he said. He brought up a computer program on the shared ship's database and transferred it to their ocular VDUs.

Ki pursed his lips as if he wanted to argue, but with a grunt, he sat his substantial frame in the chair next to D'zia.

"The initial background check on Aja came back clean. She had a degree in interspecies relations from a respectable university. No record of any wrongdoing, no living family, no known associates." Here he paused for dramatic effect. "Clean as a whistle, as the humans like to say, right up until the day she died."

"Wait, what?" Ki asked before Qay did. "Died? What do you mean?" This was interesting. Ki's department should have caught this before letting her join the crew.

In the virtual room, D'zia brought up the 3-D image of a lovely middle-aged Zerin female, wearing clothing several decades old and standing in the middle of their circle. "This is the actual Aja-ne L'len R'oxk as she looked before she passed away fifty years ago from complications in giving birth to her only child." D'zia's voice remained subdued and professional.

"The traditional background check we did on her was performed with precision accuracy. The only reason I found out this information was because I dug a little deeper than normal." Watching D'zia comfort Ki and his department was a welcome change. "Now all I have to do is find out who stole her identity to work on the ship. I'm afraid that will take me a little more time."

"Do what you can. I'm impressed you were able to get this much information in such a short time," Qay reassured his cousin. "I appreciate you wanting to find out who the imposter is, but it's more important for you to figure out where she went." He massaged his temple as he sat back in his chair. He regarded the two men in front of him as the image of the dead female disappeared. The three left the virtual room to resume a real-time conversation.

"Ki, make sure you appoint someone as the lead on the scheduled repairs the *StarChance* has to undergo before you and I head out. I want to leave as soon as possible."

Ki raised his left eyebrow. "Are you planning on acknowledging the TrueBond once we find her?"

Qay swallowed as he glanced away before admitting, "Yes." With a steady gaze, he told the rest of his shameful secrets. "I was fooling myself when I thought I could get away from what was natural by avoiding her. I wanted to stop the TrueBond process from starting." He slumped his shoulders. "I rejected her."

D'zia stared at the markings decorating Qay's temple and gave a quick snort. "And how's that working out for you?" Qay might have deserved the condescending tone, but it still hurt.

Qay's face flushed as his lips thinned. "Not so much, thanks for asking." His heart stumbled as he relived those few precious moments with her. "I panicked last time I was with her and said some hurtful things."

Ki's unusual blue-green irises widened as he asked for clarification. "Hurtful? How were you able to hurt your TrueBond?"

Swallowing his shame, he described the last conversation he'd had with Aimee. He gave a sardonic smile at their identical open-mouthed expressions. Not that he blamed them. By nature, it was next to impossible for a Zerin male to intentionally inflict pain on his TrueBond.

"Are you out of your ever-loving mind?" his cousin barked. "What is *wrong* with you?"

Qay grimaced at his cousin's harsh tone. "I thought I was protecting her. I didn't want the Imperial Forces arresting her as a traitor. You know as well as I do she might have died because of it. I was hoping she'd attend the Exchange, find a mate, and the TrueBond process would stop." He scrubbed his face in a gesture of utter weariness. "I had no idea if we could even form a TrueBond with a human." He wasn't sure who he was trying to convince with that statement. "Aside from that, even if she'd been found innocent, our laws don't allow us to take females out of the Exchange. Who's to say what would have happened then?" He fingered the itching tattoo on his temple.

Ki's loud snort announced his disagreement. "That's the biggest load of *danka* shit I've ever heard."

D'zia nodded. "What he said."

It didn't help that he'd already admitted the same thing earlier, but still, it stung to hear it voiced out loud from the two men he respected the most. He glared at them anyway.

"Qay, I've known you for a long time and I have never seen you act like such a complete dick." Ki glared right back. "You have always taken any challenge thrown at you head-on. Sometimes you don't even stop to consider the ramifications if you failed. Case in point, after your father exiled you, you didn't give up in your attempts to regain his trust. You strategized and executed a plan to reclaim your birthright and prove you deserved it in the first place."

Ki leaned forward and rested his arms on his thighs as he clasped his hands to stare with unwavering conviction. "Now you find yourself in the uncomfortable position of having an alien TrueBond, but instead of dealing with it and thanking the Goddess you found her, you shove your head up your ass and pretend like you're rejecting her for her own good. You and I both know claiming her would have been the best thing to ever happen to you." He rested back and crossed his arms over his chest with one leg over his knee. "So what is really going on with you?"

"Oh my Goddess, he's scared!" D'zia exclaimed as he slapped a thigh with mirth.

What good would it do to disagree? Denying it would be pointless since he'd already admitted the same thing earlier.

Qay shrugged and grunted his agreement. "It won't make a bit of difference if we're too late." A sour taste coated his mouth as he continued. "Even if we do find out where she is, and even if we could get her away, I've treated her so badly she may never forgive me. I'm sure she hates me, and I wouldn't blame her if she did." His fear worked overtime and tightened his sternum. "What will I do?" he mumbled under his breath.

"Oh, cry me a river." D'zia jumped out of his chair to slap Qay upside his head. Qay rubbed the offended spot and shot D'zia a confused expression. D'zia shook his head. "Earth expressions—get over it." He paced. "Everyone, and I mean everyone, has been mad at you for one reason or another. But with your natural charm and wit, she'll be putty in your hands in no time."

D'zia's colorful way with words annoyed him, but what he said gave Qay pause. Not about everyone being mad at him, but about her forgiving him. "Okay," he said. If there was a slight chance with her, he'd take it. "Where do we start?"

"Didn't the human female mention something about a frying pan?" D'zia put his fists on his hips with a slight frown.

Ki's brow furrowed before he blinked to access the ocular VDU and became unfocused. Before too long he shared the information as a red communication light blinked in their own virtual computer implants.

What he sent them was a map of an outer sector used by the fringes of their society.

"I think she was trying to say 'FiPan.'" Qay's screen came on with the information about a slavery trafficking waystation on the outer rim of the galaxy. It was one of the more disreputable outposts known to shelter not only slavers but also served as the main underworld headquarters for those working in the underbelly of the Federation Consortium.

Maggoty hell. Qay's heart sank. Aimee was a delicate human and she wouldn't last a day in a harsh place like that. He had to find her before something terrible happened. His stomach sank next. What about the baby? It was chilling to imagine his child dying before being given a chance at life.

"We don't have much time to lose, Qay." D'zia's low voice jolted Qay out of his musings. "What do you want me to do?"

Qay stood and paced with his hands behind his back before he addressed the two males. He was glad they had something to go on and nothing would get in the way of finding his TrueBond. In a clear, concise tone he began, "D'zia, I need you to continue your search for Aja. Figure out who she is and find out if she's colluding with anyone. This might lead us to where she went in case FiPan is a dead end.

I'll contact the head of the Imperial Forces to work with you on this. With your talent and their unlimited resources, you should be able to ascertain her secrets in no time." He focused his attention on Ki, who stood in front of him. "You and I will go to FiPan. I'm hoping your previous connections can help us find Aimee."

He waited for their agreement. They gave him unwavering identical stares.

"Good. As soon as you can secure us a ship, we'll be off. I would hope we could be gone within the next few solar hours." He fingered the tender area around his right temple at the MalDerVon scroll. "In the meantime, I'll tell my father everything. Maybe he'll just keep me in exile and not put a warrant out for my arrest." He gave a snort. The prospect of talking to his father and admitting his failures was daunting but not as important to him as finding his female.

Qay straightened his spine as he regarded his two friends. "Now is the time to consider your options carefully before either one of you get caught up in this mess. If we can't find the evidence against Aja, they'll view you as accomplices if they come to arrest me. You'd suffer the same penalties that I would."

Silence laid heavy in the small room as each male refused to move.

Finally, D'zia let out a whoop of excitement and clapped his hands. "Well hell, ladies, let's get this party started!" He strode out of the room with a jaunty wave of his hand, "I've got people to do, places to disrupt, and an Imperial general to annoy in my future. Keep in touch and in the meantime, I'll find that bitch come hell or high water. Later, dudes!"

Qay and Ki looked at each other in confusion and asked at the same time, "What's a dude?"

Aja

Of all the interfering—Aja thanked the Goddess she'd been on the main hangar when the intrusive clan from a neighboring sector landed. At first, she hadn't paid any attention to them until the occupants came strutting out of their ship like conquering heroes. The leader carried the flopping, dead body of the Friebbigh she'd sold those humans to. To Aja's utter shock, the last alien who disembarked carried none other than that redheaded human she'd gotten rid of. As far as she could tell, the *puntneji* was alive and well.

Well, the human was not *well*—she was unconscious and a pasty, sick color. Maybe the *hysta* would die before she woke up. Speaking of which, it irritated her the Friebbigh didn't heed her warning about mistreating the humans. But, if the human died because it didn't listen to her, well, there'd at least be one less witness.

Either way, it was time for another plan. She'd leave the *StarChance* and go back to anonymity to regroup and figure out her next move.

Going to her cabin was out of the question so she headed straight for her own personal ship she'd cloaked in the same small hangar where she'd kept the Friebbigh one. Good thing she'd planned for this type of emergency and kept everything she'd need on the ship.

Oh well, time to begin anew. It wasn't the first time and probably wouldn't be the last either. She appreciated the irony of using her dead mother's name, but she was more than ready to get rid of it. She had a couple of ironclad identities ready to go at a moment's notice.

After settling in the cockpit, she put the machine in stealth mode and slipped out of the hangar. By using small thruster bursts, she would remain undetected until she cleared Zerin space.

Going over various scenarios in her mind, she realized she had to do damage control and come up with enough credits to replace the shipment the Friebbigh lost. Maybe her best option was to retrieve Aimee from FiPan and offer her up as a bargaining chip to the Chancellor. Yes...yes, that might work. Offering the crown prince's human TrueBond would reassure the Chancellor of her loyalty to him. He could sell Aimee at an exclusive auction to make up for the other ten human slaves Aja lost.

Aja simmered. If the Chancellor didn't want the human, she had contacts that would give her a nice hefty price. There were plenty of outlying systems dying to get even with the Zerins for keeping them out of the Consortium. An image of Aimee being humiliated as a common pleasure slave under the noses of the royal house made her shiver with pleasure.

Satisfied she had a brilliant plan, her lips curled in eager anticipation. Once again, she congratulated herself on her ingenious ability to plan ahead when she'd put a tracker on Aimee's neck at the human dinner the first night. It amused her when the stupid female reacted as if she knew Aja had put something there. Of course, the human had no idea what it was.

It was a short-range tracker, but Aja was sure she'd have no trouble finding the human. Plus, she had a good idea where on FiPan Akoobjie would take her.

All she had to do was make sure she got there before it sold her. It'd be better to go in person instead of audio communication. No sense in alerting the Friebbigh she was interested in "re-acquiring" the human. There was a slight chance the grey alien wouldn't see things her way.

Even so, it didn't matter to her if it did or not. She'd eliminate the little insect herself if it came to that. After all, she was the best assassin in the business.

Confident everything would work out better than before, Aja slipped into warp space and headed to FiPan to reclaim her previous possession.

Aimee

Being alone in a cramped, gloomy room, Aimee had no way to measure the passage of time. The light never changed, the temperature never changed, and the air stayed a consistent, gritty staleness. She choked with each breath. Everything blurred. She could have been in the same place for a day, a week, or a year. She tried to find a way out of her cell several times, but her only reward was mounting frustration.

The only break in her monotony was when a tube of nourishment dropped from a small wall opening. At first, she didn't know what to do with it. It reminded her of an emergency ration she'd eaten on an outdoor adventure once. She guessed it might be something similar. It was easy enough to open and she took a tentative lick. Nothing. It was as if she'd tasted a glob of nothing. Aimee decided she didn't have anything to lose, so she filled her mouth. It was hard to swallow the slimy, tasteless paste. When her stomach didn't rebel, she squeezed it like a toothpaste tube to squirt the thick liquid into her mouth, which made her gag. Between one swallow and the next, the relief of hunger pangs overcame any queasiness she had about eating it. Though she didn't get any water, she found she didn't need it as long as she sucked up whatever was in the tube.

The only thing worse besides the "food-in-a-tube," was the pale orange liquid that poured out of the ceiling like a shower from hell. It covered everything in the small cell daily. The first time it happened, she gave a startled squeak. Her mouth was open and some of the liquid got in. A searing fire blistered the tender skin of her tongue and inner cheeks.

The next time the orange stuff fell she kept eyes and mouth shut with her head bowed. At least the liquid evaporated within seconds and left her skin, hair, and clothes in a pristine cleanliness. She wasn't too wild about the sharp astringent smell it left behind though.

Since escape wasn't possible, there were plenty of other things for her mind to stew over. Like the constant dull throb around her left temple. It was as if burning screws dug into her skin before it tapered off to ping in odd moments. Was there something growing on her temple and upper cheek? Did the grey alien somehow brand her? She rubbed the skin trying to ease the steady pulses with her fingertips. She felt tiny raised bumps along the temple, above and below her eye. There was a large one with multi-facets stuck in the middle of her temple.

To top everything off, she became nauseous after she slurped down the goop in the tube. But then again, who wouldn't feel sick in this type of situation?

Aimee rested her head on the tops of her bent knees, her back to the wall. The air was thicker than usual, as if it was uncirculated. Drifting in and out, her mind replayed everything that had happened to her in the last several weeks. Aimee focused on Qay and the first time they'd met. Their instant attraction was something she'd read about but never experienced in person. With every fiber of her being, she still believed he was the one for her. Didn't matter he'd rejected her more than once. The pain in his eyes and his pinched lips belied what he said. Plus, watching him all those nights on the vid in her room had given her insights into him as a person. The way he acted with his subordinates and other Zerins showed her he was an honorable man. He'd been fair but firm in his interactions with others.

She relived that vid she watched when he'd saved those old women, men, and children. He put his life on the line trying to protect them. The determination it took for him to take care of others at the cost of his own life was admirable.

Which led to why she went to him to help her find Shannon in the first place. In hindsight, that probably wasn't the smartest thing she'd ever done. All she did was make him run away from her as fast as possible. Who could blame him since she'd run into the room like some kind of freak screaming her head off. It was crazy how her emotions were all over the place. One thing was for sure, all she thought about was protecting Qay. Even if she could go back and do it differently, she wouldn't. She'd always want to protect him.

Go figure.

Her mind wandered toward their first kiss...and what a mind-blowing experience that had been. All she had to do was ignore everything that happened afterward.

Okay, the same went for the last time they were together. She'd hold on to the tender, reverent way he'd made love to her and ignore his parting shots or she'd start tearing up at odd times.

She jolted awake when the twilight in the room became brighter. She opened her gritty eyes as she sat straight from her reclining position on the cool wall. She rubbed her eyes before she watched her captor waddle its thin body toward her. A few feet away from the wavering force field, the creature blinked its sideway lids over its large almond-shaped black eyes.

"What on face?" Its thin, bony index finger pointed at her left temple.

What was the dumb-ass thing talking about now? Did it come to see its handiwork? Too bad. She hid her face in her hair.

"Creature, show face now!"

Creature? Who in the hell did it think it was talking to? She turned around and crossed her arms over her chest. Maybe, just maybe it might get mad enough at her and open her cell. Then she'd rush out of the cell and tackle it.

It wasn't much of a plan, but it was better than nothing.

"Creature, turn, or I punish."

Annoyed at the repulsive little twerp, she glanced at the black box in its long, sticklike fingers. Shuddering in remembered pain, she faced it but made sure she kept her hair over her left temple.

Its double-jointed finger wavered over the box. "Show now." The command came through the metallic voice box on its chest.

Thinking fast, Aimee made a motion as if to pull her hair back when she bent over and groaned as if in pain. "Oh, my stomach! I'm going to be sick! Ahhh...!" She groaned louder, clutching her hands to her stomach. She put her head between bent knees.

"No, up. I push button."

"I'm in pain. Help me, help me!" For a little added dramatic flair she raised one of her hands in a pleading gesture, "I'm dying—ahhh!"

Ha! Meryl Streep had nothing on her.

Glancing through the curtain of her hair, Aimee watched as the alien waved at the force field to turn it off. Not waiting to think about it, she jumped up, rushed the smaller alien, and tackled it to the ground. She was fighting for her life, frantic movements made in panic and fear. The force of her attack jerked the black box out of its hand and it flew in a high arc above them. As Aimee and the grey alien entwined, a disgusting reality became all too clear. Its repulsive limbs were squishy and slimy as if she were trying to hold on to a thick, sticky spider web. On the heels of thinking of a spider web, Sherri now envisioned the greasy alien as a huge, hairy spider flaying and grabbing hold of her. She had a wild vision of eight eyes that blinked independently and yellow venom dripping and pooling out of sharp fangs.

She had to get it off—get it off—NOW!

Instinct ruled as she bitch slapped the gooey alien, her hands flapping and smacking as she tried to get it off her.

The more she pushed it away, the more their limbs became entwined. With a violent jerk, she pushed its bare feet, complete with repugnant, long three-knuckled squiggly toes that matched its long squiggly fingers. She squealed in horror as she rolled around the floor with it as it made loud squawking noises out of its tiny slit of a mouth, its pink forked tongue slithering in and out.

She must feel as yucky to it as it did to her. Both were in a frenzy to untangle themselves, but in the furious fray, they couldn't break free. Not until one of their rolls resulted in the alien thumping its head with a sickening bounce on what Aimee assumed was a control panel.

A loud clanging sound reverberated throughout the small room as a tinny voice announced, "*Alert, alert! Autopilot off-line, manual override needed.*"

Panicked, Aimee blinked at the alien. It stopped moving and slithered to the floor in a boneless heap, leaving a thick purple goo behind its head, smearing down the console. She stared at it for a few heartbeats as she gulped in the rancid air.

Go ahead, Aimee. See if it's dead or not.

There it lay, comatose on its back with its large, almond-shaped eyes no longer an endless black but a milky white as if its pupils rolled to the back of its head. The freaky sight made her tummy protest with an acid roll. Putting a hand on her abdomen, she went in closer.

With extra care, Aimee crept toward the prone body, ready to jump and choke the little shit if she had to. Between each step, she waited to see if it moved. When nothing happened, she stopped and towered over the crumpled body.

"Okay, Aimee, you can do this. Just walk right over there and see if it's still alive or not." She took a few cautious steps to the body and gave it a nudge with her foot. It didn't move. *Humph*, that didn't mean it was dead. "Think, think. How do you tell if a slimy little grey alien is dead or not?" Something rolled on the floor and caught her eye. She bent to look closer. A thick pool of dark purple liquid rolled out from underneath its large, bulbous head.

"That doesn't mean anything. It could be alive. Maybe." Pushing aside her queasiness, she nudged the creature onto its stomach with her toe. "Ew!" There on the back of its large hairless grey head was a dent the size of a grapefruit. Globs of its gelatinous brain and indistinguishable goo oozed out of the gaping hole.

"Well, I doubt it survived that. Ha! Who says I can't kick some serious alien butt?" Her elation was short-lived when a loud blaring voice echoed in the small chamber as the ear-piercing siren continued to wail.

"Warning, warning! Entering atmospheric parameters. Manual override needed."

She ignored the ship's warning. She had to find the little black control box for the collar around her neck. "I'll be damned if I keep this thing on me for one more second. Come on, come on, where are you, you stupid little box? I refuse to die with this dumb thing around my neck."

"Aha!" She spied it across the room and rushed to grab it. "Now how do I get this thing to work?" she muttered, looking it over. Nothing popped out to show her how to release the choker. It was a smooth onyx cylinder whose sole purpose was to deliver excruciating pain. The smooth exterior taunted, giving nothing away on how to release her from its hold.

"Damn it! How do I get this stupid collar off?" she screamed and shook at the inert device in frustration.

"Specify." Aimee jerked in surprise as the same metallic voice issuing the warnings resonated in the small chamber around the clanging bells in the background.

"Huh?" Was the computer interactive?

"Specify the nature of your previous query."

"Are you the ship's onboard computer?"

"Affirmative. State the nature of your previous query."

Okey dokey—maybe things were looking up. "How do I remove the collar around my neck?"

"Restraint collar can be removed by the thumbprint of the master in the specified parameters on the control device."

Good thing "master" was available and willing to donate its thumbprint to her worthy cause. She had no shame going over to the dead carcass to grab one of its fingers. She held the slippery appendage and placed it a couple of places on the black box before she heard an audible click. The hated collar opened and dropped to the floor with a light clink. With a whoop of victory, she kicked the torture device across the room.

Now on to more important matters. She observed the various lights and blinking buzzers on the control panel, surrounded by a weird type of writing she'd never seen before. It was a combination of binary language, Egyptian hieroglyphs, and children's drawings. *Well, crap.*

"Where are we?" As if knowing where she was in the galaxy would help her. What a dork. On Earth, it didn't take much for her to get lost fifty miles out of Grand Rapids.

"We are approaching the outpost planetoid of Hiigar."

Well, at least it wasn't FiPan. Even if she crashed, it was better than going to the slave planet. Which, let's face it, was not something on her bucket list.

"Okay, can you land us safely?" The harsh noise continued throughout the chamber. "And can you turn off that stupid alarm?" The careening noise made her cross-eyed.

"Negative, unable to fully comply."

"What do you mean? What part can't you comply with?"

The screeching alarms stopped. *"Unable to land vehicle. The automatic pilot has sustained extensive damage."*

The ensuing silence was nice, but Aimee wished the automatic pilot worked. She glanced and frowned at the control panel where the alien had bashed its head. Clumps of gooey yellow brain matter covered the smashed controls and plopped to the floor. She swallowed an urge to throw up at the disgusting sight. Good thing her sense of smell was on the fritz because if she smelled anything rotten she'd be spewing chunks.

"Can you fix it?"

"That is not within my coded parameters."

Well, wasn't that a stupid thing to leave out of your computer system? "What can you do?" Her knuckles turned white as she gripped her fists.

"Specify."

Sheesh, she didn't have time to pick and choose. She would die if she didn't get this bucket of bolts to land in one piece. "We need to land safely on the planet as close to a town as possible without burning up in the process. Is that specific enough?"

"Affirmative. Navigation will return to manual control on your order."

Aimee snorted. Stupid, dumb-ass, worthless alien computer...

She studied the vid screen as a desert-like landscape whooshed past. Was it too much to ask to land miraculously in one piece?

She had no flying experience on Earth, much less on an alien spaceship. Swallowing her panic, she tried to think about the controls in front of her. "Can you guide me through the landing if you return it to manual control?"

"Affirmative."

She waited for a few beats to see if the computer would elaborate a little more. When nothing further happened, she took in a deep breath to control her zigzagging emotions. There'd be plenty of time to freak out later. Hopefully.

"Okay, give me manual control and instructions on how to land this ship." She sat in front of the console and buckled in.

"In this sequence, press the following controls."

In excruciating, mind-numbing detail the onboard ship's computer gave Aimee a set of instructions she could handle. Woo-hoo! Maybe the stupid computer wasn't so stupid after all.

The ship warned her it was time to land.

She'd done everything she could. The only thing left to do was see if it was enough. The vid screen gave her a frontal view of the dust-laden planet as it rapidly got larger.

"Okay, time to put my head between my knees and hopefully not kiss my ass goodbye." She bent and assumed the classical "crash" position of putting her face between her knees and her arms over her head. She tensed and braced the best she could.

Because of the oval shape of the ship, it bounced with a jarring ping as it hit the ground. The outer hull was made of some stern stuff since it withstood the violent impact before it spun like a bowling ball. At least she'd been smart enough to buckle in before they crashed. Going around and around while buckled in was far better than being thrown without being anchored. Something sharp cut across her left upper arm and several things battered the top of her thighs. All in all, she'd walk away from this unscathed. Except for her shoulders and chest bruised from the restraining straps.

Once the spinning ship stopped and settled, Aimee wobbled to sit upright in the chair. She slumped her head back against the padded headrest and whooshed out a breath. She had to wait for her thundering heart and queasy stomach to calm before she pulled open the X-shaped body buckle to slide out of the seat and land on her hands and knees. With her head down, she waited until the dizziness steadied enough for her to function like a normal person again.

She glanced around the wreckage to find the window vid was off-line. She stumbled over loose debris littering the floor. *Damn!* Now what? Ha, maybe time to get out of this lousy ship. First thing's first, she had to find something to pry open the door with. No such luck, there wasn't anything sharp or heavy lying around. Great, time to come up with plan B and explore the rest of the little vessel.

Chapter SEVEN

A fter several grueling, frustrating hours, Aimee was certain of a couple of things. First, finding the battered body of the grey alien was *gross, gross, gross*. Its mashed and mangled body looked like it went through a dryer—on high. The flayed, shredded skin on the skeletal remains with its bashed head was worse than before. Purple blood liberally sprayed the interior of the ship in a rendition of an abstract artist's painting—on steroids. It was a good thing her stomach was strong enough to ignore the grisly display.

The second thing she found was a saddlebag she could use to store supplies. Inside was a small cape-like hoodie to put around her shoulders and over her head. The fabric was lightweight, but it would at least give some protection over her clothes.

Last but not least, she found a deep container with a bunch of those tubes filled with the edible paste. It wasn't by any means her favorite food, but it was better than starving or dying of thirst. Now all she had to do was find a way to get out of the pod to find a settlement so she could get a message to the Zerin authorities.

Who else could she contact? Earth wasn't an option, so the Zerins were going to have to suck it up and come and get her. After all, it was their fault she was in this predicament.

After Aimee pulled more debris and broken bits apart, she found a medical kit complete with cloth-like strips to use on her bleeding arm. Taking her top off, she tore one of the rectangular strips and dabbed the bleeding wound. By the second swipe, the blood flow lessened and the two-inch gash closed. By the third swipe, the wound sealed itself and a small pink scar remained as a trophy. She pulled her tunic back on when she finished. She stuffed as many of the cloth strips as possible in the bulging bag, just in case.

Now she was ready to go. To where was the question.

"What am I supposed to do now?" Aimee kicked a pile of debris in front of her. To her utter surprise, the mechanized voice of the computer answered her.

"Unable to recognize your command. Please specify."

Well, at least Mister Personality was back. "Can you open the hatch door so I can leave?"

"Affirmative. Upon your command."

Okay, but where to go once she got out? "Wait, can you connect me to the Zerin homeworld instead?" She should have thought of that before. Excited, all she had to do was ask for help and she wouldn't have to leave the ship. Ugh, she'd have to clean up first.

"Negative. Interstellar communication has irreparable damage."

Well—yippee kiyah. That's what she got for thinking of things too late. Now what? What would be the next best thing? "Is there anywhere near here I can go to contact the Zerins?"

"The nearest interstellar communication is 204.68 units north."

Crap on toast. "Is there any civilization closer?"

"Affirmative. A small outpost is 15.37 units northeast of our position. It can be reached in approximately six solar days by foot."

Okay, six days sounded good. She could survive for that long. Couldn't she?

"Will I be able to contact the Zerin homeworld from there?"

"No data available."

Jeez, it was like pulling teeth. "Can I at least breathe the outside atmosphere and survive the planet's temperature?"

"Affirmative. Air and temperature are well within your physiology."

"Is there any danger from the native animal or plant population on my way to this outpost?" Hey, she'd read a ton of science fiction stories where a giant omnivorous plant attacked the heroine. Not to mention scary, pointy-teeth large monsters bent on eating tasty, slightly plump little human girls.

"Negative. Animal and plant threat is at a minimum."

"Are there any weapons on board I can take with me?" Just because the computer said there wasn't any danger didn't mean there wasn't any.

"Affirmative. A selection of blasters is available for you to choose."

A panel to her left opened and she spotted two small pistols attached to the wall. She grabbed them and held them up for examination. Yeah, like she had any idea what she was looking at. There was a button on one side, so maybe all she had to do was point and shoot.

Digging deep within for the courage she needed, she squared her shoulders. The sooner she got away from this death trap the better. Not like there were any other options floating around.

"Okay, Cortana."

When in doubt, she always found it helped to quote one of her favorite video games to feel better. Especially when she suspected she was doing something stupid.

"Open the door and let me out."

Dust—unrelenting, soul-sucking dust—wormed into every pore and crevice. Thank God for the hoodie, it came with a scarf to wrap around her nose and mouth. Even so, each movement became an excruciating exercise in futility as the fine, dry dirt rubbed and scraped against Aimee's skin with each step. The lazy wind became a consistent whine around her.

During the day, she found the fire-orange morning sun inspiring with its splash of color against a cloudless yellow sky. The nights were more breathtaking, an eggplant canopy topped with three pale turquoise moons surrounded by a myriad of blazing stars.

When dawn came and the monotonous morning stretched endlessly, it was all she could do to keep her feet shuffling in the silty, slick dust that wasn't thick enough to be dirt. There were no signs of vegetation, nor were there any hills or mountains on the horizon to break up the dreary landscape. At least the heat never climbed to unbearable heights, but it was hot enough to be uncomfortable during midday.

Aimee was grateful there weren't any signs of human-eating plants or animals but hearing birds chirping or the tittering of insects would have been nice. The only break in the heavy silence was the gentle whooshing of a light breeze as it distributed the fine granules around.

During the fifth rising of the blood-orange sun, Aimee became anxious. There were only two food tubes left, and there'd been no signs of life. Wouldn't it be just her luck to walk around in circles? Well, she doubted that was true since she followed the sun to calculate her direction. She hoped being on an alien planet didn't change the laws of physics of the sun rising in the east and setting in the west.

In her trek to find civilization, she worried about a new problem. What was she going to do once she got to a populated area? She had no way to pay for anything. Heck, she wasn't sure she'd be able to communicate with anyone. She never thought to ask how the nano translators worked. Did someone else have to have the same thing to understand her? When she thought she was talking in English, did she instead talk in their language?

Even though the Zerins insisted the humans had to be educated in several alien cultures before they attended the Exchange, their instructions lacked basic info. If Aimee had her way, she'd revamp their program to include emergency contingencies. She couldn't be the only one to find she was alone and cut off from help.

Something caught her eye on the horizon, wavering in and out as a dark outline rose from the flat ground. Could it be? She stared harder to make sure she wasn't imagining things. The sun dipped a little lower and sure enough, there stood a building outline.

Her heart pounded. Maybe she'd find help there.

Common sense reared its ugly head. Who was to say it wasn't another black market outpost overrun with a bunch of outlaws? Even on Earth, trying to find somebody to help a homeless, penniless foreigner was dangerous. She gripped the blasters she kept in the pockets of her tunic.

It didn't matter, what choice did she have? She couldn't wander in the wilderness for days on end. It would take at least another day to get there, so she might as well make camp for the night. The last thing she wanted to do was walk around in the dark and run into some creepy alien animal. Or worse, twist an ankle because she didn't see a hole in the ground.

The next morning, there was a surprising break in the constant whirling breeze. Without the dirt devils antagonizing her, Aimee took off the hoodie and gave it a couple of shakes to dislodge the silt. Her pants and tunic were next, and she shook them out the best she could before putting them back on. The black fabric clothes kept up with the abuse she'd put them through. The color hadn't faded and the material resisted tears and rips and protected her skin from worse cuts in the crash. Without the diminutive dirt clinging to her clothes, they'd be as fresh as the day she put them on.

She picked up the saddlebag she'd used for a pillow and crisscrossed it over her shoulder to rest on her right hip. The last thing to put on was the hoodie, with the hood part over her forehead. Then she shook the dirt out of her shoes and headed out.

She arrived at what she considered a small village by the end of the day. Exhausted, every part of her body protested the rigorous nonstop pace she'd set for the last six days. Her left upper arm was throbbing even though it had stopped bleeding back at the ship. In addition, numerous bruises dotted the tops of her thighs along with the ones on her chest where the seatbelt had held her in place.

Constant throbbing aside, she wished she had a mirror. How could she walk into an unknown town looking like the friendless, homeless vagrant she was?

Dwelling on that idea wasn't helpful. She shrugged and trudged into the little town as she kept an eye out for any possible threats. The village had several single and two-story buildings opposite of each other on a narrow dirt road. It reminded her of the old west, complete with open storefronts and loud noises spilling out into the street as dirt devils swirled in separate areas. The only thing missing were tumbleweeds and a soundtrack from an old spaghetti western.

The structures on both sides of the street were made of a pink clay-like adobe material, something resembling an igloo and a teepee. The "sidewalk" was the same material, firm yet spongy enough to give a little with each footstep. It was eerily surreal since the streets were empty of any living beings.

She wasn't sure if finding herself alone was a good thing or not. She shuddered at what the ramifications of being by herself on the street could mean. Maybe she'd be better off inside.

At the first open door, she took her time to peek her head around the corner. Before she went in any farther, she pulled back and shook in revulsion. She had no idea what she'd seen, but it sure wasn't anything she wanted to see again. Bodies writhing in either ecstasy or agony in complete synchronicity with the booming clamor inside. Maybe they were all dancing to some music, but because of the various alien shapes, noise and rotten smell, it was hard to tell. No way was she going in there.

She ran—no, trotted. No, ran, as she passed several two-story buildings to the next open door. She took in a deep breath for courage and poked her head in. A warm tawny light bathed the crowded room accompanied by a welcoming scent of freshly cooked food. Her mouth watered as she inhaled the forgotten scent of something edible. Itching to get a better view, she stuck her head in further. With eyes darting back and forth, she was relieved to see a conglomeration of various alien species peacefully interacting with each other. The saloon-like atmosphere of the place welcomed any-one to come in and enjoy food and drink in a relaxed environment. Loud laughter and boisterous speech further alleviated her worries of it being a dangerous place.

Just like the cantina scene in an old sci-fi movie.

Crowded bodies at various tables were having a good time eating and drinking. It was hard for her to say if that's what they were doing because they were all so different. She decided the vibe was good enough to take a chance, so she slunk into a one-person table close to the door a three-legged creature had vacated. A forcefield closed behind her and kept the dust out.

Aimee wanted to remain cautious, so she kept her hood over her face as she glanced around the room with her back to the wall. Sitting this way, she could observe everyone in the glow that illuminated from the ceiling.

In front and to the right was a long bar similar to any local pub on Earth. This one was made of the same clay-like exterior that blended seamlessly into the building. Barstools lined up in front, each occupied by a multitude of species. Some were humanoid, some...not so much.

Aimee had to blink at the giant behind the bar. He towered at least seven and a half feet with a body in the shape of a pyramid. He had a small head in proportion to the rest of him, with one large eye in the middle of his forehead. His inverted chin drooped with loose skin over a thick neck. A tuff of bright yellow feathers sprouted on the top of his pointed head and matched a feathered unibrow over his one eye. His yellow iris had a dark orange, round pupil in the center. His nose was flat over full, rubbery lips framing a soft pink, humanlike mouth which complimented his pale yellow skin.

It was hard to tell what the alien was wearing below the waist since he was behind the bar, but his bare, pale chest devoid of nipples had a smattering of tiny yellow feathers forming a T across his pecs and into a line down his protruding belly. A panel of turquoise material from his waist draped over his right shoulder and down his back like a Scotsman's kilt.

With expertise, he worked the bar grabbing and making drinks for the patrons in front of him. He had two thick fingers on each hand with a thumb just as long. Aimee was amazed to see how fast he was for someone so large. But what didn't surprise her was how observant he was to everyone around him.

Including her. His large yellow eye never wavered from staring at her. She squirmed under his scrutiny as his deft hands poured drinks and grabbed glasses.

A loud crash to her left made her jerk. One of the waiters threw the tray he'd been holding at a patron after he'd pummeled the creatures head with it. The alien with the bashed head squealed in a high-pitched sonic boom loud enough to shatter several glasses around the room. The waiter ran over to the tray, grabbed it to bop the other creature's head again, and shouted "shut up!" in a loud squeaky voice. The ear-numbing noise escalated as the wounded creature continued to scream with piercing intensity as he clutched the back of his head where the tray had smashed it.

The crazy sight had Aimee laughing aloud because the guy getting his head whacked was another behemoth. This one had large muscles resembling rough boulders along his arms as he raised his five-fingered hands to defend himself against a furry rodent-like creature wielding his weapon of choice—a serving tray. The small four-legged creature was no bigger than three feet in height but succeeded in kicking its opponent's ass as it continued to pound his frustration out on the larger one.

In a blur too fast to follow, the large bartender leaped over the counter and pulled the two opponents apart. Holding each one aloft by the scruff of their necks, he shook them.

"I's tolds yous twos befores no more fights." He gave every indication he was ready to crash their heads together. A small feminine figure jumped on him and wrapped her dual arms around his nonexistent neck and her legs around his massive waist.

Aimee touched her open mouth as the female who clung to the large bartender reminded her of an Anime character. The spry female was petite and thin with pale pink skin and large neon pink eyes framed with dark pink lashes. Her spiky pink and black hair was short in the front with long curling tresses floating past her thighs. She wore a short pleated black skirt with a white blouse tucked into a tiny waist that emphasized her perky, bountiful breasts. To finish the outfit, she had black thigh high stockings and pink Mary Jane pumps. How the thigh highs stayed in place as she gripped the bartender's waist was anyone's guess.

Other than being alive, another glaring difference between her and a Japanese animated character was she had four arms instead of two. The top set of her arms held the back of the bartender's head and stroked the feathers in a rhythmic, soothing motion. The other lower set of arms cradled the bartender's face in a gentle caress as she planted kisses around his large rubbery mouth.

There was absolute quiet in the crowded room as everyone held their breath to see if the danger had passed.

"No, no, mustn't do, mustn't do." Her singsong voice peppered between the kisses she planted on his immovable face. "No kill. No kill."

Aimee was astonished when the large male rolled his eye upward in a universal gesture of exasperation. "Alrights...alrights, Hayami. Yous wins." His face softened when his yellow and orange eye focused on the female in his arms. "Yous can gets downs nows. I's no hurts 'em."

"Good Fylgir, my good Fylgir. No dead more customers." She loosened her legs around his waist and slid off his massive body. How she avoided pulling off his kilt-like garment at the same time spoke of consistent practice. With the female stepping away from the massive bartender, Aimee noticed he had large, pale yellow legs covered in fuzzy feathers that reached to his fuzzy, split-toed feet.

Freed from the clinging female, the large male lumbered over to the front door and threw each offender outside. "Nos come backs here agains! Hayami no saves yous next times."

"Oh, Fylgir!" Hayami's singsong voice punctuated with a giggle as she playfully slapped his forearm with her top right hand. "You Hayami good so." Without warning, her round, soulful eyes filled with tears. "But Hayami needs now help. How take Hayami care without Gooshma here people?" Both of her arms went straight to her sides as each fist clenched.

Uh-oh...a crying fit was coming...one...two...

"Nows...nows, Hayami! Nos needs to cries. Fylgir nevers lets Hayami suffers. We's finds someones soon." The pretty alien's face became a blotchy maroon as she gulped in a lungful of air.

...and three!

"No!" wailed the distraught female. "Now Hayami someone needs!"

Annnnd—cue in the golden opportunity.

Reacting on autopilot, Aimee stood and said, "I'll help you!"

A heavy silence thrummed as she became the sole focus of the place. Sweat popped between her breasts and an empty feeling pinched her stomach. Talk about feeling awkward. That wasn't going to stop her, though. She raised her chin.

The behemoth, Fylgir, placed his massive knuckles against his wide hips. "Whats or whos is yous?"

"My name is Aimee and I am looking for a job." Was it called a job here?

He answered her by narrowing his large yellow eye at her. "Let's sees yous face."

Aimee had forgotten about the hood over her head, so she pulled it back and let it drop behind her. She hoped she didn't look like she'd survived a kidnapping, a ship crash, or a dusty trek through the desert for the last six days. She straightened her spine and gave him a wide, and, she hoped, winning smile.

Hayami squealed with delight and clapped both sets of hands as she rushed over and swooped Aimee in an enthusiastic hug. The feel of four sets of arms engulfing her was a bit suffocating.

"Look Fylgir, pretty how! Perfect be. I now keep." She let go of Aimee as she turned large soulful eyes at Fylgir with both sets of hands clasped to beseech him. Up close Aimee was amazed Haya-mi's eyes had white slivers in them pulsating with emotion. Huh, just like the animated versions she'd seen countless times on different shows.

The large alien male narrowed his eye at Aimee until the orange pupil was a mere slit. "Yous works befores?"

"Yes, of course! I work hard and I learn quickly."

Fylgir scratched the top of his head, which caused the bright yellow feathers to fluff out. If Aimee hadn't been in such a desperate situation, she would've laughed when a feather loosened and floated to the floor.

"Yous talks funnies."

"Hush, Fylgir. Hurt you make Pretty have." Hayami admonished as she grabbed Aimee by her upper arm with both of her small right hands and dragged her with surprising strength toward the bar. "I work show you, you work." Those expressive, pulsating eyes examined Aimee again. "Yes?"

Aimee gripped the top of Hayami's upper hands in a grateful squeeze.

"Yes."

Aja

For the first time in a long time, Aja was scared. Her two-month long trip to FiPan resulted in exactly nothing. Akoobjie had never shown up with the human and its compatriots were convinced Aja was responsible for their leader's disappearance. As a whole, the species couldn't care less what happened to each other, but the head of their ruthless society was an exception. It didn't matter that Akoobjie had to kill or maim half of their population to get that dubious distinction.

Now she had to figure out what had happened to Akoobjie's ship before the rest of its people did. If they got a hold of that human first, losing the profits would be the least of Aja's worries. She had to get back in the Chancellor's good graces and showing up empty-handed wasn't the way to do it. She might as well stay on FiPan and sell herself because her life wouldn't be worth the air she breathed.

It took her a moment to get comfortable in the hard seat of the cockpit. With deft fingers, she input the flight pattern to leave the orbit of FiPan and head into space the same way she'd come. The only thing to do was to analyze and reverse the trajectory the Friebbigh would have taken to reach the slave outpost. The beacon she'd placed on the human's neck was short range but there was a good chance she'd be able to pick up the signal along the way.

Satisfied the coordinates were heading her in the right direction, Aja put her ship on autopilot and got up to limp to the sleeping chamber. She opened an overhead compartment with a touch and pulled out a small first aid kit. Time to take care of the broken wrist and cuts she'd suffered escaping the slimy little insects.

Aja sat on a small chair and placed her broken left wrist on her lap. Various areas on her face and hands bled in slow trickles. It had taken every ounce of strength and cunning to run away from the mob of the small grey aliens when they realized who she was.

Aja was glad she'd taken precautions and brought her blasters with her. She had to use them to escape from the enraged hive mentality. Not her fault she had to kill most of them to do it. She finished mending her wrist when a light alarm sounded. She dropped the healing cloth and ran to make sure what she heard was the human's location beacon.

Yes, it was the human's signal! Where was she? Ah, the human was on a small no-nothing planetoid called Hiigar. The only claim to fame on that ball of dirt was the dregs of every known civilization went there to disappear. The dubious citizens of the various out-posts minded their own business and couldn't care less what happened elsewhere in the galaxy. They shunned advanced technology, so if the Friebbigh had to land there for an emergency it would have to stay and wait for help from one of its own.

Perfect. All she had to do was get there before the slave trader left. She doubted Akoobjie had called for help, otherwise its people wouldn't be a mindless mob. If she found it was still alive, she was going to make sure it wasn't when she took the human with her to the Chancellor's Palace.

The element of surprise was on her side, after all.

If she wasn't mistaken, there was an obscene reward offered for the death or capture of the Friebbigh leader. And she was just the Zerin to cash in on that opportunity.

Qay

FiPan was as big a cesspool as Qay remembered.

It was night as Qay strode alongside Ki. They made their way through the gloomy, narrow streets of the village called Auks that reeked in equal parts despair and greed. A rancid odor swirled around them in the humid air as they weaved through a conglomerate of buildings as diverse and eclectic as the dregs of society that inhabited them.

Having discussed the best plan of action before landing, Qay and Ki bargained for an audience with the lead criminal boss known as The Dread Pirate Maynwaring. Heading up the largest territory in the underworld, he was an enigma with no known ties to any system or species. Security was at an all-time high, and audiences spoke to his audio orb under stringent conditions. Final agreements and contingencies had to go through humanoid sexbots programmed for secretarial and bodyguard purposes.

Nearing the end of their nerve-racking journey in space, Qay was glad he'd put on his old mercenary uniform—complete with a black balaclava mask to help camouflage his identity—when they went planet side. Dark leather pants encased in black leather boots, a light natural fiber shirt open at the collar with a thick, long coat and enough pockets to house many and various weapons. Blasters, knives, and a flat phase inducing sword strapped down his spine in a custom-made holster helped him to shed the respectable ship's commander persona and become the hired gun he'd been. Resuming his old life was comforting, like spending a relaxing evening with an old friend. The familiar blasters strapped to his side gave him added assurance he would get the information to retrieve his TrueBond.

A sideways glance at Ki striding next to him filled him with an extra sense of purpose. The large male had exchanged his customary uniform for the garb he had worn when Qay had first met him. In appearance, the dark clothing was similar to what Qay wore, but looks were deceiving. Ki not only had an air of a dangerous predator, but also the dark battlesuit was a formidable weapon. The shielding technology in the suit came from some obscure race long gone. It was impervious to any known weapon in the galaxy, making Ki an indestructible warrior along with the hidden weapons in his overlong coat. Ki was definitely the more lethal of the two.

Qay had once asked his friend where he had gotten the lifesaving clothes, but the only answer he'd gotten from the big man was a blank stare from his blue-green eyes and a rise of an eyebrow.

Stopping at the end of a nondescript, narrow, shadow-filled alley, they came to the front of an unmarked steel-plated door. When the external scanners finished, the door disappeared. They walked over the threshold and met one of Maynwaring's programmed sexbots. This one was a female, humanoid in appearance, with bright orange skin, and a baldhead with three eyes in an arc across her forehead. The feminine body was lush, with three high, firm breasts over a tiny waist tapering down to rolling hips. A wisp of clothing barely covered the rosy areolas and the outline of a female's bare mound.

"The Master will see you now." The tittering voice of the feminine cyborg was a pleasant lure to his masculine ears. Her voice was a mild aphrodisiac that made his mouth water and his balls itch in anticipation. It wouldn't surprise him if the gangster used this sexbot for more than mundane office duties.

Going through Maynwaring's stronghold, the cool air was a welcome relief from the oppressive, sticky heat of FiPan's night. Qay and Ki walked side by side through a foyer rich in priceless artwork and furnishings from planet systems long extinct. It was obvious the criminal lord flaunted his vast wealth to anyone who was brave enough or stupid enough to enter his sanctum. The sexbot led them through another doorway into a circular room encased with transportation mirrors.

Having had previous dealings with Maynwaring, Ki had warned Qay on what to expect in the mirrored room. Each reflective surface was a portal to another part of the gangster's vast empire, only accessible at his whim.

"Ah, how may I be of service to the great M'alalu E'eur?" A metallic voice echoed throughout the bare chamber as a headless mannequin covered in a long, black robe rolled into view. The palms of the figurine held the round glowing orb that contained the essence of the Dread Pirate. The internal colors fluctuated as they swirled and rolled with enough separation that the rainbow never mixed.

Qay had never dealt with this criminal before and deferred the conversation to Ki, who had.

"Sire." Ki gave a slight bow in respect, his ninja mask fluttering with his movements. "We are seeking one of our slaves stolen from us by a Friebbigh named Akoobjie. We request your permission to conduct our search here on FiPan."

"Is that so?" A humorless chuckle followed. "We were not aware the crown prince of Zerin retained slaves."

Qay's body stilled. He didn't like how the thug knew his identity. He remained silent, letting Ki continue the conversation.

"As you may well know, sire, Prince Qayyum E'etu has been exiled from his home planet and is engaging in, shall we say, personal pursuits." Ki didn't miss a beat when addressing Qay's identity.

"Just so." A slight pause before the voice continued. "No matter, we are open to hearing your offer to allow you to search for your missing *slave*."

Ki gave another slight bow before continuing. "We would never be so presumptuous as to know what would be of adequate compensation. We instead rely on your most wise counsel."

This part worried Qay the most. The notorious underworld leader was like a giant *norakthed* insect, weaving its giant web to ensnare others into doing his bidding. He was quite successful at it.

"Ah, M'alalu, how we have missed you and the proper way you negotiate with us." A dramatic chuckle made the hairs on the back of Qay's neck rise. "In the spirit of gratitude for our past dealings, we magnanimously request a slight token from you."

Qay shifted his stance, keeping his body ready for any potential outcome.

"You stand in our chambers and announce the crown prince is currently exiled from his throne. However, we are certain it is only a temporary situation. Therefore, we wish for the crown prince to be in our debt for the equivalency of one request. He is to pay this debt at a time of our choosing."

Qay opened his mouth to reply when Ki put a restraining palm against his sternum. "The exiled crown prince is unable to grant you such a request. I, however, am under no such constraint." Ki crossed his massive arms over his chest and widened his stance in a demonstration of strength. "We both know my word is worth more to you than anything the crown prince could possibly offer."

Incensed, Qay opened his mouth to argue when a resounding, "Done!" rang out, followed by the booming metallic laughter. The colors in the orb swirled in rapid succession, their hues deepening and mixing.

Furious at what his friend had done, Qay grabbed at Ki's forearm. Before he could make it an issue, the gangster's computerized voice continued.

"Because we are so pleased with your offer, we will freely part with a piece of information for your benefit." The humor behind the words had Qay grinding his teeth. "There is no need for you to search for your so-called slave here on FiPan. The Friebbigh known as Akoobjie never arrived here once it left your ship. It is presumed by its people to have been killed between there and here." A dramatic, long-suffering sigh was as practiced as it was fake. "However, one of your females came here looking for it. She barely escaped with her life when the other Friebbigh tried to kill her in revenge for their leader."

Qay's heart raced at the mention of a Zerin female being on FiPan looking for Akoobjie. It could only be Aja.

Speaking for the first time in a calm tone Qay asked, "Would you happen to know what direction she was headed?"

Ki moved as if to stand in front of Qay to protect him.

"No, no M'alalu, do not be concerned. We will not request another tithe for this information. Your previous offer to us is compensation enough." The full-length mirror in front dissolved into the screen showing the coordinates Aja took when she left FiPan's orbit. "This is her last known trajectory and we anticipate she's heading for the outer rim planetoid of Hiigar."

Lead dropped in Qay's stomach. It would be at least another month and a half before they could reach that distant planet.

"This exhausts our knowledge of this topic," the booming voice from the orb announced. "You may leave our presence and resume your journey elsewhere." The surrounding mirrors blackened except for the one behind them, which lit up in a neon montage of colors. "This portal will take you directly to the dock where your ship is." Both men began to leave, but Maynwaring had to have the last word.

"Just know, M'alalu Ki E'eur, we will soon be in touch to collect our debt."

Aimee

Aimee stared at her reflection in the head-sized mirror attached to a wall in her quarters. She hardly noticed the subtle changes to her appearance. With an inner vision, she admitted she was grateful for how everything worked out, even a month and a half later. True, she was at an alien outpost, but she had found deep and lasting friend-ship at *Galaxy's End* pub with Hayami and the giant Fylgir. Good thing too, since there wasn't any other place on the small planetoid she wouldn't have ended up literally torn to pieces. The outpost wasn't friendly to outsiders, and being the only human within five parsecs didn't help much.

Fortunately, the owners of the *Galaxy's End* pub were a pair of misfits who took her under their wing. Fylgir and Hayami provided her not only with a way to support herself by giving her a job, but they also rented her a small room on the second floor at minimal cost. Though there were no communication facilities locally, Aimee learned there was one at a larger outpost about a two-week journey from where she was at the small village of Kijiji. Hayami promised to take her there after she'd saved enough credits to send out a distress signal to the Zerins to demand they come and take her back to Earth.

At least that had been her initial plan. Now she had to come up with something new.

Oh, she didn't have to change her plans because of the bizarre changes in her body. Somehow she'd developed enhanced senses—heady flavors, sharper eyesight, intensified hearing, and her sense of smell could rival any bloodhound. She had more stamina and felt stronger physically. Yep, nothing to complain about.

Overall, nothing to bother over...She put that concern in a teeny tiny worry box and shelved it in the back of her mind. She could always take it out later.

Check.

Along with her enhanced Spidey senses was the intricate tattoo that showed up on the left side of her temple. It had a Celtic knot vibe, swirling over her temple and under her eye in purple-like ink. The center had a clear diamond crystal that changed into a dark viridian green. As crazy as it sounded, the crystal changing color was reassuring.

So again, nothing important. It went into its own worry box for later.

Check.

Now her skin and hair. When she'd left Earth, her brown hair was shoulder-length, with a wide white birthmark stripe from the roots to the end. Now, overnight, her hair was longer and thicker and reached above her ass. The white stripe had lost more pigmentation and was a pure alabaster that made the new brandy hair color more luxurious and pronounced.

As a bonus, her hair took care of itself. It was sleek and supple as if she'd run a hundred strokes through it with a hairbrush and *presto*! It would braid itself into a sophisticated French twist tapering down her back.

Her skin now had a light pearlescent sheen. If she stood in front of the mirror just right, the reflecting light would shine in a soft multicolored hue like an abalone shell. It was striking, better than any tan she'd ever gotten.

Again, in the scheme of things, this was no big deal. She took that concern, wrapped it up and put it into a box with a pretty pink bow. She took that box and stuffed it next to the others in her head to take out later.

Yep...check and double check. All of that was barely a blip on her personal weird-o-meter.

Instead of looking into her normal hazel eyes—staring back at her was a stranger whose gaze was a vibrant green with a hint of gold and brown flecks. With a hand to her throat, she concentrated on keeping her breath even as her head pounded. Aimee did her best to ignore the overwhelming emotion. She wasn't panicking because of her new enhanced senses, or because of her new face art or her unusual skin and eye color or the whacked out way her hair was behaving.

She had to be pregnant.

With an alien's baby.

Now that wasn't something she could stuff into a worry box to figure out later. She wasn't ashamed to admit it took everything she had not to *freak the hell out!*

Then an unexpected small flutter moved within the growing baby bump she carried. Aimee placed a protective palm across her abdomen and a sense of joy brought tears to her eyes. She wasn't alone anymore. She had a family again. But what if something happened to the baby? Could she take care of it by herself?

Okay, this wasn't the time to lose control. She had to remember she and the baby were okay for now. She had a steady job, a safe place to sleep at night and enough food to eat to keep her and her baby healthy. Everything was fine...everything *would* be fine.

With one last sigh at her altered image, she shook off her mental musing to get on with the day. It was time to go downstairs and meet the oodles of eclectic aliens that came to see the bizarre human. Funny, to think she was the exotic alien and not the other way around. On the bright side, it gave her a chance to introduce the customers to the human art of "tips."

On the downside, the aliens who came into the pub were not the hunky specimens that graced the front covers of the erotic science fiction romances she used to devour. The aliens who came into the pub were so bizarre looking she didn't know whether to be repulsed or fascinated by the variety. Her first impression of the old cantina scene was more appropriate than ever.

Her shift started around sunset so she had to get moving. The citizens of the small village of Kijiji ended up at the *Galaxy's End* then. Tons of food and drink had to be prepared and there wasn't any time to waste before the first customer either stepped, slithered, or stomped through the front door.

Going down the rickety stone steps would soon be tricky as her belly got bigger. Right now all she had was a small protruding bump making her pants a little bit tight. Even so, Aimee loved the clothes she had on now. They were made of a soft fabric that breathed and was durable as any expensive denim. Her current khaki green top was loose at the waist and complimented the gray slacks that flared at the ankles. Her shoes were a mix of an athletic shoe and a slipper in the same gray as her pants. Pretty soon it would be time to fork out some of her hard-earned credits to buy more clothes. Maybe she'd ask Hayami tonight if they could go back to the same clothing replicator store a couple of streets over. Not for the first time, she was amazed at how close she'd become to the small alien in the last several weeks.

Aimee reached the bottom of the steps and inhaled the comforting scents of Fylgir's cooking and the heady aroma of the various beverages. She went toward the bar to join the large Orisha male polishing several drinking utensils before he put them away in a cabinet behind him. Fylgir might be over seven feet tall, but he was no match for his lover, a Merkaba female who barely topped five feet in her spiked Mary Jane pumps. Aimee watched as Hayami arranged several tables and chairs to prepare for tonight's masses. She had to chuckle as the smaller female whizzed by and, with precise motions, set everything to rights for the night's onslaught.

Boy, she'd been way off base on her previous assumptions between the large male Fylgir and the smaller female Hayami. Aimee had been convinced the dangerous one was Fylgir, but in reality, Hayami was the deadly one.

It wasn't the double pairs of arms or her ability to move fast that made Hayami dangerous. It was the cold determination she brought to the pub whenever order needed to be established. She used a warrior's skill with razor-sharp accuracy that all of the patrons respected and recognized. It wouldn't surprise Aimee if she found out her friend had military training in her background. Either way, she was indebted to them both for taking her in. She shuddered to think what might have happened if she's stepped into any other establishment along the narrow street in the small village.

"Look, Fylgir! Here Pretty ours is!" Hayami gave a little skip as she rushed over to Aimee and gave her a quick hug. The feel of the two sets of arms simultaneously was a little uncomfortable, not being a touchy-feely person, but Aimee had to admit she liked the physical affection she got from the smaller female.

Hayami stroked Aimee's braid in a soothing motion up and down her back. "Pretty good feel?" Her lower right hand caressed the small bump on Aimee's abdomen. "Baby feel how?"

Aimee gaped at her friend. "How'd you know I was pregnant?" Holy cow, she'd only figured it out this morning.

The corners of Hayami's large, expressive eyes crinkled in amusement as they flickered to Aimee's left temple before replying. "Hayami lots knows. See you, good all will be."

"Yous having babies?" Fylgir demanded in a stern, booming voice. He stopped wiping a glass with a frown. "Wes no have babies heres. Yous leaves."

Hayami stomped her foot as she placed two sets of fists against her slim hips. "Stay, Pretty! Hush, Fylgir." She sashayed in a provocative manner toward her mate. "Good here business, Fylgir? Strange human come many see to?" She was purring by the time she sauntered behind the bar to stand in front of him as both sets of her hands caressed him along his arms and his barrel-like chest. "Pretty business make good, no?"

It amazed Aimee to watch the sheepish smile replace the previous stern look in Fylgir's eyes. He reached out and grabbed her by her tiny waist to pick her up and look at her eye to eyes. "Hayami, yous goes too fars somedays." The stern tone didn't match his softened expression.

"Today not!" She leaned in and gave him a quick peck on his full lips. "Me down put. Open soon." With a resigned grimace, the large male took a while to set her down and let go.

Aimee's breath came out in a whoosh of relief. She wasn't sure why she was worried. She doubted Fylgir denied Hayami anything. In the weeks Aimee had been here, the large Orisha male never had. Which was great, especially for her.

Now that Hayami settled the first potential disaster of the day, it was time to organize, prepare, and get the place opened. Aimee's duties were everything the pub needed—part server, part cook, part bartender, and the never-ending cleanup. The work may have been physically taxing, but she liked the variety the evening brought. It was nice to meet new, um, people, and she'd built a small fan base. Most of the patrons appeared to be enamored of the strange-looking human. No one ever threatened her nor did she feel like she was in any danger.

Overall, things were going well. That is if she'd ignore when Qay's image would appear at odd times and put her in a melancholic stupor.

Humph! Aimee shrugged off the remorse and instead focused on being busy for the rest of the evening. That is until a thin humanoid figure slipped in and sat at one of the back tables. A hooded gray cloak covered the figure from head to toe. The fabric billowed when it sat down. It kept its back to the wall and the hood covered the facial features in a deep shadow. The hair raised on Aimee's neck as a shiver slid down her spine.

Tearing her gaze away, Aimee focused on serving the group of large sasquatch-looking males rowdily celebrating. They demanded all of her attention as they roared orders that made her run back and forth with drinks and food. She had a hard time keeping up with their voracious appetites. They had her going between the kitchen and the bar too many times to count. Even so, she made sure she kept an eye on the mysterious figure slunk in the corner gloom by the door.

The evening drew to a close as the large group finally left. She scrubbed and cleared the table and stayed as far away from the hooded creature as she could. As she straightened the chairs, something familiar teased her nose. She stood and took in a deep breath trying to place the scent in her memory. It was elusive, almost like a fading thought she couldn't grasp.

Aimee checked out the near-empty room and her stomach sank when the only one left was the cloaked figure sitting alone with its gloved hands resting casually on the table. The figure wasn't threatening, but for some reason, Aimee was positive the person was here for her—and not in a good way. Why did the elusive scent bother her so much? She inhaled deeply but the memory continued to escape her.

Maybe it was because the slight figure kept the gray hood over its face and its features throughout the evening. A hand covered in a dark, leather-like glove wrapped around a glass of the local brew Hayami had served to it earlier.

Wait, the glove covered only three fingers.

Maybe it was a Zerin! He might be willing to send a message to the Zerin homeworld for her. If she put in a request, they'd take her back to Earth...right?

She refused to listen to her screaming instincts to flee and instead walked toward the cloaked figure. Before Aimee made it halfway to him, he stood up and pulled a pulsating blaster that had been hidden in the folds of the dark cloak.

Aimee's stomach lurched the minute the weapon pointed in her direction. The background noise of Fylgir and Hayami working behind the bar and the last of their customers leaving out the front door soon faded into white noise.

"Well, well, well. Aren't you the resourceful sort?" The hand without the blaster reached up to push the hood away from the face it hid.

The revelation was the last person Aimee ever wanted to see again.

Aja.

Her stomach dropped as her face became hot.

"What are you doing here?" Aimee ground through clenched teeth.

The sneer on the other female's face was unmistakable. "Why, human, I would think it was obvious." She jerked the blaster toward the front door. "You're coming with me." Her eyes narrowed to look at something behind Aimee.

"You stop right there." Aja's hand that held the blaster never wavered. "Your little friend and I have some unfinished business and she's going with me."

The twittering, singsong tune from Hayami indicated her building fury. The last time Aimee heard something similar was a prelude to a serious ass kicking she gave to a stupid, unruly customer. Aimee would give anything to watch Hayami do the same to her nemesis.

Aja reached into her pocket to pull out a small cylinder. With hard eyes, she glared at Hayami, whose fresh floral scent let Aimee know she was behind her.

"I know all about you, Hayami of the Merkaba peoples. Your reputation is well founded. Nevertheless, know this—I do not have a quarrel with you. This human is my property and I plan on taking her back."

"That's a lie!" Aimee's denial echoed around the empty room. "You kidnapped me and sold me to the Friebbigh." The urge to rush the other woman was strong and she quivered as she tried to control her crazy emotions.

"Quiet, human. Your betters are talking." Aja raised the silver-colored cylinder, probably so Hayami could get a better look. "You know what this is, don't you?"

Not daring to take her eyes off Aja to look at Hayami, Aimee heard a soft whisper behind her. "Yes." Hayami moved away, taking her comforting warmth with her.

"Good, we understand each other. Don't we?" Again the ugly sneer. Aimee would love to see her face freeze in that position.

"Yes."

Aimee's body stilled as a bad feeling snuck through. What was going on?

Aja's gaze targeted Aimee. "Let's go." She bobbed the percussion blaster toward the front door before she walked around behind Aimee.

"You're out of your mind if you think I'm going anywhere with you." Aimee crossed her arms and widened her stance as her eyes followed Aja's movements.

Behind Aimee, Aja leaned behind her neck and whispered into her ear. "Obviously you have no idea what I have, do you?"

The moist breath on Aimee's skin caused a shiver of revulsion to slither down her back. She hated being this close to the menacing alien. "No, but I'm sure nothing's gonna stop you from telling me, is it?"

Aja exhaled a taunt on the back of Aimee's neck. "Just one flick of my wrist on this will cause an explosion large enough to break this *fruking* little planetoid in half." A hard nudge between her shoulder blades pushed Aimee. "Now, I don't want to have to repeat myself. Let's go."

Panicked, Aimee watched the resigned grimace on Hayami's expressive face. It was enough to convince Aimee what Aja said was true. Acid churned in her stomach. She couldn't let anything happen to Hayami or her mate so she had no choice but to follow. If Hayami wasn't able to stop the Zerin, it sure wouldn't do any good for her to try.

"Worry no! Finds Hayami Pretty!" Hayami's singsong voice gave Aimee comfort as the last syllable died when they left the pub.

With Aimee in front, they walked down in the hazy light of the dusty street, the push of the blaster at Aimee's back. Aimee glanced at the alien woman behind her. "Now what?"

"Go to the left and keep walking to the end." At the end of the deserted street, Aja pulled the back of Aimee's shirt to stop her. "Put your hands behind you."

Aimee bit the inside of her cheek—don't say anything stupid to the crazy alien with a blaster. Resigned, Aimee held her hands behind her as Aja put metallic restraints around her wrists. Once secured, Aja placed the cylinder back into her pocket and the blaster in a holster around her hip. She grabbed Aimee's shirt and pushed her with a jerk. "Not too far now, princess."

Aimee gritted her teeth. How did she end up in this stupid situation again? Her eyes darted around as she tried to figure out an escape route that didn't involve blowing up a planet.

After a couple of steps into the dark, cool desert landscape, Aimee had to find out what was going on. "Okay, what is it you want from me now? Are you taking me back to FiPan?"

A snort of amusement from the other woman surprised Aimee. "Oh, no. I have much   bigger plans for you." Aja gave her another slight shove. "Someone very important will be glad I'm bringing you to him."

Aimee's heart pounded in excitement. Qay? She took in a deep breath to calm her racing heart and asked, "And who would that be?"

"You, my dear, will be the instrument in bringing about a much-needed revolution to the entire galaxy."

"Huh? What?" A dull pain throbbed between her eyes.

Aja continued as if she didn't hear Aimee. "Finally, those of us who had nothing will be able to have a say in our own lives."

Damn alien sounded like a bat-shit crazy diva. Maybe the crazy voices in Aja's head were taking over.

Aja grabbed Aimee's upper arm, the grip holding her in place. "Stop right here. This is far enough."

There wasn't anything around but empty darkness. Even with Aimee's enhanced eyesight, she couldn't see two inches in front of her.

Tapping her right earlobe, Aja spoke a command. "Two to lift."

Aimee went from the dusty, silty desert of Hiigar to standing on a raised dais, part of Aja's ship. "This way, princess." They came to the end of a narrow corridor before Aja stopped in front of an open archway and pushed Aimee in. "In you go." She waved her hand as lines of energy locked Aimee in the small room. Without missing a beat Aja barked, "Inject gas."

Gas? What the hell…? Aimee flopped to the cold, hard floor. A sharp pain exploded inside her head before she lost consciousness.

Chapter **EIGHT**

Aimee's eyelashes hurt. How could someone's eyelashes hurt? Lift up lids...*ow*. Close lids...*ow*. Again with the lifting action...*ow*...blink...*ow*.

Now breathe...*ow*. Breathing in hurt, but hey, so did breathing out. Lift lids again...and focus on the large blur.

And why was there a dry, scratchy cotton wad in her mouth? Aimee's tongue was so swollen she couldn't make salvia much less swallow.

The numbness in her right arm screamed for attention. Aimee rolled to the other side to relieve the pressure. *Ow*—it hurt to move. Cue circulation coming back into said arm with sharp needles to follow, so *ow*...*ow*...*ow* times two.

Lift lids again...and whaddya know? *Success!* They stayed up. Focusing was another matter, though. Blink...less *ow* this time, so bonus. Blink...and wished she'd been smart enough to keep them shut when she spied Aja's hateful mug.

"Ah, poor little princess feeling bad? Hum?" Enhanced hearing was not welcome when all she had to listen to was this particular Zerin flapping her gums.

A sharp shove to Aimee's side caused an involuntary groan to gurgle out of her mouth. Aja was making use of those pointy shoes she always wore. "Get up, human. We're here and I'll not let you make us late for our meeting with the Chancellor."

"Bitch, stop touching me," Aimee said in her mind, but what came out was something like "bligh syop tucng e." As a reward, another push dug into the same spot on her tender ribcage.

"I said get up!" Aja's high-pitched voice grated on every last damn nerve Aimee had.

Aimee rolled over to get up—anything to stop the torture of Aja's grating voice. Moving was hard to do with her hands bound in the metal handcuffs behind her. Not sure what the alien thought she could do except roll around like a rubber ball.

"Oh, for Goddess sake!" Aja's firm grip on Aimee's right bicep was painful as she hauled her to her feet. Too bad someone didn't tell Aimee's legs to hold—they folded under her like a deflated accordion. Once again, Aja forcibly hauled her up...and presto! Feet and legs got the message and locked in place.

"Come on, I don't have all day."

Too bad for Aja, Aimee's stomach had other ideas. Nausea, deep and rumbling, came up her throat.

"Gonna puke!" Aimee wished her hands were free to cover her mouth to stop from spewing chunks in the alien's direction. But then again, she'd like nothing better than leave her hostess a nice parting gift for providing such wonderful accommodations.

Besides, the shimmering navy blue tunic set Aja wore was way too nice. Aimee would *looove* to mess up her pretty clothes.

Nature won the battle as her heaving stomach doubled Aimee over. Aja yanked Aimee's arm and pulled her back in the small cubicle. She slapped her palm against an indentation that produced a circular bowl from the floor and shoved Aimee's head over it.

No words were necessary as Aimee's stomach heaved its acidic content with a violent splash. After two painful dry heaves, Aimee hung her forehead toward her chest as sweat broke out on her forehead. The stagnant air wasn't any help in cooling her off.

Pleasant duty over, the lower parts of her body gurgled and de-manded attention. "I have to go to the bathroom." She hated how weak her voice sounded when she raised her head to look at the Zerin towering over her.

With her hands on her narrow hips in a perfect imitation of human annoyance, Aja waved one hand at her, "Well, get on with it. Don't look at me for help."

Asking the crazy bitch for help was the last thing she wanted to do, but she had no choice.

"Can't. Need my hands."

Letting out a puff of annoyed air, Aja released the cuffs and dropped them on the floor behind Aimee. Pins and needles pierced her arms as she rubbed her hands.

Aimee's humiliation was secondary. She didn't care the alien female witnessed her at her worst since it was her fault anyway. Once Aimee finished, she was surprised she was steadier on her feet. Thank God getting rid of everything in her stomach settled the aftereffects of the gas. She went over to a basin that gurgled cleansing water when she got near. Placing her hands under the cool liquid, she splashed her face and rinsed her mouth out. The fresh water took away the grimy taste coating her mouth. When she stepped away, the sink and toilet melted back into the floor and wall. The liquid dried fast, so she didn't have to wipe her hands or face on the gray pants or khaki shirt she'd been wearing when she left the *Galaxy's Pub*.

"Okay, let's go." Aja grabbed Aimee in a bruising grip on her upper arm and pulled her out of the small cell. At this rate, Aimee was sure to have a lovely circle of purple bruises to show off.

In a lethargic haze, Aimee let Aja drag her to the ship's mirror transportation room. While Aimee didn't like not knowing where they were going, she had to admit it was nice to leave the sweet smell of sickness back in the small vessel. Aja stepped to the raised dais in front of one of the mirrors. "Two to lift. Chancellor's receiving chamber," she barked in her clipped, no-nonsense tone. Her bright azure crystal earrings twinkled in the room's light.

A quick glance at her disheveled appearance was all Aimee caught of her reflection before the mirror disappeared and an entrance to another room took its place. Her weak stomach gave a perceivable jolt as they went through. Now her stomach acid wanted to join the party again, but a couple of dry swallows helped to keep it down. She doubted Aja would tolerate any more delays.

Aimee's new surroundings were a pleasant surprise. The room was large and airy, tastefully decorated in a wide variety of colorful mosaics along the tall walls with moving holograms of past glories and current victories. Plants, flowers, and bushes dotted around the room in a soothing display while also giving off a slight earthy scent that thankfully helped to calm her shattered nerves. The underlying warm tones of the room added to the effect of putting her at ease, but the overt presentation of manipulated warmth gave her a shiver of foreboding.

Overshadowing the pleasant surroundings was the large Zerin male across the room who sat on a chair big enough to be a throne. He lounged on the pristine white surface, his thick thighs spread as his massive hands rested on the smooth armrest. Aimee might be a city girl, but she knew a dangerous predator when she saw one. She shivered as she took in his appearance without gawking at him like a backward hillbilly.

It was hard to tell how tall he was because he was sitting, but his enormous body hinted at him being one humongous character. The recessed lighting reflected off his bald head as it emphasized the sloping points of his ears. His lower face had raven-black facial hair in an old-fashioned Fu Manchu. His pencil-thin mustache sat atop a small black beard, flowing to his waist. His tunic and pants were made of a red color so deep and rich it bordered on being black.

The deep, depthless onyx of his eyes trapped her. Every Zerin she'd ever met had dual-color eyes with iridescent pupils framed in green hues. Not this man. His eyes had no contrasting color and were as cold and dead as a snake. Her involuntary shivers increased.

"What do you bring me?" the slow boom of the giant asked in a steady inflection. His icy stare never left Aimee as he continued to stroke the sides of his satiny mustache.

"Sire, I have brought you a wondrous gift." Was that simpering, submissive voice coming from Aja? A glance confirmed it. The syrupy tone went well with the body bending routine of a subservient lackey. Well, wasn't she lucky to live long enough to see the haughty Aja scraping and bowing like a good little lapdog.

The giant raised a scornful eyebrow. "I fail to see how that is so." One thick finger beat a rhythmic tattoo on the armrest. Aimee wasn't an alien expert, but to her, he gave a universal signal of someone fast losing his patience.

"This human, majesty, is the TrueBond of Prince Qayyum E'etu." The scrambling explanations came fast, complete with a genuflecting bow.

TrueBond? What was that? Who or what was Prince Qayyum E'etu? Aimee had to resist the urge to look behind her to see if there was another human they were talking about.

His thunderous eyes narrowed and a frown pulled his facial hair with his full lips. There was no denying the annoyance on the massive man's expression. "And what does it have to do with me?"

Uh-oh...bitchzella was getting into trouble. Aimee swore panic flashed across Aja's face. "But sire, don't you see? If we expose this human as his pregnant TrueBond, we'll have the proof we need to show the Zerin people the house of E'etu is dead. They will have no choice but to give up the throne since there will be no more heirs. Chaos will erupt and you can step in and take over. During the confusion, the other systems will fall quickly in line and into your control much sooner than planned."

The hopeful, beseeching look on the taller woman's face almost had Aimee feeling sorry for her. Almost...okay...not really.

It was all too clear Aja had no clue how livid he'd become. Aimee kept a close eye on his face and body language throughout Aja's little speech. No way was the big man a happy camper. He unfolded his massive body from his throne and sauntered over to them. Aimee checked again—yep, he sauntered. No other word described how the considerable male took his time to step closer, each foot placed with deliberate care.

Taking a small chance the Chancellor or Aja wouldn't notice what she was doing, Aimee shuffled baby steps away from them. The stony, hard look on the man's face was a clear warning to her an explosion was coming. No way did Aimee want to be in the middle of it. It'd be best for her to stay as far away as possible.

"You presume to tell me what to do?" The deep masculine voice was deceptive and mesmerizing until he stopped in Aja's personal space, chest to breast. The alien female breathed faster and he...not so much. Calm, cool, and steady like a cobra coiled to strike.

"You, a no-nothing gutter *puntneji* who lost our last vital shipment of slaves at this critical time? You bring me this worthless human and expect me to overlook what you've done?" He cocked his massive head to be level with Aja. "Now the Imperial Forces are aware how we stole humans from under their noses thus closing my ability to make the credits I need." He straightened and crossed his enormous arms across his immense chest. "To add to your complete failure, I now have to find another way to make large sums of viable credits to replace those you lost with your inept handling of this whole situation," he continued in a low, calm voice. His arms dropped to his sides as he stepped closer to Aja, whose eyes were blinking in rapid succession.

He reached with both hands to cover the sides of Aja's face before he bent to make their eyes level. He whispered in Aja's ear loud enough for Aimee to hear. "I'm afraid it is time for us to part ways." With the last word, he gave a savage tug on her head. A loud crack reverberated throughout the large chamber.

Stunned at the sudden turn of events, Aimee watched Aja's body flop in a boneless heap a few feet away. Dead, shocked eyes stared at her as if begging her to do something.

Before Aimee reacted, two tall, metallic-clad figures came over and took the body away. They wore hard gray armor and triangular, matching helmets so she had no idea what species they were. She assumed they were guards.

A subtle movement to her left made her turn around and face the biggest threat she'd ever seen in her life. Abject terror made her quake uncontrollably as her mouth dried. Her only coherent thought was to protect the baby. She placed her hands over her womb and bent her neck *waaaay* back to look at the giant who loomed in front of her.

A fleeting image of how a bug felt before a booted heel came down caused her breath to hitch.

"So, little flower." The lift of a mocking eyebrow didn't give her any warm, fuzzy feelings. "What shall I do with you?"

Aimee could think of a couple of things, but she was sure he didn't want to hear them.

"So many choices." His calm, intense voice had a singsong lilt to it. Now the rat bastard was playing with her, and she hated it when anyone made fun of her. She'd be damned if she let this overblown bully make her cower.

"Look, dickhead." She couldn't help it. When she got nervous she spouted off smart-ass comments. "Quit playing with me and get on with it. I have better things to do than stand here and listen to you talk to yourself."

Was...amusement crossing his granite-like features? "So, the little flower has thorns." He slanted his head sideways as if seeing her for the first time. "No wonder the prince bonded with you." His cold obsidian gaze traveled up and down her body before resting on the tattoo at her temple. "Maybe you can be useful." He paused. "Of course, the prince will do anything to get you back."

Aimee couldn't help it. She barked an unladylike snort-laugh hybrid. "You've got to be kidding me!" Her hand was smart enough to slap it over her treacherous pie hole before she said something even more stupid. Let the bastard think some prince was coming for her. It might give her enough time to figure a way out of *this* mess.

Oblivious to whatever Aimee had said, the behemoth gave a per-ceivable flick of his fingers to something behind her. "Take her to lock-up."

Lock-up? Well, at least it was better than say...dead.

On cue, guards led Aimee to a cell. As an added bonus, the cell turned out to be nicer than the previous six-by-six hellhole Aja had provided. This one at least had a small cot and toilet facilities. The metallic-clad guards left her with a wave of their hands to activate the force field to keep her in.

Deflated, Aimee lay down on the cot on her side to face the wavering prison door. Her body raced with endorphins from her recent brush with death and she shook with violent tremors. There was no doubt in her mind she barely got out of there with her life. One flick of his ginormous hands and she'd be as dead as Aja.

Who knew having a smart mouth might someday save her life? Speaking of which, her life had become so ridiculous—trying to figure out a way to escape from one stupid cage or another.

Humph. It looks like she missed her life's calling as an escape artist.

Yeah, take that Houdini.

Qay

Qay was in the habit of looking out the main vid-screen whenever they approached a planet and began their orbit. Standing in the cockpit of Ki's ship, the *Doomed Heart*, he stood in rapt attention with his hands clasped behind his back, staring at the vibrant display of the small brown planetoid coming closer. The scene mesmerized him as he searched for answers.

This time, answers were elusive. The basic question "Is she still alive?" was a moot point since the vibrant colors of the MalDerVon scroll and the emerald crystal in the middle remained. But other questions plagued him. Was she here on Hiigar? Was she all right?

As a human, did she have any problems carrying his child? How had they survived the last few months?

He worried she was suffering and it was all his fault.

He was so engrossed in his inner musings he hadn't heard Ki when he entered the room until a slight weight rested on his shoulder. Qay jumped and faced his friend.

"Son of an asswipe, Ki! Stop sneaking up on me." He threw his braid over his shoulder and pulled his shirt down with jerky movements. "If I didn't know any better, I'd think you've been taking hints from D'zia on how to make me jump like an untrained cadet."

Ki's unflappable expression spoke volumes. "If you're going to be jumpy like an untrained cadet, I'll treat you like one." He stepped away and clasped his hands behind his back. "Speaking of D'zia, he's requesting to talk to us."

Qay scrubbed his face and concentrated on calming his raging nerves. "Did he say what it was about?" He followed Ki to the communication station on the opposing wall.

Ki shrugged. "I have no idea. All I heard was 'Gotta talk to Qay'...blah, blah, blah...before I tuned him out." His graceful descent into the chair was a sharp contrast to his gigantic frame. "It's your job to talk to him, not mine."

He ignored his Security Officer's complaint and sat down on a chair next to Ki in front of the communication console. Ki brought up the 3-D vision of his cousin sitting in a professional lounger.

"D'zia, what do you have?" Qay kept an even tone with conscious effort. The need for action drove him hard and it wouldn't be right to take his frustrations out on either D'zia or Ki.

"Well, cuz, I have good news and some bad news." As usual, D'zia got right to the point using Earth slang. His deep dimples disappeared along with his smile. "I've got more information on the liaison we knew as Aja."

Qay raised an eyebrow in surprise. He hoped they could use whatever D'zia had found. "Okay, go ahead."

"Remember how I told you the real Aja'ne died about fifty years ago from complications in childbirth?"

Qay leaned forward with his elbows resting on his thighs and gave a nod.

"Well, the person we thought of as Aja was actually the daughter she gave birth to by the name of Al'ura R'oxk Naim." D'zia winced. Qay got the impression he wouldn't like the next part. "To say Al'ura had a crappy childhood is being generous. Orphaned at birth, she got lost in the system and didn't get the appropriate care she should have. The midwife who attended the birth sold her at an early age to a less than reputable individual in the outer rim. Al'ura's life was a miserable existence as a child slave, complete with all the goodies that entails." The bitter observation was sharp and poignant. "At the age of nine, she lucked out when one of her 'customers' took pity on her and reported her to child services back on Zerin."

D'zia narrowed his teal eyes as his lips became bloodless in a tight frown. He cleared his throat and continued. "Once here, she went through a series of tests and examinations, but the end result was conclusive: despite being an intelligent individual, her damaged psyche was untreatable. By the age of sixteen, she had to stay as a permanent resident in a mental facility due to a sociopathic, schizophrenic personality disorder. She was deemed too violent for the general population, not only to others but to herself as well." D'zia picked up the end of his warrior braid and petted the tail in a childhood habit. "Despite the heavy guard she was put under, Al'ura escaped and disappeared from Zerin records. It wasn't until thirty years later when Aja'ne L'len R'oxk reappeared along with her advanced degree in interspecies relations and wound up with our happy little crew."

Qay sat back in his chair and brushed his braid to drape over the backrest. It was hard to control his anger as he realized they'd put a dangerous female in charge of the humans. He touched his fingertips into a triangle as he contemplated his cousin. "So what's the good news?"

D'zia's thunderous scowl was not comforting as he clenched his jaw. "Are you kidding? That was the good news."

Qay straightened his spine at the same time Ki did. He braced for the next question. "Okay—so what's the bad news?"

"She's dead."

"Dead?" Qay's mouth dropped open as he gazed back and forth between D'zia and Ki. *Fruk!* They had to find Aja to get her to tell them who her traitorous contacts were. Going back to the Imperial Forces only with the name of a dead traitor was not enough.

"Yep, discovered as of this morning. Her body turned up in a less than reputable part of the capital city. No specifics yet on how and when she died."

"Is there any way you can find out where her body is interred so we can claim it to have an autopsy done?" It was a slim hope, but her body could give them some clues or answer outstanding questions.

"Already ahead of you. I've filed a claim that has been accepted and I expect the body to arrive within the next couple of clicks to the Imperial Forces medical unit." D'zia answered as he sat back. "Anything I can do to help in your search for Aimee?"

"I appreciate the offer but I can't think of anything right now," Qay replied. "We are approaching Hiigar's orbit and will go down to the surface in a couple of solar hours. I'll let you know what we find before we leave there. Thanks again for all of your help. Qay out." He canceled the vid to voice his opinion at Ki.

"Well, *danka* shit, that wasn't very helpful, was it?" He rubbed the back of his neck in frustration. "On to other matters. Any ideas on how we might find Aimee on Hiigar? It's a small planetoid but there are thousands of land measures to search."

"I've been thinking about that and I believe I have an idea." Ki's large fingers waved open a computer program vid on their personal ocular VDU. "I've been running a program to see if we could find any Friebbigh materials on the surface. It'll be easier to find that than the standard Zerin ship Aja used. You know what stingy bastards they are about their ships. They'd never leave a scrap behind if they could help it." After he flipped through some screens and verified several displays, Ki stopped and expanded the display.

"Ah...here we are." He highlighted a pulsating dot on a geological screen. "Here, next to a small outpost named Kijiji is enough Friebbigh material to make up one of their small ships. It's a good place to start as any."

Qay's tense shoulders relaxed. "Can you determine how long it's been there?" Hope was such a tentative thing, but for once, he allowed the feeling.

After a couple of scans opened and closed, Ki responded. "It appears the wreckage has been there less than six solar months."

Qay watched as Ki used his eye movements to input the coordinates when a whistling hail pierced the small cabin from the small outpost of Kijiji. Which surprised him since it was general knowledge the village did not to have any interstellar communications within its borders. Qay disconnected his ocular VDU and opened the general communications to receive the call.

"Ship Zerin you are?" A female's high voice sounded frantic.

Qay gave his companion a confused expression. "Identify yourself," he demanded.

A loud slap sounded in the background as if someone stomped their foot or slapped a face. "Hayami wants back Pretty! You Zerin or no?"

Impatient, Qay snapped. "Who am I talking to and why do you want to know if we're from Zerin?"

"You listen no! Stolen Pretty taken by female Zerin bad. You Zerin, you Pretty get back right now!" The last demand ended on a loud wail as if a toddler threw a fit.

Qay's heart thudded in his chest. Wait—was she saying a bad Zerin female had someone the voice calls Pretty? "Was Pretty's name Aimee?"

"Yes! Bad Zerin female take Hayami's Pretty! You Hayami come see and Hayami show how to get Pretty. Coordinates follow." The communication ended with landing instructions.

Ki frowned and his brow furrowed. Before Qay asked him what was wrong, Ki stated, "Inputting now." He entered the information sent. "I assume we're going in."

"Do we have any choice? Sounds like Aja got here before us and we have to find out where they went." Goddess almighty! Did he miss Aimee again? The bitter taste of frustration made Qay grit his teeth and he squashed the impulse to smash the *danka* shit out of something.

"You might want to grab your cloak to keep the biting dust off Hiigar out." Ki motioned toward the dark animal-hide mercenary garb Qay wore since they left the *StarChance*.

Qay eyed the impenetrable battlesuit on Ki. Wanting one as well, not for the first time he was curious about where Ki had gotten it.

"You're right," Qay quipped. "We can't all be protected as well as you."

Ki murmured his deadpanned agreement as he landed the ship on the outskirts of a rustic village. Once they opened the hatch, a swirl of silt rolled by that caused Qay to cough. He squinted at the afternoon red-orange sun against the yellow sky through the wall of dust. He followed Ki down the short ramp as an eclectic duo came through several dust devils to meet them. The first one was a large Orisha male, complete with yellow feathers and one eye, who stood in a protective stance next to a small, rare Merkaba female.

Seeing the two was shocking enough, but what Ki did next had him opening his mouth and doing a double take.

Standing in front of the Merkaba female, Ki went on one bended knee in the powdery dirt and lowered his large head in supplication as he crossed both arms over his chest. "I serve thee in honor." A swirling wind coated in dust moaned around Ki's prone figure.

"M'alalu! Fylgir, its Zerin our own! Missed you, how I have!" The squeal of delight wasn't hard to miss as she clapped both sets of hands in obvious joy. In return, a look of complete devotion wasn't hard to miss on Ki's expression as he straightened. The dust gathered on his broad shoulders fell around him in a cloud of silt.

Qay rubbed his chin as he contemplated them. "I gather you two know each other."

"Hayami is, or was, my commander in the Alliance of Assassins." Ki's stern expression relaxed as he explained. "I have never met a more bloodthirsty, brilliant strategist in my life. I had the distinct pleasure of serving under her command for numerous solar cycles."

"Then bad Zerin leave. No tell, no reason." Her large, pink eyes pulsated in either anger or sorrow. Those expressive eyes narrowed. "Here why you?"

Qay chuckled at the rare sheepish expression on Ki's face.

"We are here looking for Qay's TrueBond." Ki gestured to Qay behind him.

Hayami crossed her upper arms underneath her breasts, the lower left hand rested on her hip and the right one waved an angry finger at him. She gestured for him to show her his tattooed temple. "MalDerVon I see must."

Qay swallowed his impatience and tilted his head to the side so she could get a better look. Those large eyes missed nothing; it was obvious she wanted to compare his mark to another one.

Hayami's full mouth flattened. She took a step back, her pulsating pink eyes blazed with anger. "You bad mate to Pretty! Deserve her you not! Zerin no ever mate let go. You always stay from her."

Qay refused to acknowledge what the Merkaba female said about him staying away from his mate. He glared at her. "Tell me where she is." He demanded as he made a move toward the village. Fylgir stepped in front to stop him.

"Yous no moves." The large Orisha crossed his arms in a menacing stance.

Qay didn't care the large alien was twice his size. Nothing would stop him from getting to Aimee. He reached for the blaster harnessed the small of his back, but Ki stopped him before his fingers could reach the handle.

"No, Qay. Trust me, it'll be okay." Ki gripped his arm before he let go.

Qay's heart thundered as he wrestled not to go against Ki's advice. Maybe his friend had a good point. "Fine. Then tell me, is Aimee here?" It was hard to maintain a calm façade when all he wanted to do was tear past the two aliens and rip the village apart looking for her. It wasn't just the dry heat that made him sweat—his stretched nerves were tight enough to snap.

"Listen no you!" Hayami's small foot stomped in anger. Puffs of the silty ground rose and fell around her pink-clad legs. "Zerin bad female stole my Pretty! I back her now."

Her large Orisha companion enfolded the petite female in his massive arms. "Nows... nows...nos gets upsets, my owns. We's finds yours Pretties." His large yellow eye skewered both Ki and Qay. "Won'ts we's boys?"

Before either of them could answer, Qay's personal communication device beeped in his ear with an incoming call. He caught Ki's eye and motioned he was receiving a communication before he mentally opened the channel. Ki gave a slight nod of understanding and stood between him and the other two.

"Qay here."

"Please hold for Chancellor U'unk's communication."

Oh, for the love of the Goddess! With everything going on, getting a communication from Chancellor U'unk was the last thing he needed.

"I trust you are on a secure channel?" Qay had never liked the elder Zerin, his slick voice grated on his nerves. Qay couldn't understand how his father could interact with the male.

"Why would I need to be on a secure channel?" Qay asked. He gestured to Ki to listen in on the conversation as he linked their communicators. Ki came over and motioned to Hayami and Fylgir for silence.

The uncharacteristic chuckle from the Zerin politician put Qay on guard.

"Why, you and I have business to discuss. Business that would benefit us both." U'unk continued.

"I can't imagine what."

"I have a proposition for you. I have in my possession a certain personage I believe you might be looking for."

Every cell in his body froze. "I'm listening."

"I am sending a visual confirmation and your ocular VDU communiqué. You must reply before we finish this conversation that you will agree to meet or I will be forced to make, shall we say, 'a permanent' solution to the current problem that affects us both."

Qay blinked to activate the communication to see the vid display. His stomach hardened as he swallowed the urge to roar a primal scream of rage.

There she was, his TrueBond, lying on a thin pallet in a standard holding cell. The vid angle didn't allow a close-up, but he had no trouble making out her eyes were open and unfocused. The brief glimpse the vid gave lasted a heartbeat, but it told a story of someone tired and worn, but not defeated.

Pride and joy warred with fear for her safety.

U'unk continued. "You will meet me here at the Consortium Palace at the Galactic Space Station so we can discuss an advantageous arrangement. Are you in an agreement?"

It was a struggle to keep his voice bland as he talked to the other male. "Acknowledged. I will be at your chambers within seventy-two standard rotations."

"Very good. Just so we are clear, you are to involve no one. If you do, it negates any further discussions." The image of the cold chancellor filled the vid. "And the reason for our meeting will disappear." Abruptly the communication ended.

Without a word, Qay headed back to the ship.

Ki caught up with him and stopped him by gripping his upper bicep. "Where do you think you're going?"

"I'm going to go to the Consortium headquarters to get my True-Bond back."

Ki's bark of laughter was without humor. "You don't think I'd let you go by yourself, do you?"

Qay tugged to remove his arm from Ki's strong grip. "You heard the male, I have to come alone. I'm not taking any chances with her life."

"Don't be stupid." Ki gave a crooked smile as he glanced between Qay and the two aliens. "I have an idea." A whine of wind stopped and held its breath.

Aimee

Three long...boring...monotonous...days passed for Aimee, stuck in a cubicle little bigger than her small bathroom at home. Someone should fire the cruise director on the lido deck for letting her sit here with nothing to do. She was a person used to being active. She groaned at her own musings. You'd think she'd be used to being a captive by now. What a great accomplishment to put on her resume: professional jailbird.

"Get up, human!" Her body jerked out of the semiconscious stupor she'd been floating in. Heart pounding, she sat up to glare at the moron standing at the door. She couldn't see his face with the helmet he wore, a triangular head covering made of the same dull gray metallic material of his armored uniform. It was hard to tell what the person underneath the uniform looked like, could be a Zerin...could be something else. Not knowing bugged her for some stupid reason.

One thing for sure, he wasn't human. Not as big and bulky as the evil creep that held her hostage, but this guy was nevertheless a huge sucker. Under the stiff-looking uniform, she could tell he had muscles on top of muscles. Steroids on crack couldn't make a human that wide in the shoulders.

With slow deliberation, the guard walked into the room and grasped her in a gentle hold by her upper arm. "Time to get up." The voice came out distorted and sounded like a chipmunk.

She wanted to laugh, but she'd left her humor back on Earth.

Aimee jerked her arm out of his tentative hold. "Okay, okay, give me a minute." She scooted off the cot and stepped as far away from him as she could and crossed her arms over her chest. "I'm sorry, I can't possibly join you. I don't have a thing to wear."

The faceless guard went behind her and gave her a slight push between her shoulder blades to make her go ahead of him. "No talking. You must go with us willingly." The gentle tone of his high voice contradicted his actions. If she didn't know any better, she'd have thought he was trying to be nice and not upset her.

Hah! Too late. Rat bastard.

"Okay, I'm coming, I'm coming. No need to twist your panties in a bunch."

He made a move to reach for her again so she wiggled away from his outstretched arm and bumped into another person. Oh great, one more masked man to push her around. This guard was the complete opposite of the jolly green giant behind her. Small, just tall enough to reach Aimee's chin, he reminded her of Hayami. Too bad this one only had one set of arms instead of two. She sure could use her Merkaba friend right about now. Resigned, Aimee followed between them like a good little sandwich filling.

Because she wasn't suicidal, she knew she'd better play along. She placed her palm over the small bump where her baby rested as if to protect him. She glanced around to see where they were going. She was disappointed the corridor resembled the one on the *StarChance*. The same golden floor made of the same soft, spongy material muffling their footsteps. The color of the recessed lighting was the same warm amber that bathed the rampant plants and flowers along the hallway. The natural scent of growing things didn't inspire calm in her this time.

They entered the large, domed room where she'd first met the Chancellor. Her nerves tightened and she had to clasp her hands to prevent anyone from seeing them shake. Aimee had no desire to meet big, bald, and scary again.

Of course, she didn't get her wish. Once again, the huge Zerin reclined on his throne-like chair, sitting back as if he owned the place. Oh wait, he did.

It was the other Zerin in front of the Chancellor with his back to her that caught her attention. His hands clasped above his buttocks, the ankle-length leather coat covered him from his shoulders to the tops of his boots. An inky braid as thick as her wrist roped along his spine. Even with his body covered by the dark leather, she'd know that luscious backside anywhere.

Qay

Her eyes blurred. What if he turned around and sneered at her? The last thing she needed was to be subject to his condescending attitude. She had a baby to protect and didn't want to deal with his confusing attitude. The tears dried as anger replaced them. He'd made it all too clear what he thought about her the last time she'd seen him. She'd be damned if she let him or anyone else see her cry.

The two metallic-clad guards stood close enough beside her for her to feel their body heat. She had to stay calm and not panic. She folded her arms over her chest and concentrated on tamping down her churning emotions.

Aimee's resolved crumbled as Qay turned his dual-emerald eyes on her. Oh, God...she swallowed hard in a dry throat. How unfair was it he was so beautiful? Everything faded into the background as she focused on his face. His exotic eyes locked on her with laser concentration before his attention rested on the small bump on her abdomen. He lifted his gaze to her with unwavering intensity that smoothed out before she could blink.

It was then she noticed he had the same intricate tattoo she did, except on the opposite temple. Well, that was weird. No matter. Right now she had to figure the best way out of this ridiculous predicament. Might be hard to do when surrounded by hostile people, but, she had to believe an opportunity would show itself.

Eventually.

Meanwhile, she'd give Mr. Too-Sexy-For-His-Own-Good a cool stare.

"As you can see, she is unharmed." The larger Zerin rose out of the chair in a graceful motion before he strolled to stop in front of Qay. "Her presence here is quite unfortunate for me. Normally, I would have eliminated her without a second thought, but being pregnant with the royal heir of Zerin has afforded me a unique opportunity too good to pass up."

Aimee's stomach dropped. *Crap!* She didn't want her pregnancy confirmed to Qay. It made her nervous. When she took in his stern frown, she became downright scared. He might want nothing to do with her, but she'd never imagined he'd want her dead. The pain in the pit of her stomach boiled as she took in a deep breath to gain control. She gripped her arms tighter, digging her nails into her skin as she struggled with her fluctuating emotions.

"I'm listening," Qay replied, never taking his eyes off her. He kept his arms loose and limp at his sides, no sign of stress in his body language. It might be a good thing or a bad thing because she wasn't getting any indication of what he was thinking. He might be wondering what to eat for lunch for all she knew.

The Chancellor took his thumb and forefinger and slid it over the satiny looking mustache, from the top of his lip to the end of his chin as if to contemplate his next words.

"You know, I always believed your exile was for show. Your father indulged you too much and allowed you to run wild throughout the galaxy before taking responsibility of governing our people. You and I both know King Abzu cannot abdicate the throne to anyone other than the E'etu heir. And since you are his only child, it's obvious who the next ruler of Zerin will be."

The next ruler of Zerin? What?

The two of them faced each other, one adversary confronting the other. The tension in the air was thick, making it hard to breathe.

It took two blinks, but what the Chancellor said made it through the sludge in Aimee's brain. The Chancellor had hinted about some-one named Qayyum being a ruler, but never in her wildest dreams did she think he meant *Qay* was the crown prince of Zerin. Confusion changed to anger.

The urge to walk over and punch him in the face was strong. Good thing common sense reared its ugly head and stopped her. She dug her nails in a little more on her poor arms as blood gathered under her fingernails. Looked like Qay played her for a fool and she was stupid enough to not see it coming.

"I don't imagine you brought me here for a history lesson." Qay stepped back and balanced on his heels as if he didn't care how the conversation went. "Get to the point."

The Chancellor frowned. "You always were a condescending little prick, weren't you?" He went to his alabaster throne and sat, his body splayed in a lackadaisical posture, lord of all he surveyed. "All right, here is what will happen. You are to go back to your father and beg forgiveness. I, along with several of my allies, will convince him you are worthy to resume your position as crown prince. Once established, your only concern is what I tell you. You'll do what I say when I say it. My agenda will be your only agenda."

The malevolent gleam in the Chancellor's soulless eyes sent a shiver down Aimee's spine. But something in his demands didn't sound right. Qay may have gotten her pregnant, but he had no emotional ties to her. No matter how much she wished he did.

"Is that so?" It hurt to see the sneer on Qay's face as he asked that question with his crossed arms. But, what did she expect? "Now why would I consider doing something so asinine?"

The Chancellor's lips thinned as he caressed his mustache. "In return, I will keep your little human here with me and I guarantee no one will know you've illegally taken an alien TrueBond. She will remain under my tender care." He glanced at the tattoo on Qay's face. "How you officially explain the MalDerVon is your responsibility."

The Chancellor sent his cold glare at her and made her want to step back. By sheer will did she stay in place and not move. She frowned, biting her lower lip to keep a smart-ass remark from popping out. She'd be damned if she ended up being a hostage for the rest of her life, ignored and forgotten.

"To sweeten the deal for you," the deep voice of the Chancellor continued, his eyes back on Qay. "I will be happy to remove the child for you once it is born. I will keep him safe in an undisclosed location unless you decide to renege on our agreement. At which time I will have no qualms eliminating the disgusting half-breed. You and I both know an abomination like that will never rule the Zerin people. I assure you, I am a reasonable Zerin and I will let you decide what to do with the human after an acceptable amount of time has passed." He sat back with his massive elbows resting on the arms of his chair with a self-satisfied quirk on his full lips. He crossed one leg over his thigh and rested his fingertips in a steeple.

That's it! No asshole was going to threaten her kid and get away with it! A banshee scream erupted out of her throat as a blind, protective emotion overrode common sense.

Before she took her first step, the metallic-clad guards grabbed her arms and held her in place. She ignored Qay as she focused on the amused smirk on the Chancellor's face.

"Restrain and silence her," he commanded his guards with a negligent wave of his forefinger.

A slave collar clamped around her neck and a small jolt of pain had her gasping for air. The guards had a tight grip on her and she couldn't move. The tiny shock was brief, but she gulped to regain her balance.

Shit, she hated those damn things.

Taking in a deep breath, she took a peek at Qay. His lack of reaction to her pain hurt her the most. Unwelcome tears blurred as her sinuses burned.

She just wanted to go home.

"So, let's be clear, shall we?" Qay faced the Chancellor. His matter-of-fact tone broke Aimee's heart a little further. His frigid attitude shattered any hope of him helping her or the baby they'd made. Aimee jerked to place a protective palm over the little bump, but the guards holding her arms made it impossible.

"You will keep the human here with you while she carries my unborn child." The Chancellor gave a wave and nod of acknowledgment. "Once the child is born, you will somehow take care of him? Be specific, what is your intention?"

"Ah, I understand your concern." The black eyes of the Chancellor gleamed and made Aimee shiver and a heavy weight lodge in her chest. "I too wouldn't want the idea of a mistake coming back to haunt me. Do not concern yourself. I assure you I will be most discreet where the child goes."

"Yeah, well, why not kill us now? Huh, buster?" Aimee struggled in the guard's grip. One day she was going to choke on that foot in her mouth. But, she'd be damned if she became a pawn for these two. She'd be better off dead than having to deal with this. She was sick and tired of being scared all the time.

Enough was enough.

Those onyx eyes under bushy brows would give anyone nightmares. "My dear, stupid human."

Oh great, just what she needed. The bad guy giving her a lecture in a condescending tone.

"We are not a barbaric society. We do not kill indiscriminately."

Oh yeah? Tell that to Aja.

"Your worth on the black market is unparalleled. Why would we terminate you when your usefulness is not at an end?" He gave a snort of disgust in her direction.

As if the exchange between Aimee and the Chancellor had never occurred, Qay continued asking questions. "And in return I am to be your pawn at the Zerin court, spying and interceding at your direction. Is that correct?"

"Yes, indeed." The self-satisfied smile morphed into a small jeer.

"Well." Qay's deep sigh dispelled any hope Aimee had of him somehow changing his mind to help her. Her shoulders deflated. "It seems I have no choice but to tell you one thing."

"Yes?" The behemoth leaned in with a gleam of anticipation, his large hands gripping the armrest of his alabaster throne. With her and the baby as unwilling pawns, Aimee stared at the floor so she didn't have to watch the bully get his way.

CHAPTER NINE

"**A**s the humans like to say...go fuck yourself." Qay's firm voice echoed in the large chamber and made Aimee jerk in surprise. He...What? What did he say? Did this mean he was turning the Chancellor down? The abrupt change in the conversation shook her. Without Qay wanting to play the Chancellor's little game, there would be no reason to keep her. She'd wind up at the slave markets without a second thought.

"I do not understand." Chancellor U'unk sat back. His deep frown pulled the hair of his mustache at a funny, sideways slant. Hysterically, Aimee preferred the smirk. "You are refusing me?"

Qay's demeanor changed. Gone was the rigid, uncaring male. Instead, he was a controlled angry alpha that vibrated with violent intent. "You dare threaten my TrueBond and unborn child?" he said in a soft tone, his fingers tight in clenched fists. "You think I would betray my family and my people?"

Aimee frowned. If she didn't know any better, she'd think he was going to attack the much larger man. She doubted the Chancellor was in any danger. His guards were right there, for God's sake. And there were a dozen more within shouting distance.

The Chancellor's lips thinned. "I believe you forget who you're talking to. Let alone where you are." The Chancellor responded in a soft voice and a satisfied smirk that matched his relaxed body.

"I can assure you," Qay said as a condescending sneer twisted his handsome features, "I have forgotten nothing." For the first time, Aimee witnessed the prince inside of the commander. There was no mistaking his ability to take control of the room in the blink of an eye.

On cue, both guards released their hold on Aimee's arms and pointed their blasters in the Chancellor's direction.

"Seal the door and disrupt communications," Qay commanded without taking his eyes off the massive Zerin. For the first time, hope loosened the terror that choked her.

Aimee could swear a sliver of unease crossed the big man's expression. Oh, it was masked quickly enough as he lifted his chin and jutted his jaw. He glared at the two guards before he focused his attention on Qay.

"I see," he intoned without blinking.

"Do you?" The soft, civilized tone of Qay's voice contradicted his body language as his hands clenched and unclenched. His nostrils flared. He exposed his fangs with each word spoken. "I'm not so sure, so let me spell it out for you." He took a few steps closer to the large chair where the Chancellor sat with a heavy-lidded eyes and disgust curling his mouth.

"You're lucky I don't kill you for what you are trying to do. You threaten my TrueBond, my child, and my family's honor all at once. The only reason I don't do it now is it might throw the Zerin people, not to mention the Consortium, into a bloody civil war it cannot afford. But know this, if you in any way try to stop us from leaving, I guarantee you'll regret it. Bloody civil war or not." Qay gestured to the metallic-clad guards behind him without taking his eyes off the man in front of him. "My friends had no trouble infiltrating your guards to join us today and I can assure you they won't encounter any difficulties coming back at my request." Qay moved to stand next to Aimee and put an arm around her.

The warmth of his body was welcome and it helped to calm her shaking, but she reminded herself it was for show. It didn't mean anything. Right now, she'd play along. Going away with Qay was better than staying with an evil emperor wannabe.

"The four of us are going to use the emergency transportation mirror you keep hidden behind you and neither you nor any of your outer guards are going to follow us." He reached into a pocket in his jacket with his free hand and pulled out a familiar silver cylinder.

Aimee's eyes widened in shock. The crazy man had the same bomb-like thingy Aja had when she'd kidnapped her from Hiigar. What? Could anyone get these dangerous things at the corner market or something?

"I will leave this present here for you. It's on a timer that will detonate unless it receives my transmission code to shut it down. Understand?" Qay's snide insinuation was unmistakable.

The malevolent glare and red flush on the man's sharp cheeks was answer enough.

"Good, I'm glad we understand each other." With a head tilt, he signaled the others to follow him as he took her hand in his. He led her to a transportation mirror she hadn't noticed before. It was weird to watch the stern reflection of the four of them getting bigger as they neared it in determined strides.

Well, at least the other three appeared determined and badass—her, not so much. She looked puffy, tired, and worn out in the rumpled and dirty clothing. She wasn't huge in her pregnancy, but the forced inactivity had taken its toll. Her waddle had a waddle, and she lumbered along like an old woman needing a walker.

She'd laugh if she weren't so tired of everything. All she wanted to do was to get off this emotional roller coaster and take a break from all the drama.

All four went through the mirror to a landing platform where a small ship rested in an enormous, empty chamber. Aimee gave a slight shiver at the sudden drop in temperature and humidity. The lone small vessel was bigger than the one Aja and the little grey alien used, but nowhere as large as the *StarChance.* Aimee stood, not sure what she was supposed to do or where to go. A movement caught her eyes as she watched the two metallic-clad guards as they took off their helmets.

The giant one removed his first and Aimee wasn't surprised to see the Zerin Qay had sparred with before. Up close, he was a handsome devil, bisecting scar across his face and beard notwithstanding. His deep mahogany hair lay flat against his skull with sweat. Maybe the ventilation in his helmet was on the fritz.

When the helmet came off the tiny guard, Aimee squealed with joy.

"Hayami!"

"Pretty!"

Both females raced toward each other in complete abandon as Hayami's dual arms pulled out of the snug uniform. Aimee breathed in Hayami's comforting floral scent and burst into tears.

Stupid baby hormones.

Hayami's arms caressed and offered a sanctuary Aimee sorely needed. She calmed and sheepishly pulled back from the smaller female.

"I'm sorry." Aimee's voice came out garbled. She blotted her eyes and running nose with the sleeve of her shirt.

"Hush, Pretty mine." Hayami's upper hands wiped the tears from Aimee's face as if she were a small child. Her lower hands patted Aimee's back in a soothing motion. "Now safe are you."

Aimee sniffed and stepped back as she wrinkled her nose at the small group. "Not that I'm not grateful, but why did you come and get me?" She hated showing any weakness to the man who'd broken her heart on more than one occasion. She kept her back to him and focused on Hayami.

Before the others could respond, Hayami took over the explanations. "Stolen you, Fylgir and me back you get." Hayami's piercing gaze sliced at Qay, who stood close to Aimee, his warmth covering her back. She moved away. She didn't need his nearness messing with her careening emotions.

Without a word, he reached over and pulled her toward him to tuck her back against his wide chest. His warm sandalwood scent wrapped around her and caused painful memories to surface.

She shook out of his loose hold and stepped closer to Hayami. "What do you think you're doing?" She faced him and demanded with arms crossed. "Why are you here?"

"I would think it was obvious." His obscure remark pissed her off and made her face flush. She ignored the way his lips pinched and his brow creased when she'd stepped away from him. She tapped her foot.

"Obvious? To who? Because it sure isn't obvious to me." She gripped her elbows for support. "The last time I saw you, you made it quite clear you couldn't get away from me fast enough." With an unexpected sniffle, she blotted her watery eyes with her soaked sleeve. You'd think an advanced culture would have invented facial tissue by now.

Qay's face became an alarming shade of purple. If Aimee didn't know any better, she'd have thought he was either embarrassed or mad.

"*Ahyoka*, please let me explain." He started toward her but the larger Zerin stopped him by placing a hand on his shoulder.

"Qay, we need to leave before the Chancellor regroups and thinks he can counterattack." He was talking to Qay, but the larger male's eyes were on her as if begging for her understanding.

She didn't want to be understanding. She wanted answers. A loud klaxon echoed in the small chamber.

"Let's go." Qay grasped her elbow and steered her out of the chamber and into the ship. He led her into a cockpit large enough to seat the four along with the mammoth Orisha male sitting in the pilot's chair. His bulk made the seat disappear under his wide girth.

Before Aimee could say anything, much less stop Qay from moving her around, he put her in a chair that automatically buckled her in. She gave up and dropped her head back in resignation. Well, maybe now she'd be able to find a way back to Earth. How to raise an alien baby once she got there was a problem for another day.

"The Chancellor's fighters are on our left," the large, shorthaired Zerin male announced from the navigation chair next to Fylgir.

"Yous nos worry," Fylgir boomed. A couple of swats and flips of his two-fingered hand and the vid display in front splashed a ripple of bright colors as the ship entered light speed. "We's at Hiigars nows."

Sure enough, the ship entered the desert planetoids atmosphere and within a short period landed outside the village of Kijiji.

Aimee couldn't help but be impressed at how fast they'd made the journey. When she'd gone with Aja, she was sure it was longer than the instantaneous trip they just took.

She sat there, watching the others unbuckle and then move about the cabin. Now what? Were the Zerins dropping her off here? Were they going to take her back to Earth? They wouldn't make her attend the Exchange again, would they?

She clenched her fists as a panic attack threatened. There was no way she was going to go through the humiliation of the Exchange again. She'd rather take her chances with the oily Chancellor.

"Thank you for your assistance." Qay gave a slight bow to the Merkaba female. "Not to mention the use of your wonderful ship." He touched the bulkhead with a reverent caress. "Are you sure you can't part with it?" The tone was teasing, but Aimee would bet the offer was genuine.

"Nos." Fylgir stooped in the room since his large frame didn't fit the interior. Now there was a firm, definite answer if she'd ever heard one.

"Fylgir, hush." It was Hayami's favorite saying to her Orisha mate. "Have take ship yours. We back to Zerin M'alalu take." Hayami went to Aimee, who hadn't moved from her chair. "Pretty, go home must?" She reached down and helped Aimee up. "But stay Fylgir and Hayami, yes...maybe?"

Tears welled in Aimee's eyes at the generous offer Hayami made by asking her if she wanted to stay on Hiigar at the *Galaxy's End* pub. Again, her stupid hormones kicked in. Wistfully she gazed into the beautiful, pulsating pink eyes in front of her. Aimee admitted it was a tempting offer. At least her alien baby wouldn't stand out too much on the isolated outpost.

To Qay she said, "It seems I should thank you for coming to get me. I appreciate what you've done, but I want to know what you intend to do with me now."

"I plan to take you home." Well, that was a quick, decisive answer.

She ignored the sharp pang of regret. What did she expect? He'd somehow changed his mind and wanted to be with her? She snorted, but she answered Hayami the only way she could. "I would love nothing better than to go back with you." She blinked back more tears. "But we both know I don't belong here and it's time for me to go home." She pulled the smaller woman to her for a heartfelt hug and enjoyed the reciprocal warmth. As the petite alien took out the remote and popped the slave collar off, Aimee stepped back and gave Hayami's shoulders a small squeeze. "I can never repay you for everything you've done for me. I am forever in your debt."

"As am I." Qay stood next to her as he addressed Hayami.

His statement annoyed her. She didn't know what his deal was and why he came with Hayami. She wasn't sure she wanted to know.

"Careful be, prince of Zerin." Hayami's expressive eyes filled with humor before she frowned in mock sternness. At least Aimee thought she was kidding. One never knew with the volatile little Hayami. "Hurt my Pretty you not. Mate save no you again neglect. *Pytki* you fate. Yes?"

Qay's normal dark complexion paled at whatever Hayami said. It would be interesting to find out what that word meant.

"You have my word she will be well taken care of, *Rouva.*" Aimee knew he called Hayami an "honored one." The title was a rare privilege given out sparingly to others by the Zerin people.

Hayami preened at the compliment. "Watch will I you. Of Pretty care take."

"On my honor." Qay gave her a salute with his right arm over his chest and a slight bow. He straightened and with a gentle nudge on Aimee's elbow, he took her out of the ship.

As they walked down the ramp, Qay asked over his shoulder, "Ki? Are you coming?"

The massive Zerin stood in the doorway of Hayami's ship and shook his head. "I'm afraid I can't. I've received the summons from Maynwaring and I have to go there immediately."

Qay frowned as he kept a light hold on Aimee's shoulder. "I understand. When will you be back?"

"Soon, the Goddess willing." The one named Ki locked his gaze with Qay. They were silent, and with the change in their facial expressions, Aimee thought they were in a silent communication before the large one disappeared back into the Merkaba ship.

Qay barked a laugh. "Great, she's going to let him use the ship. No wonder she wouldn't sell it." With a smile on his full lips, he steered Aimee through a transportation mirror on the opposite wall. This time they ended up on another hangar holding a different ship. The air was warmer and thick, which caused her forehead to break out in a sweat. The vessel waiting for them was tiny compared to Hayami's. With any luck, there would be enough room for the both of them. They walked in silence as they entered a small ship. He guided her to a chair in the control center. The doors closed in a quiet whoosh behind them. The cool air was an instant relief.

"Please buckle up. The chairs aren't automatic like on the Merkaba ship." He sat next to her and strapped in. He inputted a long sequence of coordinates then spoke in a soft voice as he gave the command for the ship to start. The thrusters fired as the hangar doors open. The splattering of stars welcomed them as their lift-off went without a hitch.

Aimee was happy her stomach cooperated and didn't make her nauseous at the sudden change in acceleration.

She leaned back into the comfortable headrest and closed her eyes before she asked, "How long before we reach Earth?"

"Earth?" Qay's sharp retort made her open her eyes and squint at him. "What makes you think I'm taking you to Earth?"

The frown on his face made Aimee uneasy. "Because you said you were taking me home. You know, to Earth."

"Yes," he said in an uncertain tone. "I am taking you home."

He paused. "But I'm not taking you to Earth." The determined look on his face should have warned her was going to tell her the last thing she wanted to hear.

"I'm taking you to our home...to Zerin."

Qay

Whoever said the female of any species was the weaker sex was delusional. In the bedroom chamber aboard the ship, Qay watched Aimee sleep and admired her delicate and soft appearance. Her demeanor was a welcome sight, the softness of her curves and relaxed profile rivaled the Goddess herself. Silky umber hair fanned across her pillow, her soft bow lips parted in slumber. The fan of lush lashes rested against the shimmer of her light, pearlescent skin. Her creamy vanilla musk teased his nose.

Too bad her inner character was the complete opposite of the gentle exterior. Hardheaded, obstinate, and stubborn were only some of the nicer ways to describe how she acted toward him.

Patience was not a normal emotion for Qay, and to be fair, his past actions had a lot to do with how she reacted to him now. Keeping that in mind, he'd been gentle with her as much as possible. No matter how she treated him, he was determined to woo his TrueBond with a tenacious and steady hand.

After they'd left the Chancellor's palace and boarded the ship to Zerin, Qay planned to take the "long" way home. Stretching the one-day journey into a solar month to give him time to undo the damaged he'd done to their relationship. Once he told Aimee how long the journey would take, she gave him a blank stare, went straight to bed and immediately fell asleep. There she stayed for the next five days. At first, he worried something might be wrong with her. He had the onboard medical computer scan her as she slept. To his immense relief, the results came back with minor issues. She was exhausted, dehydrated, with a touch of malnourishment.

It was nothing bed rest and plenty of food and water wouldn't cure.

The medic scan also came back with information about the first hybrid human-Zerin baby she carried. So far, the fetus was progressing at an accelerated rate for a human. The baby's weight and measurements were the same as a Zerin child close to the last trimester, as Zerin babies were small throughout the pregnancy, doubling in size during the last month of gestation. Which, according to the ship's medical records wouldn't happen for another two months. He wasn't satisfied with the ships prognosis, but because of his exiled status, he couldn't contact anyone on his homeworld to verify anything. He thought about turning the ship around and requesting asylum on one of the outer systems not affiliated with the Federation Consortium, but that would take too long and he didn't have the time or inclination to consider that option. He needed to settle his affairs, not just for himself but also for his growing little family. The best thing to do was go back to Zerin and convince his father to rescind his exile edict.

But first, he had to make things right between Aimee and him. She was the most important person in his life and he *would* convince her they belonged together.

By the end of the second week of their four-week journey, Qay fumed as their interactions bordered in the nonexistent category. When she did speak, it was a handful of words that repeated themselves. "Leave me alone," "Get away from me," or the ever-popular "No."

One thing he was grateful for was she didn't complain about whatever he put in front of her to eat. She never commented on the food...or her surroundings...or engage in any conversation. But Qay wasn't about to let that stop him. Every night he would sit next to her on the bed and talk to her where she'd lay without speaking. He wasn't sure if she heard him most of the time, but he persisted in speaking in low tones. He'd tell her stories about his childhood, the troubles he got into with his cousins and how he missed his mother who had passed when he was a young boy. Once or twice the edge of her lips would curl in a small smile or an amused twinkle would shine out of her exotic eyes.

When he'd run out of stories about his younger days, he'd confess some of the less reputable things he'd done that led to his father having to exile him from Zerin. He held nothing back—he told her how he'd become a spoiled, entitled aristocrat who gave no thought to his people or the responsibility he'd inherited. When he didn't show an ounce of remorse after one of his self-indulgent episodes—that had cost a citizen their respected livelihood—his father, King Abzu had no choice but to teach him a lesson. So, according to their custom, the King disowned him and stripped him of his citizenship in the Federation Consortium.

Qay fell silent after he confessed his painful past. She lay on her side with her back toward him, her hands under her head. She didn't say a word when he finished, but the tense way she held her body became loose before she relaxed into sleep. He lay there for hours, caressing her hair and watching her steady breathing. It was one of the most peaceful evenings he'd ever spent.

The next day he coaxed her out of the bedroom to join him in the upper control room. He wanted to tempt her with the colorful vid feed's full view of the distant stars. After he got her settled in a forward-facing seat, he brought her a plate of food from the replicator and enjoyed the way she absently ate the simple fare. She never said a word, but by the time she was done, she gave him the gift of a slight smile when he took away the empty dishes.

Her continued lethargic state made him desperate. He had to find a way to "jolt" her out of her fatalistic manner. He worried she would sink further into her head and he'd never be able to reach her.

By day twenty, he'd had enough. He needed to take her and the baby to Zerin for the medical experts to monitor the pregnancy. He had no idea if the ship's medical unit was outdated or able to consider the unique child she carried. That evening as she slept, he had the computer run another medical scan to make sure she was healthy enough for what he had in mind. The results came back better than he'd hoped: the prior exhaustion, malnourishment, and dehydration were all within normal human parameters.

He rubbed his damp palms over his thighs as he contemplated on how to start. He'd tried to talk to her, coax her, woo her, and engage her on every level—except one.

He had no choice but to take drastic measures.

Goddess forgive him if this backfired. But if it didn't, he was sure Aimee would thank him later...he hoped. After careful consideration, he decided it was better to do this after she'd had a good night's sleep.

Deep into the morning sleep time, he woke before she did and began. With a gentle hand, he rolled her on her back from her side. He waited until he heard her light snore before he massaged her soft skin under her sleeping tunic. Throughout his careful actions, she gave a soft murmur of protest but otherwise stayed asleep.

Determined, he rubbed his palms to stimulate the mating oils. A Zerin's natural oils acted as an aphrodisiac to their sexual partners, creating a lubricant that ramped up the experience. With extra care, he raised her tunic top to expose the round bump where his child slept. He took in the sight with a sense of awe. Reverently, he rested both of his hands to the side of the mound and received a firm kick for his efforts from his son.

The small movement under her skin filled him with a joy he'd never known before as his child welcomed his father. Overwhelmed, he leaned down to nuzzle the taut skin as the baby moved and gave another thump under his fingers and caressing mouth.

"What in the hell do you think you're doing?" Aimee put her hands on the top of his head as if to push him away.

"I am introducing myself to our son." Qay continued to caress her with his mouth and hands as he kept her firmly in place. Her own exotic oils began to seep through her pours as his tongue lapped the pungent flavor. The welcome taste of tangy female captivated his senses.

"What...I," She struggled against his firm hold.

"Shhh, calm yourself, *Ahyoka.* I would never do anything to harm you. I only want to give you pleasure." He shifted so his lower torso lay next to her as his hands kneaded and caressed, his mouth blazing a trail toward her unbound breasts. The ambrosial scent of her skin made his nostrils flare in appreciation.

"Let me go!" She squirmed to push his face away.

Her actions caused his chest to tighten, making it hard to breathe. Qay reached up to clasp her face between his hands and force her to look at him. To *really* look at him.

"See me," he muttered, holding her exotic eyes with his own. "Aimee, you have to *see* me."

She blinked and her lips pursed, causing his attention to divert to her lush mouth. Without stopping to consider what he was doing, he lowered his face to capture that temptation. His tongue swiped across the closed seam of her lips, seeking permission to enter.

Aimee

When her face had been in his large hands, Aimee had no choice but to return his hard gaze. She calmed as she searched the intent in his dual-emerald stare. Her panic receded enough to allow her to focus on him and what he was asking.

She blinked as memories of him talking to her endlessly about his childhood shifted through her mind. Coupled with waking up to the sensual feel of his lips and hands over her naked stomach had her reeling.

Then he did the most unexpected thing. His eyes left hers to fixate on her lips before his mouth covered hers. His tongue stroked over her, gentle and tentative as if asking for permission. Then, a switch flipped, the kiss deepened with bold sweeps in a masculine demand.

What in the world was that flavor? Spicy sweetness, like the tang of nutmeg mixed with an unknown taste of pure masculine bite. *Delicious.* She opened her mouth and welcomed him in.

It was all the encouragement he needed. His tongue swooped through with masterful determination. His body sidled over her side, his soft linen shirt rubbing enticingly against the naked skin of her stomach.

Lost...she was lost in an overload of sensation. When he pulled back and broke their connection, she whimpered in disappointment.

"Yes, Aimee, give yourself to me—to us." His husky whisper fueled her passions to a higher level.

Before his words seeped through her befuddled mind, he resumed their mind-blowing kiss. As his tongue lavished over hers, she returned the favor. His mouth was an intoxicating hint of savory goodness and she wanted more. She whimpered as she raised her head to get closer. Stroking, sucking, caressing, and absorbing the rush he gave her.

Her body shivered in reaction. The intense emotion scared her.

She broke away. She couldn't think. How stupid was she to let this go on? She couldn't be more embarrassed if she stood in a room full of strangers stark naked.

He moved back with heavy-lidded eyes, his lips wet and plump from their kisses. How did he end up with his lower body wedged between her thighs? She inhaled his enigmatic sandalwood scent as her clit swelled with the sensual need for friction.

No...no, this wasn't right. Aimee was determined baser instincts weren't going to rule her. She glared and demanded, "I think you should let me go."

"I can't," he leaned in and nuzzled the side of her neck. The nubs on his tongue stroked the tender skin below her ear. "We've just started."

"What? You're going to force yourself on me?" She twisted to get away. She wasn't proud of the whine in her voice, but it didn't change the fact she was terrified. The longer she let this go on, the more she'd indulge in her passion for him.

Qay jerked his head back and he gave her an incredulous stare. "I would never take you by force, my TrueBond." He shifted so she had an unobstructed view of his creased brow. "But I'm at my wits end on how to get you to talk to me. You've been unresponsive for weeks and I'm worried, not only for you but for our child as well." He brushed a hand through the side of his hair. For the first time, Aimee watched his unbound black hair fall around his handsome face and naked chest in a waterfall of silk. He sat back on his heels. The cool air between them caused her skin to pebble.

She searched his exotic features and the new ink curling over his forehead and around and under his right eye. The dark green diamond nestled in the middle of his temple winked in the soft light of the sleeping chamber.

She frowned. "TrueBond? What is that?" She squirmed as her face and neck heated under his intense stare.

His answer puzzled her. "It's obvious I am your TrueBond. It is my honor and privilege to take care of you and our young one."

"Are you kidding me?" she croaked. Confused ideas bounced back-and-forth in her head. Aimee tried to remember if Aja had used that word, but her memories were fuzzy. She'd been too busy fighting the pain collar, terrified by the slimy grey alien holding her captive, and the threat of becoming a sex slave to pay any attention.

Aimee bit her lower lip. "What is a TrueBond and why are you calling me that? You didn't before." Her throat tightened. "In fact, you couldn't get away from me fast enough the last time we were together."

An amazing shade of ochre darkened his cheeks as he frowned. "I thought I had good reasons for acting the way I did. But..." He gestured to the tattoo on his right temple. "This shows I was wrong."

This conversation was getting them nowhere. He might as well be speaking without the nano translator since she couldn't figure out what he was saying. She shifted her body as she tried to find a more comfortable position. She didn't like being flat on her back while they talked. "Okay, you want to talk, let's talk." He helped her to sit up, placing his hands on her arms to settle her in a comfortable layer of pillows. She pulled her sleep shirt down.

He scooted close as he rested his palms on the top of her thigh. She watched the mesmerizing movements as he caressed her naked thigh below her sleep shirt. She wanted to push him away, but the warm, soothing oils between his skin and hers had her purring in pleasure. What were they saying?

"Where do you want to start?" The circular motion of his hands matched the soft, comforting tone of his voice.

"Um...let's, um...what do you think you're doing?" She trembled. She wasn't about to admit she wanted him to continue. "And what is that massage oil you're using? I swear you could make a fortune selling it on Earth. I've never felt anything so luxurious in my whole life. It's better than taking a warm bubble bath while drinking an expensive glass of champagne." The intoxicating aroma of tangy citrus wrapped in soothing sandalwood teased and caused her body to react. Her nipples pebbled and an embarrassing catch rattled in her throat.

"It's the natural oils from my body being transferred to yours." He leaned into her neck. The nubs on his tongue continued to roam below her ear.

Oh my God, it's unbelievable how good...just a little lower...yeah, right there to the curve of my neck and shoulder. *Oh...that's it.*

"Shall I do the other side, *Ahyoka*?"

"Other side..." Great, her mouth filters were on the fritz. Before the last syllable tumbled off her traitorous tongue, he moved and snuggled on the opposite side. His body shifted to line his chest to her breast and proceed to rub against her. First softly then not, but always gently.

It was hard to concentrate on anything other than what he was doing. She had to keep her wits about her and asked the only thing that popped in her head. "What does *Ahyoka* mean? Why are you calling me that?"

Having moved his talented mouth to gain further access to her willing flesh, he paused. "I researched the Native American heritage of your mother's people and found a word that describes you best for me." Slow, dangerous swipes of his tongue were devastating. "It is the Cherokee word for 'she brought happiness.'" A little nip of his sharp teeth made her pant as a wave of pleasure rolled through her.

It took time, but his words penetrated her foggy brain. "I, ah...please don't stop." Wait...that's not what she meant! "I mean...stop. Please stop!" Her voice came out louder than she'd intended. She'd probably made the poor man deaf. But he had to back off so she could think.

He took his time as he sat back on his heels and raised a questioning eyebrow at her.

"Please, we need to talk. Okay?" She closed her eyes and placed a hand over her pounding heart. She had to get ahold of herself.

Aimee opened her eyes and latched onto his patient expression. She was afraid he wouldn't do what she asked—but she was afraid he would. Within a few heartbeats, he pushed off the bed to face her.

"Yes, I agree." His hair flowed over his shoulder. For the first time, Aimee noticed a white strip replaced the inky blackness along the thin braid that began at his right temple. Come to think of it, his skin wasn't as dark as before. If she didn't know any better, she'd swear their skin hues matched...

"I'd better start..." A loud klaxon pierced the air before a frantic voice boomed in the small space.

"Qay! Are you there? Qay! Answer me, damn it!" A young masculine voice. Aimee thought she'd heard it before, but couldn't place a face with the voice. "It's about your father! Answer me!"

Qay sent her a beseeching look as he kept his focus on her. "What is it D'zia? As usual, your timing sucks..."

"Shut up and listen, damn it!" Aimee understood the sharp impatience in the voice. She found she wanted to scream at Qay more than once herself. "There's been an assassination attempt on your father and he is in critical condition. You've got to come back to Zerin immediately."

Qay's face drained of color and his lips became bloodless. She didn't know his father, but the blanched look was heart-wrenching.

"What? Is he all right?" His tone may have been steady and controlled, but he stood with his hands clenched into tight fists.

"All I know is he was breathing when they took him away." She could hear the veiled quiver in the other man's voice. "Do you have Aimee? Can you come back now?"

Aimee's heart squeezed as Qay's face fell. "Yes, to answer both questions. We can be there within the next solar hour." He ran an agitated hand through his hair. "Will they allow me to land?" His lips twisted into a grimace.

A snort came through the filtered communication. "Yes, yes, everything will be all right. Your father took the exile off both of us when I came here to work with the Imperial Forces, thank the Goddess. Just hurry. D'zia out."

The communication ended and silence settled.

"I'm so sorry about your father," she whispered as she slid off the bed. "Is there anything I can do to help?"

He gave a slight jerk as if he'd forgotten she was there. "No, I don't think so." He absently patted her shoulder. "I have to go and put in the coordinates to Zerin. Please excuse me."

He gave her shoulder a slight squeeze before he walked out of the room. She didn't know what else to do so she changed her clothes into a soft hi-low tunic in bright emerald green over snug, black leggings from the ships replicator. The shorter hem in front flowed long in the back and gave her a feminine sense of whimsy and made her smile. Emerald slippers completed the outfit.

When she joined Qay in the front cockpit, he lifted the corners of his mouth in appreciation. He must have taken time to change his clothes as well. He wore a simple outfit of a dark hunter green jacket over black slacks tucked into knee-high boots. The jacket was made of a soft rolling material, with four buckles fastened on his left side with bell-shaped sleeves ending at his wrists. The austere neckline was as black as his pants but made of a shimmering material that reflected in the light of each movement.

His bound hair was in a tight queue at his neck that emphasized the sharp curve of his cheekbones. The silky tail swayed down his spine and curled at the ends. The thin braid of white hair at his temple rested on his chest.

Aimee had a sudden urge to join him on that chair. She imagined mounting his lap to sit on his ridged thighs and coax his cock with her rocking hips. She'd twine her fingers in his sleek hair to loosen it as she covered his lips with hers. Her tongue would plunge into his welcome heat and savor his unique taste....

She shook her head and gripped the sides of the chair with tight fingers. What was wrong with her? She darted a quick glance in his direction to make sure he hadn't seen her zone out. His regal profile told her she escaped an embarrassing discovery. Damn, she'd better stop with her fantasies or she'd have to change her panties before leaving the ship.

They landed at the Zerin spaceport faster than Aimee believed possible. As they disembarked, Qay took her hand and kept her close enough to him to feel the warmth of his body. She could have kicked herself for not thinking to ask him what to expect once they got here. But he'd been so distracted she didn't have the heart to interrupt his thoughts.

The hangar was massive—large enough to fill ten ships the size of the one they'd used. She would have expected such a huge room to have people working, hurrying and readying ships. This one was empty except for the vessel they'd come in.

They walked down a steel plank out of the open hatch when a group of guards rushed toward them and pointed large, scary-looking three-barrel rifles in their direction. Without a word, Qay moved in front of her. She had to peek around his wide back to see what was going on.

A slender, older Zerin male walked toward them and stopped shy of entering their personal space. He gave a slight bow that was anything but respectful.

"Prince E'etu." His dual-colored irises were an attractive apple green. Aimee would have thought them striking if they weren't filled with disgust. "You and your...TrueBond are under arrest."

Qay stiffened. "Under what charge, Captain?" One hand was loose at his side, the other held her hand in a protective grip behind his back. "It is my understanding my exiled status has been rescinded."

A great, lumbering figure caused the guards to part in a mad dash. Their scrambling boots echoed in the large chamber. Aimee snorted. Huh, looked like those guards were smart enough to get out of his way.

"There has been no official sanction from the council ending your exile status." An all too familiar voice answered. "You are illegally trespassing not only on Zerin soil but at the royal residence in particular."

"Chancellor U'unk." She heard the steel in Qay's voice.

Yep, big, bad, and menacing was right there, a few feet in front of Qay. Her eyes widened and she gripped Qay's hand tighter.

"Captain, restrain the prince and this...this human." The Chancellor waved two fingers in a gesture for the captain to do his bidding.

Qay raised his own palm out to stop the thin Zerin who first greeted them.

She flinched when Qay pulled her from his back and under his arm. While Qay's actions continued to confuse her, she admitted she appreciated his outward show of support. Aimee shivered and kept an eye on the interaction between the two formidable Zerins.

When Qay squeezed her closer, she took a chance and glanced at him. His attention was back on the Chancellor and she was impressed with his steadfast ability to appear regal and in command. He sported a deep frown that thinned his full lips with an angry narrowing of his eyes.

"My father lies at death's door and you dare come here on Zerin soil, where you have no authority, and presume to tell my guardsmen what to do?" His sharp cheeks flushed.

The Chancellor flashed his sharp teeth in a mockery of a smile. The expression was chilling in its complexity. "I have all the authority I need by the mandates of the Zerin constitution. The role of leadership naturally falls to my office when there is a void in the monarchy." A snide sneer replaced the smile. "You don't think you are above the law, do you?"

"As I have said, my exile has been rescinded. I have called for my legal representative to meet us here at the royal residence." He blinked, and an image of a 3-D legal document floated between him and the Chancellor. "As you can see, a stay has been filed and accepted by the Zerin council." He blinked again and the image disappeared. "We are scheduled to meet them in two days. Now, if you'll excuse us, we are going to check on the status of my father." He tipped his head toward his nemesis in dismissal. "Chancellor."

With Aimee tucked under his arm, he moved them around the larger Zerin. Aimee grabbed his forearm as they strolled past the giant politician. The guards kept their weapons pointed and followed them with each step they took.

"Prince E'etu." The Chancellor's smug voice rang throughout the vast space. "I can assure you this is not over." He motioned to the men behind him. "These guards will go with you. For your protection, of course." Aimee narrowed her eyes at him before she turned around to focus on where they were going.

Insufferable creep. She didn't think this would be the last skirmish between Qay and the Chancellor. She shuddered as she admitted she wouldn't want to be in the middle of their power war.

Out of the hangar, she kept her eyes down as she worried about her future and where she stood in the scheme of things. As if he sensed her inner turmoil, Qay pulled up their clasped hands and brought her knuckles to his mouth for a soft kiss. Her breath hitched as her eyes widened in bewildered shock. She didn't think he knew her well enough to have insight into how nervous she was.

Aimee gazed into the warmth of Qay's dual-jeweled eyes and relaxed. His unspoken support steadied her nerves, up to a certain point. She wished she and Qay had been able to finish their conversation so she knew what was going on with him. She got the impression what he had to tell her might save her a ton of future heartaches.

CHAPTER TEN

A fter leaving the hangar, Aimee walked with Qay into a mirrored transportation center. He murmured a command for the royal palace, and the nearest mirror distorted before a new image appeared and they wasted no time walking through. Qay stopped them in the archway as the immediate homey scent of something baking had Aimee taking in an appreciative breath. The yeasty goodness wafted around her and had the added sweetness of piping hot fruit. Her stomach rumbled a happy sound.

She appraised her new surroundings. The humongous space was a scene right out of an old medieval movie. Well, that is if you didn't add in alien technology. Twenty feet above her was the ceiling, at least she thought there was a roof since dark beams crisscrossed in the arch above her before disappearing. Instead of material intersecting between the beams, a soft lavender sky dotted with light yellow clouds floated. Sunlight filtered between the fluffy clouds, its gold and orange rays lighting the room. It reminded her of the ceiling from the gym from hell aboard the *StarChance*.

On the pine-colored marble floor, beautiful multi-colored throw rugs complimented the 3-D scenery of the tapestries adorning the high walls. Aimee would love to study the changing scenery on those tapestries—she was sure each display boasted legend or history.

Long tables with comfortable looking benches sat in the middle and a huge stone fireplace took up an entire wall to her left. Instead of fire, the glow inside was a warm wave of colors with no discernible means of fuel. Ahead was a winding stone staircase with intricate wood handrails, leading upward and disappearing into the sky scenery.

Aimee half expected a white knight to come out, swinging his sword to fight for his prince and defend his lady's honor.

Moving across the room was a small group of Zerin's who approached Qay and gave a slight bow. They dressed similarly—the men with thick black cloth tights and light linen shirts, belted tunics, and closed-toe shoes. The women wore colorful long gowns with sleeveless tunics. The only thing to complete the medieval picture was wimples to cover their hair and pointed ears.

The battalion of guards behind them disrupted the fantasy. There were several cries of alarm as the civilians backed up before they stopped and glared.

An elderly Zerin male approached Qay and gave a bow before encircling him in an embrace that Qay returned with a hearty hug. They squeezed each other before parting with a firm man slap on the back.

"Your Highness." The man's curtain of chestnut braids gathered at the nape of his neck and flowed to his knees, the ends clinking with colorful beads. His attire appeared to be made of pressed silk, the shirt a warm shade of khaki green with darker khaki tights nestled in knee-high brown boots. His dual-colored eyes were unusual, more turquoise than green. The scroll over and rounding his temple and cheek was more circular than Celtic with a clear, diamond crystal. "I am so glad you're home, nephew. You have been missed." The man's eyes filled as he laid a gentle hand on Qay's cheek. He took in a raspy breath. "Come, I'll take you to your father."

"Uncle Yaq," Qay's thick response told Aimee he was fond of his uncle. He returned the gesture to the man's face before they parted. Qay kept his hold on Aimee. "How is he?"

"Still unconscious, I'm afraid." Uncle Yaq stood in front of her and reached over to grasp her hands in his as he pulled her in to kiss both cheeks. His open expression released the tension between her shoulders. He offered her a sense of warmth, along with a welcoming smile and a twinkle in his bright eyes. "And who is this enchanting creature?"

What an old smoothie. Bemused, she broke into a wide smile. "My name is Aimee."

He released her. "I am thrilled to meet you, my dear. My son has told me so much about you."

She frowned. Who was his son? Before she asked, Qay responded, "I certainly hope you don't believe half of what D'zia tells you, Uncle Yaq." He took her hand and brought it across his chest. His heartbeat thudded and his warmth bathed her skin. "This is my TrueBond, you old rogue." He set their hands to their side. "As if you didn't know," he said with comfortable familial teasing.

Uncle Yaq's eyes shifted to the guards behind them. In a manner eerily similar to Qay, he raised an eyebrow. "And what, pray tell, do we need all of these men for?"

"I'm a trespassing, exiled prince who had the nerve to go against Zerin sensibilities to take a human as my TrueBond." Qay's nonchalant answer amused his uncle, who gave a bark of laughter.

"Well, at least you're consistent in doing the unexpected." He patted the younger man on the shoulder with a wide smile. "Come, let's go and see how Abzu is doing." He faced the gaggle of guards and spoke to the one in front. "Captain, I hardly think we need all of your men to follow us. Please select two, since the King's own guards will be in attendance." He walked ahead and didn't bother to make sure others followed.

Which, of course, they did.

Uncle Yaq led them down a wide hall, his steady stride swift and efficient. He and Qay had no trouble keeping up with each other. For Aimee—not so much. Working every night in the *Galaxy's End* pub made her toned, but with her shorter legs, it was hard to match their footsteps. She huffed and puffed between running and skipping.

Qay abruptly let go of her hand and scooped her up into his arms. He cradled her close to his chest as he followed his uncle.

With an undignified squeal, she wrapped her arms around his neck. Her nose met the crook of his neck and breathed in his masculine musk. She held on with a desperate grip—it was a long way down. She didn't know if she was mortified or impressed he could carry her around like a child. She met his amused gaze. "What are you doing?" Her soft words brushed against his skin as it pebbled.

He tightened his grip with a stark vulnerability that clouded his face. "Let me hold you."

Oh man, he did not play fair. Her mouth dried as words fled.

"Here we are." It took time for Uncle Yaq's words to reach her otherwise occupied brain.

Qay lowered her to her feet and pressed a kiss to her forehead. He held her hand and led her into a round, sterile room passing two guards dressed in emerald, complete with formidable blasters. The only thing in the room was an egg-shaped, clear chamber where a comatose Zerin male lay floating in light blue liquid. The man's arms and legs bobbed as the fluid rippled in soft waves. At first, he appeared nude, but when she looked closer she could see an iridescent, skintight bodysuit.

A tie held his long, braided hair and made his features easy to see. He had a face eerily similar to Qay's—except his cheekbones were sharper and his nose didn't have the small bump from a break. His midnight hair had a touch of yellowing strands at his temples.

Qay walked over to the pod and placed his free hand on the translucent covering. At first, he stood there, lost in thought. With a visible shake of his head, he let go of her hand to walk over to the computer display embedded in the shield near the head.

He glanced around the room. He gave a frown at the two guards standing in the doorway before he addressed his uncle. "Where are the healers?"

Uncle Yaq placed a comforting hand on his nephew's shoulder. "They have done all they can, Qay. It is up to the Goddess now whether or not Abzu awakens."

The color on Qay's cheeks deepened. "What happened?"

A comparable expression mirrored in Uncle Yaq's face. "The cowards shot him in the back with an alien weapon as he disembarked from a transport." He brought up a vid in the middle of the room. "Here is the picture of the projectile that entered his back just shy of his spine. Unfortunately, some of it stayed lodged in his muscle tissue. The healers removed as much as they could, but we have no idea how this weapon will affect him. We also don't know where this primitive, alien device came from." He gave a sigh as he studied the still form of his brother floating in the blue liquid. "But I can assure you we are diligently looking into it."

At first, it was hard to see what Yaq pointed at. When Aimee stepped closer to the display, the outline was unmistakable and she gasped.

"What is it?" Qay asked in a tight voice.

"It looks like a bullet from a gun," Aimee whispered. "Why would a Zerin use a human weapon? Don't you guys have phasers or something?"

Qay's dual-green eyes twinkled in amusement at her question. "Or something." He frowned and turned back to his uncle. "How did an Earth weapon wind up on Zerin?"

Before Yaq answered, a Zerin woman entered and walked over to their little group. Dressed in a formal tunic and pants, the turquoise and green garment complimented her dark pearlescent coloring to perfection. Her braided light walnut hair was in cornrows, interlaced with beads and jingling crystals that sparkled each time she moved her head. She had an intricate tattoo around her left eye and temple. The style was different from the one Aimee shared with Qay, and the inner crystal on her temple was clear.

Aimee found the woman's dual turquoise eyes stunning. The lighter shade surrounded the darker one before it blended into the oval pearl of her iris. She was a strikingly beautiful woman.

Aimee wasn't sure if she liked her or not.

"Qay, I am so glad you're here," the woman said. She enveloped him in a tight hug which he returned by pulling her in tighter. Eyes closed and everything.

Aimee scowled and moved closer to Qay. She crossed her arms and tapped her foot in irritation. Bah! She unfolded her arms and clasped her hands behind her back. She had no claim on Qay. It was stupid to get jealous. She hoped no one noticed her reaction as she took step back and smoothed her expression.

Out of the corner of her eye, Uncle Yaq sent her a wide smile. She tilted her head in defiance. Aimee refused to let him think Qay and his open display of affection to the gorgeous alien bothered her, because it didn't. No siree...not one bit.

Qay and the female parted after an eternity passed. "It is good to see you again, Yesult." Aimee frowned at the deep affection in his tone. "How have you been? And the twins, how are they? I've really missed them. Did they miss me?" The wistful look on his face was heart-wrenching.

A sinking sensation lodged in the pit of her stomach. Did they have children?

"Yes, you wretch!" The woman's hair beads clinked when she smacked him on the arm. Good thing he wasn't human or that would have left a bruise. Aimee was sure his low grunt was for show.

"All they can talk about is joining you in becoming space pirates." She put her hands on her hips in agitation. "I will not have it, Qay!" A stomped foot. "You have to set them straight right away."

A pained look crossed his face. "Why in the world would they think I'm a space pirate?" A distressed grimace twisted his full lips. "Has D'zia been filling their heads with nonsense? I haven't been anything but a respectable merchant for years now."

"Qay...." No mistaking that warning tone, the universal maternal threat was easy to recognize. Especially when she wagged an angry finger at him.

"But why can't D'zia do it?" Wow, who knew a grown prince could whine like a little child? "It's his fault, make him do it. Besides, I don't want them to hate me."

"Coward." She narrowed her teal eyes in warning. "You *will* talk to them and you *will* change their minds. Do I make myself understood, cousin?"

Cousin? Aimee perked up.

"Yesult, come and meet my TrueBond, Aimee." Great, now she was the change of subject so he didn't have to do something he didn't want to.

Qay gathered Aimee in front of him as he enveloped her. He crossed his arms over her chest and anchored her in a sea of warmth and masculine spice. His right palm rested on the baby bump. "Aimee, this is my cousin Yesult E'etu H'ara. She is the twin sister of my cousin D'zia and daughter of my Uncle Yaq Parvaiz E'etu, younger brother to my father." He inclined his head to his father, floating in what she assumed were healing fluids.

Yesult's lips pursed in annoyance. "We will finish this conversation, Qay. I will not let you ignore your duties to them. They are young, impressionable females who need to go on to university and not have their heads filled with nonsense." Those expressive eyes zeroed in on Aimee. Which unnerved her since she wasn't sure how Qay's family would like a having human in their family.

Aimee gave a startled yelp when Yesult grabbed her out of Qay's arms and gave her a sturdy hug, surrounding her in a light citrus fragrance. "I am so happy to finally meet Qay's TrueBond! Welcome to the family." Guess his cousin didn't care she was a human.

Stepping back, Yesult took in the baby bump and reached for it before she stopped and glanced at Aimee. "May I touch?"

Aimee started to ask Qay for his approval before she stopped. *Damn it!* She was better than this—she didn't need his approval. She pulled her shoulders back and replied, "Yes, of course."

Yesult placed a light palm on the baby bump and jerked in surprise when an energetic kick greeted her. "Oh, my! He's a strong one." Her joyous laughter was infectious and the group joined her in shared smiles.

"I hate to change the subject, but what do you have for us, my dear?" Uncle Yaq prodded in a gentle tone. He stood next to his daughter and placed an arm around her shoulders in greeting.

Qay pulled Aimee back into his embrace. "Yesult is not only my cousin, but she has the best legal mind on the planet."

Aimee watched Yesult walk over to her uncle in the floating stasis. She frowned before she directed her attention back to the group.

"Let's go to the conference chamber down the hall. There we can get comfortable and order some refreshments. Then I'll give you a status report. Sound good?"

Everyone agreed. Aimee found she was starving and the mention of food perked her up. The thought of sitting down wasn't a bad one either. She was bone-weary and would like nothing better than to rest for a bit.

It didn't take long for them to walk to the conference chamber, the two guards following. The large room boasted a round, wooden table big enough for ten to sit with plenty of room to spare. Aimee sat next to Qay on a chair padded with fluffy sections. She sat on her curled feet as she leaned against the thick armrest. Sleep beckoned her tired mind as voices kept buzzing around her. Aimee, eat this—come on you must eat something. Come on—one more bite. Blah, blah, blah. Soon her belly was full. She waved away the incoming eating utensil as she leaned back into the padded chair. Eyes blurred, the lids too heavy to keep open.

Sleep claimed the last of her thoughts.

Qay

Qay watched Aimee's every move and was aware when she fell asleep. He reached over and pulled the release on the backrest to lay it at a more comfortable level for her to snooze in. He moved a gentle hand over her hair to brush it away from her face and took a moment to study her before he was satisfied she was comfortable.

His fingers lingered on her cheek before he brought his attention back to his relatives.

The approving look on Yesult's face had him scowling back at her. He'd forgotten what an interfering female she was. Ignoring her, he spoke to his uncle.

"Tell me more about the status of my father first," he commanded.

His uncle took in a deep breath. "It's not looking good. The metal in the projectile is poisonous to our people. He's not only fighting the damage it made as it entered but also the effects of the poison." He opened a 3-D vid in the middle of the table. The images of King Abzu's vitals showed in clear detail for everyone to see. "The healers removed all of the foreign objects from here and here." He pointed to an area covered in a dark blue color denoting the injury on the meaty part of his back muscles. "By the blessed Goddess, we pray the healers will be able to find an antidote to the poison."

Qay frowned at the statistics in front of him. He regarded his uncle. "How much time does he have?"

Yaq's cheeks flushed as his eyes narrowed. "No one knows, but he's strong and has been holding his own steadily for several hours now. Let's not lose hope at this point, okay?"

Qay cleared his throat to hide his rising panic. Gritting his teeth, he concentrated on the news Yesult had. "Let's get to the legal stuff, shall we?"

Yesult's smile reassured him. "Before he was injured, your father filed an official edict rescinding your exiled status." She swiped clean the display and replaced it with her own forms. "However, since it hasn't been approved by the Zerin council, it is not legal yet." With an elegant lift of her shoulders, she sat back. "All you have to do is have a representative fill in for Uncle Abzu to state your case before the council. That's the easy part."

Qay raised an eyebrow in question.

Uncle Yaq intoned with his voice of reason. "I've got your father's written declaration ready to go. I have already submitted my intent to represent him on your behalf. I do not anticipate any opposing arguments."

"So, what's the hard part?" Qay had a sinking suspicion he knew the answer.

Yesult glanced at Aimee, who slept across from her. "The hard part is pleading your case about a human TrueBond." She frowned and raised a finger to her lips. "Not only is she an alien, but a human who was supposed to attend the Exchange. As you know, it is illegal for a Zerin to take a human out of the Exchange."

Qay sat back and smiled at his cousin and uncle. He gave a brief chuckle. "Bah! I'm not worried." He got up and grabbed one of Yesult's beaded braids and gave a quick tug. She swatted his hand away and glared at him as he went back to where Aimee slept. "How can I when I have you on my side?" He caressed the hair on Aimee's head. "When do I go before the council?"

Yesult frowned. "You and father are scheduled to appear before them in two days." She narrowed her eyes as she continued. "You realize without their sanction, you not only lose your birthright, but you put your TrueBond's life in jeopardy. Both of you might be labeled as traitors and could face subsequent charges." Yesult's eyes filled with tears.

Qay smiled and shook his head, a signal to his cousin not to worry. He reached over to pull his TrueBond into his arms. She didn't wake but snuggled closer. Warmth flooded as he nuzzled the top of her head. Her spicy vanilla musk filled him with calm purpose. Everything clicked into place and made him grateful he was with her. He chuckled at his previous obstinate idea to stay away from her. It was humbling to admit what an ass he'd been.

"Qay, you need to take this seriously!" Yesult pounded her palm against the table. "What are you laughing about?"

He hugged his female close and smiled at his family as he told them.

Aimee

Scorching heat blasted through Aimee from her toes to the top of her head. *Closer*...more...she needed more. She yearned, her body clamoring as it strove for the source of the out-of-reach pleasure. It teased and stoked—an insistent wave that crashed and pulled...over and over.

A sensual buildup glided across her eager skin. In a slow heat, Aimee's confused mind returned to consciousness.

Warm male hands, fingers, and talented tongue moved in complete synchronicity over her neck, breasts, and the wet seam between her legs. They stroked, kneaded, and caressed sensitive skin. Her ability to think coherently strangled in confusing knots. She swore an octopus was seducing her.

Aimee opened her lips to give a small squeak, but before a sound escaped, strong, masculine lips covered hers. Coaxing, demanding, the spicy taste wove its way into her, breaking through any barriers to stop him. He was one of her favorite flavors, a hint of a spicy bite that was all Qay. While Qay's tongue continued to plunder past her defenses, Aimee's hands were busy as well, plunging into his thick, loose hair.

His warm chest came closer as a large hand wrapped under her ass. Strong fingers massaged one cheek and pulled her mound closer to his long, thick erection.

Aimee moaned when he took his mouth away. She chased him with her arms around his neck and head and pulled his expansive chest to her. The new position interfered with his grip on her ass so he retaliated by rubbing his lower body against hers. Aimee's eyes opened to see him paused mere inches from her face. His exquisite eyes pulsated with longing and she drowned in the sensation.

"I promised myself I would take it slow with you, *Ahyoka*. But the chemistry between us is so strong I don't want to resist," Qay declared. He lowered and nuzzled the soft skin behind her ear. "I know you have no reason to trust me, but I swear to you, you have nothing to worry about. I am completely devoted to you and our little one."

Her body stilled as his words soaked into her lust-riddled brain. It was as effective as a bucket of ice water dumped on her naked body. It made her pause. Was she doing something she would regret?

She scrambled as she moved away from him. "Wait, wait, *wait!*" She pushed at his delectable pecs and tried to dislodge the immovable force. "Qay...oh...*no!*" A strangled moan as his tongue sucked sensitive skin.

He answered her moan with a groan of reluctance that vibrated in her ear before he drew away. He didn't go far. His chest remained flush with hers and his hand groped the round globe of her butt. She wasn't sure, but he probably wasn't aware he was massaging her ass and using it to rub her sex against his.

She watched his half-lidded reaction to them grinding together. Her body clenched in anticipation. Though the clothes they wore hindered skin-to-skin contact, it wasn't enough to stop the promise of coming pleasures.

"Qay?" Did that throaty plea come from her? She cleared her throat to try again. "Qay, please...uh...I can't think!" The last word came out in a distressed plea.

Abruptly he slid down her body. He took her pants and panties with him.

"What are you doing?" Aimee rested on her elbows and watched as he lowered his head to the juncture of her thighs. His inky black hair flowed around him and over her torso. She watched in fascination when the freed strands added a silky curtain to tease her responsive skin. It caressed and petted her as he moved.

He ignored her and continued his journey. He stopped at the juncture of her thighs and held them open with the lubricated palms of his hands. Wherever he touched, her skin absorbed the invigorating oil.

Aimee drowned in sensual overload. She was losing her sense of self. Terrified of the careening emotions, she again tried to stop the inevitable. Aimee reached for the top of his head. He eluded her to dive in and envelop her sex between his pursuing lips. His tongue lapped up her stiff bud and sucked on it.

Hard.

She detonated and flew apart. She wailed his name trying to find an anchor with flailing hands. Aimee became the throbbing, pulsating release that squeezed from her clit into a tempest that ran through her body.

As Aimee came down from her orgasmic high, Qay reached under her to flip her over onto her hands and knees. With a rare talent, he stripped off her top tunic simultaneously.

"Ah, my everlasting beauty, what do we have here?" He licked the base of her spine. Aimee's muddled mind scrambled to understand what he meant. Oh, he must mean her tattoo with its image of a starflower in blue and purple ink surrounded by a burst of color. She'd gotten the totem in her late twenties to celebrate her promotion to management.

"How did I miss this before, hum?" Qay's lips suckled the pebbled skin as he caressed and plucked at her sensitive nipples with his fingers. She shuddered at the added sensation. The air became heavy as the combined musky scent of sex ramped up her passions.

His wide body covered the back of her thighs as he caressed the globes of her butt. Strong fingers kneaded and squeezed before he parted the folds of her womanhood with one finger. Her wet, welcoming heat was ready as he slipped the thick digit in and out. His thumb joined the party and rubbed over her sensitive clit with each thrust. After a few swipes, he added another finger. As they entered he scissored his fingers apart and caught her special spot.

The buildup was too much. Aimee groaned and pushed back as she fisted her hands on the silky sheets in reaction. Her sex tightened and her body sucked him in. She was ready for the onslaught of another explosion and pushed back, seeking the elusive completion. He withdrew abruptly, and Aimee whimpered at the emptiness. She pushed her hips back, seeking his return. She turned to look at him and make her demands known when her mouth dropped open. The sight of him fisting his massive erection in a rounding, up and down motion struck her stupid.

She'd never seen anything so erotic in her whole life. Between the uncompromising expression and his forceful stare on her exposed pussy, Aimee quivered. He placed an open palm on her ass and aimed the blunt head at her soaked opening. Once the wide staff penetrated, he put both palms on the shelf of her hips and gave a forceful thrust.

She closed her eyes as unexpected bliss consumed her as his thick cock filled the empty space. He didn't move right away, except for the throb of his cock. She savored the sensation of her body wrapped around his wide girth as he settled inside.

Aimee rested her forehead on the soft mattress. Her pussy walls squeezed his hot length and she moved her hips up, craving the friction. When Qay didn't reciprocate, she turned again to see what the holdup was. The curtain of his straight, black hair covered his bowed head, obscuring his face. He stayed rigid, his hands gripping the flesh of her hips in a firm hold. His big chest moved up and down as if he was fighting for control. Awe filled her. She did this—she caused this proud, beautiful man to struggle. For the first time in her life, she enjoyed the smug sensation of womanpower.

With slow deliberation, he rocked his hips and brought his head up. Eyes closed and face tight, he sucked his bottom lip between his teeth. Aimee watched as his sharp incisors gleamed in the cool light of the room. Qay ground his groin in a rounding motion, making his cock slide and rub her welcoming walls. She sucked in a gasp at the movement. He alternated between a straight back and forth motion and a round, swaying one. Her body hung on to his wide cock with a fierce determination as her full breasts swayed with each thrust.

The friction became too much. One more stroke, one more rounding push was all it took before she came in a shower of hedonistic ecstasy. His slick chest caressed her back as he continued to plow with deep, striking thrusts, causing Aimee to push back. One last forceful lunge and he found his own release. He shuddered, his violent tremors sliding on her back as his palms rested on the bed next to hers.

After a few heartbeats, Qay let out an erratic breath as he placed his right arm around her waist. He pulled them back to the bed so they could lay flush on their sides while he kept them intimately connected. Her body relaxed after the powerful orgasms she'd enjoyed.

It didn't take long for the tension to return. At first, Aimee wasn't sure why she was reacting this way. Then it dawned on her she half expected him to jump off the bed and claim he wanted nothing to do with her. Her skin tightened and her eyes became hot as she waited for him to bolt. Instead, he pulled her closer and wrapped his leg around hers to enfold her in a soft, warm Zerin cocoon.

In the dusky silence they lay together. Neither one spoke before nature called and forced Aimee to look for a bathroom. There had to be one around somewhere...wherever she was.

She lifted her head and tried to look around, but the room was dark and the only thing she could make out was random shadows. Maybe that darker shadow along the wall across from her was a door. Just as she was about to tell him to let her up, she heard a soft snore behind her.

She bit her lip so she wouldn't laugh aloud. Well, looked like a man falling asleep after sex was universal. She had a good chance in making her escape undetected. With careful precision, she inched out from under his embrace, stopping when he gave a light snort. Heart pounding, she crept from under his heavy leg. He gave a low moan before he continued his slumber.

When Aimee disengaged his sex from hers, the sensation of him sliding out made her want to stop and give it a go again. Good idea or not, her bladder strongly nixed that suggestion.

Impatient with her urges, Aimee slid further out from under him. She grimaced when their combined fluids flowed after he slid free. Maybe she'd find a shower because she was feeling a tad sticky. Clothes, she'd worry about later.

Liberated from Qay's arms she rolled out of the bed and with careful steps tiptoed across the room. Not for the first time she was grateful for her enhanced eyesight into avoiding most of the obstacles in the way. She reached the darker part of the wall and found the indent to place her palm to open. When the soft whooshing noise signified her success, she heard Qay give a manly grunt before he rolled over. The light snoring continued.

Affection for him blossomed in her chest. No, no! Bad Aimee. Do not fall for sexy alien again. No matter how many mind-blowing orgasms he gave you. You have pride somewhere, don't you? Freakin' hussy.

Disgusted over her inner dialogue, she turned to walk in the dark room. The door whooshed behind as the lights came on. Thank God...a bathroom.

And what a bathroom it was. Huge didn't describe the luxurious bounty before her. Straight ahead, what she assumed was an enclosed glass shower stall large enough for a bowling team. To her right sat a sunken tub big enough for that team to join each other, complete with multi-level jets. She made a beeline for the obvious toilet facilities at the opposite wall.

After she was done, she went over to that stall. She walked into the large rectangular cubicle as water rained down, a soft spray that followed her in the large enclosure as the clear walls closed around her. The water was the right temperature to sooth her aching muscles. The various water streams pulsed at different parts of her body and were a welcome surprise. Immersed in the decadence of the massaging water, she never heard the sheer shower doors open until a large, masculine arm slid around her waist.

Aimee jumped and squealed in surprise. She turned around, but his big arm held her in place, keeping her from facing him. She stared at the marble outlay of the enclosure. She blinked in confusion as she focused on the solid white wall with multiple veins of color. She tried not to shiver in reaction and closed her eyes to gather her strength to resist him and move away.

"Don't turn around. Let me hold you." He nuzzled her ear as he pulled her closer. His firm cock nestled in the seam of her ass. "I don't blame you for being mad at me. I promise we'll have plenty of time to deal with that. For now, let me cleanse you." He licked the junction at the back of her neck as he whispered to her. "Let me caress you."

"Qay, really, I..."

"Let me worship you the way I should have the first time I saw you."

Well...crap. Had she mentioned he didn't play fair? Honestly, how was she supposed to stay mad at him when he said things like that? Her throat tightened. No matter what he said, a part of her expected him to walk away like he had before.

He took a soft cloth embedded with a light, nutty fragrant soap and washed her with caresses and gentle groping. Aimee's skin pebbled in reaction to his touch and her nipples tightened into hard points. When he reached between her legs and stroked, all doubts fled. Her alien mate remained true to his words. He worshiped her. He adored her. He took his time to explore every inch of her body with tender hands, a hot tongue and devastating lips.

Their loving in the shower was everything Aimee had ever dreamed of. She ignored the nagging fear of rejection that poked in the back of her mind. She was convinced she was on borrowed time. Any second now, he would cast her aside as he'd done before.

She doubted she'd survive the devastation.

The next two days Aimee found herself in a whirlwind of activity. It was a race against time as Qay and his relatives scrambled to prepare for the upcoming council meeting. Nerves were tight as she watched him work to reclaim his birthright even though he'd taken an "alien" TrueBond.

Ha! Her, an alien. The idea still cracked her up.

She spent every waking hour with Qay but they were never alone. His family was always around and that prevented Qay from finishing his explanation about why he'd had a sudden change of heart toward her. After the first day, she started to suspect he deliberately avoided the topic. Either he'd change the subject verbally, or when they were alone at night he'd use a more direct, physical route to stop her questions. She swore he was an expert in changing her from a sane, collected woman to a mindless, incoherent blob of sexual need with a glance from his heavy-lidded emerald eyes.

Even though she enjoyed their physical interludes, the more he didn't answer her questions the more nervous she got. Her fears crept up at the most inopportune times and her insecurities pissed her off. She hated the mass of blubbery nerves that ruled her life.

The morning of the council meeting, Aimee woke up alone. Her first thought was he'd had enough and left her. When she walked out of the opulent bedchamber and into the living room suite, a running vid of him explaining he'd gone down to see his cousins D'zia and Yesult with Uncle Yaq calmed her. He let her know they'd come to get him earlier than expected and he hadn't wanted to wake her. He admonished her to take her time to get ready and not to rush. They'd be back for her soon.

The vid was nice, but Aimee wished she could have gone with them. A pang of loneliness settled in her heart. What did she expect? She was an alien whose dubious ties to the family were thin. Not to dwell on the worst-case scenario, but if Qay couldn't convince the council of her legitimate status, there was a real possibility she might be exiled to the outer rim. She never told Qay she overheard him talking to his cousins when the words "possible execution" came out in hushed tones.

Well hell, they didn't have to bother with all that. She'd rather go to Earth, but if nothing else, they could take her to the *Galaxy's End* pub. The Zerins would never have to see her again or remember she ever existed. She'd get a spray tan and mute the iridescent sheen to her skin. Explaining a baby with three fingers and dual-colored eyes might be trickier, but she'd figure something out.

With that cheerful thought, Aimee went over to the closet to pull out the clothes she would wear. Yesult had a formal tunic and pants made for her in honor of the occasion. It matched the royal emerald green of Qay's outfit, a show of solidarity between them.

She wished Qay would have told her what he was going to say to the council. Whenever she'd asked, he brushed her off, telling her "It wasn't done yet" or "I'm still working on it" or "One more revision before I can share." Wasn't it funny how the chance to go over it together had come and gone?

She stood in front of the mirror and watched her long, silky hair braid itself when a horrible thought occurred to her. Once the thought took hold, she couldn't shake it off.

Maybe he didn't tell her what he was going to say because he was going to reject her again. You know...like saying, "Hey, guys, I didn't mean to TrueBond with an alien. I mean, come on...look at her! She's way past her prime, a bit chubby (if you know what I mean, wink-wink) and she's not nearly as pretty as our women are. Am I right, guys? Huh? Am I right?"

She hardly noticed the look of horror on her reflected face as the devil's advocate in her head continued. "I mean, really guys, so I banged her a couple of times. So what? (Here's where he'd give a conspiratorial wink to the good ol' boys.) What do ya say we get rid of her here and now, eh? Between us, we'll pretend nothing happened. Forgive, forget, and go on with our lives. Sound good?"

Aimee hyperventilated and hadn't notice Yesult had entered the room.

"Oh my Goddess, are you all right?" Yesult grabbed her upper arms as her dual turquoise eyes widened in alarm. The concern on her face broke something inside of Aimee.

Aimee jerked away from Yesult's tender expression waved her to stay away. "No! No, I'm not all right. He's going to get rid of me, isn't he?" She peeked behind the Zerin woman. Why wait? Why didn't he have her arrested here where no one could see? "Is he going to have someone come and get me here so no one can see?"

"Do what here? Who do you think is going to come for you?" Yesult put up her hands back on Aimee's shoulders.

Conflicting emotions choked Aimee and she didn't want Yesult touching her. "Qay!" She pushed passed the other woman to walk around her. "Don't you see? The reason he wouldn't tell me what he is going to say to the council is that he's going to tell them to get rid of me!" She choked on the last word as it tumbled out. Her face heated and her heart thundered in her ears. Her breath...she couldn't catch her breath...

Yesult had Aimee's face between her three-fingered hands before Aimee moved. "Aimee, Aimee calm down!" Yesult's eyes widened as the skin across her cheeks tightened. "What are you talking about? Qay could no sooner hurt you than he could himself. He is, after all, your TrueBond!"

"So what? It's never stopped him before!" Her fears took over as Aimee's control snapped. With an incoherent sob, she wasn't aware of Yesult taking her into the other room. With a gentle push, Yesult sat next to her on the bed and enfolded her in her arms. Aimee's emotions ran rampant.

Yesult was patient, kind, and soothing as she let Aimee sob her fears, stress, and confusion. "Tell me," she said when the sobs subsided into jagged hiccups. "Tell me everything from start to finish." The low whisper got through Aimee's panic as she considered confiding in her. Qay's cousin produced a tan square cloth for Aimee to wipe her nose and face. *Ha!* Looked like they did have facial tissues in space.

Aimee's head fought with her heart in trusting Yesult. But she had to talk to someone, so Aimee began with a stilted voice at first before she gained enough strength to share her story. She began from the moment she'd first seen Qay aboard the *StarChance* and finished with how they left the Chancellor's palace. The silence stretched out until Aimee pulled her head out of Yesult's embrace and the embarrassing wet stain she'd left on the woman's tunic top. Jeez, she probably ruined the pretty silk of the orange and gold outfit.

"Well," the other woman sighed. She gave a reassuring hug and patted her arm. Yesult's turquoise dual colored eyes narrowed as she glanced around the room. Aimee gave an involuntary shiver. For the first time, the Zerin woman let Aimee see her menacing side.

"It looks like there's only one thing to do."

Aimee braced. Was she wrong in trusting this woman with her doubts and fears?

"He has to die."

Aimee jerked her head to look at the Zerin female in shock. "What?"

Yesult shrugged her elegant shoulders. "Well, he's just too stupid to live. How can we possibly allow someone that stupid to rule the Zerin people? The easiest thing to understand in the galaxy is the connection between TrueBond mates. For Goddess sake, our children get this explained to them at a very young age. It's not complicated and the idiot should have made sure you knew about it right away. Obviously, he's beyond hope. I mean, *really*." There was no mistaking the look of disgust on her face as she stood placed her fists on her slim hips. Her beaded hair tinkled as she moved. The light brown of the small braids swayed in unison around her waist.

"Um, Yesult...."

"No...no, can't wait, it needs to be done right away." She scanned the room. "Maybe I'll do it myself. Don't you have something heavy around here I can beat his empty skull with? Where's a heavy piece of metal when you need it?"

Aimee couldn't help it—she laughed at Yesult's absurd comment. "Really, Yesult..." she wiped the moisture from her eyes with the soaked cloth.

"Yes, really, Yesult. I believe bashing my head in is considered treason." Qay stood with his hands on his hips as he gave his cousin a teasing glare.

"Bah!" She walked over to him. "It would be justifiable homicide because you are too stupid to live. Think of all of the headaches I'll save the empire." She poked him with an index finger. "Besides, it's not murder if they can't find the body." She gave him a narrow-eyed glare and another poke for good measure. "And I'm just the gal to bury your thoughtless ass where no one could find you."

"See, I'm not the only one who fantasizes about hiding your body constantly." In walked another Zerin, the male whose ear she'd chomped. Uh-oh. Aimee's face heated in embarrassment when she noticed the uncanny resemblance between Yesult and him. This must be her twin brother. D'zia?

"Shut up, D'zia."

"And you must be the lovely Aimee. I am very happy to finally meet you under better circumstances." D'zia ignored his cousin. He walked over to Aimee and enfolded her in a warm hug.

Wait—was Qay growling?

"Um, thank you?" She patted D'zia's back. "You're Yesult's brother?" Qay's cousin was a big male and it was hard to get her hands around his wide shoulders. He was handsome and smelled wonderful...but all wrong. Holding him made her twitchy.

D'zia stepped back and gave her arms a final squeeze before he let go with a warm smile and a sparkle in his bright turquoise eyes. Two deep, dangerous dimples framed his devilish lips. "Yep, guilty as charged."

Yesult made a rude noise. "Younger brother."

D'zia's eye roll was so humanlike it made Aimee giggle. "Let's not forget that important detail. Like five clicks is such a big deal."

She snorted and folded her arms across her chest. "It bothers you, great fun for me."

Wow, they were identical twins not only in looks but in temperament as well.

"Do you have any brothers or sisters?" She directed the question to Qay. Jeez, what kind of person was she that she hadn't asked him this before?

A dark flush crossed his high cheeks. Embarrassment or anger? "No." A small shake of his head. "Mother died when I was young, so no siblings."

"Your father never married again?" She'd have thought a monarch would remarry and continue having children. She'd only seen King Abzu in the stasis pod, but from what she could tell he didn't look much older than Qay. They could almost be brothers.

"See! This is why you're too stupid to live!" Yesult's exasperation was clear from the tone of her voice and the raising of her hands. She gestured wildly as she berated Qay.

"What? Did I say something wrong?" Aimee asked, confused. What was she missing?

"Honest to Goddess, Yesult. Quit doing my job for me, will ya?" D'zia heaved a dramatic sigh. "It's obvious he doesn't know Aimee is completely in the dark about Zerin physiology and what being a TrueBond means. Aren't you, gorgeous?" He winked at Aimee for confirmation.

It was uncomfortable admitting her ignorance. She gave a negligent shrug and took a quick peek at Qay. The alarm in his wide eyes surprised her.

"You're still confused about what it means to be a TrueBond?" His voice cracked as the tips of his pointed ears reddened.

His clueless question pissed her off.

"I've been trying to get you to talk to me for the last couple of days." Her face heated. "All I know about this TrueBond thing is this tattoo I've got on my face that matches yours. You guys act like it's something more, which I don't get." Now she was warming up. "When I tried to do research on Zerins on the *StarChance*, there was nothing in the data base from the VDU he gave me." She gestured to D'zia. Oops, was she supposed to admit that? Guiltily, she glanced at D'zia to make sure he wasn't upset with her. She didn't know for sure if he was the one who'd left the device, but with his unusual eye coloring, it was a safe bet.

If the self-righteous grin on his face was anything to go by, she didn't have to worry.

"You had a VDU with access to our data base?" Qay asked. He glared at his cousin in silent communication.

"Yes, so she could watch your happy ass any time she wanted to." D'zia crossed his arms as if to dare the other man. "I suspect that's how she found you in the training room the day she bit my ear off." He fingered the tip of his ear as if a ghost memory compelled him.

"She bit your ear?" Yesult demanded as she went over to her brother and pulled on his offended ear. It was a good thing it was still attached otherwise her tugging would have pulled it off.

"Ow, let go, you sadistic witch!" D'zia griped as he twisted to escape her.

Satisfied there wasn't anything wrong with him, she smacked his shoulder and told him to grow up.

"People, let's not get off the subject," Qay announced. He turned his emerald gaze her way and stood in front of her. "How much do you know about being a TrueBond?" He reached over to hold the tops of her arms gently. He pulled them together as his serious gaze searched her face. His warmth and tantalizing masculine scent washed over her. She relaxed.

She opened her mouth to answer when Yesult interrupted with a squeal. "Oh my Goddess, we're running late. We have to be at the council meeting in less than ten clicks. We'd better leave now to get there before the opening sounds."

Aimee wanted to stamp her foot in exasperation. For God's sake! Why was it every time she was about to learn something important, she was interrupted? Before she protested, Qay gathered her under his arm and hustled them out of the personal apartments.

They reached the hall of transportation mirrors in record time. Aimee took the opportunity to check out at her reflection before it changed. It was a relief there weren't any splotchy spots or tear tracks to show she'd been crying.

However, the annoyed look on her face wasn't hard to miss.

Chapter ELEVEN

T he mirror took them straight to the entrance of the council chambers. Aimee's previous fears about her future threatened to start all over again. She swallowed and steadied her breath to maintain control. She wanted to hide her emotions from Qay so he wouldn't be distracted from the upcoming trial and the speech he had to give. After all, he'd been up most of the night preparing his talking points.

Aimee walked next to Qay into an immense, extravagantly decorated domed antechamber. It reminded her of Royal Albert Hall in England she'd visited once. Of course, Royal Albert Hall didn't have an invisible ceiling that let in the natural orange and yellow light of the Zerin sun. Nevertheless, it was intimidating as hell. Intricate dark woodwork lined the curved walls, toward the round ceiling. Finely tuned acoustics allowed sounds to be comfortable enough for everyone in attendance to hear.

According to Yesult, there wasn't an empty seat in the house, with the overflow rooms outside filled as well. As the four of them entered, the multiple conversations stopped.

The rolling butterflies in her stomach threatened to riot as Aimee watched hundreds of Zerin's scrutinize her. She'd rather be anywhere but here. If it was up to her, someone could come and get her when it was all over. She didn't like being on display in front of the council and the citizens of Zerin to examine and judge. It made her feel as if she was pinned under a microscope. To say she was nervous and tense was an understatement. She tore her gaze from the crowd of seated Zerins to concentrate on the front of the room.

On a raised stage at the far back wall, seven elderly Zerin sat: three males and four females in separate large, dark brown loungers. Each wore a different colored robe, their hair piled high on their heads, their backs straight and unbending. Each face displayed an unemotional façade as they moved in unison to watch Aimee and the others walk in.

An usher greeted them and gave a slight bow before directing them to a row of seats off the side of the same dais, separated from the main stage by a small circular platform surrounded by a railing of dark cherry wood. Uncle Yaq was already seated at the end of the row, smiling as they approached.

Everyone filed past Qay as he waited on the outside. D'zia sat next to his father, then Yesult. Aimee took the next seat beside Yesult and watched Qay sit beside her on the end chair. She was impressed the seats were soft and comfortable, quite like the adjustable chairs on the *StarChance*.

Once they settled, Yaq stood up and approached the podium centered in front of the council. He gave a respectful bow to the audience before he addressed the governing body.

"Sacred Greetings, esteemed council members. It is my deepest wish the Goddess blesses you with Grace, Contentment, and Glory." He gave them a deeper bow before he continued. "We are here today to review the request by our revered ruler, King Abzu Jareth E'etu to rescind the exile status for his highness, the crown prince, Qayyum A'agnan E'etu. Before his majesty, King Abzu, could present his request to the council, a coward using an alien weapon assaulted him which resulted in his current comatose state. I am here on his behalf to present his wishes in this regard."

He paused to open up a 3-D computer program from his ocular VDU to float in the middle of the dais. Each image displayed legalese and Qay's uncle pointed out how each form was signed or initialed by the King prior to his being incapacitated. With each page, Yaq described the reasons for Qay's exile.

Aimee smirked. Looked like her man was something of a spoiled bad boy— everything from disrespecting his teachers and tutors to refusing to focus on being a part of the governing body in preparation for him taking over the throne. He'd spent the majority of his youth going out of his way to party and embarrass the E'etu family line. Aimee glanced at Qay and raised an eyebrow at him. Maybe the father of her baby had "Responsibility Deficit Disorder."

Well, as far as she was concerned, whoever he was before didn't exist now. She'd watched him night after night and how he interacted with his crew and the respect they gave him. Just her luck, his only problem was her. She snorted under her breath. He'd run away from her fast enough.

She started when Qay took her hand up to his mouth to kiss her knuckles before he whispered, "Do not worry, *Ahyoka.* I have mended my wicked ways."

She opened her mouth to say something, but he stopped her by placing his forefinger on her lips and nodded his head toward Yaq, who was winding down his narrative.

Aimee had to admit Qay's father was justified in shocking his son into taking responsibility for the life he was born to by exiling him. Per Zerin custom, it was common practice to exile young adults who were aimless and refused to take responsibility for their actions.

"Esteemed council members, here is King Abzu's sworn statement to rescind the order he placed fifty years ago."

Aimee snapped her head to look at Qay. Fifty years ago? Good God, how old was he?

According to Yaq, Qay had been a good boy in the fifty years he'd been away from Zerin. Starting from nothing, he'd worked on various space merchant ships and moved his way up the ranks. He'd also covertly worked for the Zerin people on various missions. As Yaq continued, Aimee envisioned Qay as an alien James Bond.

Yaq outlined Qay's brilliant business dealings until he became owner and commander of the *StarChance*. Once at the helm, Qay helped to organize the Exchange for the systems in the Federation Consortium who needed the human women to save them from extinction. Because the Zerin people headed the Exchange, the entire planet profited from the endeavor.

Aimee noticed there was no mention of the illegal activity of humans sold into slavery—a topic she would love to bring up with Qay when things settled down. Come to think of it, it was one of the many things she wanted to discuss with him.

By the time Yaq finished his glowing report, Aimee wouldn't be surprised if they canonized Qay into sainthood after they reinstated him.

Yaq began to wrap up his speech. "My esteemed council members, I currently rest my case in the request to have Qayyum A'agnan E'etu's exile status rescinded to reinstate him as the Crown Prince of Zerin. All signed documents are available for your approval." With a respectful bow, Yaq returned to his seat.

An elderly male council member, whose chocolate brown hair was yellow with age, moved from his seat to take his place at a small podium in front of their seating. His dark hunter green robe may have hidden his elderly body, but nothing could hide the intelligence in his matching dual light and dark hunter green eyes.

"We have all heard the testimony from his Excellency Yaq Parvaiz E'etu stepping in as King Abzu's surrogate in the request of reinstating Prince Qayyum to the royal line of succession, thus eliminating his status as an exile. Be it so noted this date in time under the Goddess's merciful judgment." He moved his head to encompass to the bank of chairs where Aimee sat with the others.

"Commander E'etu, the council will hear your case in claiming an Earth woman as your TrueBond." He paused. "Be advised, this is an extremely serious matter that may have treasonous consequences. Who is your legal representative in this matter?"

Qay let go of Aimee's hand and stood. He gave the man and council a bow before he spoke.

"Sacred Greetings, esteemed council members. It is my deepest wish the Goddess blesses you with Grace, Contentment, and Glory." He stood ramrod straight as he addressed the question put to him. "As you so rightfully pointed out, Councilman Aine, I agree this is a very serious matter. Having acknowledged that, I stand to represent myself."

Aimee heard Yesult give a quiet moan of distress. She must feel as lawyers on Earth do: representing yourself means you have a fool for a client. *Damn*, he'd better know what he was doing.

"Indeed?" Councilman Aine raised a surprised brow.

"Yes, Your Honor. May I approach the witness platform to present my case?"

The elder glanced at his fellow council members. None voiced any objections. With their silent approval, he addressed Qay. "Yes, you may state your case." He frowned. "However, I would be remiss if I did not ask you to reconsider using a professional barrister on your behalf."

Qay walked over to the podium Yaq had vacated and gave a reassuring smile. "Thank you for your thoughtful consideration, Councilman Aine. But my decision stands."

The Councilman gave Qay a bow of respect in return. "Very well. Once I return to my seat, you may begin."

Aimee took those few precious moments to admire Qay in all of his masculine glory. He stood proud, not only before the Council of Elders but also in front of every Zerin citizen through a planet-wide broadcast. How he could look so cool and regal was a mystery to her. She was a nervous wreck just sitting on the sidelines.

He stood tall—a wicked pagan god with his russet iridescent skin reflecting his muscular body to perfection. The midnight hair respectably encased in warrior braids in the front as the curtain of silk flowed down his back and whispered across his ass. The pure white strip that framed one side of his face contrasted nicely to his dark strands. One of these days she'd get him to tell her why he did that to his hair.

Today he wore his formal commander's uniform of emerald green, complete with tight-fitting pants encased in knee-high black books. A long, formal vest covered the clothes, an unbroken panel draping the back while the front two panels were open and held in place with a wide black belt that matched the boots.

He wore no jewelry except the MalDerVon scroll with the dark green crystal in the middle, which was on prominent display.

As she sat and watched him, she was stuck by how proud, regal, and downright sexier than hell he was. Startled at her musings, she came to a staggering conclusion.

She loved him. She blinked and tasted that thought for a moment. A warm flood of peace wrapped around her. Yep, there was no doubt in her mind. Not only was she deeply and irrevocably in love with her alien, she always would be.

Her eyes watered as her heart pounded. Stupid baby hormones. She pinched her nails into the palms of her hands to get a hold of her emotions. She took in a few deep breaths and focused on Qay and willed him to know she supported him.

As if he heard her, his eyes met hers and something clicked between them. Aimee held her breath as her heart and emotions settled.

"Don't worry, I've got this," his deep voice quietly echoed in her mind.

She smiled, took in a relieved breath, and sat back.

Qay

Qay focused on what he was going to say as he approached the podium. He was relieved he'd made sure he and Aimee had a quick getaway if things didn't go their way. All he had to do now was convince the entire planet taking a human TrueBond wasn't grounds to deny his father's request to rescind his exiled status. Or worse, charge him as traitorous criminal.

He stopped at the dais when an unwavering sense of déjà vu hit him. Memories came back, him in front of the council in his misspent youth. Addressing the elders was like putting on an old pair of boots small enough to pinch your toes. While you could walk in those boots, it would be as uncomfortable as hell the whole time you had them on.

Give them the standard greeting...blah, blah, blah. Yeah, they all thought he was an idiot for wanting to represent himself. But who else could give the right story but him? He would bare his soul to his people and face them to prove he was the male they'd all hoped he'd become.

Besides, Uncle Yaq laid all of his sins out in the open, anyway. There was only one reason he was here to bare his soul: Aimee, his TrueBond. He had wronged her and now it was time for him to make it up to her. The reason he hadn't shared with her what he was going to say was that he wanted to prove his sincerity and what she meant to him—in front of the entire Zerin population. Then there'd be no doubt in her mind what she meant to him. She'd know he did it all for her.

Even though she'd been amiable enough the last couple of days, she continued to hold part of herself back. Trust was a hard thing to earn, and by the Goddess, this would be his first step in earning hers.

Without warning, she was there, inside him. Her strength and support caressed, letting him know she had faith in him. He couldn't resist—he locked his eyes with hers to internally project to her, *"Don't worry, I've got this."* When her eyes widened in surprise, he knew she got his message. That was all the fortification he needed.

"Thank you again, Councilman Aine. I would like to express my gratitude for this opportunity to explain how our TrueBond occurred to not only the Zerin people, but most of all to Aimee. Therefore, I officially declare proudly to one and all that Aimee Elizabeth Gwiazdowski of Earth is my TrueBond."

There were murmurs around the room. Some were in anger and some in confusion, but he ignored the intense stares of hundreds of faces and continued with his narrative.

"In order for me to do this, I must start at the beginning. When I first met Aimee, it was aboard the *StarChance*..."

In painstaking detail, he went through his first meeting with her. How he'd seen her on a vid display at his cousin's urging. She'd captivated him, so he pretended to tease his cousin about meeting a human for the first time.

"I must admit I admired her courage in leaving all she knew behind for a chance at a better life. How many of us would have that type of fortitude given the same circumstance? Would you leave all of Zerin behind, your friends, your family, and your very way of life? Imagine what Aimee and her fellow humans have to decide in a short time with little to no information or proof. I ask you to put yourself in their place. Would you have the courage to make the same decision? We are fortunate any of them choose to attend the Exchange at all."

He shared their initial meeting and how her enthralling scent drew him in. How he had to fight his TrueBond urge to possess and claim her. But, he was determined to avoid the illegal possibility at all costs.

With a slow flush creeping up his neck, he told them how he'd become obsessed with her, following her daily activities secretly on a nightly vid.

Undaunted, he continued explaining the second time he met Aimee. He admitted his distraction with thoughts of her as he sparred with his cousin. When a blow to the nose caused his nose to gush blood, out of nowhere, a screaming Aimee attacked his cousin. Qay explained how his security officer had tracked her movements and was able to subdue and pull her off D'zia before she did more than bite off a piece of his ear.

As Qay described the abused ear, a collective groan filled the auditorium. A Zerin's ear was one of the most sensitive areas and any abuse would make any of them moan in sympathetic pain.

Qay didn't have to turn around to see Aimee's face heat in an embarrassed blush. He sensed her unease and sent her a wave of soothing reassurance.

"I might have refused to believe it, but the TrueBond process had already begun. Aimee was beginning to take on Zerin characteristics as I began to have emotional changes. She unconsciously read the Zerin language and had the instinctual drive to protect her mate. I have to admit, the sight of her attacking my cousin sent my own instincts into overdrive. It was then I had the privilege to taste her lips for the first time." His eyes unfocused and he got lost in the memory of their kiss. He jerked out of his reverie and continued by admitting the abrupt way he stopped their activity.

"Once again I fooled myself into thinking I could stop the natural TrueBond process. I was convinced it was best for the both of us to stay away from each other." He gave a rueful smile. "I was pretty successful until I received a report showing her involved in the illegal slave trade. It alleged she had been an agent and coordinator on Earth's end." His collar became tight as he swallowed his embarrassment. A low murmur rolled through the crowd. "I'm ashamed to admit how quickly I fell for that ridiculous account and believed every accusation."

He described how he rushed to Aimee's quarters, fury riding every step. How dare she come aboard his ship to conclude her criminal activities and think to escape at the Exchange?

With a stiffened spine, he went on how once he entered her room, all cognitive thoughts fled. He admitted his cousin and security chief had followed him and tried to stop him. But by that time, the TrueBond had taken over. Qay wasn't about to share his and Aimee's intimate details, but he confessed it was then he and his mate physically came together.

"However," he made eye contact with several faces. "Panic set in once the TrueBond obsession receded and I rejected her without giving her a chance to defend herself." An angry rumble came from some of those in attendance. "I somehow thought I could still prevent the TrueBond process from happening. I told her under no uncertain terms she had to attend the Exchange and find a mate because it wasn't me." Now the growls were a little more forceful. He prayed his confession didn't cancel out Uncle Yaq's previous statements.

It didn't matter. He would see this to the end.

Resolved to complete the painful story, he continued how he found out Aimee wasn't chosen at the Exchange but instead was sold to the Friebbigh. He described her later escape from bondage on the planetoid Hiigar, where she secured not only a way to support herself but also found a safe place to live.

"Now I ask you, citizens of Zerin, to put yourself in her place. Imagine being a hundred thousand light years away from your home. You are without credits in unfamiliar territory. Think of the bravery, the unwavering ability to make the best of the situation she had endured to survive. In addition, we must take into account how she had no idea what the changes in her body meant. She experienced the enhancements of her senses, hair, and skin. It must have frightened her to realize she carried my child." He lovingly gazed at her again—his beautiful TrueBond with her exotic features and alluring persona. Her slightest change in emotion, every beat of her heart echoed inside him. His lungs expanded with pride that he could call this captivating creature his.

"As every Zerin child knows, a shared TrueBond is the most sacred in our culture. Only with our TrueBond can we sire children, only with our TrueBond can we interconnect on a physical as well as a spiritual level. Only with our TrueBond can we experience the deep joy of unconditional love with someone else. It is the only time in our lives when we are free to love who we are and who we were always meant to be." He spoke, never taking his eyes off hers. He gathered strength from her exotically blended eyes, now swimming in tears as she steadfastly returned his gaze.

Turning back, he continued his narrative. "It was during this time I did some serious soul searching and came to a painful conclusion after she was gone. I'd let my fears override my common sense and my biological instinct to claim my TrueBond. My fear blinded me to the false evidence of Aimee's involvement in the slave trade. We've since been able to determine the real traitor, Aja-ne L'len R'oxk, had compiled a fabricated conclusion and replaced it in the official reports. Of course, this came after the traitor escaped from the *StarChance*. But fortunately the Goddess takes pity on fools and exiled princes and we got a lead where Aimee was."

Skipping some of the more sensitive issues about FiPan and the outlaws Hayami and Fylgir, he now was at the point in his narrative when the Chancellor contacted him.

"As we followed the latest lead on where she could be, I was contacted by..."

All at once, pandemonium broke. A thin young Zerin male stood up in the middle of the audience and screamed, "WARRIORS OF LIGHT...RESIST!" In his hands, he held a metal alien weapon that he pointed at Aimee. It discharged with a resounding boom.

Adrenaline spiked and instinct took over. Qay leaped over the barrier from the podium where he stood. He had to get to her—the urgency to protect Aimee overrode any rational thought. Heartbeat thrashing in his ears, he rushed before it was too late.

No, no, no...everything slowed in real time as he raced toward her. He choked in horror when he recognized the alien projectile as the same type that hit his father. It streamed in her direction, a tiny piece of burning metal targeted to end her life.

He was achingly close. He dug deep inside and sprinted with everything he had to make it to her first.

A soft buzzing called to Qay from the buoyant darkness. No, wait...not buzzing. It was more like an indistinguishable sound of, "Zzzz-ZZzz-hngGGggh-Ppbhww-zZZzzzZZ" gently exhaling in his right ear.

Where was he? Why was it so hard to open his eyes? He lifted his left hand to reach over and confront the hypnotic sound. Hot pokers of pain shot down his arm, from the top of his shoulder to the burning tips of his fingers. He winced at the movement and put his hand down.

"You wake her up and I'll break your fingers," Ki's deep rumble declared. "She just fell asleep."

Heavy eyes flew open as Qay turned to the sound of his friend's voice. He tried to speak but his mouth was too dry. His vision blurred as his eyes darted around the healing room in search of something to drink before he spotted a glass on a table in front of Ki. He motioned his head toward it.

"Need something to drink?" Ki asked. He ran a finger against the rasp of hair at his jawline and contemplated Qay with an unflappable expression. He sat back in a large chair next to the bed with one ankle resting on his knee.

Qay tipped his head and licked dry lips.

"Well, don't wake her up and I'll give you some rejuvenating nectar." Qay's vision was bleary, but he had no trouble making out the stern scowl on the big male's face.

Frustrated, Qay swallowed an angry retort and agreed with an impatient nod of his head.

Ki got up and brought him the glass filled with the lifesaving thick black juice. "Here you go." Qay reached out and grasped the tall, thin goblet. He lifted his head and drank deeply of the tart beverage.

He cleared his throat before he handed the empty glass back to Ki. He flopped his head onto the pillow from the strain. A wave of wooziness caused his head to throb.

He waited for the dizziness to pass before he noticed the warm, fragrant female form next to him, nuzzled in the crook of his arm. Her head rested on the meaty part of his chest as her previous sounds dimmed to a rambling, soft whisper.

Contentment, sure and swift, swept through him. She was here—sound asleep and snuggling as close as physically possible.

"What are you doing here? Last time I saw you, you had to go to Maynwaring." He kept his nose at the top of Aimee's head and inhaled her intoxicating feminine scent.

"I heard what happened to you and, uh, came to make sure you didn't need me."

Qay smiled in Aimee's fragrant tresses, hiding his appreciation from the other male. To show gratitude would only make his friend uncomfortable. "Thank you for coming, my friend. So...tell me." He brought his attention back to Ki. He kept his voice low as he recalled jumping in front of Aimee to stop the alien projectile from ending her life.

"You were fortunate the alien missile only grazed your skin and didn't penetrate."

Qay made a rude noise. His left shoulder hurt worse than if a *danka* beast sunk its enormous fangs in and gnawed on it for hours. He glanced at his shoulder. The healing liquid that solidified over his skin was for serious wounds. He was shocked at how small the injury was. He would swear to the Holy Goddess it had taken off the entire shoulder.

"The weapon used on you was the same type as the one used against your father." Ki blinked in his ocular VDU and displayed a program to show an image of an alien-looking blaster. "This is an Earth weapon called a gun, or to be precise, a Desert Eagle. It is a semi-automatic pistol that uses a metal projectile called bullets. These little beauties are made from an Earth metal called lead." The image showed how the weapon worked. "This weapon is deadly when used for its created purpose. However, Zerins are highly allergic to lead poisoning. Good thing the healers have come up with an antidote or you'd have died. They are now giving the cure to your father."

"Is he all right?" Qay's gut tightened as he waited for the answer. Ki nodded his head and the knot lessened in his chest. "Is he awake?"

"Not yet, but the healers are convinced he'll recover soon." He blinked and changed the scene. The image became one of a young, painfully thin Zerin male standing in the stadium of Council Hall.

"WARRIORS OF LIGHT – RESIST!" With that cry, the young male stood and pointed the weapon at Aimee. The image changed to show Qay's flying body as it intercepted the projectile. He'd knocked

Aimee out of her chair when the bullet struck him. At the same time, the royal guards rushed to subdue the young male. Before anyone could stop him, the male put the barrel in his mouth and pulled the trigger. The resulting blast took off half of the back of his head.

Shocked at the self-violence, Qay gaped at Ki for clarification. "Who was he and what is 'Warriors of Light'?" The slight movement he'd done earlier with his left hand caused a painful internal throb. He wasn't about to disturb Aimee, so he didn't move a muscle.

"You wake her up and I'll break your fingers." His cousin Yesult issued her dire warning as D'zia and Uncle Yaq followed her.

"What is with everyone wanting to break my fingers?" Qay complained. He glanced at his sleeping mate and allowed the subject to change. After all, taking care of her was his highest priority. "Why are you all so concerned about her sleeping?"

Yesult grunted and pulled up an empty chair to sit closer to him. She kept her voice low. "You've been out for two days and Aimee hasn't left your side the whole time. We barely got her to eat, much less sleep." She motioned to the large chair on the other side of the bed where a small pillow and a blanket laid abandoned on the cushion. "The only way she would get the sleep she needed was to lay next to you, so when she finally dozed off, Ki moved her. She needs to sleep." The last warning came with narrow eyes and arms crossed. Qay was surprised to see his cousin out in public with her gray tunic and pants wrinkled and limp. It didn't appear as if Yesult had been home lately.

He gave Aimee a soft squeeze on her hip and she snuggled deeper into him. The contact between them gave him a sense of righteous calm. He tore his attention away from her to focus past the constant throbbing pain so he could make sense of the conversation.

In a low tone, he continued with his questions. "What do we know about the shooter?"

"Not much, unfortunately," D'zia piped. He sat in a chair next to his sister. He was as disheveled as she was, his open collar shirt rumpled and left untucked over his dark pants. "He was another lost citizen at a young age, much like Aja was in her youth." A thoughtful frown creased his brow. "I bet there's a connection there somewhere." He shook his head and continued. "Anyway, there is no known link between him and the Chancellor as Ki assumed," he said. His eyes flashed in anticipation toward the larger male. "But, I'm dying to dig deeper into that idea."

Qay was relieved when Ki let D'zia and the others know what had happened between him and the Chancellor. He was exasperated, because without proof, it was a moot point. "Has the council come back with a verdict on my exile or TrueBond status?"

All four heads shook in denial.

"We expect a ruling any time now," Uncle Yaq replied. "I have faith because my, ah, inner contacts in the council are saying only positive things."

"Well, *danka* shit." Resigned, he gave a groan of frustration. He fixated on D'zia. "Do you still have contacts with the Imperial Forces?" At D'zia's murmur of agreement, Qay continued. "Since I can't give you a direct order, can you discreetly talk to someone there to look into the Chancellor's dealings, off the record?"

D'zia's smile was wide and self-satisfied at the same time. "Discreet is my middle name." Qay had to resist doing a human eye roll at D'zia's inaccurate description of himself.

"Besides, I'm already on it," D'zia continued. "Believe it or not, the Imperial Forces are a bright bunch of fellows. There have been suspicions floating around about the Chancellor's activities for the last decade. They've been trying to infiltrate his inner circle for quite some time now."

He shifted with a grimace on his face as he glanced back and forth from his father and sister. He caressed the end of his warriors braid. "I have an idea, but I'd rather talk to you about it when you're feeling better."

Yesult glared at her brother. Whatever his idea was, it wasn't going to make his family happy. Good thing his aunt wasn't in the room or D'zia would never get away with making a cryptic statement like that.

Speaking of which, "Where is Aunt Ah'Mira? I would have thought she'd be here." He addressed his uncle.

"She's visiting her family in the Western Providence because her mother is terminally ill. We don't expect her back for a while yet." Uncle Yaq crossed his ankle over his knee and held it with his right hand. "But be warned, she will expect you to vid her as soon as you're released from the healers' unit."

Since she was the mother he'd never known, he had no desire to hurt her any further than he had by his past actions. He wasn't about to start by not talking to her once the exile was lifted.

"Before we leave, I want to let you know I submitted a counter-point on the legal issues of you bonding with a human who was slated for the Exchange." Yesult glanced over at her brother. "With what you told me before you were shot, I reviewed the initial meeting between the two of you and came up with a brilliant plan to circumvent the apparent law preventing a Zerin from bonding with a human."

Qay fought a mixture of hope and dread. With Yesult on the case, Qay was certain to find a way around the alien mating law. Ignoring his heated face, he asked, "So my earlier assumption proved to be correct?"

"Well, let's see. The Federation law states a citizen of Zerin cannot legally take a mate from a non-Federation system. As we all know, Earth is not a member of the Federation Consortium and thus Aimee is not a citizen."

Qay and the others in the room nodded their heads in agreement.

"And because Zerin helped to set up the Exchange, we've agreed to have a 'hands-off' approach concerning our males intermingling with the human females. All Earth females are for the Exchange only, especially since the Zerin people aren't in any danger of becoming extinct. Thus we created a law to forbid a Zerin male to take an Earth woman out of the Exchange. There is no law that states the crown prince can only mate with a Zerin female. It is, however, one of our more sacred traditions."

Yesult's matter-of-fact tone worried him. He glanced at Ki for reassurance that the procedures were in place for him and Aimee to make a quick getaway if necessary. Ki's calm demeanor told him volumes, and he relaxed to pay attention to his cousin.

"So, having said that, what could you possibly say or do to overrule the current law?" Qay asked.

Her smile was one of smug superiority as she sat back. "Nothing." At Qay's frown, she continued. "Actually, it was quite simple since no laws were broken." She crossed her legs and tilted her head to one side. "First of all, you and Aimee consummated the TrueBond before coming to the Exchange. Thus you made her not only a citizen of the Federation Consortium but one of Zerin as well." She gave a slight smirk. "She became a citizen just like the other Earth women who mate when chosen in the Exchange. And because of your exiled status, your position of crown prince wasn't part of the equation." She gave a slight cough as she continued. "As for the rule of her not being taken out of the Exchange, it's a moot point because it's my understanding Aimee attended the Exchange. Didn't she?"

Sheepishly, Qay gave his agreement. The guilt of making his True-Bond participate in the Exchange was a shame he would have to live with for the rest of his life.

"There you have it. You never took her out of the Exchange, she just wasn't chosen while there. Therefore, the other systems can't make a claim they never had a chance with her. It's their own fault none of them chose her."

"But someone could argue she wasn't chosen because she was bonded to Qay." Uncle Yaq voiced the fear as it occurred to Qay.

Yesult shook her head. "That would be a flimsy allegation at best. It is a well-known documented fact all Zerin TrueBond mates display the MalDerVon scroll, and it had not appeared on her. And we have the vid to prove it."

For the first time since waking up, Qay briefly closed his eyes in gratitude. "I can't begin to tell you how much I appreciate everything you have done, Yesult."

"Well, hopefully, the council will see things my way. Anyway, it's time we leave and let you rest." She stood and gestured to the other males in the room. "You are not going to be released at least for another day, so you might as well get some sleep while you can."

He checked his mate; she was still sound asleep. Frowning, Qay turned back to them while Aimee snored softly beside him. "Is she okay? Is she hurt?"

Uncle Yaq gave him a small smile. "She's fine, as long as you let her sleep next to you. As a newly mated pair, separation for any length of time puts a toll on the both of you. Rest, we will come back once we have word on the council's decisions."

As his family stood, Qay took in their tired faces and rumpled appearances. "I'm not the only one who needs their rest." He waved them out. "You all look like you haven't slept in a week. Go home." He tightened his other hand on Aimee's soft hip. "We'll be fine." He looked each one in the eye. "We both thank you and appreciate what you've done for us." He closed his eyes and took in a deep breath. "Now get out of here and don't come back for at least one sleep cycle." He opened his eyes and met Ki's unusual blue-green combination. "Except you. I need to talk to you before you leave."

Yesult gave him a kiss on the cheek and his uncle and cousin gave him manly slaps on his arm before they shuffled out.

Ki waited for the others to leave before he spoke. "I will have a personal guard outside of this room at all times. People I trust with my life as well as yours."

Qay relaxed. He always appreciated Ki's ability to anticipate what he needed.

"Thank you. Until we know who tried to kill Aimee, I need help in protecting her until I can get on my feet again." He stared at Ki. "But I want your word that if the ruling comes down that my exile status has not been rescinded, you'll not to let anything happen to her. She is to be protected at all times." He paused to make sure his friend understood what he asked of him. It would be treason to go against the council to help Qay and his TrueBond escape Zerin justice. "Now would be the time to back out."

Ki's snort of annoyance was comparable to one D'zia made before he gave a smart-ass comment. "While I was away, I made arrangements for the *both* of you. Just as planned. I have to say, it's a good thing you're lying flat on your ass because I'd have to knock you on it for even suggesting I'd do anything else."

Satisfied, Qay rested on the soft bed. "You could try." He yawned. "All right, get out of here. I can't wait to hear what Maynwaring has you doing. Stay alive and come back so you can tell me all about it."

The big man gave a grunt of agreement before he left and closed off the room behind him.

Chapter TWELVE

Aimee

Aimee had no idea where she was. She brought a hand to her eyes to rub them open so she could glance around. Wait...Yeah, she'd been resting in a chair in the healing chamber with Qay. The spicy, warm scent of the muscular chest she lay on told her someone had moved her and she was now in the bed with him.

Boobs squished on his solid chest, she had her right leg wrapped around his. His big arm was around her, and his large palm rested loosely on the globe of her ass.

Her very naked ass.

Not wanting to wake Qay up, she tentatively pulled her leg back. His body tensed and his breathing changed. He was up.

Ha. He was more than *up*. She smiled. Her alien woke up just like a human man, with an erection hard as steel. The blazing heat pouring out of his protruding cock had her skin pebbling along her thigh.

She itched to slide her fingers over that bad boy. Damn, her libido was shooting off the charts. The urge to grasp him and watch his body respond up close was overwhelming. She squeezed her vaginal walls together as she visualized him embedded deep inside.

Bad Aimee! Stop lusting after the injured man.

"Going somewhere, *Ahyoka*?" His deep rumble had her tummy quivering in appreciation. Jeez, all he had to do was speak and she'd come from his commanding voice alone.

Where was her pride? Where was her dignity? Under the control of a shameless hussy, that's where.

Aimee put a lock on her wayward, lurid thoughts and glanced back at him in the dim light. His features were stamped with possessive intent that tightened his face. She shuddered in reaction but pushed away from him as gently as she could. Someone had to think about his weakened state, for God's sake.

"Qay, how are you feeling? How is your shoulder?"

He let go of her ass as he rolled over onto his right side and gingerly put his left hand around her neck. "I am fine, don't worry about me." He moved his fingers to the back and massaged her with tender fingers. Why was he moving around so much? He had to be in pain. Then the words he'd spoken in the council chamber came rushing back. Her face, neck, and ears heated in a scorching blush.

"Are you uncomfortable about something?" He moved his left hand to rest on the top of her shoulder and gave her a slight squeeze. "Tell me."

Aimee squirmed in embarrassment. "I dunno—I," She searched his face, taking in the widened iridescent dark green pupil surrounded by emerald. "Did you mean what you said?"

His eyes burned with everything she'd ever dreamed of whenever she'd fantasized about a man looking at her. "You mean in the council chambers?" His full lips turned into a lopsided grin around his scruffy beard. Her eyes automatically watched his tempting mouth as it parted with each word he spoke.

Unable to speak, she nodded in agreement. His overt sexual overtones made it hard to pay attention to his answer. He'd lowered his head to nuzzle the soft skin below her ear as a deep moan vibrated under a small chuckle. "Yes, I meant every word I said." He lifted his head as his eyes narrowed and his lips thinned. "The only thing left out was my apology to you. Can you ever forgive me for the way I treated you?"

Aimee searched his face. His wide eyes and pensive expression reassured her that his sincerity was real. She recalled Qay's apology to her with his entire world watching. If she hadn't witnessed it herself, she wouldn't have thought him capable of admitted his wrongdoing in such a way. A warm wave of love infused her and she let go of her fears and doubts. She placed her palm in the middle of his chest and gave a sincere answer as his heart thudded heavily under her fingers.

"It depends. How good are you at groveling?" She gave him a smoldering smile so he'd know she was teasing him.

"Oh, I am a master," he boasted before his lips tasted hers with a firm touch. His tongue peeked out to lap across the seam of her mouth, demanding entrance. The sweet taste of his passion had her opening eagerly to join with him.

As her tongue entangled with his, he gave a hard twitch. She pulled away from him. He had to be in pain. Aimee saw the evidence in the paleness of his skin.

"Qay, honestly. You've just been shot and have been unconscious for days. Don't you think you should take it easy?" The dilated eyes looking back at her might be because of desire and not pain. The sight of the inner ring of his green irises blended seamlessly with lighter outer rims made her tremble in anticipation. Those panty-melting orbs moved from hers and focused on her peaked nipple pointing at him. With a predatory lift of his lips, he made a move to envelop the rock-hard nub with his eager mouth.

Oh, crap. It was going to be up to her to be the sensible one. "Qay." She gave a feeble push as she tried to get him to lie down. She squirmed out of his hold and sat up. The blanket pooled away, leaving her bare upper body exposed. "If you're going to be unreasonable about this, you need to lay back and let me take care of you."

Confusion marred his features before he submitted with a slight groan. As Aimee pulled the covers back, she exposed his glorious nudity for her pleasure. She'd seen him bare before but never had the opportunity to indulge her curiosity up close.

My. Oh. My. Her previous assessment didn't do him justice and adequately describe the bounty laid out before her. While the words she'd used when she'd first seen him were a good start, adding a couple of new ones would not be amiss.

Taut flesh—to explore, caresses, and memorize.

Chiseled perfection—a virtual rolling mass of muscles to have fun in.

Okay, so she used more than a couple of words. But, come on, the man had a body Adonis would kill to possess. His seductive pearlescent tan skin reflected the low light of the room. She scrutinized him from head to toe before she stopped at his burgeoning erection. His magnificent manhood was long, wide, and thick. She reached to grasp all that masculine beauty for herself.

Yeah, come to mama.

Oral sex had not been one of her favorite pastimes, so that didn't explain how her mouth salivated at the mere thought of lavishing all his gloriousness with her tongue.

As she lowered her head, Qay touched her upper arm and stopped her.

"What are you doing?"

Puzzled, Aimee tore her focus away from her treat to gaze at him. "What do you mean what am I doing? I would think it was obvious." Her attention focused on the generosity in front of her. "This big boy and I are going to become well acquainted."

His features tightened. "How?"

"Don't tell me you haven't had a blow job before."

"Blow job?" It was cute how confusion crinkled his brow.

"You know a hummer?"

His eyes crinkled.

"Sucking chrome off a tailpipe?" Okay, bad choice, Aimee. How would an alien know what a tailpipe was?

"Okay, how about 'playing the skin flute'?"

Again, nothing except a vein popping at his neck.

"Honestly, Qay, you went down on me, is so hard to believe I would want to do the same for you?"

Now the pinch on his face cleared up. "You wish to put my penis in your mouth?" The eager anticipation matched the wide grin on his face.

She couldn't resist the urge to tease him. "Unless you don't want me to..." Show her any male in the universe who'd turn down a blowjob, and she'd show you a big fat liar.

And her mate was anything but a big fat liar.

"No, no. I would love to experience this with you."

"You're sure, now?" Her pause stretched out the teasing. "I wouldn't want to do anything to make you uncomfortable." During their conversation, Aimee had never let go of his rigid flesh. His natural lubrication made it easy for her to give him a nice steady hand job. Up and down, around and around, her fist manipulated the pliable skin repeatedly.

She giggled as he panted with his eyes crossed. She only hoped he wouldn't have a heart attack once she sucked him.

Without further delay, she lowered her head and flicked her tongue at the underside of his inflexible cock. She rolled her eyes to see his reaction and wasn't disappointed when he drew in a shuddering breath. Once again she focused on the job at hand *(snicker)* and tentatively placed the flared, crested head between her lips. A burst of salty gooeyness had her eagerly swallowing more of his length to get a better taste of the tantalizing flavors.

Lost in chasing the spicy-sweetness around and up his impressive length, she was startled when his large hands grasped her under her arms and lifted her up and onto his lap.

"No," his whispered gasp had her smiling in feminine power. "Stop, no more." His lips flattened. "I have to—have to finish inside you." His strained undertone sent shivers down her spine. Her wet pussy completely agreed as her stiff clit thrummed consent.

Together they eagerly positioned her body's opening over the wide expanse of his gleaming cock. Their gazes locked as her body encompassed him.

"Yes, take me. That's it." His hitched voice broke as he burrowed his cock deeper. She relaxed stubborn tissues to allow his girth access. As she joined physically with her alien mate, she knew he was everything she'd dreamed he'd be. Nothing in her past had prepared her for the full experience of them together and the righteous joy sharing with him gave her.

Already soaked, she settled around him with little effort. Her vaginal walls massaged as she adjusted to his thickness.

"You are so tight. I love how your pussy grips me." His lowered eyes held her captive. His stare caught her as their bodies moved in a synchronic rhythm. Masculine hips danced upward in a slow pace beneath her, steadfastly pumping low, deep thrusts while she squeezed her inner muscles.

"Yes, *Ahyoka*—take all of me." Her slick body grabbed him greedily, trying to keep him inside as much as possible. Loving the freedom of being on top, she alternated between going up and down and rounding her hips like a seasoned belly dancer. Soon the room echoed with groans of shared excitement.

She leaned down and licked his sensitive ear and breathed, "Like it? Is it good?"

In retaliation, he held her hips in place to plow deeper. The delicious friction from his natural lubrication on his chest and arms had his iridescent tan skin glowing with each dip and bump. Unable to control the impulse, she lowered to slide her chest over his to experience the slick feeling on her sensitive nipples. Conscious of keeping the baby bump protected, her hands grasped his thick forearms for added support. Their skin slipping together produced groans of pleasure as a ferocious tingling detonated with each touch. The slightest brush of her body against his brought her to the edge of completion.

"Oh, Qay...that's..." Immersed in the erotic dance between them, she jumped when he sat up and reached down to guide her legs to encircle his waist. He bent his knees to help support her back. It was such a smooth transition he never lost his pace. This new position spearheaded untouched nerve endings and caused her lady-bits to swoon in ecstatic joyful abandon. "Yes—right there—oh!"

Low and slow, her inner walls convulsed. The working of this thick cock had her complete attention and it was hard to notice Qay's stumbling movements as the carnality bloomed inside and threatened to overwhelm her.

No...no, she had to hang on. She wanted to...savor....the...experience a little longer before she let her body detonate. Too bad, her lover had other ideas.

He reached between them to rub her clit between his fingers. "Come for me now!" he growled in demand.

Her body obeyed.

The unexpected force of gratification made her wrap her arms around his neck to hang on for dear life. Unable to keep pace with the depth of his forceful strokes, she had no choice but to follow with natural abandon. Gasping for air, she reached up to the tips of his ears, the overly sensitive part of her mate. The touch guaranteed to tip him over.

She leaned in to whisper, "Come for *me*, lover." When she stroked the sensitive skin, he gave a loud roar of completion.

Hot and heavy, his pulsating cock spurted steaming jets of seed, coating her welcoming channel as it pushed her orgasm harder. Sharp and swift, her convulsing body burst open like a flower unfurling in the morning sun. Transformed, she joined her mate on a sensual, emotional level she'd never experienced before.

An eternity passed when the journey back to the physical plane left her dumbfounded. She hated to leave such a glorious place. However, when Qay tightened his arms around her, all was well in the universe again.

A sharp grunt of pain from Qay told her he'd overexerted himself. "Qay, lay back down before you hurt yourself more." She tried to keep her tone more concerned than bossy.

"She's already bossing me around like a TrueBond." The indulgent smile came before he grimaced. He laid his palms on her thighs, and he lay flat on the mattress.

"I'm glad you're here." His soft words warmed her heart. She gave him a gentle kiss before she straightened up and disengaged their bodies, savoring his rigid his penis rolling through her once more. She lay beside him on his uninjured side and pulled the light covering over them before she rested her arm on his lightly slick chest.

Aimee waited until her breathing slowed before she asked. "How did I end up naked next to you?"

At his appreciative chuckle, she raised her head. "I asked an orderly to help me." He rested his hand on top of hers, over his heart.

Her fingers caressed his warm skin. She swirled the silky, short chest hair as she put her thigh between his. Tired, she closed her eyes. Yep, time for a little nap.

The door to the healer's room faded open and his cousins strolled in.

"Lights on. Hope you're both decent in here," D'zia announced.

"I could have sworn I had the orderly lock the door," Qay grumbled next to her ear.

"Ha, no locked door can keep me out," his younger relative boasted. Yesult rolled her eyes. It amazed Aimee how many humanlike gestures the Zerins sported.

"D'zia, let the adults talk. So go sit over there and mind your manners." Yesult waved to a chair against the wall. She wore a fresh tunic and pant set in a brilliant lavender while her hair was smartly styled in a chignon ponytail. Her stern features mirrored her no-nonsense clip. Aimee's dry tongue stuck to the roof of her mouth. Usually, someone only had that expression when giving bad news...

Yesult's set expression lasted only about two seconds before she let out a loud whoop and reached down to hug Qay in a bone-crushing embrace. "We did it! We did it!"

Confused, Aimee searched D'zia for answers. No help there, he was busy hugging Yesult hugging Qay. Obeying his sister to sit in a corner didn't seem to be a high priority for him.

She pulled her arm away from Qay where it'd been laying. Aimee sat up and pulled the light blanket to cover her nakedness. "What's going on?"

The three Zerins were too busy talking over one another to hear her. Good thing Uncle Yaq walked in and went over to her side of the bed. He wore a light turquoise open-collar shirt tucked into formfitting black pants. Today, he wore a silver hoop in the tip of his right ear with his tawny brown hair pulled back at the top in a loose bun while the rest of his tresses gathered in a man pony to flow down his back. "How are you feeling this morning, my dear?"

"Fine, I'm fine." She gestured to the group of three next to her as she pulled the sheet tighter around her breasts. The hug between the three was over, but a loose circle of arms kept them together. "What is going on?"

"Don't mind them. The Zerin people are a family-oriented society and Qay's exile has been hard on us." Even with the yellow at his temples and the slight crow's feet at his captivating eyes, Qay's uncle was a handsome man. His calm demeanor appeared to be a constant personality trait, something Aimee appreciated whenever she was with him.

He pulled a chair over and sat. "The word from the council has come down, and the news is good. They unanimously approved the rescinding of Qay's exile, ensuring the continuation of the E'etu family rule."

"Do you mind if I ask you something?" He gave her an encouraging gesture to continue. "If Qay were out of the picture, wouldn't you be king? Or your son?"

Qay and his cousins must have heard her question since they stopped talking to give her equal expressions of horror.

"Shut your mouth!" D'zia's overdramatic screech would have made any diva proud. "Even if I could, I would never—I mean *never* want to take bugly's place!" He shuddered for emphasis. He'd pulled the light acorn brown of his hair back with a lift over his forehead and the sides sectioned into a French braid. The rest of the tresses were in a thick tail, held in place by a band of hair. His blinding white pullover shirt molded to his wide chest, which he left untucked over loose navy tunic pants.

Uncle Yaq frowned. "Who or what is a bugly?"

Aimee had to smile at D'zia's use of English slang. "It's the words 'butt ugly' meshed together. Hey!" He'd better not be talking about Qay. "Who do you think you're calling bugly, mister?" She was going to jump up and bite his ear off again. She directed her glare at the tip she'd previously munched on before.

"Ouch, lady! Lay off the ears." D'zia's whine was genuine enough as he sheltered his threatened appendage under a cupped hand.

Ignoring his son, Uncle Yaq continued. "Neither my children nor I could lay claim to the throne. By Zerin law only the eldest child of the eldest child may rule."

Before she asked more succession questions, Yesult took over the conversation. "Attention people! That is not the only good news I have."

Qay raised an eyebrow in anticipation.

"Your father is awake and asking for you."

"Why didn't you say so?" Excited, Qay jumped out of bed, uncaring about his nudity. "Where are some clothes?" His head whipped back and forth as he searched the room. D'zia got up and produced dark pants and a light green tunic from a hidden drawer on the furthest wall. While Qay dressed, his hair automatically straightened itself and plaited into a loose braid down his back.

Aimee loved watching his excited reaction. He acted like a kid at Christmas morning getting his favorite toy. She admired how much he wanted to see the father who'd exiled him. Her eyes prickled with unshed tears as she gave in the wistful memory of her own parents whom she'd lost several years ago. The three of them had been so close, both Mom and Dad had been only children of elderly parents. They'd had the normal difficulties any family experienced, but she always knew she had their unconditional love.

She missed having a close family. As she watched Qay interact with his uncle and cousins, her heart filled with contentment. She was a part of this family now. No one could replace her parents, but the E'etu family was a good start. She placed a palm across her tightening pregnant belly. She was ready for her family to expand.

Before she knew it, Qay was dressed and ready to run out the door. He stopped at the foot of the bed. "Come on, Aimee. You have to meet my father." He was like a child, bouncing from foot-to-foot in impatience.

Oh, hell no. "There is no way I'll meet your father for the first time looking like this. I need to shower and find some clothes..."

"You three go ahead. I'll stay and help Aimee get ready." Yesult, the lifesaver, stepped in.

Indecision warred on Qay's features. Though he was eager to see his father for the first time in years, she realized he'd wait for her to join him.

"Please go," she told him. There wasn't any reason to hold him up. Besides, he'd only make her nervous hovering around her. "Don't worry, I'll be right behind you."

He nodded at Yesult. Before he left, he vaulted over to her and gave her a kiss hot enough for her toes to curl. No doubt about it, the man sure could work the lip lock.

"You must come right away. No delaying." A stern command if she'd ever heard one.

Well, you can take the commander out of the ship and all... She sighed. Arrogant cutie. That's what she got for wanting her own alpha mate. "Just go. I promise I'm right behind you." At least she hoped she would be. Good thing Yesult was staying to help her get clothes and show her where to meet up with him.

"Go, Qay! We won't be long." Yesult shooed him and the rest of the family out. "Tell Uncle Abzu we're coming."

He squinted at Yesult before he agreed and moved away. "You have five clicks."

"Oh sure, I'll get right on that," Yesult replied. Aimee rolled her eyes behind his back. Five clicks, my ass. She would not meet his father, much less the king of an entire planet, with only a few moments to get ready. Delusional much?

She and Yesult shared impatient looks when the males left. "Okay," Yesult said as she whipped off the blanket Aimee had in a death grip. "Let's get you dressed."

She went to the same place D'zia had pulled out Qay's clothes and retrieved a gorgeous set of sunny yellow pantaloons and matching tunic top. She shook out the ensemble for Aimee. The clothes had a silken, satiny appearance. The material was so luxurious she couldn't wait to touch it. It wasn't slippery like satin or silk, but soft like a fluffy pillow made of the finest cotton.

"Oh my God, it's beautiful." Aimee gazed at Yesult, confused. "What, this was lying around?"

Yesult's tinkling laughter made Aimee smile. "No, of course not. I ordered clothes for you and brought them here as Qay recuperated." She went to another part of the same wall and opened it with a press on an indent. A bathing facility was inside, similar to the one she'd used aboard the *StarChance.*

"Do you need any help in there?" Yesult asked taking the clothes over to the bed and placing them there before she added a pair of flat yellow slippers to match.

"No, I'll be okay." Aimee walked into the other room.

"Qay's under a lot of stress right now, so I wouldn't, um—what's the word?" Yesult paused. "Dawdle? Yes, don't dawdle if you can help it."

"No worries, I'll be right out."

True to her word, she rushed as quickly as she could, scrubbing her hair and body in record time. When she came out of the refresher room with towels around her head and body, she walked over to the bed.

She bent to unwrap her hair and flipped her head back. Her hair took over and straightened into a loose braid that tapered into a low tail down her back. She secretly enjoyed the awesomeness of her hair as she concentrated on drying so she could put on her pretty clothes.

She donned the decadent outfit and put on the footwear. She flexed her foot and admired the stitching around the top in a darker—honey color. She rushed to the mirror in the refresher room and had to gasp at her reflection. With her darker hair braided, showing the white birthmark running near her right temple, the bright coloring of the tunic and pants offset the iridescent sheen to her pale skin. She looked like a fairy princess.

With Qay reinstated as crown prince, she guessed she was a princess. Imagine, her, Aimee Elizabeth Gwiazdowski from Grand Rapids, Michigan, a princess of a whole planet. The idea was so outlandish she had to snicker.

Reality crashed. Well—*crap*. She knew nothing about being a princess. She'd better sit her TrueBond down and have him spell things out for her as soon as possible. She didn't want to mess up their lives if she could help it.

"Everything okay in there?" Qay's cousin walked toward her with a puzzled look on her face.

Aimee beamed as a smile curved her mouth. She'd deal with the whole "princess" business later. Bottom line, she didn't care if Qay was a prince, a commander of a spaceship, or an exiled citizen running from the law. She loved him no matter what and wanted to be with him. Whatever challenges their life brought, they would face them together. For now, all she wanted to do was get out of this room and find him.

"Yep, everything is just perfect."

Qay

Qay hadn't had sweaty palms since the last time he'd seen his father. He chuckled at the memory. Back then, he'd been an arrogant male escorted to face his father's wrath in his private chambers over the latest stupid stunt he'd committed. At the time, he assumed it was no big deal and it wouldn't differ from all the other times he'd been in a similar situation.

But by damn, he'd been wrong. He took in a deep breath. Now wasn't the time to bring up the painful memory of when his father exiled him. He picked up the pace to the healing recovery chamber.

He'd seen his father since he'd been back, but watching a comatose form floating in the restoration chamber wasn't the same as seeing him awake and coherent. He stood outside the closed room and ignored his uncle and cousin as he took a moment to compose himself. Straightening his shoulders, he put his hand on the indent to open it.

And there he was. His father might be a pale, gaunt shadow of his former self, but he was still the daunting man from Qay's memory. His throat tightened as he swallowed his concern. It wouldn't do to have his father open his eyes and the first thing he saw was his only son with unshed tears.

He went to his father's bedside, amazed he was awake.

The familiar electric green orbs swam with unshed tears.

"Qayyum," his father's choked voice rasped. Qay enveloped his parent and held him close, as he had not done for over fifty years. The knot in his chest loosened and dissipated into a small wave of contentment at the familiar fragrance of wood spice. The years melted and he was once again a small child in the arms of his beloved parent.

"Father." He couldn't say anything else. He stayed in his father's thin arms before he straightened to clasp his elder's hands. "Father, I am so glad to see you."

The smile on his father's face was priceless. "Much better than the last time we spoke, eh son?" A slight frown creased his brow. "Are you all right? I hear you were injured by the same device that was used against me."

"I am well, only a little sore." A nudge at the back of his knees told him Uncle Yaq brought him a chair to sit on. Not taking his eyes off his father, he kept a grip on his parent's hand as his companions pulled their own chairs over.

The warm smile his father gave Uncle Yaq and D'zia told him they'd already been there. His father's eyes wandered around the room. A puzzled expression crossed his face. "Did you forget some-one, son?" His gem-green eyes so like his own narrowed on the MalDerVon scroll and the dark moss-colored crystal in the middle.

"My TrueBond, Aimee, is hopefully right behind us. Yesult stayed with her to help her get ready to meet you." He needed reassurance, so Qay brought the frail hand to his chest. "You will love her, Father." He paused to make sure he had the man's full attention. "But I want to make sure you understand something first."

A firm expression clouded his face. What happened next would determine the rest of his life. "Are you aware she is a human?" His father gave him a slight nod and squeezed his fingers in an encouraging sign. Continuing, Qay said, "The council has rescinded my exile status, but they have not ruled on me having a human as my TrueBond."

An alarmed expression crossed his father's face. "How long ago did the council meet about this matter?" His father's voice was weak, but the royal inflection was present.

"Same day Uncle Yaq submitted your request. Unfortunately, be-fore I could finish giving my argument about our TrueBond status, we were attacked." Thank the Goddess the burning pain in his shoul-der was bearable now. Even so, something as inconvenient as pain didn't stop him from making love to his exotic mate earlier. The memory of their shared ecstasy made his cock stir in interest.

Enough. Time to move on to more pressing matters. "Father, I am so grateful you rescinded my exile status. I will do everything within my power to make you proud of me and I beg that you forgive me for the pain I've caused you. Nothing could bring me more joy than to rule at your side." He laid his father's hand back to rest on the bed but kept it on his own. "But please understand, if the council comes back with a ruling that Aimee cannot be accepted as my TrueBond, I will leave Zerin forever and take her with me."

Silent tears gathered on his father's unlined face and rolled down toward his temple.

"I am so sorry, Father. I would do anything to not disappoint you again, but..."

"Son, stop." His father was too weak to sit up on his own, but with a flick of his wrist to the controls next to him, he had the bed move him into a sitting position. "You are misunderstanding my emotions." He pulled Qay toward him and once again his father was the formidable force that ruled a planet. "These are tears of happiness because you have finally become worthy of ruling our people."

Qay pulled back and stared at his father in confusion. He glanced at his uncle and cousin for help. Normally their identical looks of exasperation would be amusing, now they only confused him.

"Lord love a duck, cousin..." D'zia smirked at Qay.

His father's eyes rounded first at D'zia and then to Uncle Yaq. "What is a duck?"

"Ignore him, he's an idiot. Papa dropped him on his head several times," Yesult announced, walking through the door.

"Oh come on! How could you even know something like that?" D'zia crossed his arms in defense. "You were a baby the same time I was."

"I'm talking about last week." Yesult rushed the last few steps to her uncle to hug him, unwittingly breaking the contact between Qay and his father. "Uncle Abzu, you are looking wonderful!" She stood up and wiped the tears from her eyes. "I am so glad to see you finally awake."

Qay took advantage of the distraction to stand and look behind Yesult for Aimee.

Shouldn't she be with Yesult?

"Yesult." Impatient fear caused his heart to race. "Where is Aimee?"

He stood and stopped. There she was, straight and proud at the threshold.

Time stood still.

She was resplendent in the bright yellow outfit she wore. The iridescent sheen to her creamy white skin glowed as her otherworldly, multicolored single iris eyes shone with love for him. He didn't need a TrueBond bridge to know what she was thinking. It was clear for anyone to see.

His lungs expanded with pride. Here she was—a supposedly fragile human female who taught him the meaning of what was strong and important in life—family and putting them first. His responsibility was to ensure not only for their safety but also anything which could affect them. For the first time, he was excited about being a prince, with a say in what shaped their culture and overall guiding the galaxy. Not just for his people, but for his TrueBond and their children and all sentient beings in the Milky Way.

With her by his side, he could hardly wait.

He had the urge to grab her and run to the nearest level surface to make love to her for a long time, again and again...

He stepped toward her but his uncle grabbed his forearm. "Qay, introduce your TrueBond to your father," he admonished.

Oh, right. Introduce Aimee to his father.

Then he'd take her somewhere to get horizontal.

She bit her bottom lip as she clasped her hands in front of her as he approached. The shy look on her face caused him to enfold her in his arms.

"I love you, Aimee of Earth." He never wanted to let her go. By the Goddess, it was so good to hold her in his arms. He shuddered to think he was almost stupid enough to not let this happen between them. He held her tighter as her sweet flavor surrounded him.

"Come, *Ahyoka*. Meet my father."

Aimee

Aimee had hung back when Yesult entered the room. At first, it was because she didn't want to intrude on a family reunion, but when she heard the heartfelt joy in his father's voice, she didn't want to interrupt. Qay might have been confused about his father's tears, but Aimee got it.

His father was proud his son was ready to take an immovable stand about something important. It humbled her that he was talking about her—she was the reason this proud man was able to return to his family and reclaim his birthright.

Edgy and excited, Aimee heard Qay asking Yesult where she was. Though nerves sizzled along her body, with pride she stepped through the doorway.

Qay came toward her. Her TrueBond enfolded her into his arms and brought her home.

EPILOGUE

Lora

The next day, deep inside the Chancellor's Palace on the Federation Consortium space station, orbiting the planet Zerin

The first thing Lora Callahan became aware of was the sludge coating her brain. The second was the burn that squeezed the back of her neck. The third thing...well, there was no third thing. She jerked awake.

Where was she?

Crap! Wait...the last thing Lora remembered was attending the Exchange, a program an alien race, the Zerins, created. Once there, it never occurred to her she was in danger. For God's sake, she'd been in a room filled with hundreds of people under the Zerin's watchful eyes. She should have been safe. Boy was she wrong. Like a frantic crazed person, she'd been busy searching through a smorgasbord of lusty, beautiful alien males when—*ow!* A sharp pain pinched her neck.

Did she fall?

She didn't remember falling. One minute she'd been in the middle of hundreds of bodies, and the next...she was...here.

"Here" was where she lay on a damp, cobbled floor. The uneven rocks painfully dug into her head, back, and bottom. With a wobbled, shaky breath, she coughed at the moldy smell of rotten eggs. Her tongue was thick and dry as she shivered in the damp air.

Oh, eck! Even her tunic and leggings stuck to her skin.

Okay, time to sit up. After a few pathetic tries, she finally levered her body into an upright position and panted, completely exhausted. Now for the next problem...she couldn't see anything. It was so black it was hard to tell if her eyes were open. At least nothing hurt, except for her head. Yay for small favors.

A distant, stomping sound made her tilt her head. What was that? Her stomach dropped with a hard thud. Was someone coming?

The blackness eased into a murky gray. Wait, was it getting lighter? She blinked for her eyes to adjust. The dimness morphed into simple gray as a dull light filtered through the small door window. As the image of her surroundings became clear, she shivered and shut her eyes. Like that was going to help. There was no way to unsee she was in a tiny prison, complete with rock walls slathered in dirt and green slime.

Looks like "Dungeons-R-Us" had a sale and she was the lucky recipient.

Counting to ten, she opened her eyes. Nope, still here with her butt squished against the slick floor. The smell got to her so she covered her nose with her fingers, which didn't help since the filth from the floor covered them. There had to be a way out, but nothing jumped at her to say, "Exit." Well, unless she immediately lost a hundred pounds to squeeze through the small, open window in an old-fashioned wooden door. Yeah, like that would happen on a good day.

The clumping noises returned, coming closer. Stamping, heavy footsteps stopped in tandem outside the heavy door as it flung open. Lora jumped as it bounced against the wall with a solid thud. Her heart hammered as two humanoid guards with heavy footsteps came in. Their bodies were covered in dull metallic gray suits, complete with triangular, matted helmets. They stopped inside the door and raised long firearms with three-hole gun barrels pointed at her.

And...right on cue...in strolled the villain of this absurd melodrama.

Holy cow was he a *big* sucker. He had to be over seven feet tall. Lora swallowed a nervous burst of laughter. He resembled the bad guy from an old movie her mom used to watch. Complete with a shiny bald head and a thin, long black Fu Manchu mustache and goatee. He wore a robe of deep burgundy with long bell sleeves embroidered with black piping where his hands were hidden.

His irises were empty pits of darkness, black and soulless, indistinguishable from his pupils. With pointy ears, he was a Zerin or an evil Vulcan. Could go either way.

She was getting a crick in her neck looking up at him. Sitting on her ass wasn't the best place to be, so she stood.

"Ah, there you are, my dear." A wide, fake smile showed his pointy teeth.

Oh, okay Zerin it is.

"I am so pleased you are finally awake. You've been in stasis for several months and I feared my operatives may have given you too much of the narcotic necessary to bring you awake." He moved around her into a weak light that reflected the pearlescent sheen to his skin.

Well, whaddya know...aliens abducted her anyway. She glanced around her dingy quarters. Lucky her.

"Yeah, gee thanks for waking me up, I guess." She put on a brave front as she crossed her arms to calm her shivering. "So, who are you and what do you want?"

"Ah, getting right to the point I see." His smarmy smile made the pit of her stomach drop while it quaked and churned.

He stepped into her personal space and leaned down to meet her eye-to-eye. A whiff of sour onion cooked in curdled milk had her fighting the need to gag.

"Plans have been changed according to unfortunate circumstances." His chuckle came across as practiced and phony. He pulled his three-fingered hand out of the bell of his sleeves and stretched out a long, thick finger to caress the skin on her cheek. She jerked back. "The Council's ruling came down and Prince Qay's TrueBond with a human was approved and met with no opposition." He narrowed his cold, obsidian gaze at her. "Distasteful decision on their part—however, a unique opportunity for me."

He stepped back and Lora could once again breathe through her nose. She had no idea who in the hell he was talking about or how it concerned her. His next words didn't help clear things up, either.

"You see, my dear, you are going to help me take over the galaxy."

...to be continued in "D'zia's Dilemma"

A SMALL ASK...

Now that you finished reading this book, it would mean the world to me if you left an honest review on Amazon here. After all, your candid feedback will help others find my work so I can keep on creating wonderful worlds of romance for everyone to escape in.

Thank you!

ACKNOWLEDGMENTS

What is an author but a collection of experiences and good friends? I wouldn't have had the courage to plunge ahead in my dream career without the help from these excellent people...

To Jacqueline Sweet - Gorgeous, gorgeous cover!

To ELF - Magical Editor Extraordinaire

To my friends and mentors at "Barany's School of Fiction" - Beth and Ezra. You both rock the Kasbah. Of course, a quick shout out to Trent and Mary - fellow students and editors extraordinaire.

To my very special BFF's Barb and Marsha. Barb who loved me enough to let me know my hero was an asshole. Hate to admit it, but she was right. So Qay got a makeover. Thank God you've never changed over the years... you trying to sell me off to some horny old guy all those years ago notwithstanding. And to Marsha for teaching me the true meaning of friendship and loyalty. Not to mention she's the best damn cheerleader anyone could ask for as I danced a jig on a bar counter.

To my talented, stupendous offspring. Over the years you've kept me honest and (in)sane... not to mention giving me a greater purpose in life. You are practically perfect in every way. Just ask me, I'm not biased.

And last, but never least, to my hubs. You still see me as that shy eighteen-year-old redhead you first met all those years ago. I couldn't love you more for it. Open that wine bottle and let it breathe, baby. I'll be right there.

ABOUT THE AUTHOR

Keri Kruspe, award-winning "Author of Otherworldly Romantic Adventures" loves nothing more than to write about romances that feature "feisty heroines who aren't afraid to take a chance on life... or love". Her writing career started when she became irritated that most SciFi romances had women kidnapped before they could find love. Determined to create something different, she turned "the alien kidnapping trope upside down" (Vine Voice) and the ALIEN EXCHANGE trilogy was born.

Keri's latest SciFi Romance series, ANCIENT ALIEN DESCENDANTS, is taking the Ancient Alien motif and mixes it with a sensual, romantic twist.

A native Nevadan, Keri is a lifelong avid reader who lives in Northwestern Michigan with her hubby and the newest member of the family, a Jack Russell Terrier named Hestia. When not immersed in her made-up worlds, she enjoys discovering the fascinating landscape of her new home and pairing red wine with healthy ways to cook. Most of all, she loves finding her next favorite author.

If you want to know when Keri's next book will come out, please visit her website at http:/kerikruspe.com, where you can sign up for her mailing list. You'll get a **FREE** copy of the novella, *The Day Behind Tomorrow* that is a prologue to the ALIEN LEGACY series. Not to mention being kept updated on the life of a dedicated, obsessed author.

Facebook: https://www.facebook.com/klkruspe15

Twitter: https://twitter.com/keri_kruspe

Instagram: https://www.instagram.com/kerikruspe/?hl=en

ALSO BY KERI

Alien Legacy: The Shapeshifter

Alien Legacy: The Psychic

Alien Legacy: The Vampire

Alien Legacy: The Mage

An Alien Heritage
Three tales from An Alien Exchange and Alien Legacy Universe –
Coming Early 2023

Alien Legacy Brotherhood
Coming soon

www.ingramcontent.com/pod-product-compliance
Lightning Source LLC
Chambersburg PA
CBHW020559260626
47157CB00003B/786